D1042746

"Lowell's finely wrought characters don't have it easy when it comes to navigating restrictive Victorian society, but even their most outrageous actions ring true. Readers will be swept away by this entrancing, intelligent romance."

—*Publishers Weekly* (starred review)

"It's a lush, sensual, and outstanding romance that makes the heart ache in the very best way."

—*BookPage* (starred review)

"Impeccably researched, Lowell's latest emphasizes justice. This love story tackles weighty issues but remains suspenseful and spellbinding."

—*Library Journal* (starred review)

"Lowell's prose is vivid and evocative, and issues such as class inequity, women's rights, and alcohol addiction complement the intense on-page evolution of the love story. . . . Those looking for a happy ever after for complex and passionate characters will be very satisfied here. A new voice in historical romance that will keep readers riveted."

—*Kirkus Reviews*

Titles by Joanna Lowell

THE DUKE UNDONE
THE RUNAWAY DUCHESS
ARTFULLY YOURS

ARTFULLY YOURS

Joanna Lowell

BERKLEY ROMANCE

New York

Berkley Romance
Published by Berkley
An imprint of Penguin Random House LLC
penguinrandomhouse.com

LIBRARY OF CONGRESS CATALOGING-IN-PUBLICATION DATA

Names: Lowell, Joanna, author.
Title: Artfully yours / Joanna Lowell.
Description: First edition. | New York: Berkley Romance, 2023.
Identifiers: LCCN 2022025638 (print) | LCCN 2022025639 (ebook) |
ISBN 9780593198322 (trade paperback) | ISBN 9780593198339 (ebook)
Subjects: LCGFT: Romance fiction. | Novels.
Classification: LCC PS3618.U568 A89 2023 (print) |
LCC PS3618.U568 (ebook) | DDC 813/.6—dc23/eng/20220602
LC record available at https://lccn.loc.gov/2022025638
LC ebook record available at https://lccn.loc.gov/2022025639

First Edition: February 2023

Printed in the United States of America
1st Printing

For Frankie anyway.

ARTFULLY YOURS

CHAPTER ONE

May 1885

ALAN POINTED TO the painting on the drawing room wall.

"Fake," he said. The maid dropped the tea tray with a crash, so he repeated himself, in case his brother hadn't heard.

"That painting. It's a fake, not a Rembrandt. It's no more Dutch than the devil. Or perhaps the devil *is* Dutch." He shrugged. "I've always pictured him as an English aristocrat. Better the devil you know, as they say."

"*Your* devilry is my only concern of the moment." Geoffrey sat rigid in his chair, face as starched as his collar. "Lord *Death*."

"De'Ath," corrected Alan absently, still eyeing the picture. He'd adopted his nom de plume thirteen years ago while a student at Oxford, the same summer their father died and Geoffrey himself assumed a new name. Duke of Umfreville.

All of Alan's enemies called him Lord Death. Geoffrey was as original as . . . well, that bloody Rembrandt.

A ringing thud. The maid had fetched up the silver sugar pot only to let it slip again. Judging from the sound and the sugar pot's location on the floor, Alan surmised that it had struck the edge of the marble tabletop on the way down.

"Leave that alone," barked Geoffrey. The maid was on her knees, scooping the sugar back into the pot. She scrambled up. All around her feet, the Turkish carpet glittered with crystals.

"Send a competent parlormaid to clean up," said Geoffrey. "And see that she brings a fresh tray."

Alan leaned over the curved arm of the settee and felt for the teacup he'd seen bounce toward the flower stand. He hooked the bone china handle with his finger, set the cup on the table, and smiled at the maid.

"Don't mind him." He tipped his head toward Geoffrey. "His dander's up about his sham masterpiece."

Among other things, none of which pertained to a bumbled tea tray.

Upon inspection, the maid appeared less mortified than Alan had expected. She was staring at Geoffrey with open hostility. She had the sort of round, short-nosed face associated with angelic sweetness. And yet her expression left no doubt. There was more than one devil in the room.

"*Now*," said Geoffrey, and the maid wiped her sugar-coated hands on her tea-splashed apron, turned on her heel, and marched out.

"She's new." Geoffrey inspected his cuff as though his very proximity to the mess might have left a smudge. "She won't last long."

"I'm sure she won't," murmured Alan. Geoffrey and his wife, Fanny, went through maids and footmen faster than they went through flower arrangements.

"In any case." Geoffrey lowered his hand with a frown. "You didn't call to discuss my domestics. Or my art."

"It's not art," said Alan automatically. "Your Rembrandt is a forgery, which, in fact, degrades art."

He'd called to discuss money. But presented with such an opportunity, Alan couldn't resist.

He unfolded himself from the settee and crossed to the painting, avoiding the scattered saucers and spoons. It was only a few paces, but he leaned on his stick, a slim ebony baton with a flared gold knob. A dress cane. The sort an antiquarian gentleman might tuck beneath his arm. Brandish for emphasis. Wield in menace. Combined with his side-whiskers, spectacles, and velvet frock coat, the stick seemed a sartorial flourish. Its function was hidden in plain sight.

Alan De'Ath. The consummate persona. His performance was finer than most he saw upon the stage.

"Behold." He whipped up his cane, hovering the ferrule an inch from the painted panel. "No glaring errors. Plausible wood. Plausible subject. *Too* plausible, perhaps. *Introspective old man* is the lowest common denominator of Rembrandts. But never mind that." He glanced at Geoffrey and back at the panel. "Look closely. The brushstrokes are too smooth. The drawing itself is too blurry. Rembrandt was *rough*, but Rembrandt was *precise*. That was his particular paradoxical magic. This picture has no magic whatsoever. Because the forger, however talented a draftsman, painted to order, without a trace of vision."

Geoffrey laughed. "Alan *De'Ath*." He spread his arms and addressed an imaginary audience. "He even criticizes Rembrandt for being too much like Rembrandt." He stood and strode to Alan's side, pushing down the cane, fixing the picture with his ice blue gaze. After a moment, he gave a sage shake of his head.

"Authentic," he pronounced.

"Ah." Alan smiled with mock deference and sketched a bow. "So *you're* the expert now?"

"I don't need to be an expert." Geoffrey bristled. "I bought it from Chips Sleaford, a highly reputable dealer. He represents a reclusive collector, in Friesland. Sells the finest golden-age pictures on the market."

"Reclusive collector," echoed Alan, and brightened his smile. "The lowest common denominator of provenances."

"The provenance is impeccable." Geoffrey wheeled about to face him. They were inches apart. Alan could smell his brother's cologne, mixed with another odor, rank and gamy. Male anger.

"I could show you documents attesting to that picture's history," said Geoffrey. "Every sale, from Rembrandt's workshop to this drawing room." He had to look up at Alan, who topped him by half a head.

Alan kept smiling. "Please do."

Geoffrey's nose was a touch longer than Alan's, his lips thinner, but the set of his eyes was the same, as was the angle of his jaw. They resembled each other. Although—who could ever have guessed?—Alan the invalid had become the larger man, taller, more heavily muscled, more *vital*.

Perhaps Geoffrey, too, was drawing comparisons. He stalked away, kicking at the teapot, which the maid had righted. The pot tipped. He kept going and flung himself onto a sofa. In Parliament, he'd cultivated a reputation for sangfroid. In his household, and in his dealings with Alan, he reverted to a child.

"Sleaford's pictures are genuine." He bit out the words. "Even Lloyd Syme goes to Sleaford. He acquired a Rembrandt, a Brueghel, a . . . a . . ."

Alan raised his brows as Geoffrey cast about for the names of old masters.

"Shall I list possible candidates?" he inquired.

Geoffrey scowled. "It's whoever you'd think. All the greats. For the art collection at the South Kensington Museum."

"Syme's judgment is flawed. Clouded by ambition and animosity." Alan felt the dampness beneath his boot as he returned to the settee. Tea was still seeping into the carpet, staining it with an irregular rosette. He felt the urge to halt the flow, to stand the teapot on the tray, for the sake of the servants. But he wouldn't kneel in front of his brother.

"He looks like a wise old owl, but he has an ophidian heart. *Ophidian* means snakelike." He sat, throwing his arm across the settee's back in a casual pose. "How many pictures did *you* acquire?" he asked. "If you want to build your collection, I can introduce you to the best artists of our age. You can buy a painting wet from the easel."

"Stuff your advice." Geoffrey spoke through gritted teeth. "That's an order. I've had enough of your opinionating, and so has the rest of society."

"So has Count Davanzo, you mean." Alan sighed. "It's not my fault if your cronies produce abysmal operas. If you so dislike my opinions, don't read my reviews."

"The bloody review in question took up a full page of yesterday's *Times*. It was deuced difficult to avoid. And Davanzo found it horribly insulting." Geoffrey leaned forward. The tea table interposed between the sofa and the settee, and he looked poised to lunge across it. "By God, he's the *Italian ambassador*. Central to the efforts of the Home Office to protect the nation from foreign terrorists."

"So I should flatter him?" Alan shook his head. "He perpetuated a musical atrocity on our nation. What of that? I've yet to meet an anarchist who's done worse."

"Ha." Geoffrey snorted, then drew a sharp breath. "Let's come to the point, shall we? You're here because I closed your bank account."

"Not exactly." Alan smiled. "I'm here to make you open it."

"I will open it, and return the funds." Geoffrey smiled back unpleasantly. "When you learn to comport yourself. When you resume use of your *family* name. And when you stop dipping your pen in poison."

"It has come to this." Slowly, Alan removed his spectacles and polished the lenses on his sleeve. Window-glass lenses. His vision was perfect. Better than perfect.

He met Geoffrey's eyes. They'd never been close, but they'd made, on several occasions, a fragile peace. Every time, the peace fractured, due to pressure from beneath, the bubbling up of what they'd covered over to achieve the semblance of fraternity.

The secrets. The rancor.

Their latest peace—such as it was—had ended.

"If you won't honor our arrangement, I won't either." Alan replaced his spectacles on his nose. "Perhaps you don't remember? I inherited *everything* dispensable." Not only the properties in fee simple, which he'd sold immediately, investing the sum in railways, shipbuilding, and steel, but the books in the libraries, the portraits in the galleries, the silver plate, the very settee upon which he sat.

A muscle flexed in Geoffrey's jaw. Of course he remembered. That final proof of parental preference had put the seal on his brother's resentment. No matter that Alan had presented him with the investment portfolio, given him control of the capital he'd needed to resuscitate the dukedom. To avoid a loveless marriage, if he'd been willing to forgo extravagances, live more reasonably; that was, like less of an Umfreville.

He hadn't been willing, in the end. He'd married Fanny, about whom Alan had, to date, heard him utter only one approving statement: *At least she's not American.*

"Open the account," Alan said. "Or I'll sell every stick." Starting with anything to which Geoffrey attached a sentimental value. Let him buy it all back at auction.

"The portrait of Great-Great-Grandmama is a Gainsborough," Alan mused aloud. "It's certainly worth more than your Rembrandt." He tilted his chin toward the forgery.

Geoffrey gave a strangled cough. He looked, for an instant, overcharged, like his twenty-five-year-old self, reeling from their father's death, and from his crushing patrimony. The estates had been so encumbered he couldn't borrow enough to pay the interest due on the preexisting loans. The night before the funeral, he and Alan had talked until dawn, drinking straight from the bottle. *That* was the closest they'd ever come to each other. The first and only time they'd shared confidences. It was the night Alan had learned of Geoffrey's desperate, doomed love for Lady Patricia Kempe, third daughter of the penniless Duke of Harewood. It was the night Alan had revealed his darkest suspicions about their mother.

Sometimes, Alan recalled those impassioned, drunken hours and imagined doing them over, saying something different, something that would have made Geoffrey believe him, that could have changed the whole course of their adult relationship.

"You haven't asked after Claud," said Geoffrey, his tone suddenly slippery. "He was poorly after his swimming lesson."

"I'm sorry to hear he was poorly." Last Friday, Alan had spent an hour with Claud in the Serpentine, his nephew's first time in the lake since last September.

"*Light* exercise is recommended." Geoffrey's eyes glittered. "You pushed him too hard."

"The lesson included quite a bit of floating." Not the most exertive activity.

"He was chased by dogs until he wheezed."

That was one interpretation. Either the nurse, Miss Milford, had given Geoffrey the report he wanted to hear, or else he'd twisted it himself.

"There was a spaniel after a duck." Alan sighed. "Claud splashed with them in the shallows. He wasn't wheezing. He was laughing. I don't wonder the nurse didn't recognize the sound." He paused. "Would you?"

Geoffrey's lips disappeared. "With God's grace, I intend to raise a duke. Not a clown."

Alan didn't take the bait. "How is the future duke today?"

"Poorly," retorted Geoffrey. "Consider this Friday's lesson canceled."

All at once, Alan's composure snapped. He wanted to *smash*. Hurl the closest bauble at the equally worthless Rembrandt, right at the head of the introspective old man. Only Geoffrey could do this—shatter his control.

"He's a child." Alan fought to keep his voice steady. "Not a bloody bargaining tool."

"You're right." Geoffrey came to his feet. "He's *my* child. And I have no interest in striking any kind of bargain."

Alan rose smoothly and stood without bothering about his cane. It was a good day, for his bones at least. The cane was topped with a heavy gold pommel. If he touched it, he might succumb to temptation and split Geoffrey's skull.

"Perhaps he's under the weather," he said. "We'll cancel this Friday." He took a breath. "I'll look for him next Friday."

"You'll look in vain." Geoffrey squinted, twitching his thumb against his thigh. "I am through indulging your delusions at the expense of my son's health."

"How convenient." Alan sneered. "Make a virtue of your envy and self-interest. I'm deluded? Brother, your life is a lie."

"Brother?" Geoffrey charged around the table. "If I had any choice in it, you'd be no brother of mine."

"Pity that you don't." Alan stepped to meet him.

"They're yelling and scrapping! The duke and his brother."

Nina looked up as Clara burst back into the kitchen, still carrying the loaded tea tray.

"I can't go in there." Clara was panting. "It'll be the end of me."

The duke's brother. Nina kept creaming castor sugar with butter in the mixing bowl.

Since she'd made her graceless retreat from the drawing room, she'd thought of no one else.

The duke's brother was Alan De'Ath. The art critic. The most discerning man in England. And the most devoted to Art, with a capital *A*.

Nightmare development. She'd resorted to blinking extra blinks. Nightmares could be blinked away.

She blinked at Clara as the girl set down the tea tray, and Amy, a scullery maid, set down her stack of dirtied dishes and rushed to her.

"There," said Amy, touching Clara on the shoulder. "There, now. Don't be afeard."

A bowl of beaten eggs appeared at Nina's elbow, the wraithlike kitchen maid who assisted the cook fading back into the cabinetry. Nina added the eggs mechanically to the creamed butter. She could mix faster now, and her thoughts accelerated with the motion.

When thieves cut a Botticelli from its frame in the National Gallery and replaced it with a copy, Alan De'Ath was the man who noticed the substitution. And in Paris, the directors of the Louvre had had him barred from entry, to prevent further national embarrassments after he published a list of fraudulent artworks.

That was De'Ath. Legendary. All the parvenues, eager to display their taste, quoted from his articles. All the artists thronged him at the galleries, hoping he'd launch their careers with a word. And all the art forgers did their damnedest to ensure their pictures didn't pass before his eyes.

Her brother, Jack, must have known. Sleaford must have known. Umfreville and De'Ath—brothers! And yet Sleaford had sold the duke Jack's worst work. Three more of Jack's Dutch knockoffs were hanging in the duke's picture gallery. And three of *her* landscapes. She'd glimpsed them the day she'd arrived, the day before yesterday, when Mrs. Fletcher, the housekeeper, had toured her through the wings.

What had they been thinking? Had their greed overridden their sense of self-preservation? Sleaford's carelessness was the reason she was here in the first place, sneaking about, risking her own neck.

She hadn't blamed Sleaford, precisely. Anyone might put a note in the wrong envelope.

He'd sent a letter intended for Jack to the duke. It was only a short note, nothing incriminating on the face of it. Except for the tongue-in-cheek salutation: *My dear Dutchified Dauber.* Likely, the duke would have glanced at the note with a moment's puzzlement and put it aside. He wasn't the type to keep Jack's nickname in his mind. After all, more than a decade had passed since the Dutch-ified Dauber had figured hugely in the papers, during and immedi-ately after the trial. Still, it didn't do to leave in his possession a document connecting Chips Sleaford, the art dealer, to Jack Reeve, the convicted art forger.

Just after the luncheon, she'd breached the duke's study, and, by the grace of God—or more likely the devil—she'd retrieved the blasted letter. A triumph. But for what? They had bigger problems if Alan De'Ath was prowling the grounds like a wolf in the fold.

"Nina." Clara stepped away from Amy, swiping at her nose. "What are you doing?"

Nina glanced down the length of the table to where Mrs. Hen-derson stood, chopping furiously. She didn't want to embarrass the cook.

"Mrs. Henderson needed an extra pair of hands with the Victo-ria sponge."

In fact, Mrs. Henderson's Victoria sponge had failed to rise, and, seeing the woman's stricken expression, Nina had offered to help. But for that, she'd be halfway to Hatton Garden by now, and good riddance to this miserable household.

The horrid, pinch-lipped duchess was entertaining for tea *and* dinner. Mrs. Henderson had fallen desperately behind, even more so with the failed teatime dessert.

She couldn't help but help. For Mrs. Henderson's sake. And be-cause she'd longed to bake something in this magnificent kitchen, enormous, whitewashed, and orderly, with an iron double range and stacked ovens, all plumbed with gas. Shelves and racks lined one wall and held more molds, pie pans, wire sieves, bowls, quart and pint measures, rolling pins, graters, ladles, and dippers than she'd ever seen.

Someday soon, she'd have a kitchen of her own, housed in a little bakery in the village of Hensthorpe. Far more modest, and far better suited to her needs.

But an opportunity to handle equipment in a kitchen such as this might never come again.

Clara was nodding uncertainly. She looked down at the tea tray, and her chin started trembling.

"I can't go in there," she said again.

The past two nights, Nina had shared Clara's room, and they'd whispered before going to sleep. She knew that Clara had only recently arrived at Umfreville House herself.

If she were fired without a reference, she might not find another place.

"Don't," said Nina firmly. "*I'll* take the tray. Only let me get this in the oven." She'd already sifted together the dry ingredients, prepared the tins. It would be the work of a moment.

Clara flashed her a grateful look, then just as quickly shook her head.

"Then he'll send *you* packing," she said. "Better no one takes it."

"Then Mrs. Fletcher will get the licks, and she'll make everyone suffer." Nina frowned as she added the flour, leavening powders, and salt to the wet mixture. She'd begun to learn the roles and relationships of the different members of the staff. And to learn something of the complex system of reprisals. Mostly, reprisals were deferred down the chain, from those ranking highest to those ranking lowest. Sometimes they reversed direction. Regardless, they always found a target.

Just this morning, the duchess had sacked Nandini, the nursemaid, because the evening before, the youngest of the three children had refused to press a ritual good-night kiss upon her cheek. And she'd sacked Harriet, the new kitchen maid, because the eldest had received a pot of hot chocolate with his breakfast, the same as his sisters, which in his case violated the doctor's edict.

Jack's tyranny seemed rudimentary by contrast.

"The situation is my fault for dropping the first tray." Nina couldn't help but blink as she said it. When De'Ath had latched his strange silver eyes on Jack's picture and said *fake*, her heart had stopped beating. Her fingers had stopped gripping.

"Two minutes," she said. "And off I go."

And off with my head.

But it didn't matter. Like Clara, Nina was an orphan, or at least she preferred to think so. It was worse to imagine that her father had abandoned her mother when Nina was just four years old—nearly twenty-two years ago now—and never thought once to reunite with his daughter. That he'd never inquired what had become of his wife, who'd died a week before Nina's tenth birthday. For all practical purposes, she was an orphan. No stranger to hard work. But unlike Clara, she hadn't made a life in service.

She'd made a life of crime.

Or rather, Jack had made it for her. In any case, she planned to leave Umfreville House today. Whether she quit or was fired, it was the same to her.

"Thank you!" breathed Clara.

Nina nodded, looking into her bowl, away from the gratitude and guilt playing over Clara's wan face.

"Keep mum," Clara advised her, and then added doubtfully, "You might get off with a dressing-down."

Five minutes later, Nina was knocking for the second time on the drawing room door.

CHAPTER TWO

"You."

As the maid entered, Geoffrey straightened and balled up his handkerchief. He'd been holding it pressed to his nose. The blood had ceased to flow, but his white cravat was stippled with crimson. "I said send a *competent* maid."

The maid paused on the threshold.

"You did, your grace," she said at last. Agreement, perhaps, seemed the wisest course. Alan could have told her there was no wise course. No way forward for her, not here. She'd been picked out to pay for the intemperance of her betters.

They usually were, those who could least afford it.

She swept the room with wide, dark eyes.

Geoffrey stood in one corner, and Alan leaned against a chiffonier in another. The wreckage of their contest lay strewn between them. Broken majolica. Dented wax fruits. Toppled plant stands.

The maid started for the tea table with a resolute tread. Alan frowned, cradling his swollen hand. He didn't relish her imminent humiliation.

Geoffrey, its all-too-willing agent, had already begun to pace toward her.

"Carelessness I can overlook." He spoke with cold precision, the consonants brittle as glass. "To a certain extent, I *must* overlook it, today's servants being what they are. However, I will not tolerate disobedience."

This was how he salved his hurts and disappointments, his frustrated vanity. This was how he sweetened the sourness of the life he'd chosen. He vented his spleen at the weak.

"You disobeyed me," he continued, heat building in his voice. "Or perhaps you mistook my meaning. Either you lack the proper deference, or you lack sufficient wit. Which is it?"

The maid walked more quickly, her reply breathless. "I wouldn't know, your grace."

Alan glanced down at the Qing dynasty vase that stood by his left elbow on the chiffonier. The sunlight pouring through the windows lit the copper-red glaze. The vase glowed. Most of the decorative objects in the drawing room were Fanny's purchases. Not the vase. Their mother had displayed it in the breakfast room when Alan was a boy. The vase belonged to *him*.

Now that he'd mastered his rage, his brain worked with cool efficiency. Smash nothing. Sell everything. Force Geoffrey to capitulate to *his* demands.

Geoffrey intercepted the maid before she reached the table. "What's your name?"

"Nina Finch." The maid stopped short, shifting her grip on the freighted tray. Geoffrey didn't care, of course, that he detained her, that her arms strained to support all that weighty silver. Or, more likely, the fact increased his satisfaction.

Frown deepening, Alan pushed off the chiffonier.

"I'll be speaking with Mrs. Fletcher about *you*, Nina Finch. What do you recommend I say?" Geoffrey looked down his nose, straight as the Umfreville line of succession. Seven generations, father to eldest son. The blow he'd suffered hadn't bent it. *Self-inflicted* blow. When Alan had dodged his first wild swing, Geoffrey had tried another, a close-range jab that ricocheted off Alan's forearm, smack into his own face.

In the heat of the moment, Alan had decided to drive his fist— not into Geoffrey—into the tabletop. The crunch of knuckle on marble had disturbed him more than the pain. But at least Geoffrey had snapped his jaws reflexively and retreated, falling silent.

"Whatever pleases you, your grace," murmured Miss Finch, her humility undercut by a hint of condescension.

Geoffrey's face blazed and he spoke in a ringing voice. "It pleases me to dismiss you."

"Very good, your grace." Miss Finch lifted her downcast gaze. "But you shouldn't trouble to tell Mrs. Fletcher. I can convey a message more competently than I can a tea tray. *I'll* tell her." Incredibly, she smiled. The smile sank dimples in her cheeks.

Such dimples. Each deep enough to enfold a fingertip.

Fascinated, Alan halted briefly on his approach. He hadn't given nearly enough thought to dimples during his life to date. How they advantaged the dimpled party, if dauntless aplomb was at a premium. He almost applauded.

Well done, Miss Finch.

With that merry, impertinent dimpling, the girl had shown herself undefeated. Certainly, she'd robbed Geoffrey of his desired response. A torrent of tears, apologies, pleas.

Geoffrey's cheeks hollowed.

"*Without* notice," he added crisply. "Don't think of asking for my reference."

"Discharged on the spot." Alan drew up beside him and clapped him hard on the shoulder with his uninjured hand. Next time he was deciding between striking his brother and striking solid rock, he'd decide differently. "Bold move, old boy. Now you have to ferry your own tray. Go on, then."

He gave Geoffrey an encouraging push. Miss Finch's eyes met Alan's. Large, round eyes. But her gaze was narrow, knife-edge sharp.

"That's quite all right," she said. "I'm content to drop it." And drop it she did. The tray crashed down.

Geoffrey flinched, then went rigid, white to the lips with wrath. "Perhaps I won't speak with Mrs. Fletcher. I'll speak with the authorities."

At the mention of authorities, a shadow flitted across Miss Finch's face. She blinked it away and steeled her spine, standing taller. "Is it a hanging offense, dropping a duke's tea tray?" She flicked the carpet with her gaze, now a midden for silver, porcelain, sugar, and pastry. "They'll have to hang me twice, then."

"Mark my words, this is your last situation." For a moment, Geoffrey watched the tea lap his boot. Then he showed Miss Finch his tight, ugly grin. Teeth tinged pink. "I guarantee that no respectable household in England will have you."

"Capital." No more humility, not even a semblance. Miss Finch put her hands on her hips. "I won't have another respectable household, if it's anything like this one."

Geoffrey stepped toward her, cracking a saucer beneath his sole. "This household is one of the finest in the realm."

"Watch yourself, brother." This time, Alan caught him around the shoulder and gripped.

"It's fine as you please, your great big house." Miss Finch stared at Geoffrey. "And about as cheery as a grave, with everyone fretting about getting the sack, and you and the mistress stalking the halls with faces that could curdle milk."

Alan laughed aloud and she looked at him, a line between her brows.

"Don't stop on my account," he said, as Geoffrey gave a violent shrug, elbow connecting with Alan's ribs. Miss Finch backed away slowly, edging around the debris.

"Your servants eat crusts I wouldn't feed my marmoset." She nearly spat the words. "If I were you, I'd be ashamed of myself. You're the richest, stingiest crosspatch I've ever met in my life."

"Get out," bellowed Geoffrey, ripping free of Alan's grasp.

She whirled and threw open the door, exiting with a touch more haste than Alan supposed her pride might have preferred.

"Both of you." Geoffrey brushed at the garnet crust of dried blood on his left nostril and grimaced. "Out," he repeated, but he didn't wait for Alan to move. He was the one who left first, striding from the room.

By the time Alan had picked his way to the settee, retrieved his cane, and followed, the hall was empty. Which suited his purposes. He headed not for the front door but deeper into the house.

ALAN OPENED THE door to Claud's bedchamber without knocking. He knew from experience that nurses grew dull on their vigils and dozed. If he were lucky, he might discover Miss Milford slumped in her chair, lulled to sleep by the warm, eventless afternoon.

He wasn't so lucky. The nurse's chair faced the bed, but he could hear the grim, godly cadence of her voice, a rhythm he associated with Anglican funerals.

She was reading aloud from the Bible.

The familiar sickroom smell made his muscles tense as he shut the door silently behind him. The same odor had permeated his own boyhood bedchamber, the strong blend of the medicaments combined with something sour and disquieting. *That* bedchamber lay at the end of the hall, by the nursery. Alan had stepped foot in it only once since he'd moved to Oxford at seventeen, and only then because he'd felt compelled to search every room, the whole house from top to bottom.

Geoffrey had provided him with the opportunity, two and a half years ago now. Of course, he hadn't understood it in those terms. He'd had his own reasons for begging Alan to tenant Umfreville House while the family wintered in Italy.

Fanny wants her parents to take up residence in our absence. He'd explained the predicament with a look of horror. The Smiths' money—which he spent freely enough—could never, in his eyes, absolve the Smiths of their original sin. Namely, that of being *Smiths*. A generation removed from coal heavers.

You have the clear precedence, Alan. Say yes. If it's you, she can't insist.

Alan *had* said yes. He'd hoped to uncover something, anything, to corroborate his understanding of the first half of his life, years blurred by drugs, by pain, by fear.

As the Italian stay extended at Claud's doctor's behest, Alan's three-month tenancy had transformed into six. He'd dredged secrets from the depths of locked drawers. But not the answers he needed. He hadn't turned up a shred of evidence to prove he wasn't what Geoffrey had said he was. *Delusional. A thankless wretch.*

Claud saw him and gave a happy cry. "Uncle Alan!"

Alan shook off his reverie, grinned, and approached the bed. "Have I interrupted a battle?"

Claud was lying propped by two pillows in bed, toy soldiers scattered on the counterpane.

"Lord Alan." The nurse rose. Miss Milford had silver hair and a youthful face, which bestowed upon her an oddly eternal quality. Last summer, a different nurse—less formidable—had brought Claud into Hyde Park for his swimming lessons. That nurse had looked the other way when Alan slipped the boy toffees and peppermint candies. Miss Milford's watchful eye forbade the slightest deviation from her employers' directives.

She trained it on him now. "There aren't to be any visitors."

"I'm family." Alan sat on the edge of Claud's bed, leaning his cane against the bedpost. A quandary for Miss Milford. Run and report his transgression—abandoning her charge—or stay put and permit *Uncle Alan* to flout the rules.

Which would rankle Geoffrey more?

Alan frowned. It seemed that his presence was to make mischief for *two* women in fewer hours. Unfortunate. But not his chief preoccupation at present.

He turned his attention back to Claud. "Zouaves." He rested his swollen hand on his thigh and used the other to pick up one of the soldiers, a wonderfully intricate construction of wood and papiermâché. The Zouave uniform—blue jacket tasseled with gold, red trousers—matched the bedchamber, the red rugs and blue curtains, the red counterpane. He wondered fleetingly if Fanny curated Claud's toys, if she'd selected this particular regiment because it fit best with her palette.

"Who are they fighting?" he asked Claud. "The Prussians?" He heard the click of the door that denoted Miss Milford's departure.

"They're not fighting anyone." Claud sat up and soldiers tumbled. "They're not Zouaves. They're Martians." His thin face grew serious and hopeful.

Alan's heart squeezed. The child wanted a playmate—not a nurse, ready to apply a compress to his forehead whenever he began to flush with boyish excitement, but a friend, ready to share his adventures. Romping with Arabella and Mary would do him more good than turpentine vapor and pills of copper sulfate.

"Martians! Better yet." Alan tried to balance his Zouave—Martian—upright on the red counterpane. "So, this is Mars." His gesture encompassed the wide bed, and Claud nodded eagerly.

"That's one of the canals." Claud pointed to where he'd pinched up the fabric, forming the sides of a long trench. "It goes to the sea." He leaned to pinch the sides higher. Strands of dark hair plastered his forehead, curled damply at his temples. Heat radiated from his body. Not fever necessarily. A combination of thick blankets and the windows, their western exposure. On sunny days, the room marinated in afternoon light.

"Are the canals for shipping?" Alan asked, to cover his unease. Claud glanced up at him. Alan used to see that very expression in the mirror. The look of a boy who wanted to escape his body through his eyes.

"Boats aren't allowed." Claud picked up a soldier. "The canals are for swimming." Claud laid the soldier facedown in the trench. "The water's cold, but Felton doesn't mind."

"Felton?" Alan bit the inside of his cheek to keep from smiling. "The Martian's name is Felton?"

Claud picked up another soldier, bigger than the others, all wood, a relic Alan recognized from his own boyhood. "This one's Captain Basil. He's racing Felton." Into the canal with the wooden soldier. "Captain Basil is stronger, but he only knows the breaststroke. Felton knows the other one, the one we practiced."

Alan didn't ask how the Martians had learned terrestrial swimming styles. He nudged Felton, giving him the lead.

"The trudgen stroke," he said. "An overarm motion. It's what they use in the Americas." He raised an arm above his head and arced it down, outlining a half circle. "Plus, a scissor kick. Beats the breaststroke every time. I'm backing Felton."

"I wasn't as good at the scissor kicks." Claud wiggled his legs under the counterpane and more soldiers tipped. "But there's a new kind of kick. Not scissor. It's called the pudding kick."

"Ah," said Alan. "The pudding kick, did you say? I sense it will revolutionize the sport. Your invention? Very good. How's it done?"

"You move your legs like a spoon when there's pudding. You'll see how fast I go."

Claud smiled at Alan, then looked toward the bright windows. Nothing to see from that angle except sky, but they both knew that the gardens stretched immediately below, and beyond, Hyde Park, with the Serpentine shining in the sun.

"I hope the funny dog is there again," added Claud wistfully.

Alan cursed his brother with silent, filthy thoroughness before he spoke. "We'll have to wait and see about the dog, and about the pudding kick, too."

Claud's head whipped around. His eyes seemed to fill his face.

"No swimming this week, I'm afraid." Alan tried to smile without gritting his teeth.

"Why not?"

White lies. Alan rarely trafficked in them. He purveyed uncomfortable truths.

Because your father is a petty bastard.

"The weather needs to warm a bit more," he said. He cleared his throat. "It won't be long."

He made the promise to himself as much as to Claud.

He'd force Geoffrey's hand on this, and every other vicious imbecility, posthaste.

"Perhaps in the meantime, we can go to an exhibition at the Royal Aquarium." He'd apply to Fanny. She might facilitate it, secretly, if she knew Geoffrey disapproved. A simple outing. He could take the girls as well.

Claud's lower lip was trembling.

"I've told you about the Royal Aquarium," said Alan. "This month the Bramleys are back, and the living mermaid. Do you remember about the Bramley family?"

Claud bit his lip and slid his gaze away, nodding without conviction.

"They do everything regular people do, but underwater." Alan paused to gauge the effect of his words. "They lace their shoes and walk around. And sing."

"Underwater?" Claud looked at him. "In a tank?"

"A whale-sized tank." Alan smiled. "Nancy Bramley is the star. She won't perform until the end of the month, but if we go sooner, we'll see her mother and father. He sits at a table at the bottom of the tank and drinks a bottle of milk, while she eats a cake."

Claud tucked his chin and gave Alan a suspicious glance. His lip had stopped trembling. "What kind of cake?"

"Any kind." Alan laughed at the question. "Carrot."

"I don't like carrot." Claud wrinkled his nose.

"No?" Alan raised his brows. "We'll leave it to Mrs. Bramley, then."

"I could eat a different cake." Claud leaned forward, hugging himself, and took a great breath. "I could eat a *chocolate* cake underwater!"

"And it would be the death of you."

At the sound of his brother's voice, Alan turned his head.

Geoffrey stood framed by the doorway. He'd changed his cravat. Every strand of hair had been slicked into place.

"If you can even think such things, I don't know that we should let you eat cake at all." He strode into the room, Miss Milford on his heels. "In fact, I know we shouldn't. No cake. And you can thank your uncle for it."

Claud slumped back into the pillows and rolled onto his side, facing the windows.

Alan released air through his nose. He wouldn't engage Geoffrey here. Best to ignore him.

"Soon, Claud," he said, and touched the boy's shoulder. Reflexively, he touched with his left hand and had to suppress a wince. Claud didn't move.

After a moment, Alan stood. As he turned to take his cane, his eyes lit on the chess table by the fireplace. A Carton-Pierre casket sat atop it. The elaborately modeled black box had castellated corners and figures of the royal court in relief along the sides. He'd recognize it anywhere, recognize it blindfolded, by the feel. It contained their father's chessmen and used to sit on the table beside his sickbed.

"Where did you find that? The Staunton chess set?" Without thinking, he started around the bed. "I thought Father left it at his club. When I was here—those months—I looked all through the house."

"It wasn't in the house when you did us that honor." Geoffrey reached the table only a moment after he did. "I took the set with us, to Italy."

Alan's gaze shot up. Geoffrey's smile might have been etched across his face with acid. The bastard begrudged him that too: the chess tournaments he'd played against their father, while flat on his back. Those tournaments—another instance of stolen attention.

And yet, Geoffrey had thought to continue the tradition, to sit with Claud and alleviate his boredom. Despite himself, Alan softened.

"Claud trounces you, I'm sure." He said it for the boy's benefit, glancing over his shoulder to see if he'd elicited a grin. Miss Milford blocked his view. She was hovering over the bed, gathering the soldiers.

His stomach tightened.

"I've yet to open the box." Geoffrey picked it up. "The moment never seemed right. I only lately dug it out again." He ran his fingertip over the lid, tracing the design. His voice had regained that sly quality. "You wouldn't take the set? Before I can teach Claud how to play?"

"Not in a thousand years." Alan snorted at his brother's transparency. On principle, he should seize the box. But Claud might very well enjoy the game. And the time with his father.

"Consider the set his." He met Geoffrey's gaze. "It's a gift, not a gambit," he added in a quieter voice. *He* wouldn't use Claud to gain advantage in this idiotic struggle.

"Of course," said Geoffrey, too smoothly.

Alan turned from him abruptly, stepped to the closest window. The view of the grounds—the vast green sweep of the lawns, the brilliant flowers, the easy movement of whoever roamed below—contoured the stifling confinement of the bedchamber. Tantalized with its *beyond*. He'd grown up with the same vista.

Today, only one person roamed below. A woman, walking along the forking path. Her white cap perched precariously on her head. She carried a valise. Miss Finch. Freshly dismissed and failing dismally to vacate the property. She was going the wrong way, heading not toward the gate, but toward the rose garden. She'd wander in circles until sunset.

He watched her tidy, determined, misdirected movement a moment longer, then turned and started for the door. He paused only briefly as he passed Geoffrey.

"I'll write with a list of items for the auction house. Unless you write to me first and suggest an alternative."

"I'd rather write the Reaper," growled Geoffrey.

"Soon, Claud," Alan called to his nephew as he opened the door. "This summer will be the summer of the pudding kick."

CHAPTER THREE

ALAN CAUGHT UP to Miss Finch in the center ring of the rose garden. She'd set her valise on the ground and was staring down into the lower basin of a tiered fountain like a disappointed lover resigned to drowning.

"My God," he said as he approached. "It's not so bad as that."

She started, spun around, saw him, and started again.

"It's not," she agreed after a short pause. Her hand drifted up to her cap, and she scowled. "And I'm not exactly the Ophelia type, either."

She'd removed her soiled apron, but the white cap, black dress, and white collar and cuffs announced her degree. A servant. Plain in appearance, unprepossessing. A far cry from a beautiful young noblewoman of Denmark.

Her look dared him to argue.

He didn't. Purveyor of uncomfortable truths, and all that. No flattery. Besides, what had Ophelia to offer but the poetry of a romantic death?

"Splendid," he said simply. "Hers is a fate to be avoided."

"Hey nonny-nonny." Miss Finch muttered it and directed another longing look at the fountain. "I wasn't about to cast myself into the water. I was wondering if it's good to drink. I feel I've a hedgehog in my throat."

He smiled at the image. He appreciated a picturesque turn of phrase. And a puckish delivery.

He'd been hasty, perhaps, in judging Miss Finch plain. Worse than hasty, in fact. He had followed the herd and defaulted to the current vogue. Yes, Miss Finch lacked the emphatic bone structure and jewel tones prized in society. But her spirit and her mobile expression gave her ordinary features a lively cast. Despite her mouse brown hair and her gloomy livery, there was nothing drab about her.

"Good to drink?" Alan shifted his attention back to her words. "I've never tried it." He peered at the fountain. Portland stone and marble. He'd wager drinking from the basin was far more wholesome than drinking from the standpipes that sourced poorer Londoners with their water. Not Nina Finch. He'd wager that as well. Her accent wasn't polished, but neither was it rough. She had a clear, pleasant voice, sonorous vowels. Familiarity with the works of Shakespeare. Too much pride to bow and scrape to a bully, even though that bully paid her wages.

Many servants hailed from the country, or from rookeries, or descended from maids and footmen. He discarded each possibility, particularly the last.

No one with forebears in service would ever have dropped a tea tray. Twice.

Daughter of a clerk perhaps, fallen on hard times.

Miss Finch sighed and picked up her valise. "I've had enough in the way of unpleasant surprises for one day. I'd rather not get a mouthful of mud and tadpoles." She took one last longing look at the fountain, then she squared her shoulders. "I won't die of thirst."

The breeze picked up. It carried the heated, drugging scent of the young roses, the earliest of the year. A strand of hair floated across her face, where it grazed the curve of her cheek.

Rosy cheek. Overly rosy, perhaps. She'd been walking quickly, and to no purpose, for at least a quarter hour.

"That is, if I ever get out of here," she added, pivoting to examine the curving hedge—a solid wall of green—for hidden openings. "Clara told me the garden gate would be open for her grace's guests. But I can't find the gate." She made a face. "And by now, it's probably stuffed up with countesses."

Alan raised his eyebrows. Countesses crushing into the garden for the duchess's tea. Like something out of *Alice's Adventures in Wonderland*.

He couldn't deny it. Miss Finch amused him, even when she wasn't busy mortifying his brother. She was irreverent, bold, clever—and for these admirable qualities, she'd been abundantly punished.

Bloody hell. The longer he spent in her company, the more the injustice irked him. The more responsible he felt for it. For her. He frowned.

"Where will you go?" he asked.

"Home." Miss Finch held her valise higher, tighter to her body. He had the distinct impression that she was barricading herself against his curiosity. As she turned her head to meet his gaze, her sunstruck eyes seemed to flash. "I'm happy to go back. I missed it more than I'd expected."

"You have family, then."

She nodded, relaxing perceptibly at the relief in his voice, as though she'd just understood his interest as a species of concern, rather than a prelude to predation.

Appalling thought. But what *was* she to think? A dismissed maid pursued by a lord of the manor?

He glanced at the splashing fountains so she wouldn't suppose herself the target of the disgust in his eyes. Why *had* he pursued her through the garden? She'd seemed lost, but the mazy grounds weren't a forest primeval. She'd have found the gate eventually or retraced her steps to the house. He'd acted before he'd thought it through. The scrap with Geoffrey had rattled his brain.

"I am sorry for my brother's behavior," he said, a bit too stiffly. "He's an exemplary ass. They should print his likeness in the dictionary to illustrate the word."

She smiled a demure smile. It didn't dent her cheeks.

"On the subject of the duke, I defer to your lordship." Her knees dipped, a whisper of a curtsey. "Yours is the longer acquaintance."

He laughed, impressed and slightly unnerved. Her face was so sweet that each glimpse of her steely self-possession registered as a shock.

"Defer to me on this next subject as well." He looked her straight in the eye. "I have a vacancy. A position to fill, immediately." He heard himself speak aloud before the words had sounded in his mind. It wasn't the first time he'd formulated one of these offers. But usually, the impulse to extend employment responded to more obvious encouragement from his future employee.

Miss Finch seemed stunned. Her smile vanished as her eyes widened. Honey brown in the sun, ringed with cinnamon.

"I can't imagine you didn't notice." Slowly, she shook her head. "I make a dreadful maid."

"Depends on how you look at it." Alan felt his lips quirk. "From my perspective, you performed your duties marvelously. But I'm not seeking a maid."

She went rigid with confused suspicion, not an unreasonable response. But the idea he'd formed made a kind of sense, given the circumstances.

He raised his left hand. "I'm seeking an amanuensis. Someone to write for me."

For a moment, they considered his hand together, skin stretched like a balloon and already darkening.

"I doubt I can scrawl my own name," he said, rotating his wrist with a frown.

Her eyes flicked up to his. "That's your left hand."

"Observant." He stilled, holding her gaze. "You're quick thinking, Miss Finch. It's an attribute that recommends you to the position."

He lowered his hand, which throbbed. The ache was persistent but bearable. He judged every type of pain against the *one*. The one that, when it came on, overwhelmed categorization, overwhelmed him.

He'd heal from *this* injury, but, in the meantime, it would prove a nuisance.

She was still staring, a line between her brows.

"I write with my left hand," he explained. "Moreover, I write constantly. Books, but also reviews of art and theater. Perhaps you've read some of them?"

Her nod was scarcely perceptible. Of course she'd read him, or at least heard of him. Anyone literate had.

"You understand, then, what will happen if I go on hiatus? If the threat of my pen no longer strikes fear in the hearts of hack dramatists and moth-eaten history painters?" He smiled. "Culture itself will go to the dogs."

"Then you do need an amanuensis." She licked her lips. They were full as halved plums, but pale. Parched by her exertions.

"An *experienced* amanuensis," she said emphatically. "From an agency."

"I prefer a *serendipitous* amanuensis." He did, God help him.

Why hire from an agency if you could instead hire from a rose garden?

"Miss Finch," he said, "the job is yours."

"PARDON!" NINA GASPED, twisting away from Mr. De'Ath. "I've a midge in my eye." She clapped a palm to her face. Mercifully, the world went dark. She pressed her eyelids closed, stilling them. She'd been blinking like the blazes.

"Early in the season, isn't it?" Mr. De'Ath's drawl sounded humorous. Encouraged by his tone, she lowered her hand, untwisting so she faced him.

Maybe he hadn't been serious? Surely he wasn't so eccentric—or guilt-stricken—that he wanted a parlormaid as his secretary?

"Not a midge." She swallowed. "Dust." She gave a dusty cough.

His eyes glinted behind his spectacles. His lips curled.

No, he didn't look serious.

"You can start tomorrow," he said. "In the meantime, I'll show you to the gate. If there's a crush of countesses, we'll divert to an alternate route."

He started strolling down the path, back in the direction from which he'd come.

Bloody sodding son of a whoreson's frog's bollocks in hell. Jack's oaths strung together in her mind as she grabbed her valise and darted after him.

Of course, Mr. De'Ath didn't *look* serious. Did he ever? He had the devil's own face for cleverness. Long, wicked lips lazing between a smile and a sneer. Perpetually arched black brows, their slant suggestive of skepticism or mockery. And those quicksilver eyes, their expression keen, and keenly amused, as though he were always glimpsing something in the world that confirmed his sense of the absurd.

Damn bugger blast.

"I'm very grateful." She caught up with him. "But, you see, it's impossible. I don't know anything about the theater or . . ." Her throat clamped down on her voice, and she had to swallow hard.

"*Art*," she managed. Drat it all. Did she *smell* of deceit? She'd been sweating in all this ghastly black wool, and now she felt clamminess beneath her arms, in the crooks of her elbows. Not from the day's heat, but from her mounting dread.

"It's what *I* know that matters." He glanced down at her. "An amanuensis takes dictation. I speak, you write. You *can* write?"

"Slowly, though." She sighed, a regretful sigh, and tried to look dejected. "I couldn't keep up."

"You'd improve with practice," he said comfortably. "Are we settled, then?"

No! She smiled, close-lipped, to keep the cry from slipping out. As a sacked maid, shouldn't she jump at the opportunity? She needed to act the part. Too much blundering now and he might begin to wonder. Maybe he'd return to the house, inquire after her reference. Maybe he'd read it—two paragraphs singing her praises, signed daintily by Jack, with the name *Margaret, Baroness of Cynddylan.* Jack had been proud of his handiwork. But maybe Mr. De'Ath kept in his head a list of Welsh peers. Maybe he'd spot the invention. Ask questions. Connect her to the other anomaly he'd glimpsed in the house: Jack's blasted Rembrandt.

Maybe he suspected her already.

The position he offered was a lure. He planned to reel her in, to catch her.

Her heart hammered.

They were passing out of the rose garden. She looked across the sweeping expanse of grounds. In the distance, the house towered above the lime trees. Tables covered with white linens had been arranged on the lawn. Footmen went back and forth on the ribbon-lined walks, arms loaded with winking silver.

"Good," said Mr. De'Ath, as if her silence gave confirmation. He drifted under a cherry tree and stopped. She pulled back so she didn't have to crane to look at him. He was surprisingly tall. Broad through the shoulders.

Nothing about his physical person corresponded with *renowned art critic*. His proportions seemed unscholarly in the extreme. Shouldn't he have a stoop? And he was half as old as his intellectual celebrity suggested.

How many times as handsome?

The answer had no relevance. *She* didn't give a fig if a man was *fizzing, absolutely gorgeous*, as her friend Ruby would say. Men were much the same to her.

"What did my brother pay you?" he asked. "I'll double it."

The breeze riffled the leaves overhead, sifting light from shade. The lenses of his spectacles twinkled.

Spectacles, side-whiskers, long black frock coat, wide trousers, ebony cane—his antiquated costumery certainly set him apart from the general run of young men about town. He didn't aim for *fizzing*, that was obvious.

"I should warn you," he continued, "there's a small chance you'll wait longer than a month for your wages. My brother and I are in the midst of renegotiating our financial relationship."

He turned his head and glanced toward the house. His profile was all hard planes: strong nose, shelflike cheekbones, peaked upper lip, the fullness of the lower more squared off than curved.

Nina lowered her valise onto the petal-strewn grass. He *couldn't* suspect her. He had a prodigious brain, not the second sight. Her bad conscience was playing tricks on her. He didn't offer her employment to catch her or to catch Jack. The explanation was simpler.

He liked her because she'd annoyed his brother. Hiring her, he'd annoy his brother further.

She remembered the duke's bloodied shirtfront, the cold rage in his eyes.

"*Renegotiating*," she said. "Is that what the gentlefolk call it? You were giving each other a good slogging."

He looked back at her and laughed. So often laughter—male laughter—grated. She was accustomed to guffaws, grunts, chortles, barks, yips, honks. Mr. De'Ath's laughter was different. It was like molasses rippling off the back of a spoon.

"Whatever you call it, the disagreement will be decided in my favor." He shrugged. "Without further fisticuffs. Or broken Bohemian glass." The corner of his mouth turned down. "I shouldn't have reacted as I did. Next time, I'll count to ten."

She knew she was staring, but it was so unexpected. The critic turned his criticism on himself.

Arrogant Mr. De'Ath—chagrined by the destruction in the drawing room.

She'd been chagrined too, for her part in it. Clara and the other parlormaids would have to clear the mess. She'd apologized profusely as she said her goodbyes.

She prayed her dismissal would suffice by way of retribution, although she feared it wouldn't. The Duke of Umfreville was sour, vain, humorless, petty . . . a beef-headed boor. He placed blame reflexively.

Alan De'Ath—he was a different sort of creature. Infinitely more complicated and compelling.

And, to her, infinitely more dangerous.

"I'm very grateful," she said again, more steadily this time. "But I can't accept your offer. It would be different if I were going back home to stay. But I've the thought to leave London altogether." Lying went more smoothly when one based the ruse on fundamental truths. Now her words flowed. "I'd rather move to the country than start *any* new job here. I like the country air. My aunts have a lovely cottage with a spare room, and behind it there's a little hill covered with gooseberry bushes. My plan is to open my own pastry shop and sell gooseberry tarts." She felt a buzzing in her veins as she spoke. Ever since she'd spent those golden months in Hensthorpe as a girl, she'd imagined returning for good. Living in the cottage. Herbs overhead, cats underfoot. How surprisingly giddy-making, to reveal her most cherished hopes to a stranger.

A fizzing, gorgeous, legendarily shrewd, *lordly* stranger, famous for unflinching judgment.

Foe of banality and contrivance. Foe of fakers.

Her foe.

"I never intended to remain in service." She realized her gaze had dropped to the grass, fixed on the pink petals clinging to the metal tip of his cane. She forced her eyes up. "It's a good thing, really, that things turned out as they did."

"You plan to open your own shop?" He tipped his head just enough to indicate . . . incredulity.

She flushed. *Blast.* Not well-trodden, was it? The road from service to shopkeeping.

"More of a dream than a plan," she said hastily. "I'd never afford it."

She could, though. Now. For years, she'd kept account books. She'd saved enough cash to put down on Mr. Craddock's bakery in Hensthorpe. Mr. Craddock was fond of her and amenable to the transaction. His slugabed sons reserved their elbow grease for lifting tankards. Mr. Craddock would sell, and *she* would be the one to buy.

"I distinguish between dreams every day." Mr. De'Ath was looking at her thoughtfully. "Often dreams are self-indulgent fantasies. A tone-deaf Italian count thinks he's Verdi." He made a derisive gesture with his hand. "I smite those kinds of dreams with my pen."

She tracked the motion. His knuckles had all but disappeared, bones submerged in the angry puff of surrounding tissue. He couldn't smite anything with his pen at the moment. He noticed her gaze and smiled with all his sharp white teeth.

"But sometimes they're visions," he continued softly. "Sometimes dreams are maps of the future scrawled behind our eyelids. A way of seeing what doesn't exist, what only we, the dreamers, can bring into being. This second type of dream produces art. *True* art. And other marvels." Behind his lenses, his gaze had a pale, intense dazzle. He seemed to peer *into* her.

"This is my florid way of saying that *you*, Miss Finch, strike me as the sort who dreams that second type of dream. A visionary who makes the impossible happen." He placed his swollen hand on his heart. "And so, while I regret that you won't accept the position, my disappointment is offset by the expectation that you will someday bake the gooseberry tart equivalent of a Mozart concerto."

No, he didn't look serious. He'd found his speech comical. He found *her* comical.

Not *only* comical. His eyes glinted. His lips curled. There was mockery in his face, but also appreciation.

She couldn't tear her gaze from his. His teasing belief in her made her knees wobble. Almost instantly she locked them. Her stomach twisted. Mr. De'Ath had insinuated that *she* was a true artist! *She.* The finest falsifier in England. Discomfort prickled down her spine, making her want to squirm.

"A bit much, for pastry," she murmured, and managed to avert her eyes. "There can't be a *Mozart* of gooseberry tarts."

"Why not?"

She glanced back in time to see the smile laze across his face.

"The material doesn't matter. Flour. Gesso. Marble. Butter. Hammers and strings." His smile widened. "A man—or a woman—can dignify anything. But people so rarely take the time to cultivate the necessary skill and intention."

"Or *have* the time." She looked pointedly at his gold watch fob.

A pause, and then:

"Touché." His laugh rippled warmly. He swung up his cane, pointing at a copse of trees. "To the gate, then."

DESPITE HIS HEIGHT, she didn't find herself hopping to keep up as they wound deeper into the gardens. He set a languorous pace. She had to hold back and fight the impulse to rush ahead toward freedom.

Almost there.

They'd walked half the length of the garden before he spoke.

"You deferred, before, on the subject of my brother." His tone was light, conversational. "But I find myself remembering your colorful language. Face that curdles milk. Stingy crosspatch."

She grimaced. Ranting and raving in a duke's drawing room. She should have known she hadn't heard the end of it.

"That was *me* being florid." She shifted her valise from her right hand to her left. Her grip felt greasy on the handle. "I didn't see much of his face, or anything really."

"Your impression of the household owes something to gossip, then." Now he sounded pensive. "Servants talk."

Nearby, a gardener was kneeling in a tulip bed. He glanced up as they passed, eyes skipping from Mr. De'Ath to Nina. There'd be talk of *this*, no doubt.

She and Mr. De'Ath made improbable strolling companions.

She stared at the low hedges. "I suppose everyone talks, your lordship."

"*Lordship*." He snorted, slowed, stopped walking altogether. "It sets my teeth on edge. Call me De'Ath."

She took a few more steps, hoping he'd follow, then turned. Would he tarry from now until doomsday? Looming in black velvet, wings of black hair across his brow.

Lord Death, indeed.

"De'Ath." She nodded, stretching her lips in a smile to hide her agitation.

He smiled back. "You can talk to me. I won't betray your confidence to *his grace*."

She breathed an inaudible sigh of relief as he began again to saunter down the path. She fell into step with him.

"I want you to tell me what you heard of my nephew." He paused. "I'd consider it a kindness."

Kindness. The word sat with her strangely. *Kindness* might provide another explanation for the actions De'Ath had taken in regard to her.

Certainly no one described Alan De'Ath as *kind*. Or handsome, for that matter. Perhaps there were too many other things to say about him first.

She thought about the little boy. She'd only glimpsed him once, when she'd helped Clara change the curtains in his bedchamber. Eight or nine, she'd guess, overthin and unnaturally pale. But De'Ath didn't need her to tell him that. What did he want to know?

"Everyone says he's a sweet child," she ventured. "To be fair to the duke and duchess, some of their irritability must stem from anxiety, about his health."

"Must it?" De'Ath's voice had thinned to a cutting edge.

"Of course." She licked her dry lips, aware that she'd said the wrong thing and unsure how to repair the damage. "Tuberculosis is a terrible disease. And he's the heir."

The garden was gay with spring flowers, and the sun diffused its light evenly across the unrelieved blue of the sky. But De'Ath's eyes looked like black holes.

"Why do you think he has tuberculosis?" he asked, with that new, unexpected sharpness.

"Doesn't he?" She took a small misstep and winced as her ankle wobbled. "I don't remember who told me he did." It was a fact of the house. She'd known within the first hour that the little marquess wasn't well.

"He has his own doctor," she pointed out, "and a live-in nurse."

"Dr. Thayer. Did *he* tell you? He won't speak with me. Geoffrey's orders. I darken his door, and he pretends he's rushing into surgery."

"I never glimpsed the man."

She found De'Ath's eyes too unfathomable and looked away.

"And the nurse, Miss Milford?"

"I don't know what you mean." She worked her throat hard to swallow. As soon as she reached the street, she'd arrow for the first ginger beer seller. She could drink a *barrel*. "What about her?"

They turned into the trees, and she glanced at the house over her shoulder, a final look.

"Does she agree? She spends more time with him than anyone. What does she say belowstairs, when Geoffrey isn't there to censor her words?"

"We haven't spoken. I haven't heard." His intensity, the line of questioning—she couldn't make heads or tails of it. All she knew was that she wasn't giving him the answers he wanted. She angled up her gaze and gave a helpless shake of her head. "I'm sorry."

De'Ath released a breath and his face cleared. "*I'm* sorry," he said. "I'm interrogating you." His voice was smooth again. "Geoffrey and I inhabit different realities. I have to glean my information from other sources."

"I have no information."

"I gleaned that." His mouth tipped up.

She smiled back at him, relieved. His eyes had lost their tarnish and shone with silvery brightness. His mood seemed light again, and hers lightened too. With every step, she drew nearer the street, ginger beer, freedom. Her blood began to sing. Suddenly, he shook his head and laughed.

"We even see different paintings. I look at the painting he hung in pride of place in the drawing room, and I see a picture manufactured by a criminal, someone who aped seventeenth-century techniques to dupe insensitive buyers. He sees a Rembrandt."

Bloody hell. Her whole body tensed.

"That," she said, with all the composure she could muster, "is rather minor, in the scheme of things."

"Minor?" He drew to a halt. They'd entered an enchanting wilderness in miniature, the manicured trees divided by narrow, winding footpaths banked with tulips. A tiny pond glimmered between the trees. It was spanned by a high-arched wooden bridge. Just beyond, the tall iron gate offered passage through the garden wall.

So close.

"No, Miss Finch, a lethargic imitation passed off as an original work of art is nothing *minor*. Do you know—until the 1850s, collectors bought old masters nineteen to the dozen. Counterfeits, for the most part. Why so many fakes?" He gave a professorial flourish of his cane. Nina didn't answer. She understood the genre of masculine lecture, its various cues.

This pause—it was mere punctuation.

"Because the rising demand all but *required* fakes," he continued. "One of the perversities of the art market, but that's another conversation." He shrugged. "I credit the *Art Journal* with reversing the tide. Its writers appointed themselves watchdogs, sniffed out forgeries, did whatever they could to stamp out the trade. And what happened?"

Again, a perfunctory pause.

"You'll tell me," predicted Nina in a murmur, before biting the inside of her cheek.

De'Ath's eyes flashed, but then his mouth quirked.

"I'll tell you," he agreed wryly. "The public shifted its attention to *living* artists. Contemporary painting blossomed. New styles, new movements, began to usher British art into the modern era.

But we must remain on our guard. Forgers and crooked dealers don't merely respond to the market; they shape it. There's no such thing as *one* fake Rembrandt."

His gaze swept the pretty grove and his chiseled lips softened into their habitual half smile. "Forgeries crop up in rings, like toadstools. Find a fake Rembrandt in the drawing room of *this* imbecilic aristocrat, check the drawing room of *that* imbecilic aristocrat. You'll discover that the whole social circle has gone and paneled their homes with them. Soon, the next tier of society will be foaming at the mouth for *their* old masters. Which will prompt the forgers to double their efforts. Which, Miss Finch, sets us back forty years and imperils the interests of artists painting *now*. Imperils art itself."

He brushed a row of tulips with his cane, and she had the sense that if a toadstool had presented itself, he would have whacked cap from stalk.

"So. Not minor." He flicked his eyes to her. "But I'll grant you, more easily resolvable than some of the other issues."

A chill dove deep into her bones. He was standing in front of her, not a yard away, tall and strongly built, a man who could overpower an adversary with sheer brawn. But he used a steel nib instead, black ink.

With his smiting pen, he could condemn her, Jack, Sleaford, Laddie, even Ruby, to a British dungeon. If he was determined to *resolve* the issue of the forgeries, how long would it take him to trace Sleaford to the rest of them?

"Well." She dragged her valise up to her hip. Her dry throat—it was like a rusted bell without a clapper. "There's the gate."

He pivoted. "No countesses yet. Let's both make our escape, shall we?"

On the street, she turned from him immediately and could have kicked herself.

Don't bolt, you ninny, like a bloody cutpurse.

She schooled her leaping nerves, forced herself to rotate.

"This is goodbye, then," she said.

"I rather wish it weren't." He studied her with an odd expression. "Now I have to go to an agency."

He smiled. She smiled.

"Miss Finch," he said, "it was a privilege to know you. I'd doff my hat, but at the moment, my doffing isn't up to snuff. If you were my amanuensis, I'd ask you to doff it for me."

Her lips parted involuntarily at the idea. How close to him would she have to stand to doff his hat?

"If I see you again," he continued, "I hope it's a serendipitous encounter in a village pastry shop. *Your* village pastry shop."

"Me too." The phrase emerged as a croak. Ginger beer, now, gallons of it. But for a moment, she didn't turn. She watched him walk away. His movements were leisured. His gait rolled slightly, the suggestion of a hitch smoothing out as he stepped. He didn't look back.

With luck, they'd *never* see each other again.

If they did, she might not be in a bakery. She might be with a bailiff. Clapped in irons. Her ankles felt heavy as she ducked her head and hurried blindly down the sidewalk, racing to put as much distance as she could between herself and Lord Alan De'Ath.

CHAPTER FOUR

THE RELIEF NINA felt arriving home lasted all of a minute. *Home* was a relative term. Even though she and Jack had lived above Laddie's barbershop for nearly seven years, the commotion in the downstairs parlors still jangled her nerves. Laddie didn't limit himself to barbering. He'd inherited his trade—and the house—from his father, slowly transforming the establishment into a wonder of the world—the underworld, at any rate. It wasn't known as Ladbrooke's anymore, or even Laddie's, but rather as the Knackatory. The Knack for short. Knickknacks galore.

Most days—and nights—assorted swells, swindlers, and the occasional uppish collector circulated through the rooms, poking the mummified crocodiles, trying on the morbidly dented morion helmets, nudging one another with ribald significance and chortling at the sight of the narwhale tusks. This afternoon was no exception.

Nina sidled through the front parlor. Customers were clinking through Laddie's bottles of shaving lotions and hair oil. One man was standing on the leather barber chair, batting at a gilded sunfish that dangled from the rafter. His friends crowded around the basins, trying to teach Polly the parrot a dirty limerick as she splashed in the water.

"There was a young lady of Trent."

Nina ducked around the folding screen, heading for the back stairs. Flash gentlemen filled the gaps between the furniture, paste jewels glittering on their watch chains. She shoved, making unsteady progress, tripping over male feet. The cologne in the air was thick enough to pickle the tapestry pillows.

"I'll be blowed!"

Nina staggered as an elbow clipped her shoulder. The elbow owner was young and bullnecked, dressed in a howling mauvine cutaway jacket and checked trousers. He was making a beeline for the shelves that laddered the far wall.

"By gad." Another man started after him. "Is that a rat?"

Nina jerked around, barking her shin on a trunk. She scanned the highest shelves, cluttered with a dusty hodgepodge of trinkets, antiques, and curios.

When she and Jack had first moved to the Knackatory, Laddie's offerings had been even more haphazard and disorganized. Junk he collected from job lots heaped the divans. Old parchments made drifts on the naked floorboards. Napoleonic memorabilia threatened to collapse the spindly-legged cabinets. Clocks beyond number told motley time and chimed continuously.

Thanks to Jack's practiced eye, the type, quality, and arrangement of objects had improved markedly.

The men, though, hadn't gasped at an unexpected treasure.

They'd spied Fritz.

Nina saw him too, curled up on a shelf beside a stack of French novels. He looked *nothing* like a rat. He was rat-*sized*, perhaps. But his nose didn't protrude rudely like a rat's. He had a sweet, squashed little face, with big black eyes. They were closed at the moment. His long tail curled around him.

She opened her mouth but Laddie spoke first. The rumble of his voice—loud, startlingly deep—silenced the general chatter.

"Rat? You're off your chump."

Nina's gaze flew to him. He stood by an open display case, where he was fanning out hand-painted German playing cards for the admiration of potential buyers. He swept the cards back into the deck, split it, and shuffled the two halves together.

"*That* charming creature," he said, pointing the deck at Fritz, "has no more rat in him than Grigsby."

The man who'd exclaimed *By gad*—presumably Grigsby—turned to glare.

"Pure South American marmoset." Laddie grinned. He bleached his teeth religiously. They were white as an advertisement.

Until today, Nina had thought them matchless in brilliancy.

Alan De'Ath's Cheshire cat smile materialized before her eyes. She blinked. She blinked again. It lingered.

"How much?" asked the first man, he of the elbow and the bull neck. He'd reached the shelves and was straining upward, pinching at Fritz with beringed fingers. His offending elbow swung perilously close to a faience vase filled with peacock feathers.

Nina glanced at Laddie. Surely he'd direct Bull-neck's attention elsewhere, perhaps to the case of artificial gemstones, which Ruby shone with vinegar. The bloke already twinkled with colored glass, but Jack always said Laddie could sell clouds in Cardiff.

"Twenty pounds." Laddie snatched two cards from the deck and held them aloft. Both tens. One patterned with hearts, the other bells.

Nina gasped. Treacherous blighter! Was this his return on her friendship? How many times had she mended his broken lamps? Baked him Victoria sponge and shortbread? The morning she'd left for Umfreville House, she'd fried thin rosy-gold pancakes for the lot of them—Jack, Laddie, Ruby, *and* Fritz—mixing plenty of wine and cream into the batter, the way Laddie liked it. They'd all been pally then.

"Lawrence Ladbrooke, you're the rat!" She pushed aside the gaping oafs who blocked her path and charged at him. "You'd sell your own mother!"

He caught sight of her, and his face registered surprise, then chagrin, then a droopy, overacted sorrow.

"What's this the girl says of the dear departed?" he rumbled to the men around him, pressing the cards—the ten of hearts the topmost—to his breast. "She was a saintly woman, my mother, God rest her soul."

"She raised a reprobate!" Nina stopped short, gripping the finials of a tall-back chair. She glared, neck craned. Laddie was a mountain of a man, widest around the middle, body tapering toward his head, sunny blond hair shining with macassar oil. His grass-green corduroy suit completed the impression. "If you knew any saints, you'd be fencing haloes."

A few of the bystanders hooted, so she widened her glare.

"The marmoset is a member of my family and most definitively *not* for sale."

She whirled and almost smacked into a bust of Homer. The blind bard gazed at her blankly, without a shred of sympathy.

"You're as bad as the rest," she muttered, and edged around him, looping toward the shelves. She could hear Laddie's low rumble.

"A sweet girl, but, as you can see, a bit daffy. Never had a mother herself."

The nerve. Nina sucked in her breath. Laddie and Jack had met as boys in the schoolroom and had maintained a friendship through all Jack's vicissitudes of fortune. Laddie knew more than almost anyone about their mother. He knew Nina wasn't motherless, not in the way Ruby was motherless. Ruby, who'd lost her mother—Laddie's sister—the day she was born. Maybe he erased Nina's mother out of delicacy, because he thought the truth more damning.

Now Nina's face felt hot. After Jack's father died and her own father disappeared, their mother had managed the best she could. She hadn't many options, a young Irishwoman from County Cork, still legally married, with a toddling daughter and a son on the brink of adolescence. She'd met Mr. Farrar while selling combs on the street outside his jewelry shop. After Mr. Farrar, there was Mr. Nelson. And then Mr. Hessey. And then Mr. Bowes. Mr. Dilly. Mr. Thistleton. The list went on.

They weren't all rotters. Mr. Bowes had broken a chair on Jack's back, but Mr. Thistleton, a color mixer for a cloth-printing firm, had recognized his artistic talent and facilitated his application to the Royal Academy Schools. Mr. Dilly used to pull toffees from behind Nina's ears.

But none had done right by their mother in the end. During her last illness, Mr. Mucklow hadn't called the doctor until it was too late. Fever dwindled her to bones and staring eyes. Nina was nine that bitter December. Old enough to remember plenty. If she concentrated, she could still feel the gentle tug of her mother's hands in her hair. She could still hear her voice.

Much comfort in cats, little in men. That was one of her mother's sayings. Unforgettable. The world provided constant reminders.

For example, in the form of Laddie. The lying, scheming *backstabber*.

"Fritz!" She stepped on Bull-neck's heel, then, when he turned, wedged herself between his body and the shelves. "Fritz!"

The white tufts on Fritz's ears pricked, and his eyes opened. He ricocheted off the French novels, zigzagging his way to the floor, and jumped up onto Nina's skirt. She nuzzled his fur with her cheek as he settled onto her shoulder, tail wrapping her neck.

"Look lively." She scowled at Bull-neck and Grigsby and barreled forward. They sprang out of her way.

"Cheeky maid." She heard Bull-neck behind her. "I'd give her the sack, Laddie."

"That's not what I'd give her!" The shout came from across the room. Nina spared a single glance for the offender, who was waggling one of the narwhale tusks for emphasis.

Rats. The lot of them.

Guffaws followed her down the hall.

JACK WASN'T UPSTAIRS. Nina poked her head into the empty painting studio, then banged on his bedroom door. She went down the back stairs and found him in the small, foul-smelling kitchen, kneeling by the open oven in his shirtsleeves.

"Laddie tried to sell Fritz," she announced, and moved a sauce-boat off a chair so she could sit. There was a dormouse in the sauce-boat. She set it carefully atop the plates stacked on the table.

"Dirty-arsed little bugger." Jack shut the oven door and rose, wiping his face with his sleeve.

"Do you mean Laddie? Or Fritz?" She grimaced as Fritz snapped a strand of her hair. He liked to groom her, fingers scratching over her scalp. He groomed Boggs, the spaniel, too, and Dora and Mop, the cats, when they allowed it.

"Laddie, of course." Jack grinned the dimpled grin that made the girls at the Baited Bear sigh. *Sweet Jack*, they called him and forgave his displays of temper. "Fritz is a prince. He missed you sorely."

Nina bit her tongue. Jack had pledged to watch over Prince Fritz in her absence. He should have kept the marmoset close. And cleaned up after him! Laddie roared whenever Fritz rubbed himself on the upholstery or piddled down the curtains. If Jack had let Fritz run wild, ignoring the puddles, she should thank her lucky stars Laddie hadn't gutted and stuffed him.

She would *not* be thanking Jack.

"I expected you yesterday." Jack's smile faded. "You didn't run into any trouble?" He held out his hand. "Let me see the letter."

"Yesterday!" Was he accusing her of lollygagging? She frowned. "You can't just put on a mobcap and waltz into a duke's study saying la-di-da, your documents could use a dusting." She felt on her head for the cap and wiggled the fabric free of the pins.

"The job required cunning." Cunning, and Ruby's lockpick set. She tossed the cap and stood to fetch the biscuit tin down from the shelf above the sink. The sink was filled with greasy pans. To think, she'd left the kitchen spotless!

"I had to bide my time." She sat back in the chair, piling crockery to make room for the biscuit tin on the table. "And by *biding my time* I don't mean *twiddling my thumbs*. They run servants off their feet in that house."

"Poor Birdie." Jack curled his fingers, a quick, repeated motion. "Hand it over."

He didn't doubt that she had the letter. Nor should he. When had she ever failed him?

They had a pact, the two of them. They were bound to each other. By blood and by love, and by their collective enterprise, source of profit and peril.

Of course he didn't doubt. She was his Birdie. His best and only apprentice. Best accomplice. Best friend. She worked miracles with her clever fingers.

Sighing, she fished Sleaford's letter from her boot and passed it over.

Jack gave a short laugh as he scanned the lines. He crumpled the paper and sent it sailing through the air toward the dustbin.

"You did well," he said, and dropped again into a crouch. "Umfreville's an easy mark. And a damn good client." He opened the oven door and warmth wafted out. The acrid smell in the room intensified. "He'll like this Titian."

Nina yanked the lid off the biscuit tin and peered inside. Crumbs gathered in the corners. Not a biscuit remained. She plucked up the biggest crumb and offered it to Fritz, who shifted his weight on her shoulder and emitted a happy chirp. The rest of the crumbs she shook into the sauceboat for the mouse.

"I'll bake more," she murmured to Fritz. But he'd have to wait. No baking a fresh batch of biscuits until Jack was through baking the Titian.

The "Titian" was her work, a portrait of a young man in green. She and Jack began any given forgery by matching their materials as closely as they could to those the artist would have used in his own time. Old wood, old stretchers, old canvas from the scrap shops. Old pictures, if possible. But preparing the finished product for market still required special techniques. He often heated pictures in the oven, to harden the paint. Nina had learned to air out the kitchen before switching to pastry. Otherwise her cakes tasted of varnish.

"Umfreville's an easy mark, to be sure." She fitted the lid on the tin, pounded it shut with her fist, and put it aside. "But what about his brother?"

Jack shut the oven door slowly, sitting back on his heels. There was no sweetness in his expression now. His hazel eyes were hooded. "What about him?"

"You knew!" Nina jerked forward, and Fritz gripped her ear, either for balance or in protest. She offered him her fingertips, still staring at Jack. "Aren't there toffs enough in London without us selling to the one who shared the womb with *Alan De'Ath*?"

"It was Umfreville who walked into the showroom. Chips didn't seek him out." Jack gave a one-shouldered shrug as he stood. "The opportunity was too good to pass up." He scraped another chair back from the table and sat beside her. "Umfreville doesn't consult De'Ath on his purchases. Not on friendly terms, those two. It's a well-known fact."

"He was at the house," said Nina tersely. "Nothing friendly about it. They had a knockdown fight. Didn't stop him from seeing that new portrait of yours. The old man with the bowed head."

"And?" Jack asked, his voice soft. He reached for the sauceboat and rested it on his thigh, looking at the mouse with a strange, anticipatory smile. He was waiting on tenterhooks for her to speak.

It wasn't only about the money for Jack, their manufactory of old masters. He forged—boldly—to thumb his nose at the art establishment that had rejected him. She understood him better than he understood himself. Part of him had wanted Alan De'Ath to assess his work. He relished gulling the gatekeepers. Giving the lie to their touted powers of discrimination.

What is *the difference between a master and a mimic, if the critics themselves can't distinguish? I'll tell you, Birdie. The difference is as many pounds sterling as we can pocket.*

"Not a Rembrandt." She sighed. She wouldn't tell him that it had taken De'Ath less than three seconds to pass judgment. "He said it was a fake."

"The bloody bastard." Jack's brows lowered as he raised his head. A vein throbbed in his forehead. Warning signs. He was about to fly into a rage.

"I don't think Umfreville believed him." Holding his gaze, she pried the sauceboat from his hands. Jack—when he was *Sweet Jack*—had a way with animals. He'd brought Dora and Mop home as kittens, after scooping them, half-drowned, from a rain barrel. Fritz was the gift he made to Nina on her twentieth birthday— rescued from an eccentric drunkard's courtyard menagerie, skinny as a worm from neglect, bald in patches, with gummed-up eyes. He doted on his dormice.

But once his easy affection heated into explosive fury, he was capable of anything. Capable of dashing the sauceboat to the flags with the little mouse inside.

Nina cradled the sauceboat protectively.

"When all's said and done, the picture is Umfreville's business." Jack kicked back in his chair and studied the ceiling. After a long moment, the front legs of the chair crashed down again. He looked at Nina, his expression milder. "If Umfreville himself is still satisfied, then perhaps that's the end of it."

Nina shook her head. "De'Ath makes every picture his business. He's very . . ."

Drat it, she was blushing. Too many descriptors butted up against one another in her mind, none of which seemed entirely apt.

"What?" Jack's look sharpened. "Go on, Birdie. Seems he made an impression. I've never met the man myself. De'Ath is very . . . *what*?"

"Full of himself." She swerved her eyes and stared over Jack's shoulder, at a jar of Aunt Sylvia's hedgerow jelly. Someone had left it open on the shelf, a spoon protruding from its sticky depths.

"A right prig and typical smellfungus." She was parroting Jack's own words, the ones he used when he raved about Academicians, critics, gallerists, and their ilk. "Thinks forgery is worse than child murder. You know the type. He won't let it rest."

"Aye." Jack was rubbing his right hand with his left. A habit of his. His mangled fingers increasingly limited his dexterity and the number of hours he could paint. In recent years, Nina had found herself correcting his shaky brushstrokes, as he'd once corrected hers. "Did Umfreville mention Chips?"

"Not in my hearing." She hesitated. "But I'm sure De'Ath asked after the dealer." It was the obvious starting point. Even if Umfreville had refused to answer, a man with De'Ath's connections wouldn't be long in assembling a list of art dealers whose recent sales included a glut of Dutch masterworks.

Jack leaned forward. "Has De'Ath seen the other paintings?"

"Just the one. But . . ." She hesitated, then quoted: "*There's no such thing as* one *fake Rembrandt. Forgeries crop up in rings.*" Again, the image: De'Ath's smile. She cleared her throat. "That's what he told me."

"Told you," repeated Jack softly. His brows lifted. "De'Ath told *you*, the maid?"

Her blush deepened. "I wasn't the maid at that point." Briefly, she related the scene in the drawing room.

"Of all the . . ." Jack dropped his head in his hands before rearing up. "You were to keep your mouth shut! Slip in and out. Instead you give the duke a tongue-lashing and smash his heirloom china. What if he *had* called the coppers? Did you see the maker's mark on the cups? Not Staffordshire, I can guarantee you that." His eyes fell on a dirty Staffordshire mug squatting between them on the table, decorated with a cock-eyed portrait of Victoria and Albert, to celebrate the coronation. "He could've had you on the hook for every farthing. A fool reason to get thrown in the clink! If you won't use the sense God gave you, then—"

"*I'm* not using sense?" Nina's patience snapped. "You should never have agreed to sell our pictures to Umfreville in the first place! If we end up in the clink, *that's* the bloody reason why!"

Fritz scrambled down from Nina's shoulder to the table and leapt to the counter, where he hopped, screeching.

"Christ," muttered Jack, glancing with surprise from Nina to Fritz.

"*Fake!*" Nina's voice rose with Fritz's. "I dropped the first tray in shock. *Alan De'Ath* not three feet away from me calling your picture a *sham masterpiece*! He followed me into the garden, and I thought the game was up. He's that keen." Nina swallowed, a silvery shiver moving through her. She had to blink.

"But it wasn't up."

"No thanks to you," she muttered, focusing. "He offered me a *job*. As his amanuensis. I nearly choked! Then he all but swore he'd bring England's art forgers to justice. I'd say we're bloody well in for it! And it's not *my* doing, it's—"

"You said no."

"What?" Nina heaved a breath. Strange reversal. *She* was yelling, and Jack . . . Jack was regarding her calmly. His eyes, emptied of emotion, held pure calculation.

"To De'Ath's offer. You said no."

"Of course I said no!" She tried to lower her voice. "If he finds me out, he'll drag me to Scotland Yard. I'm not going to take his dictation."

"That's exactly what you're going to do. You're going to note down every word. We need to know what he knows. What he discovers."

"Ha." She stared at him. He had to be joking. Fritz began to shriek, as though in disbelief.

"I'll warn Chips." Jack's smile was grim. "He's the weak link. Can't trust him not to squawk if he stands to save his own skin. *You* stop squawking." He looked irritably toward Fritz. "My ears are bleeding."

Nina opened her mouth to protest, but no sound emerged.

"Shutter the showroom," Jack continued, half to himself. "Shove off to France, Holland, somewhere. Give it a few weeks to blow over. De'Ath will get some other bee in his bonnet before long."

"Let's all shove off." Nina hugged herself. "For good. You and I can go to Hensthorpe. Mr. Craddock's getting old, Jack. Summer's too hot for him by the ovens. He might sell now, if I ask."

"Capital." Jack barked a laugh. "You'll be a baker, and I'll be a farmer. I'll get myself some pigs and a plow." He made a disdaining gesture. The gold rings on his fingers clasped *real* gemstones. Jack would go to hell before he'd go to Hensthorpe. She knew that. He wanted to leave the Knack for a custom-built castle, to live large in society's shadow, a counterfeit lord.

Her fantasy was simpler. A village pastry shop, brick and flint, with a bright new sign. NINA'S SWEETS. Her canvases, cake tops. Her paints, buttercreams.

Jack knew *that*.

"I *will* bake," she said stubbornly. Jack often mocked her aspirations, made it clear he preferred she put their partnership first—if not forever, at least for the foreseeable future. *Focus on scones in your dotage*, he'd say. He didn't want her to be the Mozart of gooseberry tarts.

She felt a prickle. The way De'Ath had looked at her . . .

Ridiculous. The Mozart of gooseberry tarts. She could never pronounce that phrase to Jack. Princess of Counterfeits was more to his liking.

But he'd come around eventually. She wouldn't give him the choice.

"I'll bake," she repeated, then coughed. "And not pictures, either."

"Hell." Jack started, diving for the oven, from which thin black smoke was seeping. Nina tensed. Once *she'd* left a painting too long in the oven, one of Jack's. She'd gotten lost in daydreams as she'd rearranged her small store of spices, and the next thing she knew her eyes were stinging, her lungs bucking in her chest, resisting the caustic air. The painting had burst into flames. On that memorable afternoon, Jack's hollering could have raised the dead.

Luckily, the Titian emerged relatively unscathed. Disaster averted, Jack swung back to face her. Fritz had quieted down. In the front parlor, a clock was chiming.

"We're not turning tail," he said. "Not because one critic took issue with one painting. De'Ath wants to play detective? Like he did in the National Gallery, with that bogus Botticelli? Righto. You'll be there to put him off the scent."

"How?" Nina hugged herself tighter. Dear Lord, was she really entertaining the notion? Alan De'Ath's amanuensis! By this time tomorrow, she might be doffing his hat.

"You'll think of something." Jack shrugged. "At the very least, he won't be able to surprise us. We'll stay one step ahead of him. Don't forget, we've got the king of the smellfunguses in our pocket, that blowhard Oxford don. What's his name?" He drummed a sooty forefinger on his temple. "*Syme.* Lloyd Syme bought a half dozen of our pictures from Chips. If Chips gets caught out selling fakes, then Syme looks a fool. Ergo, King Smellfungus will defend Chips to the death." He gave a snort. "And they say *we're* the fraudsters."

Nina felt a gentle impact. Fritz had leapt to her. He climbed her shoulder and she reached up to stroke him, gratefully.

"No more nonsense about Hensthorpe." Jack shook his head. "You're not going, not at present."

Why? She tamped down on the question. Of late, they'd been making money hand over fist. Jack doled out a weekly pittance, but she knew the full amounts, what was his, what was hers. They both had enough, surely. To start over.

"There's too much at stake." Jack was looking at her.

She lowered her eyes. *He* was why, the reason she'd stay.

When their mother died, Nina had been left with no one in the world to care for her. No one but Jack, scarcely nineteen, too young for the burden. He'd turned up on Mr. Mucklow's doorstep.

It's you and me, Birdie, he'd said. *We'll stick together, come what may.*

He'd sacrificed to keep her with him. His attic room in the mansion let by his fancy artist friends in Chelsea. His place at the Academy Schools.

She wouldn't have picked the life he'd given her, but the alternative would have been worse. The orphanage. The workhouse.

If she fled when he needed her . . . who would she be? Someone unrecognizable.

But this . . . to be Alan De'Ath's amanuensis. It was absurd, a hazardous proposition.

Her mouth felt dry again. She peered into the Staffordshire mug. The contents looked murky, curdled. Undrinkable. She gave a groaning sigh.

Blast. Fritz butted the soft underside of her chin with his head, which was hard beneath the fur.

She looked up and met Jack's eyes.

"Do you think I'd better bring my own pen?" she asked.

Jack dimpled. *Sweet Jack.*

"That's my Birdie," he said. "Alan De'Ath is no match for you." He laughed. "How keen can he be? He didn't recognize *your* worth. *Amanuensis.*" Shaking his head, he stepped forward, reached out to take her hands. His fingers were hot and damp, the rings cool.

"These were made for more," he said, lifting her hands. "And he'll never know."

Chapter Five

Casa De'Ath stood riverside in Chelsea. The largest of the houses on Wyvern Walk, a redbrick Georgian mansion, five bay windows wide. Nina hesitated between the gate piers. She touched her fingers to the chain of her chatelaine purse. The purse held a notebook, a pen, an ink bottle, and assorted nibs.

Ready as she'd ever be.

She walked the short garden path to the entrance, admiring the rectangular beds of shrubs and herbs, most unfamiliar. She recognized the olive trees from Italian paintings, all those narrow leaves.

Not surprising, really, that even De'Ath's botanical taste distinguished him.

Scrolled wrought-iron rails framed the steps to the front door.

She knocked, waited, and knocked again.

At last, the door opened. A man squinted at her. He was bald with a gray, pointed beard. He held a small book bound in fragile-looking ochre cloth against his narrow chest. His brown suit was mostly made of patches.

"No ham?" he asked, peering about, as though he couldn't believe his eyes. "No wine? Sausages?"

His thick accent transformed *w*'s into *v*'s.

The letters stamped across the book he held resembled none she'd ever seen.

"Nothing?" he asked. "Ah well. You are trusting talent, then."

He nodded his approval but added, softly, half to himself, still peering at Nina, "I had premonition. This time, *ham*."

"This *is* Mr. De'Ath's residence?" Nina heard the uncertainty in her voice. But there was no possibility of error.

Casa De'Ath, as the wags called it. Number 11 Wyvern Walk.

"Yes, yes." The man waved her inside. "You are prima donna? What opera?" He said something in Italian and, when she didn't answer, switched to another language. German, she thought.

"I'm not a prima donna," she said. "I don't sing at all. I'm Nina Finch."

"And he?" He pointed to Fritz, who was flopped on Nina's shoulder like a roll of hair, an element of coiffure inattentive eyes might slide right over. She'd hoped to delay this moment.

She tried to smile.

"Fritz," she said, and the marmoset gave a lazy chirp. Coiffure never chirped. Wishful thinking, that Fritz made for a subtle companion. It was hardly sensible—porting a monkey to a lord's abode, particularly when you planned to petition said lord to renew an offer of employment. But Jack was too distracted to mind him properly, and Ruby was always in and out, on errands for Laddie. It was all too easy to guess what Laddie would do if Fritz stayed behind without a champion.

She'd made a rash decision.

"Fyodor!" The man smiled. "I call him Fyodor. He has big soul."

He slid the book inside his voluminous coat and pulled out an orange, like a gleeful magician. He began to peel it, holding out a bit of rind. Fritz leapt to him and seized it. The man tucked Fritz into his waistcoat, beaming.

"Are you . . . the butler?" Nina felt her eyebrows knit together. Who else but a butler opened a mansion door? But the man wore no livery, and what he did wear was impossibly rumpled. He had ink on his fingers.

"I am Nikolai Anatolyevich Kuznetsov," he said. "The novelist. I work as butler. You speak French?"

Nina shook her head, embarrassed. A well-bred woman—and any *real* amanuensis—would no doubt be fluent in foreign tongues. At the Knack, Laddie sold French novels, French postcards, and

French letters. Whenever she got the chance, she pored over the novels and the postcards. She'd examined the French letters too, which she'd found particularly confounding until Ruby demonstrated their function by sliding a carrot into the rubber sheath.

"It is good." Kuznetsov looked up from Fritz, his expression fond. "We speak English." He fed Fritz another piece of rind with his blackened fingertips and led Nina down the hall. Pictures lined the walls. Regular in size, they showed no continuity in style or subject. Medieval and romantic subjects. Scenes from modern life. Views of Venice. She wanted to study each in turn, but Kuznetsov walked briskly. They passed under an arch and turned left down another hallway. At the hall's end, a spiral stair with an iron balustrade wound steeply to the upper stories.

Nina paused at the threshold of an open door. A lovely parlor, Pompeiian red and gold, but disordered, with wooden packing crates levered open, straw strewn about. One young man, thin and dark, sat on a closed crate, long legs stretched out. He was peeling an orange. Another young man sat at the piano, pressing an odd melody from the keys, stopping and starting, his head cocked. His sandy brown hair fell past his shoulders.

"They are Kessler and McAdams." Kuznetsov came to stand beside her. "Poet and composer. Also, footmen. You like orange?"

Nina spied the trove of oranges glowing in an opened crate.

"Oh, I'm quite all right. Don't trouble yourself," she began, but Kuznetsov was already crossing into the room.

"Not trouble," he said, and then to Kessler and McAdams, "Gentlemen, meet Miss Finch and Mr. Fyodor."

The music broke off. Both young men looked at Nina with abstracted smiles before turning their attention to Fritz.

"Brilliant little fellow!" cried Kessler, springing to his feet. "He deserves a sonnet."

"A ballad," called McAdams, pressing his fingers again to the keys, banging out a sprightlier tune.

"What is he, though?" asked Kessler. "I must seek the rhyme."

"He's a marmoset." Nina stepped into the room. "Nothing rhymes with it."

"Omelet," mused Kessler. "Bilboquet. Or—has he a taste for

fine cheese? How's this for a beginning? *He set out at dawn, the marmoset. But he hadn't arrived in Parma—yet!* It continues, interweaving the marmoset's progress with that of the cheese itself. Cow to cauldron. Yes?"

"No!" called McAdams, banging an emphatic, negatory chord.

"Watch the nail," added Kessler, an afterthought.

Nina narrowly avoided it, skipping awkwardly to the side. The floor was littered with nails, discharged by the lids of the packing crates.

"What *is* all of this?" she asked as Kuznetsov handed her an orange.

"Homage to the great De'Ath," said Kuznetsov, waggling his eyebrows. Nina's eyes roved. One crate contained a bronze Medici lion. Another, bottles of wine. And there, a cured ham.

"These are just from today," said Kessler, nudging a crate with his boot. "They flood the house whenever an opera opens, or a ballet. Or an exhibition. Last week, a tenor from Parma brought a wheel of cheese so heavy he had to roll it down the hall. De'Ath made him roll it back." He sighed his regret. Clearly, *he* had a taste for fine cheese. "De'Ath won't accept any gifts. Except if there's no card. As with these oranges."

"It's obvious who sent the oranges." McAdams spoke over his shoulder, still playing. "Signorina Bonaccorso, who stood in the garden and warbled that song about the orange groves of Sicily."

"Pure speculation." Kessler wore a mischievous grin. "We can't return the oranges on a hunch. If we're wrong, the signorina will suppose De'Ath sent a gift to *her*. No, we must eat them, my friend. We have no choice."

McAdams banged another chord and laughed, spinning around on the piano stool. He had a freckled, mirthful face, with bright eyes that he fixed on Nina.

"*You're* not a desperate chanteuse, showing up empty-handed," he observed. "Or do you mean to give De'Ath the marmoset?"

"No!" Nina almost tugged Fritz away from Kuznetsov. But he looked contented. Kuznetsov, too, looked contented. He was rubbing Fritz's head with his thumb as he continued to peel his orange using one hand and his teeth.

Kessler and McAdams—they looked rather contented as well. Did they spend their days lounging in this parlor, picking out songs on the piano, chasing after rhymes, unpacking and repacking crates, sampling the delicacies?

Footmen in Casa De'Ath led far merrier lives than their equivalents in Umfreville House.

"Mr. De'Ath offered me a position," she said. "As his amanuensis."

She stiffened, prepared for ridicule, skepticism, even an impromptu interview, during which she'd try, and fail, to prove her credentials. She could imagine the men shaking their heads.

Doesn't speak French.

Doesn't know any words that rhyme with marmoset.

Kessler nodded mildly. "Finch, was it?"

"Welcome," said McAdams.

The pieces clicked into place. The men weren't incredulous, because De'Ath *relied* on serendipity to fill every position. Agencies didn't deliver the likes of Kuznetsov, Kessler, or McAdams to lords in search of dependable domestics.

She'd wager De'Ath's entire staff was serendipitous, a collection of down-at-heel bohemians he'd encountered in coffeehouses and literary salons.

He'd collected her as well. He hadn't broken the mold. He'd acted true to form. His offer—it didn't signify suspicion, or any inordinate interest, either.

Good. Better that she didn't seem special in any way. To him, to anyone.

Still, a bit lowering, wasn't it?

She was squeezing her orange. The sharp, sweet scent tingled her nose.

Kessler took a breath.

"Charming pet, the marmoset," he intoned. "Compared to the kangaroo. The koala bear's not half so fair, when you see him at the zoo. The platypi, I won't deny, are—"

"Enough monkey business," interrupted Kuznetsov, and looked at Nina. "I take you to De'Ath."

SHE DIDN'T SEE De'Ath when they entered the drawing room. Her first impression was of the room itself, long and bright, bay windows looking onto the garden. A molded frieze topped the walls, pale owls in flight against a background of midnight blue. The room wasn't cluttered, but neither was it sparse in its furnishings. It combined perfect comfort with perfect taste.

She couldn't see *him*, but the room revealed his sensibility.

"And he might be the next surveyor of the queen's pictures! Did you hear *that*? The *wretch*."

Nina's eyes moved to the speaker, an agitated young woman in aesthetic dress, the pleated apricot silk a striking complement to the deep blue tones of the room. Wispy curls had escaped her loose chignon and stuck every which way, adding to her look of bristled indignation. She broke off as Nina and Kuznetsov approached, swiveling in the upholstered armchair.

De'Ath was sprawled on a love seat, his cane propped beside him. He turned his head.

"Miss Finch." He smiled with more satisfaction than surprise. "You've reconsidered. How fortunate." He raised his left hand, wrapped in a neat bandage. "Not broken, but not functional either. Did you bring your things? It's best if you live in. Mrs. Dormody will prepare your room."

"I didn't want to presume," Nina murmured. She'd purposely left her packed valise at the Knack. An excuse to disappear for the evening, so she could report to Jack. "You might have filled the position."

De'Ath looked as contented as his footmen, with that languid posture. His hair kicked up in waves, full and black. She balled her fist against the urge to comb its thickness with her fingers.

Dear Lord. She blamed Fritz for his bad influence. She wasn't a marmoset, to groom De'Ath as though for nits! But his hair—it beckoned, wildly strokable, tauntingly soft in contrast with his hawkish features. She itched, as well, to feel his jaw beneath the side-whiskers, to map its obscured dimensions.

"So I did. The position is filled as of this moment." De'Ath gestured, tipping his head, a lock of hair falling across his brow. "Get your things later. For now, take a seat. Do you need a pen? Paper?"

She fumbled with the clasp of her chatelaine in her eagerness to extract the pen and the small blue morocco notebook.

"I brought the essentials," she said. "And one other thing." She hesitated. "Not a *thing*. That is, I apologize, but I had to bring . . . I hope you don't mind. I brought . . ."

"Fyodor!" Kuznetsov finished for her, stepping forward proudly. Only Fritz's head was visible, peeping out of his waistcoat. Fritz chirped, then stuck out his tongue.

"Dear goblin!" The woman in the armchair leaned forward with a delighted cry. "Aren't you an imp! I want to put you in a picture."

This time, Nina did reach for Fritz, but he wouldn't go to her. Too much stimulation. He wiggled out of Kuznetsov's waistcoat and bounced between them down to the floor, skittering over the rug to a carved cabinet. Within moments, he was perched on top, beside a blue vase. *Bollocks.* An expensive blue vase.

"He's very well-behaved," asserted Nina, less a lie than a fervent wish. *Dear God, if he starts breaking china . . .*

De'Ath had removed his spectacles and was polishing the lenses slowly on his sleeve, watching Fritz with that amused smile. If the fate of the vase concerned him, he didn't show it.

"He'll fall asleep in another moment," she added, another wish. "No one will notice him."

"I'll continue noticing, if that's all right." The woman hauled a large bag onto her lap and pulled out a sketchbook.

"Quite." Nina fixed a smile on her lips. She'd worried about the impropriety, introducing a loud, potently aromatic, ill-tempered mammal into Casa De'Ath. But he'd already won the hearts of the occupants. Well, perhaps not De'Ath's heart. Everyone else's, though. Soon, he'd figure in poems, ballads, pictures, novels. With luck—lots of luck—he wouldn't transform himself from hero into villain.

Kuznetsov clapped a hand to his heart and said something in French to De'Ath, who laughed and responded, also in French.

Nina drifted to a Morris chair near De'Ath and plopped into it, ears burning. She felt—*oafish*. Embarrassingly inadequate. Kuznetsov was disheveled, yes, but his very raggedness seemed proof of intellectual preoccupation. He had a cultured mind. Everyone did in Casa De'Ath.

Praying that they wouldn't *all* begin speaking in French, she set her ink bottle on the side table, opened the blank notebook to the first page, and composed her face. She had a secretarial demeanor at least, with her pursed lips, and her plain dress, navy with thin white stripes.

She couldn't concentrate. New worries intruded. What if Fritz had eaten too much orange? Fruit rarely sat well. The finely knotted Persian carpets on the floor looked older and rarer than those in Umfreville House, intricately ornamented with dense, curvilinear designs. If Fritz messed them . . .

Her lips screwed tighter. She began to scrawl with the steel nib of the pen, spelling out the only words of French in her vocabulary.

Boudoir.
Volupté.
Merde.

"Miss Finch," said De'Ath, and her pen skipped. Hastily, she scribbled out the column. She realized Kuznetsov was heading for the door and almost rose in a bid to make him stay. Too late. He disappeared into the hall. Her benevolent guide. Suddenly bereft, she turned her eyes on Alan De'Ath.

He was settling his spectacles on his nose, an arm draped across the back of the love seat. "Let me introduce the Duchess of Weston and Miss Holroyd."

Nina kept her lips together. Secretary. That was her role. No gaping. Elegant deference. But how to display it? She dipped slightly in her chair, a discreet bow. The duchess didn't notice. She'd twisted around to sketch Fritz, who huddled against the vase, very much awake.

"He's a perfect gargoyle," said the duchess. "I might add wings."

Nina cleared her throat but thought better of speaking.

This was the East Ender who'd painted *Endymion*, a massive, mythically styled nude modeled on her future husband, the Duke of Weston. Even Jack, who on principle ignored the hullabaloos that attended the Royal Academy's Summer Exhibitions, had taken note of *that* sensation.

The Duchess of Weston formed part of a clique of modern painters, all female. The Sisterhood. Aside from the ubiquitous engravings of *Endymion*, Nina hadn't encountered their work. Over the course of her life, she'd spent thousands of hours in the National Gallery, copying the paintings in the collections, training her eye and her hand. But she never set foot in the galleries devoted to the latest canvases. Jack wouldn't allow it. Too risky, rubbing elbows with the habitués of those exhibition rooms—critics and collectors, the very people who'd evaluate and buy their forgeries. She had no personal acquaintance with any artist of any fame.

She and Jack focused on the *dead* artists exclusively.

Until De'Ath had lectured her on the relationship between the trade in old masters and the depressed sales of new pictures, she'd never considered the negative impact forgery might have on living painters.

Did it make her conscience prick?

"We were just discussing Lloyd Syme's impenitent stupidity," said De'Ath's other guest. Miss Holroyd, by process of elimination. Also a member of the Sisterhood, if memory served.

Nina turned her head. And stared. At a handsome dandy, with close-cropped hair, dressed to the nines in a double-breasted mulberry jacket and fawn trousers. The dandy leaned back in the chair, throwing one slim leg across the other.

Nina had seen women in breeches at the burlesque with Jack. Something pinged differently here. Miss Holroyd's bright arrogance as she returned Nina's stare brought a blush to her cheeks.

Why, Miss Holroyd *was* a dandy, an absolute rake!

She winked at Nina, a friendly wink.

"Mark this down," she commanded. "We'll need De'Ath to make hay with it later. Lloyd Syme, the old crank, told Henley, *William* Henley of the *Magazine of Art*, that *all* our pictures are quote *a wicked folly and a blight on womankind* unquote. He wants to see them burned! He said this in front of us, last night, at Sir Wyndham's dinner."

Nina's pen sped across the page.

"Old crank," repeated Miss Holroyd, for Nina's benefit. "That's key. And don't bother with *Duchess of Weston*. Write *Lucy Coover*. That's how she signs her pictures."

The duchess was still sketching, looking between her sketchbook and Fritz, who suddenly screeched and raced down the side of the cabinet.

"Blast." The duchess lowered her pencil. "But I must say, my mood has improved tremendously. Fyodor is a love."

"Fritz," said Nina automatically, but no one seemed to hear. Miss Holroyd had started talking again.

"*My* mood won't improve until that *old crank* is taken down a peg or two. Do I balk at honest criticism? Never! But I refuse to tolerate bigoted abuse."

She turned to De'Ath. "You *will* attend the private view tomorrow at the Olgilvie Gallery? We don't ask for flattery. We demand pure aesthetic judgment, delivered without grudge or prejudice. Something to counteract the misogynist claptrap of that doddering old . . ."

She took a breath.

"Crank?" suggested Nina, pen flying.

"Bastard," said Miss Holroyd. "You don't object to obscenities, I hope?"

"Not at all." Nina shook out her hand. "I have a brother." She studied the notebook pages, spidered with close script, the lines slanting up. "I'm afraid I missed a bit."

"Crank. Bastard." De'Ath raised his brows, directing a wry smile in her direction. "I'm certain you captured the essence. When my hand is healed, I'll resume my own note-taking. You'll copy out and organize the notes. This state of affairs . . ." He lifted the bandaged hand. "It's temporary. So for now, record what you can."

His voice was warm. He'd spoken to put her at ease.

Nina shifted in her chair. Dammit, her conscience did prick. She'd taken her place among Casa De'Ath's peculiar, likable assortment of individuals as a deceiver.

She almost preferred the cold atmosphere at Umfreville House. At least there, in the service of the unjust and despicable rich, she'd felt righteous. More Robin Hood, than, well . . . *robber*. It *was* robbing, in a sense. Signing a stolen name to a picture, which would be sold under false pretenses.

She realized she was still staring at De'Ath. His lashes were so long, they touched the lenses of his spectacles.

"I'll do my best," she said with a shiver, far too late.

De'Ath had already looked away from her, to his guests.

"I have good news," he said. "The old crank's day may well be done. There's no danger of his becoming surveyor of the queen's pictures." A smile spread across his face—a devilish smile. "Not unless Her Majesty has a taste for fakes."

ALAN HAD GUESSED that Holroyd would react first. A victorious yawp, followed by Coover's barrage of questions.

But Miss Finch beat them both.

She gasped.

"Huzzah!" cried Holroyd as she pounded the arm of her chair.

"What do you mean, *fakes*?" asked Coover, eyes narrowed.

"I shouldn't have spoken so soon." He shook his head, but he was grinning. He could see it all unfolding, see the end result with a clarity both giddy and pitiless, almost preternatural.

Like when he was a boy, during those chess games with his father. Counting the moves to checkmate before he touched his first pawn. Then and now, an addictive feeling.

"Do you know an art dealer named Sleaford?" he asked.

Holroyd glanced at Coover, who shrugged a shoulder. "Doesn't ring a bell. He mustn't organize exhibitions."

"I'm making inquiries about him now." Alan rested his left hand on his left thigh, neatly stacking his physical discomforts. The throbbing of his knuckles. The burning in his hip, dull and persistent, a hot coal nested in the socket. He sealed off his awareness of that portion of his body.

All mind. His existence began and ended right behind his eyes. Easiest to pretend when he had a puzzle to solve, a game to win. He was almost grateful to Geoffrey, to Syme, to Sleaford. *Almost.*

"From what I've gathered," he continued, "his inventory consists of old masters. It's a small firm, with a showroom in High Holborn.

He sold my brother a fake Rembrandt. Syme buys from him as well. No proof, as of yet, that Syme purchased forgeries. But . . ."

"Cracking!" Holroyd pounded the chair again. "This isn't good news. It's *glorious*. Syme buying fakes for the blooming *museum*!"

"Purely speculative at this point." Alan said it warningly. Holroyd was hotheaded, passionately devoted to her own art and the art of her Sisters.

"Don't hie off to the newspaper offices just yet," he added. "I'll need time to investigate, confirm, build a case. You'll know when it's safe to gloat. You'll be the *first* to know. The Sisters. And Miss Finch, of course."

He inclined his head toward Miss Finch.

Miss Finch had stopped writing. In fact, she'd laid her pen in the gutter of the notebook and wore a fixed expression.

"Gah!" Holroyd let out a gusty sigh, which recalled his attention. "Even so. Let's ring for a drink."

"It's hardly noon." Coover jammed her sketchbook back into her bag. "Let's not. What about our meeting? We should go."

"Obviously we should go," said Holroyd with another sigh. "I was suggesting a solitary, celebratory, *valedictory* glass of cognac."

The gardenia had slipped down from the buttonhole of her jacket, and she plucked it up and sniffed the white petals. Despite articles—by Syme, but not only Syme—that spilled as much ink denouncing her degenerate personal habits as her paintings, she dressed, with increasing frequency and boldness, in exquisitely tailored three-piece suits, with every accessory male vanity allowed.

"We're talking about a meeting of the Sisterhood," said Coover to Miss Finch helpfully. She, too, had noticed that Miss Finch's pen had stopped moving. "We're a circle of artists who support and critique each other's work."

"Thank you." Miss Finch gave herself a little shake. She bent again over the notebook.

"Do you take an interest in art yourself?" asked Holroyd, threading the gardenia back into her buttonhole.

"No." Miss Finch looked up. "I was told it's not necessary for the job."

"More boring that way," observed Holroyd, lifting one brow

and one corner of her mouth, poking fun. "Tomorrow, at the gallery, I'll demand your opinion of my pictures."

Miss Finch frowned. "I'm only the amanuensis." She gestured to herself, to her dress, which buttoned up to her chin. She could have modeled for a fashion plate in a magazine devoted to bluestockings. She'd scraped back her hair into a painfully severe bun. Shocking that her eyes didn't water.

Alan bit back a smile. Yesterday, she'd insisted she was moving to the countryside. She'd even appeared in his dreams, tramping toward him down a hillside, holding up the corners of her apron, which sagged with the weight of its cargo, enormous gooseberries, greeny-gold in the sun. Today, she'd appeared in his house in her version of scholastic garb, with an old-fashioned reed dip pen, eager to claim her place as his assistant. His curiosity at the reversal manifested as admiration.

She was one of a kind, this Miss Finch. It would be a waste for her to note down his thoughts without ever sharing her own.

"You're entitled to your own taste," he said to her. "Which I can help you refine."

"Lofty, isn't he?" Holroyd winked at Miss Finch, then looked at him indignantly, wrinkling her nose. "Before you do any *refining*, we must give her context. She doesn't even know who Lloyd Syme *is* and *why* his ruination tickles us pink!"

"Miss Finch has gone quite pink," said Coover gently. She was right—Miss Finch's cheeks had flushed. "Don't put her on the spot."

But Holroyd couldn't be stopped.

"Lloyd Syme," she said. "Crank, chump, tosser, *bastard*. Evil mossback. Shibboleth-spewing dinosaur. Puffed-up duffer. Not to mention . . ."

Coover groaned. "Kate."

"Very well." Holroyd glowered and started again. "Lloyd Syme. He is a liverish art critic, beloved of the hidebound elements of high society. He has a remit to purchase pictures for the South Kensington Museum." She tapped a finger to her lips as though wracking her brain.

"Oh, and he slanders women artists! There's *that*." She snapped her fingers, face darkening.

"Women artists, yes, but also *any* artist that De'Ath cares to champion," amended Coover. "De'Ath and Syme have a long-standing enmity."

Miss Finch cut her eyes at him. It still took him off guard, the needlelike quality of their gaze.

He smiled. "All true. Syme was once Slade Professor of Fine Art at Oxford University. That's how we met. I, the lowly undergraduate. He, the high-flown luminary. For a time, I was chief among his acolytes. But in the end, I didn't fancy myself a follower."

Understatement, all around. Syme had been a god, bestowing favors, elevating select students, introducing them into the highest echelons of the literary and artistic worlds. He'd made Alan his particular protégé.

But Alan had blasphemed. He'd violated Syme's commandments by thinking, and writing, for himself.

Now, at thirty-three, he could look back on his behavior and see how he might have tempered it. But then . . . angry, arrogant, untested, scarcely nineteen years old, and out of his mother's sight for the very first time—he'd had too much to prove.

"What happened?" asked Miss Finch, pen poised but motionless.

"I objected to his theory of art. Published an essay that argued with his seminal work. An eviscerating essay, I'll admit. I quoted him extensively. Critiqued his style as well as his ideas. For that betrayal, he tried to ruin my career—tried and failed. I turned the essay into a book." He shrugged. "I still object to his theory. Instead of responding to my objections, he continues his attempts to discredit me. And so the feud goes on."

"*We* will have a feud on our hands." Coover stood, heaving her bag onto her shoulder. "A feud with our Sisters if we're late for this meeting. *Kate.*"

Holroyd leapt to her feet, and Alan rose as well, the gallant host. He tested his legs. The hot coal in his hip socket always burned, holding its heat in some dark, compacted, inaccessible place. Nothing cooled it. Today, though: a low smolder. No flares of pain. Nonetheless, as soon as the Sisters had dashed from the room—Holroyd yawping and pummeling the air—he sat again before addressing Miss

Finch. He always sat, when the option presented itself. No point in squandering even a moment of strength he might need later.

Miss Finch was looking at him, lips pursed, pen still slanted at an attentive angle. Waiting. He rubbed his forehead, fighting the urge to laugh, at himself. *He* had created this situation, inviting this young woman into his household.

He hoped to God she would stop pursing her lips at him. The schoolmarmish expression only emphasized her fresh face, the full-ness of her mouth, that sweetly creased lower lip.

He cleared his throat. "Are you prepared for an excursion? If you need refreshment first . . ."

"I have refreshment," she said promptly. "I put one of your or-anges in my purse. *Oh*." She bit her lip and turned crimson.

Now he did laugh. "Already partaking of my ill-gotten gifts? You'll fit right in, then."

"Do you want it back? The orange?" she asked, a line between her brows. "To return to . . . Signorina Bonaccorso?"

"Heaven forfend." He shook his head. "House rules, Miss Finch. Rule one. No bribes. I don't accept them. Sometimes packages ar-rive anonymously. Those are to be destroyed. The staff's preferred method is ingestion, particularly when the packages contain wine, cheeses, cured meats, fruits, or bonbons. I look the other way. Rule two. No Signorina Bonaccorso. The woman is indefatigable and mustn't be encouraged. Once she went so far as to hire housebreak-ers who smuggled her through the back door, so she could hold a midnight concert." *In his bedchamber.* She'd continued with the aria even as he ejected her.

"I don't write notices under duress," he added, and frowned as he thought of Geoffrey. "And I don't allow considerations beyond the artistry itself to influence my judgment."

"I'll make a note." Miss Finch lowered her eyes to her notebook. "For myself." Her pen wanted ink and scratched as she wrote, a sound like tearing fabric.

An evocative association.

He realized his eyes had slid down from her face.

At first glance, Miss Finch's bluestocking getup was prudish as you please. But the impression didn't stand up to closer inspection. The buttons strained at the bust. Her dress did her—and the world— a disservice, trying to pinch and mold her figure into wasp-waisted slimness.

She belonged in a canvas by Peter Paul Rubens, celebrant of female curves.

Another scratch, louder.

He cleared his throat. "On the way out, I'll fetch you a fountain pen, or a pencil. Your writing implement—it's antique. You need something less cumbersome than a dipping reed and an ink bottle."

"I have a pencil." She closed the notebook and considered the reed. Eighteen ten would be his guess.

"But this pen seemed more official," she said. "It probably belonged to a barrister or a banker. I picked it for luck."

She blushed again—at the admission—and turned her head toward the window. Thought she needed luck, did she? Well she might think so. Her last post had terminated in unmitigated disaster.

A triangle of light gilded the flushed crest of her cheek.

He leaned back on the love seat so he wouldn't be tempted to rub his thumb across that rose-gold wedge, the sun-warmed satin of her skin.

It helped that his dominant hand was wrapped up like a mummy.

"Fyodor won't be welcome where we're going," he said. "You can leave him with Kuznetsov, in the butler's pantry. But—where is Fyodor?"

He scanned the room.

"Fritz," said Miss Finch. "His name is Fritz. He's dozing behind that curtain." Her voice held a touch of uncertainty. "He's like a cat, but . . . lazier."

"Lazy, you say?" Alan caught the motion out of the corner of his eye a moment before she did.

"A lump of a thing," she affirmed. "Just lies around and . . ."

Fyodor—or Fritz—flashed out from behind a pillar, head crowned with tufted white fur, mouth opened wide to emit an ear-splitting yowl.

"Oh, damn bugger blast!" Miss Finch was up in an instant, darting this way and that, trying to block each objet d'art as Fritz careened on his zigzag course. She made a futile grab, then another. He leapt onto a table, then to a chair, then to her shoulder, then launched himself into space. She gasped, spun on her heel, and gave chase, thundering back in Alan's direction.

Before he could blink, Fritz was flying toward him, truly as though he *did* have wings. A furry gargoyle in flight. Screaming like a banshee.

Alan grunted a laugh as the monkey struck his chest, scrabbling up his jacket to his shoulder, twisting its claws into his hair. Miss Finch was only a second behind.

"Get off!" she cried. "Don't be a beast!" She made a final grab and tripped over Alan's cane.

All that rounded softness.

She came down on him like a sledge.

CHAPTER SIX

DEAR GOD. IF this wasn't grounds for a sacking . . .

Nina found herself half on the floor, half on De'Ath, gripping his lapels for dear life. His face was very close. And looked rather green.

She'd *injured* him. *Pardon.* She'd say *pardon.*

She couldn't say it. She had no air in her lungs. And yet—air abounded, fathoms and fathoms of it, now as always. Dumbfounded, she stared into De'Ath's eyes.

"Miss Finch," he said coolly, despite his clenched teeth, "has anyone ever told you that you're an exceedingly memorable woman?"

All at once, her lungs filled, painfully. She heard herself make an odd moan.

"Blow to the solar plexus." His face drew closer still. "Take slow breaths."

His throat was thick, a column of muscle. Her eyes latched to it, to the segment of exposed skin above the fussy folds of his cravat. She breathed. He used Brown Windsor soap. The bergamot—the soap's signature note—made her nostrils flare. The blend of spices seemed subtly altered. Darker, headier. More enticing.

His face dropped another half inch. She let her own head fall back, dragged her eyes up, to his mouth.

He was going to kiss her.

His lips parted.

"And when you're quite recovered," he said, "release my coat."

She gasped and opened her fists. He straightened instantly, rubbing the back of his neck.

Blood boiled up to her cheeks.

Kiss her! He'd been trying to keep her from snapping his spine. She pushed off his thighs, scooting back so she could regain her dignity, stand on her own two feet. His thighs were rock hard, but the muscles leapt beneath her hands.

Hell, hell, hell, went the refrain in her mind. *Bloody hell, Nina!*

"If you'd be so kind . . ." His voice sounded strangled. "Please detach the monkey from my head."

He'd raised his right arm and was tugging gently at Fritz, whose back was bowing, legs stretching longer and longer. Each of his paws was wound tight in De'Ath's black hair.

"We might have to cut him out." She hugged herself. *Hell*. "Once he got wrapped up in my hair, and my brother resorted to scissors. Your hair is bit long, isn't it? You might look well with a shorter style."

De'Ath made a sound of disbelief, extending his arm farther. Fritz twisted in his grip, gave a vicious yank. She heard a silky rip. *Oh dear*. A tuft of black hair floated down onto De'Ath shoulder.

"I'll try, of course." Nina inched forward and lowered herself delicately onto the love seat beside him. Ladylike. As though she hadn't just flopped about in his lap. What a mercy it would be if the cushions sucked her down and swallowed her whole. She'd live out the rest of her days as a sofa. Worry-free. Sofas hadn't a care in the world. They were comfortable by nature.

"While I still possess a portion of my hair, Miss Finch."

She started, reaching up, but De'Ath was too tall, and the angle was wrong. She had to tuck a leg up under her, leaning into him. Her breast nudged his side.

"You'll have to bend a bit."

He complied. She was fully pressed against him now, his muscled bulk radiating heat. But his hair. His hair felt cool, cool and soft, faintly springy in its thickness.

Slowly she worked the strands from between Fritz's claws.

"It's *like* doffing your hat," she suggested. To her gratification, he laughed. His breath blew hot against her ear. She shifted her eyes and looked at him.

Mistake. For the second time, the air left her lungs completely. His face was an inch away.

His color had returned. His olive-toned skin renewed the shock of those pale irises, extravagantly fringed with black lashes. It looked as though he'd lined his eyes with kohl.

"You laughed." She tried to swallow. Her throat seemed to have shrunk with words stuck inside. "Does that mean . . . I'm not sacked?"

"Unfortunately." His smile bared those flawless teeth.

Relief flooded her. Now that the danger had passed, she could imagine it: Jack's reaction, the scene at the Knack if she'd slunk through the door, sacked, with nothing to offer but the assurance that De'Ath was hell-bent on flushing them out.

"Thank God," she said fervently, and tried to focus on her detangling. One paw free. She squeezed it between her fingers, remonstrating. Fritz gave an unapologetic chirp.

She redoubled her efforts on the next paw.

Don't ask, Nina. Concentrate on the task at hand. But it was too late. She was already shaping the words.

"Why . . . *unfortunately?*"

The silence vibrated.

"Ah," he said. "Because of house rule three."

She couldn't help herself. She looked. His expression was complex, communicating amusement, irony, regret, resignation, all with the slant of his brow, the curl of his lips.

"Which is?"

"No dalliances. Not between me and my employees."

"Oh." She let go of Fritz's paw. A moment passed before she realized her hand had dropped to De'Ath's shoulder. She couldn't blame herself for *that*. His shoulders were massive. They were everywhere. *He* was everywhere. This whole operation required extensive contact. She brushed at that stray tuft of hair, as though its removal had been her object. Grooming. Not groping.

Hell.

"No bribes, no Signorina Bonaccorso, no dalliances," she repeated secretarially. "I've got them. The rules." She gave a fractional nod. Too vigorous a motion and they might bump noses. "Are there more?"

"Let's start there."

His face filled her entire field of vision.

She couldn't form complete thoughts. Better not to speak. But if she didn't speak, what would she do with her mouth?

He was looking at it, at her mouth.

Her breath caught—the blow, probably, to the solar plexus. She *hadn't* recovered.

"They're not—" she began, with an embarrassing croak. "They're not difficult for you to follow?"

"Not usually. I'm very disciplined." He was smiling faintly. "And you? Are you disciplined?"

Disciplined. She could work at her easel until her paintbrushes went bald. Jack had seen to that.

"Exceptionally," she said.

"We have that in common, then." His eyes glinted. Slowly, he raised his arm, searching in his hair for Fritz's paws. "Fyodor, however, is conspicuously lacking in discipline."

"Fritz," she said. "His name is Fritz." Her breath hitched again. "No one listens to me."

"Oh?" His eyes narrowed fractionally. "Who do you want to listen?"

"What?" She'd hardly been listening to herself. Her fingers kept brushing nervously at his coat.

"Is there someone in particular?"

"No. It's just—" She sighed. What had possessed her to say such a thing? "If you're a person like me, you're often ignored."

"A person like you. A woman, you mean."

"A woman." She made a face. There were as many differences between types of women as between women and men. "A woman in service," she elaborated. "People listen to the queen."

"And if you were the queen? What would you say?"

"Me? The queen?" She shook her head, amazed. Her senses were swimming. The scent of bergamot and clove teased her nose, and his torso felt warm and hard against hers. She could scarcely think, much less muster an answer to a patently ridiculous question. But he was watching her intently, waiting for her to speak.

He'd listened to her, in the duke's garden, as the words had tumbled out, about Hensthorpe and her pastry shop. He'd listen to her now.

Her fingers stilled, even as her pulse sped up. "I suppose I'd tell all the aristos to buy my Victoria sponge."

The corner of his mouth tilted. "You're practical rather than political."

"Was that a test?" She flushed and took her hand from his shoulder. "Should I have used the opportunity to promote a cause? I can't vouch for any causes. I *can* vouch for my Victoria sponge. Besides, the scepter isn't a magic wand. The queen isn't all-powerful. It wouldn't do any good, demanding the moon."

"Like I said, practical." He was making fun of her.

She glared. "What if you were the queen?"

"I'm very glad I'm not." The slant of his smile was sardonic. "Her Majesty and I don't get on."

Nina bit her lip. Of course he knew the queen!

"As many people listen to you as her," she muttered.

"Hardly."

"Close enough," she insisted. "There's more said *about* her. But you say more, in the papers, and people go around repeating it. Do you enjoy the attention?"

His smile twisted. "I don't do it for the attention."

"No," she agreed, and put up her chin. "You do it for art."

"Miss Finch," he murmured. "How well you know me already."

"I know you enough to know I don't know you at all. I don't think anyone knows you." She'd spoken too quickly and too boldly. The light went from his eyes. He looked at her, humorless, as though shaken. In a sense, this meant progress—wasn't she here to figure him out, to help Jack stay one step ahead? Even so, she wanted desperately to recant. She covered her discomfort with a bright smile.

"Is there someone in particular *you* wish would listen to you?" She focused again on the complicated intersections of hair and tiny, razor-tipped fingers.

There was a long pause.

"It can be anyone?" He didn't sound shaken. The question had an idle lilt. "Alive or dead?"

"Why not?" She freed one of Fritz's paws and held his arm up by the wrist. "Rembrandt?"

No answer.

"Shakespeare?"

"Does the person only listen?" His voice had changed. Now there was a grimness to it. "Or can the person respond?"

"Both."

"And will the person entertain *anything* I say? Hear me out, even if my words are shocking?"

She pulled back so she could see his face. The room's light played over his features, but his eyes held that unfathomable darkness she'd noted before, when he'd asked about his nephew.

"Yes," she whispered. Her breathing was too shallow. She could feel her pulse fluttering in her throat. "What do you want to say?"

Before, when their gazes had fused, she'd gone tense. The alertness had transformed into an urge, the desire to lean forward, to put her mouth on his skin.

She was tensing again, and she couldn't tell if she wanted to lean in or lean away.

A muscle twitched in his jaw. His gaze unfocused.

She sat motionless, but something inside her teetered.

"What do you want to say?" she repeated. He was very near, and as they stared at each other, it seemed to her that they were mutually off-balance, that they could topple together in an instant or retreat to safer ground. And it seemed to her, too, that if it were up to her alone, she might choose to topple, to spiral with him into something unknown.

Fritz had set off this bizarre chain of events. It was Fritz who restored equilibrium.

Suddenly, he dug his claws into De'Ath's forehead and pushed off, springing into Nina's arms.

De'Ath didn't flinch, but his gaze sharpened. A red line slashed down toward his eye, dotted with blood.

"Drat it." Nina clutched Fritz to her chest. "You're bleeding."

"A scratch." De'Ath had regained his composure, if he'd ever lost it. He dabbed at his brow with a handkerchief, his half smile aimed at Fritz, ironic and vaguely hostile.

"You," he said to the marmoset. "Get used to the name *Fyodor*. You're staying here, with Kuznetsov."

"I'd understand if you sacked me." Nina heard an undertone of hope in her voice. Perhaps a sacking would be for the best, after all.

She didn't know what she'd expected from her first hours as De'Ath's amanuensis, but it wasn't this.

"You're not sacked." De'Ath felt on the ground for his cane. "I've picked a person, by the way. And he *will* listen. And then he will tell all."

"Who?" She gripped Fritz tighter.

De'Ath stood, smile widening. Perhaps she'd imagined his grimness, imagined that he'd been on the brink of sharing something of rare import. Their exchange had been a game from start to finish.

"Chips Sleaford," he said. "We'll find him in High Holborn."

THEY DIDN'T, PRAISE be. When they arrived at Sleaford's showroom, Nina saw with relief that the door was locked, the windows shuttered. Jack had done his part. She paced the length of the street at De'Ath's side as he played detective. He walked even more slowly than he had in the garden. Her nerves strained with every measured step. The longer they prowled, the greater the chance that the proprietor of one of the shops would emerge and recognize her. She often bought pale vermillion and rose madder lake from Mr. Summer, the import and color merchant. And pencils, crayons, stumps, and paper from Mr. Steucklen, whose sign advertised drawing supplies, wholesale and resale.

What if De'Ath decided to interview the shopkeepers?

He didn't enter any of the shops. Instead, he instructed her to jot down names and addresses. Gathering information for a more thorough canvass to be conducted at a later date.

Thank God De'Ath wasn't such a capital detective that he noticed the tiny letters marching up the barrel of her pencil: *Steucklen*.

She wiggled her fingers higher as she wrote, to cover the incriminating imprint.

It wasn't until they climbed back into the carriage that her tension eased. As they pulled away from the curb, she let herself sink into the seat. If the circumstances were different, she might enjoy driving in such a resplendent vehicle. The cushioning, all covered over with butter-soft claret-colored leather, smoothed the ride. It was as though London's streets were made of glass.

De'Ath didn't seem inclined to dilate upon the discouraging conclusion of their trip. In fact, he didn't seem discouraged at all. He sat across from her, resting his right heel on his knee, his left arm flung across the seat back, and began to detail her duties. Temporary assistance with note-taking and correspondence. Copying, filing, organizing more generally.

She supported the open notebook on her palm, scribbling as he spoke.

When they reached their next destination, she had to struggle to hide her shock. Sleaford's very digs! How in the bloody hell did De'Ath know where Sleaford lived? Perhaps he had real detectives in his employ.

She and De'Ath approached the terrace of houses and stood together on Sleaford's doorstep. Nina realized she was holding her breath as De'Ath knocked on the door, her shoulders tight with apprehension.

Nothing stirred inside. The drapes were drawn.

After a moment, De'Ath turned.

Back in the carriage, they took up where they left off. De'Ath said words. She wrote the words down, increasingly distracted.

But two hours ago, she'd been on the cusp of kissing him. Her own perversity astounded her. *De'Ath*, of all people. She couldn't kiss a man she deceived. A man who threatened all she held dear. She'd never wanted to kiss *any* man before today. And no man had ever wanted to kiss her, or not so badly that he'd risk a thrashing from Jack.

Unfortunately, De'Ath had said. *No dalliances.*

He'd wanted to kiss her too.

Her pencil lead snapped.

As she bent over the notebook, she realized, to her horror, that her hand had betrayed her. Sometime in the last minute, she'd stopped writing and started sketching.

She was staring at a drawing of a mouth, very decidedly De'Ath's mouth.

She slammed the notebook shut.

"Is something the matter?" De'Ath was studying her.

"No, not at all. I wonder, though, if there's been an accident." She peered out the window. The coach had slowed to a crawl. Dimly, she registered the raised voices: cabbies yelling about the right of way, hawkers crying their wares.

"And?" asked De'Ath.

"Only traffic." She turned back to him.

He slipped off his spectacles, rubbing the lenses lazily on his lapel. She'd wadded that lapel in her hands, and she'd stroked the silk velvet of his frock coat where it hugged the dense flesh of his shoulder. The fact that the pads of her fingers felt swollen as a result meant she was going soft in the head.

"How does it strike you?" he asked.

"It?" She swallowed. He didn't mean his face? He didn't mean . . . he knew she'd been sketching certain parts of his face?

"The position," he said. "Does it suit?"

"The position? The secretarial position! Oh yes, certainly." Her voice, overemphatic, filled the small compartment. She felt a perfect fool, but he looked satisfied.

"Good. I'm told my home is a convivial place to work." He set his spectacles back on his nose and smiled. "Inspiring, even. You met Kuznetsov. Did he mention he was a novelist?"

"He did." She answered instantly. "Before he mentioned he was a butler."

De'Ath laughed that molasses-ripple laugh. "He spends more hours writing than he does buttling. I can't comment on his prose style. My Russian is only fair. But he impresses with the sheer volume of pages. We despoil entire forests in this household, between myself, Kuznetsov, and the poets. I include paper with room and board." He shook his head. "My stationer is a rich man."

This glibness irritated her slightly. Stationers weren't rich. They were tradesmen. *De'Ath* was rich. He was rich by birth.

Money trouble with the duke notwithstanding.

"I hope you're well stocked." She crossed her arms. "Rotten luck, if everyone's waiting for their wages *and* their paper."

"Indeed." He regarded her thoughtfully. "A small chance, I said, that wages would be delayed. The possibility is so remote, I see no need to worry the rest of the staff."

She couldn't mistake his meaning.

"Of course," she murmured.

"The scales will soon fall from my brother's eyes."

"You tried to knock them off." She looked pointedly at his bandaged hand. "How'd that work for you?"

De'Ath laughed again. "You're memorable, Miss Finch, and memorably blunt. Something else you picked up from your brother?"

Her stomach tightened. *Drat it.* She'd mentioned she had a brother, hadn't she? So what, though? She had a brother. Many women had brothers. Thousands. Millions. Her numbering among them revealed little.

"Aye," she said, something she *had* picked up from Jack. "He's a blunt, honest, decent man, my brother."

"With the capacity to out-curse Miss Holroyd?" De'Ath raised his brows, amusement still stamped on his face.

"He's a bit rough-spoken." She chewed the inside of her cheek. Jack had been subject to ridicule at the Royal Academy for his accent and his slouch. Rich men like De'Ath had refused on sight to believe he possessed a great or genuine talent.

"You're close, the two of you." The way he said it, she knew it wasn't a question.

"He raised me." She looked away, uncomfortable. De'Ath had a strange knack for eliciting truthful responses.

She could feel his gaze on her.

"Your brother," he said at last. "He told you to take me up on my offer, didn't he?"

Her eyes flew to him. He wore a slight smile and was trailing his fingers idly through the fringe on the window curtain.

"I've been wondering why you changed your mind. What about the countryside, the cottage, the pastry shop? The gooseberry tarts?"

He *wondered* about her.

Her temples pounded. A shiver moved over her, dread and something else. Giddy, stupid excitement.

"We discussed your offer and decided it was the more sensible option." She suppressed a sigh and did her best to wipe the bitterness from her voice. "I can bake scones when I'm sixty."

His eyes narrowed. "I hope you won't have to wait so long as that." The corner of his mouth crept up higher. "But who knows? You might develop a passion for art in the meantime that's just as fulfilling."

"I doubt it." She frowned. De'Ath had no idea how misguided the notion was. Her love of baking had burgeoned as her love of painting had dwindled. These days, she looked at pictures in the way a coroner looked at bodies. *Dis*passionately. She used to feel moved, standing in front of certain pictures, long ago. Sometimes—though rarely—she still felt swept away, painting one.

Nothing—no one—could fan those embers into passion.

"What's a picture?" She borrowed his professorial style. "Smears of color on a window blind." She lifted her chin. "I prefer to look out the window, at the real world."

"Careful." The gleam in De'Ath's eyes had turned dangerous. "I can't resist a challenge. Are you daring me to change your mind?" He leaned forward. "Pictures can't show us the world, not literally. But the best of them can give us new ways of seeing. Windows don't possess that power."

"Says you." She turned her face deliberately toward the window, assuming a look of rapt appreciation that the view hardly warranted.

De'Ath laughed quietly at her performance of the point. The sound melted something inside her. God above, she *should* be careful. She was proving idiotically susceptible to the slightest sign of interest. She'd asked De'Ath if he enjoyed attention. Clearly, she was the one who craved it.

The way he laughed, and listened, and looked at her . . .

She sat straighter. "Where are we going now?" She'd imagined they were returning to Chelsea, but the coachman seemed to be maneuvering toward the side of the avenue, which was lined with towering stone buildings.

De'Ath glanced at the window. "We've arrived, then." He smoothed back his hair, which sprang back into disarray, still mussed by Fritz's paws.

He caught her looking.

"Your hair," she muttered. "On the side there. It's still snarled." Her heart began to beat in her throat. Would he ask her to work the knots loose?

His fingers moved deftly through the black waves, snagging and then sliding more freely. For no discernible reason, the simple motion mesmerized her.

"Voilà." He raked his hair roughly, then turned his head this way and that. "Am I restored?"

Restored. Bloody gorgeous was more like it.

"Restored," she agreed, too sullen, so she forced a facetious smile. "No one would ever guess a monkey had sat on your head."

"One wouldn't ever guess," he drawled. He arched a brow and seemed about to speak further, but at that moment the coach rocked to a halt. They'd arrived. Somewhere.

Hell, thought Nina, and let De'Ath help her down from the step onto the sidewalk.

CHAPTER SEVEN

BROUGHTON'S AUCTION HOUSE was smaller than its more famous rivals but led the pack in its sales of English and Continental old masters.

"First things first." Alan passed the porticoed entrance to the Great Auction Room. The offices were at the rear. Once inside, Miss Finch walked close beside him. He caught her eye and winked.

"Wages," he said. "Paper. We shall see what Bancroft Broughton can provide."

She didn't answer but stared about with a furrowed brow. She seemed cowed by the auction house. Or perhaps she was cowed by the prospect of entering Bancroft Broughton's office, an elegant and thoroughly masculine domain.

If the latter, she needn't have worried. Alan's announcement redirected Broughton's curious gaze away from Miss Finch.

"The family portraits," Broughton repeated, leaning across his desk. "From the picture gallery at Umfreville House."

"Three Gainsboroughs, two Reynoldses . . ." Alan began to tick through the list again.

"Are you acting as the duke's agent?" Broughton interrupted, studying Alan over his tented fingers.

"I'm acting as *my* agent." Alan smiled. "The pictures belong to me."

Only a flicker of Broughton's eyelid revealed his surprise. He rose smoothly. "One moment."

As soon as he'd left the room, Alan turned to Miss Finch, seated beside him in a matching leather armchair.

"This is about to become more interesting."

"Interesting how?" She fixed him with her razor-sharp gaze. That gaze—a reminder that she was disturbingly perceptive. She'd unnerved him in the drawing room with her claim that no one knew the real him. He'd felt suddenly transparent. His friends and acquaintances and readers numbered in the thousands. He hid from them all, inside a fortress of words.

She'd seemed to understand this instantly. Nina Finch. Geoffrey's saucy maid. His serendipitous amanuensis, with the ridiculously kissable lips. Who was she really? Who knew *her*?

She was still studying his face.

He cleared his throat. "I spent the morning perusing auction catalogues. Sleaford has a lot of six paintings coming up for auction here, at Broughton's. They're on view now. I'm going to put them to the test."

"The test . . . of your opinion?" The crease in her lower lip deepened as she compressed her mouth in something like a frown.

"The test of my flawless connoisseurship." He said it dryly. "The pictures are by an eighteenth-century British landscape painter. James Berney. Perhaps you've heard of him?"

"No." She looked away. "Where would I have heard of him? Oxford?"

He cocked his head. She had sharp eyes, and a sharp tongue when nettled. More employers than Geoffrey would scold her or sack her. She must have been thinking the same thing. She looked back at him, rueful, a wince puckering her forehead.

"Please do go on," she said, and opened her notebook.

Where had she worked, before Umfreville House, and how had she fared? Did her intelligence and temper often land her in trouble? Perhaps she'd stayed at home, with that brother, cooking and cleaning, baking Victoria sponge.

He had to shake himself to proceed. "James Berney. He was an obscure painter, relatively speaking. He lived and died in Norwich and never showed in London. Not the most profitable proposition for a forger. But he does have a bit of posthumous fame to recommend him. Or to ruin him, as the case may be." He paused. "I blame myself."

"You blame yourself because . . ." She looked down at the notebook, not at him.

"Berney's a favorite of mine. I was the first critic to write seriously about his body of work." He gave a small, immodest shrug. "And I'm the critic best equipped to determine the authenticity of his pictures."

"Of course they're authentic." She raised her head. "The auction house wouldn't sell them otherwise."

"Is that right?" he murmured, lifting his brows. "I'm sure Mr. Broughton would appreciate your vote of confidence."

"What would I appreciate?" Broughton was lumbering back into the office, looking well pleased. "Mr. De'Ath, you'll appreciate this. I conferred with Mr. Goldthwaite. To secure your consignment, we're willing to offer an advance."

Alan shook Broughton's hand as Miss Finch noted down the terms.

The advance would answer to the purpose, in the short term.

Wages. Paper.

Of course, Broughton wouldn't ever receive the consignment. Geoffrey would yield, restoring Alan's funds to keep the family collection—and his dignity—intact.

Alan didn't mind wasting Broughton's time. After all, he was poised to do the man a professional service.

A few minutes later, the three of them were climbing the marble staircase, heading for the private viewing room where Chips Sleaford's lot was on display.

Broughton was the first to approach the six pictures.

"James Berney," he said with satisfaction. "Some of the finest I've seen."

Alan studied the nearest picture. A narrow, rutted road winding through trees, a great deal of dusky sky above. A picture with uncommon depth.

He studied the others one by one, lingering on the last. It showed a farm cart on the edge of a forest and triggered a memory. He'd spent a summer holiday—the first after his father's death—trekking Norfolk with his friend Neal Traymayne. They'd gone up to the heights in the north, and to the lowlands, where vast shallow lakes gleamed between sedges. Glorious swimming, everywhere. On the days his leg hadn't permitted tramping, they'd ridden together in farm carts. Neal had never pressed him on it. He'd taken it as a matter of course, juggling potatoes to amuse the farmers' children as they bumped along.

Were there potatoes in that cart? The corner of his mouth kicked up in a smile. When he looked up, he met Miss Finch's eyes. She was standing awkwardly, *behind* the easels, as though she didn't dare to face them.

"What do you think?" he asked her.

She went scarlet. "It's what *you* think that matters."

He tilted his head in encouragement. "I think I want to know what you think."

Broughton ran his thumb across his mustache, bushy eyebrows raised as he looked between them.

Miss Finch didn't move. Her big brown eyes beseeched him. He smiled more broadly and beckoned.

Frowning, stiff-backed, she came around the easels. One might suppose the pictures were a firing squad. He felt a stirring of self-reproach. But he hadn't expected this extreme reluctance.

Perhaps it was cruel, to force her to speak. He'd imagined she would rise to the occasion. If not . . . well, he'd no wish to humiliate.

Broughton was watching Miss Finch's toe-dragging progress. Alan turned to him.

"I shouldn't have asked her," he confessed. "She trusts your house to auction unimpeachable pictures. Genuine articles."

Broughton gave her a nod in acknowledgment.

Alan let the pause lengthen. "And she knows that I have reason to doubt."

"What's this?" Broughton's head whipped around. "*Doubt?* Mr. De'Ath, I am not in the business of selling *doubtful* pictures."

"It's this lot in particular that gives me pause." Alan kept his expression bland. "Chips Sleaford was the consignor?"

"Yes." Broughton sounded baffled. "But he represents the owner, Mrs. Beechey. Berney's granddaughter."

"Hmm." Alan considered. "Have you met this granddaughter?"

"No, I haven't met the woman." Now Broughton sounded annoyed. "She lives in Norwich. I deal with Sleaford. But provenance aside, De'Ath—*look* at them." He gestured at the pictures. "The quality is unmistakable."

Miss Finch reached Alan's side. She raised her chin and stared, unblinking, at the picture in front of her. A change came over her. She looked almost frightened, spellbound.

"Well?" he asked her.

Her face relaxed into a smile, and she turned bright eyes in his direction. "These pictures are very fine indeed."

AFTER SHE SPOKE, Nina felt light-headed. She focused on holding her body completely still.

"Do tell," said De'Ath. He looked bemused. He wasn't displeased that she'd sided with Broughton. He'd meant what he'd said in the drawing room, that she was entitled to her own taste.

She *did* judge the pictures fine. Her best work, in fact. She excelled at Berneys. If Jack had let her paint them exclusively, she might not have grown to loathe painting altogether.

James Berney had rendered the countryside she loved. He would set out from Norwich and paint the surrounding fields and heaths, ponds and trees. He had painted Hensthorpe. Her favorite place. Her favorite subject.

It felt less like faking when she painted Hensthorpe, even though she deliberately adopted Berney's methods. Berney was long dead, of course, but . . . they understood each other. The *way of seeing* De'Ath had mentioned. She and Berney shared it. Painting in his style allowed her sense of wonder free rein.

De'Ath prodded her. "What makes them fine?"

"I can't describe it." She clutched the notebook to her breast. A special circle of hell, this—a forger evaluating her own canvases in front of a gimlet-eyed critic.

De'Ath raised his brows.

She coughed. "There's just . . . something about them."

To her dismay, his brows crept higher.

What else could she say? Her mind raced.

Suddenly, he surprised her by giving a satisfied shrug. "There *is* something about them, isn't there?" He pivoted back to the pictures. "No mere copyist could achieve such effects."

She caught her breath, afraid to hope. "You also agree? That they're fine pictures?"

"I do." He stepped toward the closest easel. She'd titled it *Forge and Oak*. Berney himself had painted a different view of the same smithy, which stood across the green from Aunt Sylvia and Miss Lolly's cottage.

"You frightened me for a moment." Mr. Broughton laughed, pulling out his handkerchief, pressing it to the back of his neck. "You don't doubt any longer? Good, good." He wagged his head.

"You see, Miss Finch." He shot her an indulgent look. "You did well to offer your thoughts. As it turns out, Mr. De'Ath was the one who erred in his assumptions." His mustache twitched. He resembled, suddenly, nothing so much as a happy old walrus. "To err is human," he intoned. "Mr. De'Ath, it comes as rather a relief to know that you, too, are wrong from time to time."

"Alas." De'Ath smiled and stepped back. "I'm not wrong. I'm never wrong. It's a gift and a curse." His expression was sardonic as he swept each of the pictures with his gaze. "Fakes." He proclaimed the word.

Mr. Broughton's face reminded Nina to school her own features. A happy old walrus speared by an Arctic explorer.

Damn bugger blast.

She pressed her lips together.

"They *are* wonderful." De'Ath had derision in his voice. "I'd buy them myself but for that." He pointed with his cane at the lower right corner of *Forge and Oak*. The signature was a scrawl, the *B* distinct. "The forger is talented enough to sell his own work. But, as we all know, a famous name fetches a higher price."

Mr. Broughton was as white as his hair. "How can—"

"Shall I analyze and compare the styles of these pictures and genuine Berneys?" De'Ath sighed. "I could but I don't want to delay you. You have your work cut out for you. Canceling the sale, locating Chips Sleaford. If I were you, I'd send someone to Norwich to pay a visit to that convenient descendant."

Mr. Broughton hesitated.

"You doubt *me*?" De'Ath whipped up his cane again. "Perhaps this will convince you. These cracks—here. The pattern looks natural, but if you examine these closely, you'll see ridges. Someone drew them on by dragging a pin through the wet paint."

Thwack. The notebook had slipped from Nina's hands, smacked against the marble floor. She crouched to pick it up. Now. Now was the moment to close her eyes tight and wake up in Hensthorpe.

She rose on a deep breath. De'Ath was firming his mouth against the suggestion of a smile. He thought her clumsiness funny, endearing perhaps. Harmless.

For the time being.

"Ready?" he asked her, and glanced at Mr. Broughton. "It seems Mr. Broughton would find a stylistic analysis helpful. Do take this down, Miss Finch."

Nina opened the notebook. Her fingers were trembling.

"The palette is characteristic of Berney, as is the pictorial organization, even the sensitivity to the details of the natural world." De'Ath tucked his cane beneath his left arm and removed his spectacles, rubbing the lenses on his sleeve. "But Berney's figures—human and animal—are crude, almost merging with their surroundings. Background, not foreground. That cow, there, by the farm building, has far too much definition and personality for a Berney cow." He broke off. "Am I going too quickly?"

"Oh no. Well . . . a bit, rather." Nina resettled the pencil in her hand. She hadn't written a word.

She'd lavished too much attention on Mr. Middleton's cow, Winnifred. She'd known it at the time. But Winnifred wasn't fashioned for crude representation! She had such a stately demeanor, such long-lashed eyes. Her butter made the best batches of gooseberry tarts.

The Mozart of gooseberry tart.

She could sense her future receding.

"Mr. Broughton." De'Ath spoke with fastidious politeness.

"Would you be so kind as to have a porter bring us stools or a bench? This might take some time. I want to be thorough."

He shifted silver eyes back to Nina. All her muscles clenched.

"Let me back up. Berney's techniques." Again, his words flowed. Descriptions of Berney's undermodeling, his brushwork, the fullness of his paint. Descriptions of the forger's deviations, idiosyncrasies, telltale flourishes.

As De'Ath spoke, she saw a picture of herself emerging. Dear God, how could he reconstruct her very posture as she plied her brush, identify *everything* about her . . . and miss the fact that she, the culprit, stood beside him?

Stood close enough to touch.

"Miss Finch," murmured De'Ath.

She'd stopped writing again.

"A cramp in my hand." She blinked. "It's much better now. Go on."

She bent her head, gritted her teeth, and recorded every damning word.

CHAPTER EIGHT

ALAN WAS LOUNGING in his study, in a wingback chair, legs stretched out, boots crossed at the ankle, resting on a footstool. It was a louche pose, and a necessary one. The position eased the pressure in his hip.

Miss Finch's eyes had widened when she'd entered the room, shortly after breakfast, and widened further when he'd directed her to take a seat behind his massive desk, all gleaming dark oak, with papers, fountain pens, inkwell, silver stamp, sealing wax, and other accoutrements meticulously arrayed. But she'd gone and sat. And she'd set to work, first making a clean copy of the notes she'd taken down yesterday at Broughton's, then writing out the new version as he read from the copy, amending and elaborating on his points.

He imagined they'd have finished it last evening, but Miss Finch had left directly from the auction house to gather her things, and she hadn't arrived back at Casa De'Ath until he was headed out, on his way to a show at the Royal Pavilion. For a split second, he'd considered asking her if she'd care to come along. Then he'd given himself a stern shake.

She'd have nothing to do at the Pavilion as his secretary. No, her presence would have served a purely social function, spicing the attractions of the night. He couldn't justify the indulgence. He'd seen her to the butler's pantry—where Kuznetsov was playing violin for the ratty little monkey—and then he'd bid all four a rather crisp adieu.

Today, she seemed determined to make up for lost time. She wrote swiftly—far more swiftly than she'd led him to believe she could—and when he inspected the pages she'd produced, he found her letters well formed, slim, and even. A very fair hand. Her spelling, however, was atrocious. Multiple rounds of correction would be required before he allowed any document she prepared to reach a typist, editor, or correspondent.

As he began to dictate his letter to Geoffrey, an indescribable sound punctured the calm.

Miss Finch lifted her head. She'd tortured her hair into another painful-looking bun, an extravagantly unflattering style. Any female veteran of the marriage mart would advise a softer arrangement of those heavy locks to de-emphasize the fullness of her cheeks and to hide the angle of her ears, which stuck out a touch too far.

The sound gathered itself and veered, flew up, up, up to the heavens on crystal wings. Overshot the heavens. Set a course for Mars.

There was no ignoring it, but Alan increased his own volume and plowed on toward the period.

". . . and I will next dissolve the family silver collection comma followed by the bronzes full stop," he said, and paused for Miss Finch to catch up.

She was staring into the distance.

"Double *s* in *dissolve*." He nodded encouragement. "*D-i-s-s-o-l-v-e*."

The sound cut off. Silence descended on the study.

"I can spell *dissolve*." Miss Finch's gaze focused. "As in *dissolve one ounce of isinglass in water. Dissolve the dark moist sugar in the stew pan with the rhubarb, lemon peel, and cloves.*" She frowned at him. "I read copiously in recipe books."

He cleared his throat. "A useful lexicon." Or it would be, if he wrote restaurant reviews. "Scratch that sentence. We'll start over from the beginning." He let his head fall back against the chair and looked up at the Venetian chandelier.

"Brother mine comma," he dictated, using his right hand to

emphasize the punctuation. "Your brain has macerated to an unwholesome mush period. Instead of beating you like an egg comma I am disposed to . . ."

A new vocal line began, with impressive purity of tone.

Miss Finch shot up. Her gray dress had a square neckline that bit into the distinctively circular swell of her breasts. When it came to her attire, he could not approve. It generated in him too strong an urge to liberate her figure from the insane impositions of all that rigid cloth.

"What *is* that?" She tipped one of those winsome ears, listening.

"That? That is a high and rather alarming C-sharp." He sighed and reached for the snifter of cognac beside the lamp at his elbow. Signorina Bonaccorso had an undeniably agile voice. If she were singing outside his study, well, she was agile in body too. He prayed to God she didn't break her fool neck.

Miss Finch took a few steps toward the French windows. "But . . . where is it coming from? Not out *there*?" She motioned toward the windows. "We're on the second floor!"

"Horse chestnut. Huge. Spreading. One might even say *tentacular*." Alan swirled his cognac and sipped. The hour called for tea, but, on days like today, when the pain sprouted teeth and claws, he required something stronger.

Miss Finch was staring at him.

"It's not a tree but a behemoth," he said, lowering the glass, putting it from him. "Takes up most of the back garden. I should have it chopped down."

"You can't mean—" Miss Finch threw open the windows. The curtains billowed around her, filling with the spring breeze and that soaring melody. Alan detected the freshness of the air. Soon, the clouds would thicken. Rain would patter down.

His blasted hip made a damn fine barometer.

When the curtains settled, Miss Finch was gone, except for the curve of her posterior. No padding in that dress. It was the non-bustled variety, flat backed. Or it would be flat, if Miss Finch didn't round it out so splendidly. A moment later, she burst back into the room.

"A woman!" She radiated wonderment. "A beautiful woman."

"Mmm." He couldn't resist. He let his gaze wander deliberately from her glowing eyes down to her parted lips. Homely, hoydenish Miss Finch. How wonderment became her. Stroked by morning sun, lit up from within, she appeared, suddenly, in the fullness of her beauty. One second, he was detached, appraising. The next, sensation hit him like a wave. He felt ambushed. It wasn't beauty alone that worked on him. Miss Finch was all contradictions, engaging too much of his mind as he attempted to parse her sweetness from her sharpness. His overstimulated thoughts made sweat break out on his skin, changed the tempo of his pulse. He couldn't remember the last time desire had dissolved so many of his carefully maintained boundaries at once.

Dissolved them like dark, moist sugar.

Miss Finch was turning pink under his prolonged regard.

"A woman balanced on a branch." She folded her arms under her breasts, creating an unwitting frame. His lingering attention accused him.

Cad.

He adjusted his legs, and the pain used his left femur as a trumpet, blaring a loud, agonized note. It effectively chilled his ardor. The pain had more power over him than a choir of his better angels.

"She's high in the air," marveled Miss Finch. "And she's singing."

"Singing?" He sighed. "I'd say *wailing*."

"Who?" Miss Finch looked back toward the window.

"Signorina Bonaccorso." He rolled his neck on his shoulders. The problem with keeping still during a cramp—everything else began to stiffen up. "Shut the windows. And draw the curtains."

"*That* is Signorina Bonaccorso." Miss Finch sounded impressed. "I can't imagine how she climbed that tree. If you could *see* what she's wearing. Plumes, and a train that pours right over the branch like a waterfall. She has so many beads on her gown it must weigh more than chain mail, and—"

He interrupted. "*Lock* the windows. Barricade them with that cabinet. Prepare for siege."

With a sigh, Miss Finch turned to pull the windows shut, pausing between them to give Signorina Bonaccorso an apologetic wave. She stepped back and leveled Alan with an admonishing glance.

He lifted his brows. "What?"

The notes were flurrying as Signorina Bonaccorso launched on a delirious cadenza, so dizzying it seemed impossible she wouldn't tumble from her perch.

He grimaced. When the aria ended, he listened for the thud. Nothing, thank the Lord.

"I've never heard anything like it." Miss Finch drew her hands together, a spontaneous clap. Her brown eyes were shiny. "Why won't you give her a chance?"

The excitement in her voice made it seem, suddenly, a grand idea. Forget the day's business, fling open the windows, while away the time flirting with Miss Finch as Signorina Bonaccorso intoxicated them with her song.

A cozy notion, it made him laugh at himself, or rather, at the new version of himself Miss Finch called into being. A romantic idler.

"Why won't I?" He smiled, brushed away that other Alan. "Because she's cheating."

He sat up, swinging his legs off the footstool, and pushed down through his left heel experimentally. Good. The worst of the cramp had passed.

"I don't invite prima donnas to sing in my chestnut tree. She can wait her turn to be heard." He caught the shadow as it flitted across Miss Finch's face. "What now?"

"Nothing. But . . ." She bit her bottom lip. "Certain people have to wait much longer than others for their turn. And for some, it doesn't ever come. Not unless they take matters into their own hands."

Curiosity pinged. He studied her.

"Are we speaking of Signorina Bonaccorso?" He took up his cognac.

"We shouldn't be." She turned her head as she lowered it, light sliding over her hair, sleek as mink. "You were dictating your letter, to the duke."

"That I was." He looked into his glass, swallowed the last golden drops of liquor. His curiosity didn't ping, no. It was ringing carillon bells. So many contradictions. Miss Finch disarmed him with her whimsy, a dreaminess that encouraged his own honeyed fantasies. But there was something feral about her as well.

He'd take infinitely more pleasure in charting her mysteries than he would in writing to his bloody brother.

"We'll continue, then." He set down the glass, too forcefully. It made a sharp rap against the table. As if on cue, Signorina Bonaccorso began to sing.

"Bring the lap desk and pull up a chair." The signorina's singing was growing louder. He raised his voice. "I don't intend to shout myself hoarse."

As soon as Miss Finch had settled herself, he tipped back his head. "Once more from the beginning. Brevity is the soul of wit." He resumed dictation. "Geoff comma. Enclosed you will find a list of the pictures consigned to Broughton's Auction House period. There is one way to stop the sale period. Open my account forthwith period. Until then comma, I remain comma, the vendor of your patrician pride period."

He put out his right hand. Miss Finch passed the letter over.

"Perhaps *Geoff* lacks an *f*?" she ventured.

He looked. *G-e-o-f.*

"Geoff lacks a number of things," he told her. "The extra *f* is the least of his worries." He handed the letter back. "Perfect. You'll enclose the list you wrote up and seal the envelope."

She hesitated.

"Your brother . . ." She licked her bottom lip, full as a drupe. *Dear God.* He couldn't look at her mouth without comparing it to a damned fruit. He pinched the bridge of his nose.

He could have hired a male amanuensis, a former parliamentary shorthand writer, twenty years his senior. A man who jotted down 150 words per minute with one hand and churned out fair-copy transcripts with the other. Thin-lipped. Bald as an egg. The sort who never made an error, or asked a question, or fell into his arms.

This was *his* doing. Entirely.

"He doesn't own the things in Umfreville House?" Miss Finch leaned her forearms on the mahogany slope of the lap desk, which he used on his worst days, in bed.

He gave a small shrug, shaking off the thought of *her* in his bed, flushed and tousled. He'd know, then, if her lips tasted like plums or berries, or perhaps peaches.

He spoke in a roughened voice. "He owns the things he's bought with his wife's money." He extended his legs again and propped his boots on the footstool. He tried for a smoother tone. "The ancestral portraits, however, are mine. And the heraldic tapestries. The storied davenports. That majolica ewer, the one Geoff dashed to pieces. You might have noticed the fragments."

"Dunno." She shot him a frank look. "There were rather a lot of fragments."

He scoffed. "Not all fragments were created equal. That ewer was fabricated in a maestro's workshop during the Renaissance." He glanced at the letter in her hand. "I might have you add a post-script to my letter. Geoff owes me compensation."

"But *he* is the duke." Her brow knotted. "Shouldn't *he* own the ancestral everything? And you—you should be an army captain."

"Do you admire men in uniform?"

She rolled her eyes. "The jackets are smarter than the men, usually."

He laughed. Another thing about Miss Finch. In her presence, he kept forgetting their formal arrangement, a convenient oversight that allowed him to indulge their pleasant rapport. He didn't draw hard distinctions between employees and friends, but he did make sure he remembered that he held power over people he paid.

He would not take this flirtation too far.

"So you were never in the army?" she asked.

"I hate to disappoint." He poured himself more cognac. "But I'm a consummate civilian. And I inherited everything, anything that wasn't strictly settled on the heir."

"The account you mention in the letter. Why does he control it?"

Signorina Bonaccorso was still singing, more softly now. Miss Finch sat very close. He could smell the scent diffusing from her hair, roses, and he could smell citrus as well, diffusing no doubt from the fresh oranges crammed in her purse.

His hand tightened around the glass of cognac. "Perhaps you'd like to manage my finances as well as my correspondence?"

"I should manage my mouth." She slumped, a full-body cringe. "It's not my business. Forget I asked."

"No, it was a reasonable question." He drew a breath through his nose. "I descend from a long line of notorious bankrupts. Their debts never kept them from gambling, or collecting silver, or adding wings onto the manor homes. My grandfather broke the entail and sold off the castle in Ireland, the Scottish hunting lodge, the house in Somerset . . ."

Miss Finch's round eyes had grown even rounder. He decided to skip the rest.

"In short, he repaired the family fortune, somewhat, but my father and . . ." His voice caught in his throat. "*Mother* spent it freely." On, among other things, his treatments, his stays in private sanatoriums, the residence at Bournemouth, where he was meant to fade out of existence.

"I was nineteen when my mother died," he said evenly. "My father died a year later. I inherited enough real property to invest substantially in ventures that have continued to prove profitable. While my beleaguered brother drowned in debt. So, I, *loyally*, signed over those investments, as a lifeline." His lips curved into a humorless smile. "But shortly thereafter he took his own steps to secure the dukedom. He married an heiress, Fanny Smith. As you know, they lived happily ever after."

She gazed down at the letter, straightening it so the corners of the paper lined up with the corners of the desk.

He continued slowly. "Over the years, our dealings have been friendlier than the other day might lead you to assume. At the very least, we've stayed out of each other's way. I never threatened to sell his rugs out from under him, and he deposited income into my account each month. That is, until this week, when he closed the account altogether. He hopes to influence what I write. No more insulting his friends." Now he bared his teeth. "My good word isn't for sale."

Claud's face popped into his mind. Geoff knew exactly how to tip the balance in his favor.

"Hence this letter." He was grinding his teeth. "He's the duke. But I have the power to gut the bloody house. And I'll do it, so help me God. Once Geoff understands that I've gone to Broughton's, he'll reconsider. Our parents' wedding portrait up for auction?" He snorted. "An abomination."

A pause, during which Signorina Bonaccorso's voice made several runs and one notably flexible leap.

"*You* wouldn't mind it, though?" Miss Finch asked the question carefully, with a sidelong glance. "Auctioning your parents' wedding portrait?"

"No, my dear." He knew he had frost in his eyes, but there was no helping it. "I wouldn't."

"Oh." Her voice was small and told him everything. *She* had no such keepsakes of her parents and would have valued one dearly.

She still fiddled with the letter. He felt the urge to still her hands.

"But they gave *you* all they could." She met his eyes squarely. "You were the favorite. It's obvious. And that must be part of why the duke—"

"Enough family history." He rose abruptly. His leg didn't waver. *The favorite.* God help him—it was true.

And he'd barely survived.

Miss Finch's eyes were huge and dark, angled up at him.

"Holroyd will be pacing ruts into the floor at the gallery." He managed a smile. "Get an envelope. We'll post Geoff's letter on the way out."

Cane in hand, he strolled for the door, but a new tumult pulled him back. Men were shouting, and the signorina was stretching a string of Italian curses across three octaves. He veered for the window and used his cane to spread the curtains. One glance confirmed his impression. Kuznetsov and Kessler had arrived on the scene with the gardener's ladder.

Signorina Bonaccorso *was* a sight to behold. Dressed in burgundy and gold, she stood on a wide branch, one hand gripping a branch above, the gray sky peeping with pearly brilliance through the green canopy of leaves. Her plumes defied his understanding of ornithology. Surely the bird plucked for that headpiece had been the last of its kind.

Neal's conservation-minded natural scientist sisters would scream bloody murder.

At the mere thought of adding female screams to the cacophony, he felt his temples throb. He looked forward to the half hour's drive to the gallery in his quiet coach.

Movement caught his eye. A vigorous squirrel was leaping between yet higher branches, trilling in its own distinctive manner.

Ah. Not a squirrel, then.

"Fritz!" Miss Finch joined him at the window, her side pressing his as she fumbled at the latch. "Mr. Kuznetsov swore he wouldn't let him out. Fritz!"

"Will he run off?" Alan studied the little monkey and wondered how he'd fare if he were free, roaming London's verminous streets.

"He'd never, not for good." Miss Finch tugged again at the latch and Alan dropped his bandaged hand to her wrist. She froze.

"He might gorge himself on slugs, though." She met his eyes, a blush staining her cheeks. "It's unpleasant."

"I can imagine," he murmured. "But there are no slugs in my garden. My gardener is superb." One of Neal's trainees.

He applied more pressure to her wrist. "Let him have his frolic."

Her throat moved on a convulsive breath. And just like that, his heart began to gallop. In his life to date, he'd admired all sorts of women in all sorts of ways. His lovers, though, hewed to type. They were disillusioned, practiced, averse to long attachments. Pleased to exchange pleasures without the exchange of confidences. They saw the scars that wrapped his hip, but if they asked once, they didn't ask again. Wealthy widows exulting in their unfettered sensuality. Self-assured bohemians.

Certainly not the help. Not anyone subordinate.

Even if the subordinate in question possessed velvet dark eyes, like some farouche woodland creature, and lips like plums, or cherries, or— *God*.

He stepped back from the window, dropped his half of the curtain. "Time for *our* frolic." The only kind they would have. Fully clothed, and well within the bounds of her job as he'd described it.

"To the gallery, Miss Finch." He turned from her, too warmly aware of her gaze on his back. "The trembling paintings await my verdict."

CHAPTER NINE

THE OLGILVIE GALLERY was an opulent temple of art. Like always, upon entry, Alan was greeted as a high priest. The crowds made way for him, then drifted along behind. Why look at the paintings when you could look at an esteemed art critic as *he* looked at the paintings? Easier that way to glean a fashionable opinion.

"I thought this was a *private* view," said Miss Finch. Two women right in front of her stopped short, and she sidled toward him to avoid being pincered between their bustles.

"All the more reason to be seen at it." Tall as he was, he could see plenty. He looked between, and even above, the seas of top hats. There. Lloyd Syme. He stood on the crimson-carpeted marble stairs that swept up to the main galleries. His snow-white hair waved back from his wide brow, and his spectacles blazed, reflecting the electric lights. He was speaking—orating, more like—to a small group of elegantly dressed young men clustered on the lower steps.

Alan tightened his grip on the gold top of his cane. He had a vast collection of canes: shafts of ebonized bamboo, malacca, rosewood, porcelain, horn, topped with every conceivable handle in coral, ivory, silver, gold. Some contained secret compartments for tobacco and matches, or liquor. And some concealed blades.

Not this one. A good thing, given that the urge to cross swords with Syme twitched his every muscle. How viscerally satisfying it would be: literalizing the duel of ideas, steel against steel.

He quickened his pace toward the stairs, striding around the pillars. Striding—almost as though he didn't need to think about the placement of his feet.

And just like that, he stumbled.

Fitfully dormant on the carriage ride, the pain lashed as it came to life. A lightning bolt streaked down from his hip, liquefying marrow, setting it to boil. He had to lock his knee to keep the leg from buckling. A dead halt. All around, people continued streaming this way and that. Thank God, they didn't register his distress.

Miss Finch, though. She was close enough to feel his awkward step. She, too, stopped walking and looked up at him, a questioning line between her brows.

"Hazardous, these bustles." He heard himself say it, heard his plausible drawl as he waved at a grande dame and her lace-festooned daughter, whose swaying skirts might *almost* have impeded his own movements as she passed.

Miss Finch opened her mouth, but then—

"De'Ath!" Nelly Knotwood elbowed toward him. In her formless terra-cotta gown, she presented a splendid example of the room's other faction of females, those who eschewed bustles and garbed themselves like medieval maidens, or, in Miss Knotwood's case, Roman statuary. Alan held himself upright and molded his lips into a smile.

"It's a circus!" She grinned at him, exposing the gap in her front teeth. "I'm fleeing downstairs. I can't answer another question about my bronzes. Everyone wants to know why I didn't finish them. They're *meant* to be partial!"

Alan imagined his body were a bronze, or rather, a figurine of wood and papier-mâché, something he could manipulate from on high, like a plaything or puppet. During these episodes, he had the uncanny sensation that he ventriloquized himself.

He shook his head. "You'll never convince the literal-minded." How adroit he'd become at handling this situation. His voice hit all the right notes. "Better to tell them you ran out of clay."

Miss Finch hadn't removed her eyes from his face.

"Miss Finch." He addressed her. "This is Miss Knotwood, the sculptor. Her latest series is on view upstairs."

Miss Knotwood acknowledged Miss Finch with a friendly nod.

"Are you a suffragist?" she asked. "You might prefer my portrait statues. Lady Dewhurst commissioned ten, of historically significant women. Sappho, Hypatia, Mary Wollstonecraft, Joan of Arc . . ."

Alan's good hand began to ache where his palm pressed his cane. Sweat was dampening his brow. He felt like Joan of Arc, like his leg was a burning stake. He could maintain his composure, but only up to a point.

He swung his gaze to the left . . . and glimpsed a way out.

"There's Lady Dewhurst now," he observed. "Talking with the Baron of Ludlow. She seems ready to spit in his eye."

Miss Knotwood's chin jerked around. "Oh no." Her brows lowered. "It *is* Ludlow, isn't it? Excuse me while I save her from herself." She stalked off.

Alan glanced at Miss Finch. Her expression was troubled.

"De'Ath!"

This time it was William Henley, the editor of the *Magazine of Art*. He roared at Alan good-naturedly as he crutched by, flanked by poetical youths in fringed shawls.

"Where's that biography you owe me?"

Alan exhaled slowly through his nose. He needed to collapse in the wings, but he was still in the footlights, still Alan De'Ath.

The show must go on.

He responded smoothly. "I sent it straight to Mammon."

Henley laughed. He knew well enough that Alan disapproved of the artists' biographies he published, bowdlerized narratives meant to promote their careers and their dealers' galleries. Bloated, gossipy advertisements. They'd had the same exchange countless times before.

"An essay, then," conceded Henley, with a waggle of his tufty eyebrows. "On something controversial. Impressionism?"

Alan levered up one shoulder and let it drop, a passable shrug. "If you'll accept a defense."

"By June," Henley called over his shoulder, grin half-hidden by the red thicket of his beard. "Go long. I like to chop at verbiage."

He disappeared into the crowd.

Alan felt the pain knife through him. One wrong step and his hip would pop like a cork.

Where to go? Stairs were unthinkable. The exhibition lay up one flight, the shops and lounges down another.

The old smoking room.

But today, what with the crush of gallery-goers, he risked leading two dozen hangers-on to this forgotten sanctum.

He had no choice. Pale dots blotted the edges of his vision. He had only so many moments, so many steps, before the pain blinded him. The episode would pass, if he could sit.

He walked forward. He had the trick of it from years of practice. Body in motion, mind afloat. As if by magic, the crowd began to flow in the opposite direction, back toward the entrance. He could hear the reason why. *Princess Louise.* Her name emerged from dozens of lips, a collective sigh.

He kept putting one foot in front of the other. He passed between the potted palms, fighting the dizzying notion that the hall was stretching out before him, his destination ever-more distant. *Almost there.* Eons later, he saw his hand pushing aside red brocade. He was entering the smoking room. Only a few paces across the Persian rugs remained. He collapsed onto the rococo chaise longue.

And with his molars grinding, he molded another smile and aimed it up at Miss Finch.

"DON'T STAND THERE." De'Ath stretched out in the chaise longue like a lazy cat. "Come in."

He'd abandoned hat and cane, and he'd folded his right arm behind his head, the left draping the chair's scrolled frame. He looked languorous, flamboyantly at ease. Except . . . his face was white and set, a smiling mask.

Nina hesitated, the heavy red drape bunched in her hand. The room was dim and sultry, walls covered with crimson silk damask, air scented strongly with sandalwood. She could imagine peering through Laddie's stereoscope at a pornographic scene set in exactly this sumptuous little chamber. Propped on a pillow, hair wild, De'Ath was the indolent libertine, exhausted by bed sport.

But he hadn't ducked into this alcove to seduce her. Why, then?

"I thought the paintings awaited your verdict." She said it in a light tone.

"They can wait a little longer." His tone was also light. "I'll let Princess Louise inspect them first. As soon as she leaves, the crème de la crème will pour out on her heels. I'll have more room to think."

"That's why we're here?" She let the drape swing down behind her. "You want to avoid the crème de la crème?"

His waxen smile didn't budge. "Exactly."

She lived with professional liars. But even for an amateur, De'Ath was doing a piss-poor job.

"You're not unwell?" She took a step forward. Darkness rolled off him in waves. She recognized this kind of unsustainable tension. It was Jack's, right before his calm shattered into rage.

"As a matter of fact, I'm thirsty. Aren't you?" The curve of his lips scarcely shifted as he spoke. "Two coffees. Mine, black. Yours, how you like it." He unfolded his arm, produced a leather billfold from inside his jacket, and held it out to her. "Straight down the stairs. Show the monogram and they'll let you carry away the cups."

She stared. He'd bid her come in because he didn't want her to be seen lingering on the threshold. And now he wanted to be rid of her.

"Buy a fountain pen while you're at it. Go past the coffee room, and the billiards room, and the dining rooms, then take a left at the library. You'll see the shop. It caters primarily to hobbyists with pin money. Sells prints of the most popular pictures and artistic paraphernalia. Overpriced tubed oil paints, porcelain mixing pans . . ." He rolled a shoulder in a supine shrug. "The pens are acceptable. Pick your favorite."

He wanted to be rid of her *badly*.

"Why—" she began, then broke off. It was pointless. He wasn't about to explain himself.

"Why," he repeated. "Why should a gallery have the amenities of a gentlemen's club plus a department store?" His tone retained its lightness. "Reassures the patrons. Olgilvie created a luxurious venue to distract from the frightening spectacle of art that doesn't sentimentalize, moralize, or otherwise conform to prevailing expectations."

He tossed the billfold, which slapped down onto a small serpentine-topped table.

Nina approached cautiously. She could sense it still: an elemental disturbance. De'Ath didn't move, yet he vibrated the air around him.

Something *was* amiss.

What?

Now, that's a very good question, Birdie. I propose you find the answer.

Jack's voice in her head. Last night, she'd gotten an earful. Her brother had forced her to repeat each of De'Ath's observations, interrupting every few words to damn De'Ath to hell as the devil's whelp, or—just as often—to affirm his critiques.

Complained of the blasted cow, did he? Well, sure, and he would. No surprise there. Sticks out like dog's bollocks! How many times did I tell you? But do you ever listen? It's like shouting at a bloody post. Christ, Birdie! No, it's my own fault. I'm the one to blame. I'm too soft with you. Always have been. Hate to chivvy my own sister. Rather take a chance with a deficient picture. A whore's pox upon my bleeding tender heart because we're well fucked for it now. What else? What else did he say?

He was still cursing when he'd flung himself into a chair at the writing table, and he'd cursed even as his pen flashed. When he'd finished, he'd given her the letter to read over. It promised Mrs. Beechey such a sum that Nina had felt a pang. Half would come out of her own savings. But she'd agreed. Jack had the right idea. Mrs. Beechey *was* James Berney's granddaughter. She was also a gin-pickled old widow, willing to say or do almost anything if she stood to profit. Over the years, they'd paid her a king's ransom for her provenance. Now they would pay more, to ensure she stuck to her story.

In the end, Mr. Broughton might not accept that the landscapes were forged, not if Mrs. Beechey insisted that she'd found them rolled up in the attic.

De'Ath's assault might fail on that front.

But what if he kept opening new theaters of war?

Find something, Birdie. Those had been Jack's final words to her, uttered fiercely as he'd handed her into the cab, his grasp too firm. *Anything we can use against him.*

She reached the table and scooped up the billfold. "Coffee's better with cream. Everything's better with cream."

"Black," De'Ath repeated through that horrible smile. He was seething beneath the skin, nerves and muscles perceptibly out of tune. Or at least, the dissonant jangle was perceptible to *her*. But she'd spent years attuning herself to the weather of men's moods.

His distress was electric, stirring the fine hairs on her arms.

Alan De'Ath wanted to scream.

She stepped backward. Here was an opportunity. Her quarry lay helpless before her, gripped by a powerful emotion. If she discovered what, or who, had felled him, she and Jack might step closer to freedom.

And yet she stepped backward, again, and then again.

Jack started up again in her head, a rant. He was telling her to keep at it, to natter on, to make the bloody toff snap.

Heat bloomed in her chest. Her hands went damp. De'Ath had treated her well, as well as anyone ever had, and better than most. She liked his amiable, eccentric household. She liked *him*.

Sorry, Jack. She couldn't press harder. Deception was bad enough. This would be cruelty.

Turmoil must have shown on her face.

"*You* aren't unwell?" asked De'Ath, eyes pinning her.

"I'm very well." She almost let loose a wild laugh. What a pair they made. Both of them—right as rain. She swallowed hard. "Black coffee."

She spun around with such force her skirts snapped, and she marched from the room.

THE CROWD IN the gallery made for a formidable barrier. Nina imagined herself in Hensthorpe, pushing through a hedgerow, a fantastical hedgerow of particolored silk, with elbows instead of branches and ruffles instead of hawthorn berries.

She hadn't fully realized how much space De'Ath had been af-
forded by the throng until now, as she found herself bumped and
trampled. She hadn't considered, either, that she'd been enjoying a
feeling of consequence as she'd walked by his side. Now she remembered that invisibility had bruising repercussions.

"Pardon," she gasped as two laughing gentlemen with linked
arms attempted to walk through her. They continued as one, without acknowledging her exclamation or awkward hop to the side.

"Bollocks," she muttered, before following in their wake.

The gallery's lower story was less congested. She peeked into the
coffee room, which glittered with mirrors and glazed ceramic tiles.
She continued on past the trio of lavish dining rooms, from which
drifted the murmur of voices and the tinkle of cutlery, and savory
aromas that made her stomach growl. If she kept going, she'd reach
an archway that led into a courtyard garden. She could see the
greenery, shiny with damp. The rain had begun.

She could turn left, find the shop De'Ath had mentioned. Buy
herself a pen with his money.

Her stomach wasn't growling. It was groaning, and the groans
bore no relation to hunger. She felt as though her insides had
twisted up. She went back down the hall and into one of the dining
rooms, stopping just inside the doorway and leaning against the
wall. She could feel the plasterwork pattern against the small of her
back, willow branches or olive boughs. Strains of conversation
reached her ears. Cultured prattle about theatrical performances
seen or anticipated. A lofty debate between juveniles about the du-
ality of the Greek spirit in art. Even the prosaic complaints about
the weather seemed rarefied by the speakers' accents and exquisite
boredom.

This was the world into which Jack had craved admittance. No
beggarly attics for these young artists and writers. No meals of dry
bread.

Nina pressed her back harder into the wall, as though to stamp
her flesh with the decorative motif. At the Royal Academy, Jack's
pennilessness had at first appealed to his fellow apprentices. They'd
found it piquant, to include a roughneck among their boon companions, to pay his portion of the rent on their great big house, to

make offerings of their cast-off finery and send dinner trays up to his room when his pride kept him from the table. *She* had changed all that, taken the fun out of the arrangement, made it impossible.

Hovering on the perimeter of the gorgeously embellished dining room, she felt as though she'd entered an alternate reality. There sat phantom Jack among the bohemians, as lighthearted as any of them. This was the life he would have lived, if she had never been.

A waiter moved into her line of vision, striding purposefully in her direction. She lowered her head and slipped back into the hall.

This time, she entered the coffee room and walked straight to the bar, where she stood for a moment, staring at her distorted, dispiriting reflection in the silver urn of the Napier machine. Bulbous cheeks, snub nose, eyes sliding together, cyclopean. She stuck out her tongue.

And that was when she heard her name.

CHAPTER TEN

"Miss Finch!"

Nina turned slowly. Miss Holroyd, in a dove gray suit with a lilac in the buttonhole, the Duchess of Weston in crimson silk, and another woman, a beauty in blue, with a dreamy expression, sat together at a little table scattered with cups, sketchbooks, and half-eaten slices of cake. As Nina fixed a smile on her face, the ringleted Miss Knotwood appeared from behind a pillar. In her pink tunic, with those imposing collarbones, she looked like a goddess come to earth.

"Miss Finch," said Miss Holroyd again, waving her over. "Where's De'Ath? Has he gone up to see the pictures? In case you're wondering, the old crank already opined. Gave a whole lecture, in fact. On how we Sisters must cultivate dainty ways and paint for children! He had the audacity to—" The next word became a hiss. "Speak of the devil."

She narrowed her eyes, and Nina twisted in time to glimpse a white-haired bespectacled man in the entrance to the coffee room, his black cane tucked beneath his arm, a coterie of lanky half-grown boys dogging his heels, jostling one another for position. That would be Lloyd Syme. De'Ath's nemesis. Her and Jack's un-witting accomplice. She threaded her fingers tightly together, neck prickling. However much Syme reviled the Sisters, and women generally, she and Jack needed him, and that trumped all.

But the longer she looked at him—at his thin, pale, supercilious face—the more her twisted insides shriveled.

Finally, he sneered, flicked at an invisible speck on the lapel of his full-skirted frock coat, and swung around so quickly the boys around him collided as they scattered. He vanished down the hall.

"Too many chattering women." Miss Holroyd gave her assessment calmly, gaze wandering the tables, at which young ladies predominated. "He'll have gone to the billiards room for respite. What say ye, fellow musketeers of the brush and the chisel?" She pulled a silver cigarette case from inside her jacket. "Shall I breach the gentlemen's redoubt?"

"If you want to aggravate yourself for no reason," sniffed the duchess. "By all means."

Miss Holroyd shrugged. "I'm already aggravated." But she tucked the cigarette case away and picked up her coffee, black.

Black coffee. Nina shifted her weight from foot to foot, glanced over her shoulder at the bar.

"Miss Finch," said the duchess. "You *will* join us?"

Nina gave her head a regretful shake. "You're very kind, your grace. But I can't stay. Mr. De'Ath wants his coffee."

"He sent you for *coffee*?" Miss Holroyd's nostrils pinched. "You're his amanuensis, not his body servant."

"Amanuensis." Miss Knotwood paused with a cup halfway to her lips. "I wondered about your connection. I took you for one of his political friends."

Nina tried not to look sour. Obviously, she didn't belong among his artistic friends, the vivid and alluring Sisters, dashing musketeers of the brush and chisel. But she wasn't political, either.

"Has he many of those?" she asked. "Political friends?"

"Oh yes." Miss Holroyd leered. "He's especially fond of suffragists."

"*Kate*." The duchess cut her eyes at Miss Holroyd.

"What?" Miss Holroyd's leer tamed instantly into a decorous smile. "I intend to supply Miss Finch with context, about artists, critics, *suffragists* . . ." She waved her hand. "Everything. To make her job more interesting." She kicked back in her chair, smile widening as she scrutinized Nina.

"De'Ath's *favorite* suffragists," she said, "are the ones who practice free love."

A napkin flew across the table. It smacked the grin from Miss Holroyd's face before dropping onto the table, where a corner splashed into her coffee.

"You can ignore her," Miss Knotwood told Nina.

"Kate," said the duchess again. "Miss Finch wasn't asking about De'Ath's romantic entanglements."

"Of course she wasn't." Miss Holroyd's grin reappeared, more wicked than before. "She doesn't have all day."

"You're a terrible gossip," commented the dreamy beauty, resting the back of her head against the pillar.

"I'm an astute and interested observer of the human condition in all its manifestations," corrected Miss Holroyd. "And so is De'Ath. Our motto is the more, the merrier."

"One *can* observe the human condition by studying a single person in such depth as to reveal multitudes." The duchess crossed her arms. "And in so doing can get just as much fulfillment by it." Her fiery blush made it clear what she meant by fulfillment.

She was referring to her husband, the naked duke.

Nina was used to men talking, in the most forthright and vulgar terms, about various and sundry parts of the anatomy and what they did with them. But hearing the Sisters discuss matters of the heart, and other bits—albeit circumspectly—made her feel slightly dizzy. It was highly disconcerting.

"Well," she said, at a loss. "I should be getting back."

"You can't leave just yet." Miss Holroyd plucked the lilac from her buttonhole and pointed with it, first at Nina, then at the dreamy beauty. "You and Gwen haven't been introduced. Miss Finch, Gwen Burgess, the finest painter in Albion."

"I'm not *yet* the finest painter in Albion." Miss Burgess shrugged. "For now, it's Augustus."

"I say! Augustus." Miss Holroyd made a face. "You're not very complimentary to your Sisters."

Miss Burgess's expression remained bland. "It's nice to meet you, Miss Finch."

Nina bent her knees in an absurd little curtsey.

"Before you run off!" The duchess held up her sketchbook. "Let me show you my drawing of Fyodor." She flipped the pages. "Here. I fear I didn't do the dear monkey justice."

"I saw the little beast myself." Miss Holroyd propped her cheek on her hand. "You've got the likeness. Miss Finch, do you agree?"

"Yes." Nina tore her eyes from the drawing, avoiding the duchess's gaze. "You've got the likeness."

The duchess blinked. "But?"

"But . . ." Nina paused. There were so many *but*s. The duchess had no idea how to model Fritz's body, no understanding of its particularities, the shape of his skeleton under the muscle and fur. She'd relied on inference and analogy.

"It's just, you see . . ." She groped for diplomatic phrasing. "*All* of his grandparents were marmosets."

The duchess turned her sketchbook around and stared grimly at the drawing. Finally, she nodded.

"I understand. He looks like one of his grandparents was a cat." She lowered the sketchbook and regarded Nina thoughtfully. "You *don't* take an interest in art, you said?"

All of the Sisters were peering at Nina, four sets of lovely, *curious* eyes.

She cleared her throat. "I'm terribly sorry. Mr. De'Ath is waiting."

DE'ATH LAY SPRAWLED in the chaise longue just as Nina had left him, except his color had returned and he was writing—right-handed and with evident dissatisfaction—in a black duodecimo notebook. He didn't look up until she'd set the coffee and the billfold on the table.

"Where's your coffee?" He slid the notebook into his breast pocket, reached for the billfold, and sent it after the notebook. "Or wasn't there cream?"

"There was cream. But there weren't any Chelsea buns."

He looked at her blankly.

"To drink coffee I need both," she explained. "Cream *and* Chelsea buns."

"That's your dietary law?"

"One of them."

"Noted." He sat up, a nimble motion, swinging his legs off the chaise longue, setting his boots on the floor.

She was the secretary, the spy. *She* should be noting things about him, not the other way around. Why, then, did she feel a little thrill whenever he seemed curious about her?

"I'll speak with Olgilvie about the situation," he said. "No Chelsea buns. A travesty." He tsked, then smiled a real smile. Clearly, he'd recovered from whatever ailed him.

The air no longer thrummed with tension. The room felt cooler, the musk of old incense and tobacco thicker.

She gave an awkward cough.

He pointed his chin toward the doorway. "Has the human flood ebbed?"

"Not a bit." She frowned. "That's why your cup's half-full. I was jostled."

He peered down into the cup. "It's a third full."

"I was jostled repeatedly."

"You weren't burned?"

The concern in his voice stopped the blood in her veins. It was a moment before she shook her head. His eyes narrowed, and he beckoned, the gesture commanding. She went around the table, stopped right in front of him, holding out her fingers for inspection. Her hand—it wasn't soft or delicate like a lady's, but he took it gently and held it as though it were precious, examining each finger for injury with the minute focus of a jeweler.

He touched only her palm and her knuckles. But as she looked down at his bent head, her whole body began to tremble.

"You weren't burned," he confirmed. "But you *were* splashed. I detect a residue." He glanced up, a gleam in his eye. "So. You brought me a third of a cup of *lukewarm* coffee."

She snatched her hand away, rubbing at a dark stain with her thumb. "You're lucky I brought you anything. I'm not your . . ." What had Miss Holroyd said? "I'm not your *body servant*."

"No," he murmured, falling back against the cushion with a smile. "You're not."

Her cheeks flamed, and her pulse scattered. What might it be like if she *were* tasked with attending to his brawny body?

No more whiskers. In the mornings, she'd sit him in a chair, soap him and shave him, and soothe his stinging skin with lavender water. She'd help him into his shirt and waistcoat. She'd wind the silk cravat around his bare throat. In the evenings, she'd reverse the process. The clothing would come off, piece by piece.

Unbidden, her eyes had begun to roam over him, shoulders, arms, torso, thighs, taking his measure.

She met his hot, amused gaze with a start. She'd forgotten he had the power to look back.

She blushed brighter and stared at the wall above his head.

And nearly choked.

A long, gold-framed painting was centered over the chaise longue. Sleeping lovers entwined on a lavishly rumpled bed. Their flesh had the shocking color of life, a warm, swollen, sated quality.

"Do you like it?" De'Ath didn't turn, didn't take his eyes from her.

She shrugged, as though her heart wasn't battering her ribs. "I have no interest in art, I told you." She paused. "You didn't listen."

"I listened. But I don't believe you." He leaned forward. "I saw how you stood before those forgeries at Broughton's. You turned your face toward the painted light as though you could feel it on your skin. And I saw you just now. Your posture changed. Your *breathing* changed."

Her breath left her entirely. Her eyes bounced between the picture and his face. "And?"

"Paintings move you. You don't see smears of color on a window blind. You see beauty. And you respond to it."

She felt dizzy. There were too many things to say.

I don't see beauty. I see labor. I see money. I see hope and fear.

Nonetheless, he wasn't wholly wrong. She crossed her arms.

"I feel something," she admitted. "When I look at paintings, I feel something."

But he already knew that.

"Is beauty an emotion, then?" Her earnestness surprised her.

She'd often longed to ask Jack this type of impractical question but never dared.

De'Ath raised his brows. "Some people say beauty is the image of God." His smile was crooked.

"Do you say that?"

"I say beauty is a pleasure particular to each of us but available to all."

She cleared her throat. She was in a very red, very plush, very small room, alone with a man, and the conversation had turned to *pleasure*. According to Miss Holroyd, De'Ath sought pleasure freely.

"To put it another way," he continued, "beauty is the experience of becoming human."

She gave him a close-lipped smile. "I'd rather experience a Chelsea bun than a Botticelli. Does that make me *less* human?"

His ears seemed to prick. He spoke softly. "You know of Botticelli?"

"Old Italian bloke. Famous." She cursed herself, and in a back compartment of her brain, Jack did too. "I saw a print in a shop, once. Madonna and child." She made a vague motion with her hand. "Some lilies. I don't understand the fuss."

After a moment, De'Ath nodded. "I'll take you to the National Gallery to see an original." His head tipped to the side. "If you'll bake me a Chelsea bun. We will widen each other's spheres of experience."

She wanted to laugh, and then she wanted to cry. For years, painting and baking had pulled her in opposite directions, two incompatible pursuits. De'Ath brought them together seamlessly, each a fit return for the other.

"First you have to try my Victoria sponge," she said, afraid that tears sparkled in her eyes. Oh, the Jack in her head was howling now.

"And someday," De'Ath said, "I'll try your gooseberry tarts."

The silence thickened.

He'd placed the two of them in the same *someday*. In that someday, her pastry shop bustled with customers. Rows of tarts cooled on trays, and she'd set one aside for Alan De'Ath.

Of course, it meant nothing.

He turned abruptly and looked up at the picture. "It's called *The Dreamers*. Miss Holroyd painted it."

"Miss Holroyd?" Nina's eyes flew to the lovers in shock, landed on the curves of the woman's breasts, damp with sweat, nipples rosy. The other figure was partially concealed by the woman, and by the twisted sheet. Nina's eyes glided down a lithe-looking arm, which draped the woman's waist.

She read the name in the corner. "Kit Griffith."

"Signatures can be deceiving." De'Ath turned to face her. "Or haven't you learned that by now?" His expression was humorous.

She suspected her answering smile was weak.

"I can tell it's Holroyd's work," he said. "It's no mystery why she didn't put her own name to it. Wholly inappropriate subject for a female artist. And too realist. Invites a scandal no matter who painted it. Olgilvie tucked it away because he didn't want to risk another protest by the British matrons." De'Ath's laughter shaded into an ironic sigh. "England can't abide an original work of art, not if it challenges the canons of purity. The public prefers forged Berneys."

"Those forgeries, though." Her throat squeezed. "You said yourself they were wonderful. It's *real*, the experience someone has, looking at them. Even if the pictures are fake."

"You're right that a wonderful forgery presents a conundrum." He brushed back a wing of raven hair. "What does one do with a beautiful crime?"

His eyes were two steel points, inscribing the question on her skin.

Her gaze dropped. De'Ath's ambivalence about decent forgeries didn't extend to the forgers themselves.

She knew what he'd do with her, with Jack.

"The coffee," she whispered. He hadn't touched it. "Should I get more?"

"No. I've decided I'm in the mood for whiskey. Holroyd will have a flask."

Nina lifted her gaze as he stood. He looked taller than she remembered. Was he ready to go? She still didn't understand the reason for this odd interlude, and perhaps she never would.

He picked up his hat and cane.

"Miss Holroyd is in the coffee room," she told him.

"Is she?" De'Ath moved toward the doorway. "In that case, I'll drink Henley's whiskey. You and I are going up to the galleries."

NINA WASN'T SURE if she felt relieved or disappointed by his sudden distance when they left the smoking room. As they walked, he fell into conversation with first one gentleman, then another, and she trailed behind.

But as they topped the stairs, he waited for her to catch up with a smile. "Notebook?"

She drew it from her chatelaine.

"We'll start with the sculpture. And, Miss Finch." He leaned over her and lowered his voice. "If you find yourself developing a passion for art, you can tell me. I won't gloat."

She didn't move for a beat but watched him stroll away. And then she followed. She stood at his side before the sculptures and paintings, taking down his words. Several of the paintings stunned her, moved her with their beauty. But to make himself heard over the din, De'Ath had to press close and speak with his head bent to hers. If she were honest, the swirl of emotions in her breast had as much to do with him as with the art.

CHAPTER ELEVEN

THE NEXT MORNING, Nina sat at De'Ath's desk and wrote out his review of the Sisters' exhibition. Strong light poured through the French doors, and no signorinas sang.

The day was fine, and De'Ath's mood was playful. He made no mention of forgeries or of his brother, and sent her off early to lunch.

He summoned her that afternoon, and they rolled in his coach to Trafalgar Square. The fountains were splashing, and all sorts of people were milling in the sun. Clerks, soldiers, errand boys. Ladies and gentlemen swanned about, looking as though they owned the world. Tourists gaped up at the statue of Lord Nelson.

When she stepped down to the street, she swayed. The grand portico of the National Gallery had never filled her with such dread.

"I'll introduce you to Botticelli," said De'Ath. "And Bellini. And Raphael."

Inside, Nina dragged her feet on the stairs. She could tour De'Ath through the rooms of the National Gallery blindfolded. She could explain how Bellini's *The Assassination of Saint Peter Martyr* exemplified the Venetian Renaissance. She could share Jack's theory about Botticelli's varnishes or his use of tempera.

She let him lead her on a slow circuit, her stomach all knots.

She couldn't concentrate on anything he was saying. Even so, his enthusiasm touched her, as did this whole misguided expedition. She couldn't decide if he meant to impress or improve her or, more simply, to befriend her. Perhaps all three.

In any case, he was enjoying himself. That much was obvious.

She had never wandered the National Gallery, open-mouthed, in awe. She'd only come here to work, every bit of her hard and small and tightly focused.

De'Ath said nothing when they came to the Botticellis. She looked at him expectantly.

"Well?" she prodded. "Aren't you going to tell me something?"

"No." He folded his arms, eyes locked on *Venus and Mars*. "This is enough."

They stood for a time, looking, in companionable silence.

Finally, De'Ath directed them to two oak chairs, and they sat side by side, light filtering down from above, glinting on the golden frames of the pictures crowded on the crimson walls.

"*Bacchus and Ariadne*." He followed her gaze to the Titian. "Ariadne saved Theseus from the Minotaur. Do you know the myth?"

Nina nodded. "She gave him a spool of thread so he could find his way out of the Minotaur's maze. And for her pains, he abandoned her on an island."

"Where she found love, with Bacchus, god of wine and rapture."

Nina studied the painting, which she'd copied several times, practicing Titian's techniques. *This* painting moved her, the blue of the sky and the sea, Theseus's ship disappearing in the distance, Ariadne twisted away from Bacchus, himself suspended in midair.

"Love?" she echoed, and shook her head. "Ariadne looks frightened. And she's turned toward the man who left her." She sighed. "I doubt the god of wine is more trustworthy than Theseus. Those cheetahs, though, are darling." Titian had included two gorgeous, shadowy cheetahs, positioned *between* Bacchus and Ariadne. They were her favorite part of the painting, a reminder of her mother's adage.

Much comfort in cats, little in men.

"Ah yes, the cheetahs." De'Ath laughed. "They pull Bacchus's chariot. Do you see the dog?"

"Also darling." His laughter made her smile. It felt rather delightful, to sit with him in this cool, airy room, people drifting past, nothing demanded of her.

She tipped her head toward his.

"But I prefer cats," she said. "My brother and I have two, and our aunts have seven."

"Your aunts. These are the ones with the lovely cottage?"

"Yes, the only ones. Aunt Sylvia and Miss Lolly."

Aunt Sylvia was Jack's aunt, technically, sister to Jack's father. Miss Lolly wasn't related to anyone. She'd lived with Aunt Sylvia for decades.

"Two aunts, seven cats, and a room to spare." De'Ath tapped his fingers on the arm of the chair. "Yet it fell to your rough-spoken brother to raise you."

A cold current moved through Nina's veins. Her sense of delight chilled into an awareness of danger. Suddenly, the chair felt hard and ungiving, a chair fit for the accused in court.

De'Ath's pause was expectant.

Surely it was *more* suspicious to say nothing.

"We made their acquaintance when we were already grown," she said. "Or I did. My brother knew them a little, but only as a very young child. They're on our father's side of the family, and he died first, before I was born. In the village, he was a harness maker, but he moved to London, and that's where he met our mother."

De'Ath shifted in his chair so he faced toward her, signaling that she had his full attention.

She went on. "He worked in a carriage factory. Something broke, a hoist. He was killed, quite *crushed.*" She winced. Jack had given her details she wished he hadn't. "Our mother didn't talk about him much. And she never took us to the village or talked about our aunts either. I think she blamed herself for keeping him in London and imagined that his sister blamed her too."

Nina stopped, a tickle in her throat. It was all true, except John Reeve hadn't been her father. Her eyes flicked back to the Titian, to the left edge, Theseus's boat poised to sail out of the picture forever.

She'd rather not speak of *her* father, Richard Finch.

She heard De'Ath's chair creak.

"England's factories produce nearly as many tragedies as matchsticks." He sounded grim.

She turned her head. He'd taken off his spectacles. He was looking at her, his gaze unreadable.

"Then Mother died," she said. The banality of this sort of sentence still shocked her. It was so impersonal, and the loss had been so overwhelmingly specific. She wanted to ask De'Ath if *he* ever felt that words fell short, failed to express what mattered most. He was a person with whom one could discuss such things. He might have answers, or better questions.

"I'm sorry," he said. *There* was a threadbare phrase. But something in his voice filled it with a hundred shades of meaning.

Slowly, he lifted his hand. Her breath caught. Would he touch her? In the middle of the National Gallery? He laid the hand on his own arm, near the elbow.

"How did you reunite with your aunts?"

She lowered her eyes.

Funny story. Aunt Sylvia read about Jack in the paper—you did too, I'm sure. The Dutchified Dauber? She thought he might very well be her nephew, and she wrote to him during the trial. He sent her a letter back, along with me.

She gave a stiff shrug. "My brother remembered the name of the village. We went to visit, and it's such a small place—we found them at once. They're spinsters, no children of their own. Aunt Sylvia can seem a bit fierce, but they're both terribly kind. They offered to take me for a year. I was thirteen and missing my mother, and my brother thought it a suitable idea." She'd stayed over a year, in fact. The whole length of Jack's sentence.

"And they taught you how to bake?"

She lifted her eyes to De'Ath's. She had the distinct feeling that he hadn't looked away from her for a moment.

"Lumpy plum breads, at first." Her tight muscles began to ease. "I learned how to make hedgerow jelly and how to build houses for hedgehogs." She smiled at the memory. "Miss Lolly loves hedgehogs. She bakes a special hedgehog cake at midsummer. It doesn't have hedgehogs in it. It *looks* like a hedgehog, with almond bristles all over. The whole thing is soaked in fruit wine. I learned to bake that. Mr. Craddock—the village baker—he let me help him in the bakery. And Mr. Middleton from up the lane taught me about clover pie. It's a great favorite among his cows. You take a large leaf and fill it with clover, then you put it on your palm, bring it to the cow, and she eats it in one bite."

She realized she was holding her hand, palm up, as though offering De'Ath an imaginary pie. Which would make him the cow in the scenario.

"Never mind," she said. She glanced about at their very dignified surroundings and giggled.

He gave her his wicked smile, the one that showed his sharp white teeth. "A remarkable education."

"At the same age, *you* were learning other things. You were learning about art and poetry. Myths and empires. History." She made a face, teasing. "Probably in Latin. Isn't that what they speak at Eton?"

"I don't know." His gaze hardened slightly. "I didn't go to Eton."

"Oh. Don't you all go to Eton?" A thought occurred to her. "You went someplace even *more* posh than Eton!" She grinned in triumph, but his face made her smile slip. His look had turned caustic.

"I went everywhere and nowhere." He untwisted, putting his back flush to the chair. "But we were talking about you, about village life."

She looked at his stark profile and spoke in a subdued voice. "I was going on a bit."

Seconds ticked by. At last, De'Ath stirred. He cut his eyes to her, and his expression softened. "Did you ever tell your brother?"

"Tell him what? The recipe for clover pie?"

De'Ath slanted his head, gave her a slight smile. "When the year was up. Did you tell him how badly you wanted to stay?"

She drew a sharp breath. Her hands clutched into fists. Hell's bells. De'Ath had taken a scalpel to her story and cut straight to the festering heart of it.

She looked furiously at the Titian. She hadn't told Jack. But the moment he'd set foot in the cottage, he'd known. He'd seen it in her eyes, and she'd seen him see it. His smile crumpled, and she'd wanted to crumple too. Instead, she'd hurled herself into his arms.

"He knew," said De'Ath. "And he took you back to London regardless."

"We agreed it was best." Nina stood, too rapidly, nearly knocking into a woman passing by. The lady let out a shocked huff.

"Pardon," Nina muttered. De'Ath had come to his feet beside her.

She gripped her ribs, angling her body away from his.

"It's a sensitive subject," De'Ath observed. "I shouldn't have persisted."

She didn't answer.

You all rub along well, don't you? Jack had said it to Aunt Sylvia. They'd been talking in the garden where they thought Nina couldn't hear. *I've never seen her so blooming.* And Aunt Sylvia had touched his arm. *We can keep her, Jack.*

He hadn't refused. He'd gotten out his cigarettes and moved off, to smoke under the plum tree. He'd been considering it, letting her live in Hensthorpe.

Then Miss Lolly had shown him the drawings and watercolors Nina had been making, of oak trees, and the Saxon ruins at Priory Pond, and cows. That moment marked the change in the intensity of his intention.

He'd understood, in a flash, what she was worth to him.

Her heart cramped.

De'Ath spoke again. "You're tired," he said. "We can go."

She braced herself, then pivoted to face him. It wasn't his fault that he'd sent her thoughts winging down the darkest road.

"Thank you," she said. "Thank you for introducing me to Botticelli, and Bellini, and the others." She managed a smile. "I owe you Chelsea buns."

"I'll take anything but clover pie." He was studying her.

She gave a snort. "Not to worry. I wouldn't feed London clover to a rat."

He looked as though he wanted to say something else.

"Well," she said briskly, and started across the room.

It wasn't until they'd returned to Casa De'Ath that she noticed he'd left off his spectacles and that it didn't seem to affect his ability to see at all.

THAT EVENING, NINA discovered that Monsieur Rouget didn't stock the kitchen with castor sugar.

"Currants?" she asked, with fading hope.

De'Ath's chef chuckled behind his fan of cards. Dinner preparations over, he'd cleared the table and dealt a game of five-card loo. He and Kessler and McAdams were gambling with oysters from a bucket.

Nina opened another cabinet and a shining wave of utensils clattered to the stone floor.

"Ouf!" cried Monsieur Rouget. "The can opener! You found it!" He squinted at the open cabinet and sighed. "All this time. If I had but known . . ." He turned back to the game.

Nina collected the forks and knives and set about rearranging the cabinet. She brought the can opener to Monsieur Rouget. "Cinnamon?"

Monsieur Rouget pointed the can opener at a shelf. Nina lifted a sauce-crusted apron and uncovered a rotating spice rack. Cinnamon. Cloves. Nutmeg. Rosemary. Fennel. She gave the rack a satisfied spin, hung the apron on a peg, and went on the hunt for cake tins.

Once she'd finished her inventory, she wrote out a shopping list in her notebook. The kitchen wasn't orderly, but it was clean enough, with the oven well swept and Monsieur Rouget's bed made up neatly in the corner. The range wanted polish, but she'd been blessed with hardy elbows and planned to blacklead it herself. If De'Ath was willing to buy the ingredients and equipment she required, she could make miracles in this place. Unless Monsieur Rouget resented the incursion.

"Monsieur Rouget." She approached the table. "You're quite sure I'm not stepping on your toes?"

McAdams caught her eye. "No onion soup."

"That's his specialty," said Kessler. "Off-limits."

"And rooster poached in white wine," said McAdams.

"And rousing tales from the Paris Commune," said Kessler.

Monsieur Rouget cocked his head and sniffed. "My soup, my poulet au vin blanc, my stories of revolution—wasted on buffoons."

"He'll let you bake," said McAdams. "If you let him talk your head off."

"It's a perfect arrangement." Nina smiled at Monsieur Rouget. "Revolution, you said?"

McAdams and Kessler exchanged a glance and dropped their cards as one.

"Drink?" asked Kessler.

McAdams stood. "I'll get the glasses."

While Kessler poured the absinthe, Monsieur Rouget began his tale, a jaunty one, about building a barricade out of carriages requisitioned from the nobility by order of the common man. Nina laughed and sipped from her glass. Kessler and McAdams groaned and finished the bottle.

"There's more," said Kessler, as Monsieur Rouget paused his narrative and rose to rummage the shelves. "There's always more."

"I'll hear more tomorrow." Nina rose too. "When I'm back to bake Chelsea buns."

Monsieur Rouget returned to the table, a bottle of wine in his hand.

"English baking," he said. "I like it not too much. But perhaps you can persuade me."

"Persuade me, please," said Kessler. "With a cheesecake."

"Chocolate tarts," suggested McAdams.

By the time Nina closed the baize-covered door behind her they were singing "La Marseillaise." She hummed the tune on her way to the butler's pantry. Kuznetsov was writing in such a storm of inspiration he didn't lift his head. Fritz's tail waved by his ear. She left them to it.

Instead of walking to her room, she walked out the front door and stood in the small front garden. The warm, clear day had become a cool, clear night. Across the street, beyond the embankment, the river was slipping by. A bone-white moon hung overhead, nearly full. She started toward the gateposts with the idea of look-ing out at the water, watching the barges float under the bridge, counting the bobbing lights.

She was still gazing up as she walked and so almost struck De'Ath as he came down the path.

They both stopped. He was a dark figure in evening dress, his top hat casting his eyes in utter blackness.

"Miss Finch," he said, low. "Out for a stroll?"

"It's a lovely night." His sudden presence made her heart flip in her chest.

"Lovely," he agreed. He took off his hat and tipped his face to-ward the sky. "But only a scattering of stars."

"It's lovely, but it's still London." She shivered as the wind riffled her dress, fluttered the silver leaves of the olive tree. The city always smelled vaguely rotten, but here, surrounded by aromatic garden herbs, the wind carrying the bergamot scent of De'Ath's Brown Windsor soap, she found herself breathing deeply, like she did when she stepped off the train in Hensthorpe.

"I'd wanted to point out the Corona Borealis, Ariadne's crown." He shrugged and straightened. "It's there in the west, but too faint to see."

"We saw it once today already." She smiled. "In the painting. The circle of stars above the clouds."

He took a step nearer. "You noticed."

She sucked in an inaudible breath.

Titian's sky is ultramarine and lead white, she could have said. *The sea beneath is azurite. He used fourteen different pigments to paint the whole.*

Her throat filled. She despised her omissions and lies, and not entirely due to conscience. No, her *selfishness* gave her guilt another dimension, a layer of reckless, frustrated longing.

She wanted more, more from their conversations. She wanted to speak unguardedly. She wanted them to look at paintings, or at the stars, or at each other, without this awful bulwark of dishonesty keeping them apart. She wanted to lean close to him, and . . .

Lean close to him?

Nina, she chided herself. *Nina, Nina.*

"You notice everything," De'Ath murmured, "don't you, Miss Finch?"

Despite the shadows, she knew he was looking her dead in the eye. His gaze seemed to heat the darkness.

"I wish Bancroft Broughton possessed a fraction of your powers." He closed the distance between them. "Enjoy your stroll."

He blocked the moon and seemed a shadow himself. Then he was moving past her, entering the house.

Bancroft Broughton, of Broughton's Auction House.

Hell. She wasn't here to look at the bloody stars.

"Mr. De'Ath!" She hurried after him, and he waited on the threshold in a wedge of light, holding the door.

"Do you have the time?" she panted, climbing the step. "It's too late to stroll, I think."

They both turned as Kuznetsov banged down the hall. He was conducting two sides of a conversation in thunderous Russian. Nina considered plucking Fritz from his waistcoat, for comfort, but Kuznetsov spun too quickly, racing back to the butler's pantry, shaking De'Ath's hat and overcoat as he spoke, like puppets.

His voice faded. The house was silent.

The gaslit vestibule in which Nina stood with De'Ath felt overly warm.

De'Ath laughed. "He's staging the conflict between faith and doubt. It's bound to be his greatest novel yet."

"About Mr. Broughton." Nina linked her hands. "Were you just out with him?"

De'Ath glanced at her, the smile still playing on his lips. "We had a drink at the club."

"And he hasn't changed his mind?" She didn't dare to hope. "He still believes those pictures are by James Berney?"

She reddened under De'Ath's narrowing gaze. She shouldn't have inquired, and certainly not with such eagerness.

"He must be dreadfully stubborn," she added, with a reproving shake of her head. "After you laid out all your reasoning too. Shame."

She offered De'Ath a frown of commiseration.

His brows pulled together. He was only a foot away and looking at her with far too much scrutiny.

"You smell like absinthe," he said.

"Oh." She licked the corner of her lips, tasted anise and something elusively botanical. "I had a drink too, in the kitchen."

"I wish I'd drunk with you, then. Broughton was rather tiresome."

"Oh," she said again, and tried to imagine De'Ath in the kitchen, tipping the bottle. Did he go so far as to socialize with Kessler and the rest? Good Lord, did he sing "La Marseillaise"?

"Absinthe has an unusual flavor," she said. "I had the idea of using it in a glaze to drizzle on little cakes. Orange and almond cakes."

"Absinthe-glazed cakes." He sounded amused but not derisive. "They'd be popular at poetry salons. Why not persimmon?"

"Absinthe and persimmon." Instead of orange. Intriguing. Nina nodded slowly. "Perhaps I'll try that too."

Her frown was reversing itself. Mr. Broughton had dug in his heels! That alone was reason to rejoice. And De'Ath had joined easily in her favorite activity, the invention of new recipes, experimental combinations.

The light in his eyes made her giddier than alcohol.

"Do you know," she said, "that you don't own a rolling pin, or a jelly mold, or a pastry jigger? Or modeling tools or brass crimpers? Or a dough docker? Or even a pinch of bicarbonate of soda?"

"No," he said dryly. "How have I lived without a dough docker?" He leaned his shoulder against the wall. "What's a dough docker?"

"A device for putting holes in dough, to let out the steam."

"Essential," he murmured. "Letting out the steam. I'll purchase two."

"I wrote a list of what I'll need to bake Chelsea buns." She hesitated. "As well as a few other things."

"Other things?" His voice was drier still, but his lips twitched with a suppressed smile.

"Things to make Victoria sponge." For some reason, she wanted to hug herself, as though she could trap the little bubble of happiness rising inside her. "Queen cakes. Cheesecake. Tartlets. Wine biscuits. Petits fours."

De'Ath's eyebrows traveled higher and higher. "Let me see your list."

She extracted the notebook from her chatelaine.

"Perhaps I'll invite Broughton over for tea and tartlets." He said it musingly. "Or cheesecake. He seems the sort to take consolation in cheesecake."

"Consolation?" Nina blinked. "But why does he need consolation?"

"Because it pains a stubborn man to admit himself in error."

Now her brow creased. "You said he won't admit any error." *Lord love him.*

"Not at the moment. But after tomorrow . . ."

"Tomorrow?" She lost her grip on the notebook.

She knelt, but De'Ath was quicker.

"He's making the trip to Norwich," he said, rising, notebook in hand. "Berney's granddaughter lives there, she who discovered the paintings. In an old pigsty, or so goes her story." He shrugged. "Broughton will question her. The story will fall apart. And that will be that."

"Will it be?" The blood drained from Nina's face. Jack had sent a letter to Mrs. Beechey. But what if she'd been sick with drink and hadn't opened it? What if the promise of money wasn't enough to buy her silence? Mr. Broughton would scare her silly, all gentlemanly, with his fine suit and his fine voice. She'd buckle, unless Jack appeared in the flesh to charm and cajole her and press coins into her hand.

"That will be that when it comes to Broughton's stubbornness," said De'Ath. "There's work yet to be done, to find Sleaford. And to catch the forger. Why, Miss Finch." His voice changed. He'd given the notebook an idle flip, and now he stared down at it. "How incredible." He held it up, open.

She looked with horror. Beneath a column of addresses, there it was, her sketch. It was slight and unfinished. But the lines were sure.

The mouth it rendered was surely De'Ath's mouth.

She forced herself to shift her gaze back to him.

He wore an expression of intense interest. "You did this."

She couldn't deny it.

He turned the notebook around and studied it. "You've been withholding. This required skill. When did you study drawing? With whom?"

"It didn't require skill." She shook her head, heart stuttering. "It felt intuitive."

"I inspired you? Or more precisely, my mouth inspired you?" That mouth shifted into a crooked smile. It seemed to hook something inside her.

"Yes," she whispered. His eyes widened, infinitesimally.

But it was enough.

The space between them shivered, or *she* was shivering. She held still. She held her very breath.

He took off his spectacles and dropped them into his pocket. His gaze seemed to fly at her, a silver arrow fletched with long black lashes.

"And are you in want of further inspiration?" It was a soft drawl, perfectly ironic. But his eyes drilled into her. Heat surged through her veins. She scarcely realized she was pressing through her feet, rising up on her toes.

He dipped his head. His lips hovered over hers. It wasn't a kiss. It was a new way of understanding his mouth, in relationship to her mouth.

Her eyelids drifted down. Her palms settled on his hard chest.

"Does this help?" His breath was hot.

She didn't move. She was flush against him, plunged in velvety darkness. She sighed her next words. "Now I could draw your mouth with my eyes closed."

"Just my mouth?" His lips were *on* hers now. "With your natural talent, you could widen your scope."

She could taste the brandy on his skin. Were they going to stay like so? His heart pounded against her hand, furiously fast, and yet he remained immobile, controlled, body solid as rock.

Was this the *more* she'd wanted from their conversations, the two of them mouth to mouth?

Breathing.

Tasting.

It wasn't only brandy on his skin. His lips had some other savor, dark like chocolate, tantalizingly familiar. She pressed up the barest fraction. She touched his lower lip with her tongue.

He inhaled sharply. She curled her hands in his lapels, pulling his face closer, and she licked the curve of his mouth, a tentative stroke with the tip of her tongue.

De'Ath was tall and broad, dense with muscle, a man of enormous mental and physical strength. It felt strange, and desperately exciting, to explore this silky, vulnerable part of him. This softness. This sweetness.

Chocolate, yes. Date sugar. Clove.

She slid her hands up to his shoulders, to his neck. It was rigid beneath the folds of his cravat. She moved her tongue, tested his upper lip.

He growled, and his arm clamped around her waist.

"What are you doing to me?"

His grip tightened, and then something seemed to break inside him. With a groan, he bent her backward, drove his mouth onto hers. She gasped, knees loosening, but his arm was like iron. He held her upright, his teeth dragging her lower lip down. He was licking *her* now, stroking his tongue into her mouth. She met his tongue with hers, and this combination—dear God, it was the very essence of deliciousness.

The slick slide of tongue on tongue turned her molten. Her scalding blood pulsed in an urgent rhythm. His hands roamed over her, kneaded her backside, lifted her into him, closer and closer still. Her nipples were pebble hard, bright with sensation, like tiny stars. And between her legs, she felt a strong, quickened beat, like her heart had dropped down and lodged at the tops of her thighs. She canted her hips, and the jut of his cock rubbed right where she ached. She heard a thin, unraveled cry and realized a second later it had emerged from her own throat.

She froze. Delirious sensation transformed into stark awareness.

She had been writhing in De'Ath's arms. Her hands were still clasping his neck. His tongue was deep in her mouth.

Oh, bloody burning hell.

Sweat trickled down between her breasts, and that heart between her thighs beat on—needy, greedy beats.

She forced her head to the side, breath shuddering.

"Nina," he said, hoarse, fingers smoothing back her hair, tracing down the side of her face.

Slowly, she turned her face, met his gaze. His pupils were huge, ringed with thinnest silver, their wildness almost frightening. For a moment, they stared. Then he loosened his grip and let her step back. Coolness rushed in. She walked backward until her shoulders bumped the wall. The notebook lay between them on the floor. She hadn't heard it drop.

She bent and seized it.

"My list." She was breathless. "I'll find it for you." She paged through the notebook with trembling fingers. "Here."

De'Ath's face was composed, eyes hooded. His chest rose and fell more evenly than hers. But his hair was disheveled, the knot of his cravat loose and askew. His mouth gleamed with damp.

No pretending this hadn't happened.

She wasn't shivering now. She *quaked*, like a wobbly pudding.

Her first kiss. It had been delicious and atrocious at once. She had kissed De'Ath, mindlessly, when she should have been thinking, formulating a plan, deciding, perhaps, to sneak away to the Knack in the middle of the night. She'd wake Jack, tell him he needed to get on the train to Norwich.

No. No, more sensible to wait, to leave with permission.

Sensible. Nothing about any of this was sensible.

De'Ath was searching her face, his look dark and unreadable. He seemed about to speak.

"I have cake tins at home," she spoke first, voice unsteady. "And a rolling pin. Even a dough docker. There's no need for you to buy your own. If you don't object, I'll take the morning to fetch mine."

"Take the time you need," he murmured. "Miss Finch—"

"Just the morning will do." She fetched up her pen and struck lines through items on the list. When she was finished, she tore the page free. She passed it to him, and he caught her fingers. Electricity arced through her.

"Miss Finch," he said. "You are more than memorable. More than remarkable. You exceed my capacity for remarks."

He lifted her hand and kissed her fingertips. When he raised his face, she had to look away.

She was deceiving him. What could her kiss have been but a lie?

"Well." She withdrew her fingers. "Good night, then."

She could feel his eyes on her as she walked from him down the hall. Once she'd closed herself in her room, she fell back against the door and pressed her hand to her chest, where the bubble of happiness had popped.

CHAPTER TWELVE

THE VIOLIN SOLO ended, and the guests at the Earl of Bettany's musical afternoon resumed their conversations or rose to seek out more appealing company, drifting between the chairs toward the perimeter of the immense room. Alan glimpsed Neal out of the corner of his eye. His friend's hands were in his pockets, and he was bouncing on the soles of his feet, all but running for the door. *Philistine.* Neal preferred rocks to Bach. For years, he'd gallivanted the world digging up plants for Varnham Nurseries. Now he managed the nursery—a large operation with locations in London and Truro—which kept him in England. As did his wife. Lavinia didn't share his love of foliage, or of sleeping al fresco on frigid mountaintops. She was certainly the reason he'd attended today's party, and the reason he hadn't already bolted.

Alan started after him. Neal was never hard to locate. He'd be in the wildest corner of the garden, jacket on a bench, sleeves rolled up, grubbing for God knew what in a flower bed.

"Lord Alan." Bettany blocked his path. "Are you enjoying the music?"

Alan stopped. Geoffrey joined Bettany, his face alight with fury. He hadn't responded to Alan's letter, but his expression proved he'd received it.

Alan smiled at both men. "Very much."

"Henri Chevillard is my personal discovery." Bettany gestured to the red-haired violinist who leaned on the piano making eyes at the accompanist as the peevish baritone tried to recapture her attention. "I found him on the hot pavement, in Paris, playing to beggars and birds. A talent like that!" He shook his head. "I invited him to London for a proper debut." He paused to wet his lips with champagne. He'd debuted many of his discoveries over the years, usually very young chanteuses, their salient attributes not always musical in nature.

Alan didn't like him *least* of Geoffrey's friends.

Bettany disburdened himself of his empty champagne flute, pushing it into a passing footman without looking away from Alan, his expression aggrieved. "Umfreville says I should be prepared for you to debase his performance."

Alan glanced at Geoffrey. "Then my brother wasn't listening to it. The performance was brilliant. I'd as soon debase Bach himself."

"Brilliant?" Bettany drew in his chin with surprise and smiled, before his forehead crinkled with suspicion. He thrust his head forward. "Where's your notebook, then? Your pen scratches away when you're favorably struck."

Alan cut his eyes again to Geoffrey. "Perhaps my brother has something to say on that subject as well."

Geoffrey's gaze dropped to Alan's left hand, and his lips tightened.

Alan hadn't bothered with the bandage. The swelling had subsided somewhat, but the middle knuckles were livid, and his fingers had a greenish cast.

His secretary's pen should have been scratching. But two days had gone by since Miss Finch left for cake tins, and she'd not returned.

At random moments, Alan felt her absence anew, a sudden tightness in his chest, followed by a violent thud of his heart.

"Brilliant," repeated Bettany. "And you'll put that in a music column? I want Chevillard to be the rage."

Alan gave him a cool look. "Henri Chevillard will receive the review he deserves." *Not the one you deserve. Or Geoffrey.* "If you'll excuse me."

He continued toward the door, a smooth saunter. Painless today, at this pace.

"You've come to your senses." Geoffrey overtook him. They passed together into the garden.

"Don't be absurd." Alan chose a path at random. "That violinist is extraordinary. I wish he weren't. I'd rather annoy your associates."

"Bettany was pleased, which pleased *me*." Geoffrey linked his hands behind his back as he walked. "He'll have a cabinet position in the next ministry. Perhaps I will too."

"Angels and ministers of grace defend us," quoted Alan, turning through a gap in the hedges.

Geoffrey followed. "I accept your atonement, even if you won't admit to it."

Alan said nothing. The sunlight felt strident. He looked at the beds of colorful flowers lining the path.

Miss Finch appeared before his eyes, as he'd first seen her, in a maid's livery, with those enticing dimples and plush, petal-soft lips.

He'd forgotten himself, kissing her. If she hadn't stopped him, he would have rucked up her skirts and taken her there, in the vestibule. Is that why she kept away? She'd chosen to protect herself from the amorous attentions of her employer. Or else—had some harm befallen her?

His heart gave a thud.

"How does this sound?" Geoffrey was at his elbow. "A monthly allowance, beginning tomorrow. Contingent, of course, on your continuing to publish gentlemanly, agreeable essays."

Alan focused. "Sounds like rubbish. As pathetic as Count Davanzo's opera. You'll open the account, without conditions, and give me back full control of the investments. Otherwise, Great-Great-Grandmama's portrait is going on the auction block."

Geoffrey wheeled around and seized Alan's shoulder, breathing hard. His breath smelled of champagne.

"Gentlemanly and agreeable," murmured Alan. "Shall we try it on? For the sake of yon innocent maidens?"

Pairs of giggling debutantes in pastel silks were sweeping toward them along the path.

With a growl, Geoffrey dropped his hand. They parted, each to one side of the path, to permit the girls' passage, then remained where they stood, looking at each other.

"You've already taken enough," said Geoffrey at last. His chiseled face seemed suddenly haggard. "From the very beginning, you . . ." He choked off the words, compressed his lips to whiteness.

"Yes, I know. I took our mother away from you." Alan pushed down on his cane, driving the ferrule into the dirt. "My first sin." His laughter was cold enough to blight the blossoms on the trees, to stun the butterflies wafting between.

He shook his head. "I didn't ask to be sick, Geoff." He held Geoffrey's gaze and continued, slowly and deliberately. "And I was never so sick as she pretended. Until she made it so."

Geoffrey's whole face had gone white. He stood as still as the marble figure on the fountain behind him.

"And if it's true?" The breeze flattened his hair against his forehead. "She had a nervous disposition. I don't deny *that*. If her mollycoddling worsened your symptoms, what of it? Look at you. Healthy as a horse. All's well that ends well." Now he laughed, a laugh like Alan's, like winter night. "You got better. And still their pity drove them to give you what by all rights belonged to me."

Alan's smile tasted like acid. "Their pity can drive them through the fires of hell."

For a moment, he considered trying again, begging this time. *Geoffrey, listen to me. Please.*

He'd make his brother understand, at last, that their mother had sickened him. He'd add the missing piece and explain that she'd meant to cripple him too. That, in a sense, she'd succeeded.

But he'd rather die than beg.

He'd rather go to hell himself.

"All's well," he said instead, and quoted more Shakespeare. "Health shall live free and sickness freely die."

"You're insane," said Geoffrey simply. "If you were a woman, I'd have you locked away."

"Or a child." Alan sneered. "You lock away your own son."

"To *convalesce*, you lunatic." Geoffrey stepped forward into the center of the path, and Alan met him there. Nose to nose. "Better a bedchamber than a crypt. Now, listen to me." He lowered his brows, voice tightening. "I don't care what you claim to own, or what papers you can adduce to prove it. Umfreville House is mine. I won't open the door to your auction house appraisers. The portraits will stay on the walls, where they've hung for decades, some for nearly a century." His irises were washed out with sun, white and uncanny. "Complain to your solicitor. Let him spring into action. I'm a duke, dammit. I dine with the lord chancellor and the home secretary. They oversee the courts, Scotland Yard." He snapped his jaws. "*You* will bend to me, not the other way around. You'll write what I like. What I uphold, *you* will uphold. Your nonconformist capriccios end today. All of them. The preposterous name. The preposterous apparel." He took hold of Alan's lapel.

Alan looked down his nose, expanding his chest, maximizing his extra inches, which he knew made Geoffrey's blood boil.

"How *is* Claud?" he asked conversationally, as though he hadn't heard a word of Geoffrey's frothing speech.

"Believe it or not, he's in a bad way." Geoffrey released his lapel. "You won't see him, or hear a word of him, or the girls. And I won't let them hear a word of you. Not until you demonstrate that you have respect for family. Which begins with you telling Broughton that you've changed your mind about the sale."

"Your grace!"

Geoffrey didn't turn, reluctant to look away first.

Alan leaned to the side and peered over his shoulder. A couple was circling the fountain, arm in arm, headed their way. Lord Kilderbee and his wife, Lady Kilderbee, née Lady Patricia Kempe. Geoffrey's youthful passion for her hadn't blinded him to the sacrifices the union of two pauperized aristocrats would have required. Nor hers for him. They'd both married for money. Alan doubted their spouses knew how these two pragmatists carried on whenever their backs were turned.

"Ah," he said softly. "What were you saying about respect for family?"

Geoffrey turned abruptly. Lord Kilderbee, rich and portly, good-humored and insensitive, hallooed again. He had nearly reached the path. Lovely as ever, Lady Kilderbee trailed behind, twirling a sprig of blossoms in her hand.

"I'll leave you to it." Alan pounded him on the back, two hard friendly-looking slaps, and walked on.

He found Neal just beyond the avenue of rhododendrons, crouched by a shrubby conifer.

"*Wellingtonia gigantea*," called Neal. "From California. Biggest tree in the world." He sat back on his heels, feeling around its base. He wore no jacket, and his sleeves were rolled up to his elbows.

"You'd never know it." Alan sat down on a stone bench and stretched out his legs.

"Wait five hundred years." Neal grinned, at the tree and at Alan both, exuding satisfaction and marvelment and simple joy. That was Neal. The man had a wellspring of goodness inside him. No awful knowledge weighed him down. No childhood hurt curdled his mind.

Alan stared. "However do you manage?"

"Manage what?" Neal stood, dusting his hands on his trousers. Something in Alan's face made him ask: "What's wrong?"

"Fraternal strife." Alan shrugged. "Insignificant, if we take the long view." He waved his hand at the Wellingtonia. "What will it matter in five hundred years?"

Neal was at the bench in two strides, eyes narrowed. He distinguished between leaves, between blades of grass. Of course, he noticed that Alan's fingers had changed color. "Broken?"

Alan curled the fingers experimentally and shrugged. "They'll be good as new in a week's time." He frowned. "Can't hold a pen to save my life. That's the worst of it. Yesterday, I had to resort to the bloody typewriter." He didn't add that his desire for a certain woman's company had greatly increased his impatience as he'd stabbed at the keys.

"You can't compose on a machine," he said. "Unless you want to write telegrams."

"I thought you were modern." Neal sat beside him on the bench. "Mechanization is the future."

Alan laughed, recognizing the offer. A debate, for distraction. Neal had grown up in a household that specialized in cheerful intellectual argumentation.

"What about your wife?" he asked. "Don't tell me she types her novels. Surely her sentences flow from a crimson quill."

Neal tipped back his head, exposing his neck. Alan bit the inside of his cheek to keep from ribbing Neal about its attractively tanned skin and virile dimensions. Lavinia's first novel featured swooning descriptions of a Neal-like pirate. Alan liked to recite choice passages.

"I might write a novel myself." He stretched out his legs. "A novel of Mars."

The idea arrived, wholly formed. A novel of Mars, for Claud. For other children marooned in their beds.

"What else does the future hold?" Neal was looking at him. "Not five hundred years from now, five years from now."

"For me?" Alan folded his arms. "Beyond my novel of Mars?"

"Yes, and don't say a novel of Jupiter."

"But that's just it. Followed by a novel of Saturn."

"Evasive as always." Neal crinkled his brow, resigned.

Miss Finch's words echoed in Alan's ears.

I don't think anyone knows you.

He didn't let anyone know him, even the people he loved best. It was a kindness.

He sighed and offered a minor confidence. "I'll open my own art gallery. I have my eye on the building, an old fruit market. Satisfied?"

"Will it satisfy *you*?" Neal folded his arms, left hand resting on his biceps. He wasn't a man to wear rings, but since he'd married, Alan had never seen him without his wedding band. The gold winked.

Alan ignored the question. "In five years," he predicted, "you'll have three children, and you'll have planted Wellingtonias for them to climb, and Lavinia will have put them in an adventure story. And when I visit, I'll incite them to acts of deplorable mischief."

"Of course you will." Neal snorted, then laughed. "Be careful I don't return the favor. I expect by then you'll have a family of your own."

"My good man." Alan started. "Are you cracked? Why in God's name would you expect that?"

"Because you've always wanted one." Neal shrugged. "And you're the sort who gets what he wants." He leapt from the bench before Alan could react. "Help me find my jacket? I can't sit through Chopin's 'Impromptu' in my shirtsleeves."

Disconcerted, Alan rose from his seat. "I think I saw it in the rhododendrons."

On the walk back up the slope to the earl's house on the hill, he glimpsed a little monkey darting around the base of a tree.

This time, his heart's thud felt bone cracking.

Miss Finch hadn't packed the few belongings she'd brought into his house. He'd checked her room. Three sober-looking gowns still hung in the wardrobe. Her hairbrush lay on the table.

Didn't that mean she'd intended to return?

But she'd taken Fritz.

Perhaps, that fateful morning, she hadn't yet made up her mind. By taking Fritz, she'd given herself the option to go and stay gone. Everything else was dispensable.

He stopped walking, eyes tracking the monkey. But it wasn't a monkey. It was an ordinary squirrel.

That a *squirrel* could produce in him this yearning—laughable, really.

He should tell Neal the whole story, turn Miss Finch and her marmoset into a little joke at his own expense. It would illustrate how very far he was from living up to Neal's expectations. Children of his own. Marital bliss.

He wasn't in a joking mood. He continued up the hill in silence, deafened by the *thud-thud-thud* of his heart.

CHAPTER THIRTEEN

ON HER THIRD day back at the Knack, Nina decided to tear apart the studio. Jack would have fits if he could see her, but, well, he couldn't.

Jack was gone.

When she'd discovered this, the morning she'd departed from Casa De'Ath, she'd considered taking the train to Norwich herself. But Jack safeguarded their money—*where* she'd no bloody idea. Perhaps a bank account. More likely, a locked box under a floorboard. In any case, she couldn't scrape together more than a few shillings. Without cash, she'd provide Mrs. Beechey nothing extra by way of incentive. Besides, Mr. Broughton knew her face. What if they crossed paths at the station or outside Mrs. Beechey's house?

She'd almost headed straight back to Chelsea. She'd stacked her cake tins in a box. She'd pulled her dough docker from the drawer and stared at it, running her finger over the metal spikes.

De'Ath had never heard of this useful little tool. She wanted to show it to him, to introduce *him* to something. A person could feel powerful emotion in front of a Botticelli. And also, in front of a tray of golden brown Scotch shortbread.

She'd turned her head, and there was Polly, in the sink, fixing her with a bright yellow eye.

"Give me a kiss," creaked Polly, and puffed up her feathers.

"Hush," Nina muttered, feeling hot and faint, a notably absurd reaction to a parrot's routine patter.

Hearing the word *kiss* in the Knack's tiny, grimy kitchen twisted her insides. In that very room, she'd let Jack convince her to spy on De'Ath. The space was acrid with the smell of cooking paint. Probably that smell clung to her hair, the odor of deceit. It was only a matter of time before De'Ath sniffed it out. If she gave him the chance.

She'd put away the cake tins and headed out, not to Casa De'Ath, but to Jack's favorite haunts. Two thankless days spent alternately combing the streets and waiting at the window, like a faithful dog.

The time had come to act.

At the moment, she was sweating profusely, arms overloaded with rolls of worm-eaten canvas. She heaved them onto the pile and heard one of the antique picture frames crack. She didn't pause her labors. She began to fling Jack's supplies off the shelves. Chipped dishes of old glue and flour paste. Boxes of rusty nails. Vials of soot and bone dust for tinting and foxing.

The pile grew bigger and bigger as she added their library, partially dismembered books of prints and heraldic emblems. She tipped her own novice canvases away from the walls.

The more items she shoved into the middle of the room, the more flagrantly the studio announced itself as what it was: a forger's workshop.

She needed to dispose of the proof. If Jack had been nicked, the bobbies might pound up the stairs at any moment. As soon as night fell, she'd bring the whole mess to the river and dump it in. She'd sink this whole bad endeavor and start fresh. That meant goodbye, Knack. Goodbye, London.

Goodbye, Alan De'Ath.

She hadn't *said* goodbye. A pang sharpened in her chest.

Alan De'Ath made her feel more than any Botticelli, more than any batch of shortbread. And she'd disappeared, without a word of explanation.

But then, there was so much she hadn't explained.

Footsteps sounded on the stairs.

Her first, foolish instinct was to duck behind the pile. But the tread was delicate. No police constable had such a light step.

Ruby swept into the studio with a tray, on which she'd balanced a teapot, two cups, and the biscuit tin.

"Lor'," said Ruby, eyes climbing the pile. "You've been busy. Laddie says the plaster's shaking down on his head. Keep this up and you'll collapse the floor."

"I'm going to haul it all out."

"Then what?" Ruby set the tea tray on a paint-smeared table that stood by the upholstered chair, big and battered, Jack's throne.

Nina bit her lip. "Toss it in the river?"

"You need a cart, then. Have you asked Laddie?"

"No." Nina was hit with a wave of exhaustion. She dropped into the chair. Ruby put a cup of tea in her hand.

"I'll see to the cart," Ruby said. "Could be Jack'll turn up, though. He usually does." She frowned. "Like a bad penny."

Nina shifted in the chair. Jack's throne had lumps.

"He might turn up," Nina acknowledged. "But either way, we're done. I've told him." Her voice dwindled. "I've told him and told him and *told* him."

Ruby nodded, her sympathy plain.

"You sit," said Ruby. "You ain't eaten a thing, I can tell. Fritz neither." She opened the biscuit tin and handed a pastry to the marmoset. He was nestled in a smock Nina had left wadded by her easel. "And what do we have here?" She stooped and picked up a sheaf of papers, unsalable sketches in the style of Veronese.

Nina let out a helpless groan.

"Right," said Ruby smartly. "Might as well burn what we can."

She bustled to the fireplace.

Nina sipped the overdrawn tea and felt herself calm. She lacked a Sisterhood, sure. But she had Ruby Ladbrooke, and that was something. She watched Ruby pitch the papers into the fire. Her auburn hair seemed threaded with flames.

Ruby was fiery and fast. She kissed men, and had done more, and never minded much about it.

What would Ruby say if Nina confessed that De'Ath had gotten under her skin, and that his tongue had been inside her mouth?

"Birdie!"

Jack's bellow made her jump. Tea sloshed onto her hand.

He strode through the doorway. "What the hell are you doing here?"

"About time you blew in." Ruby slapped at the smoke. "Poor Nina was worried sick."

"Is that so?" Jack smiled, a flinty-eyed, dimpled smile that made Nina's stomach drop. "She wouldn't be worried if she was where she was supposed to be."

"And where were *you*?" asked Ruby.

"Jealous, my treasure?" Jack knocked his hair back, revealing red-threaded eyes. Stubble gritted his jawline. "I missed you sorely meself. Now, get out."

Ruby's shoulders went up around her ears. She curled her hand. She looked ready to strike.

Nina pushed out of the chair. "Go on, Ruby. It's all right."

"He ain't all right," said Ruby.

"She's always down on old Jack. Don't it make my heart bleed." Jack sighed to Nina, then met Ruby's narrowed gaze. "You heard my sister. She and I are due for a little chin-wag."

Ruby hesitated. The fire popped behind her.

She looked a question at Nina. *Come along?*

Nina gave her head a slight shake and tried to look unconcerned. *It won't be so bad.*

Ruby swished by Jack without another glance.

"Ta-ta," he said, and rounded the pile. He approached Nina, kicking aside canvases and stepping over books.

"You're here," he said darkly, and threw himself into his chair. "De'Ath found me out? Is that it?"

"No." Nina shifted her cup to her other hand so she could dry her dripping fingers on her skirt. "No, I came back to tell you about the man who owns the auction house."

"What about him? Must be bloody awful if you couldn't put it in a letter."

Nina's cheeks blazed. She hadn't considered posting a letter. She'd been all muddled up.

"Mr. Broughton," she said. "He went to Norwich to put the screws to Mrs. Beechey."

"So? Mrs. Beechey won't welch. I paid her well."

"You went to Norwich?" She sagged. "You could have mentioned that to Laddie. I was thinking the worst."

"And that's why you destroyed the studio?" His pleasant tone brought up gooseflesh on her arms.

"The aim is to destroy evidence." She deposited her cup on the table and took a deep breath. "Jack, it's over."

"Not if you do as we agreed and stick to De'Ath."

"Even if he doesn't find us out this time, we can't sell more pictures."

"Not in London, perhaps." He steepled his fingers, rings twinkling. "Not at auction. Not at the moment." He shrugged a shoulder. "All those industrialists up north want art."

"Blast the industrialists!" She stumbled to her paint box, where she stowed her two account books, and seized the larger.

"All my Hensthorpe plans and calculations." She fanned the pages so he could see how closely written they were. "I've been saving, for *years*. For this." She went to him, book held open. On one page was a sketch of Mr. Craddock's bakery with its big bow window, the bricks and flints lovingly shaded. On the other, a floor plan of the kitchen as she imagined it, the prices of the new equipment penciled around the edges. "*You* make art for Manchester, if you're so keen on it."

Jack's eyes were fixed on his steepled fingers.

"Not in the cards." He extended his hands to her. Together, they observed their tremor.

She swallowed her resentment with a bitter draft of shame. Those eighteen months' hard labor at Pentonville had ravaged him, giving his fingers a permanent crook. He'd broken his right thumb breaking flints. Even as that time receded into the past, the damage revealed itself more fully.

"I'm sorry." She lowered her book. "I'm sorry for every mean thing you've endured, for *me*. But I can't paint Titians 'til kingdom come. I *won't*. And even if I were willing, what then? Sooner or later, someone will catch up to us." She took a shaky breath. "Luck only holds so long. You know it as well as I do."

"A far sight better than you do." Jack leaned back in the chair. His collar looked greasy, and his trouser cuffs were soiled.

"Jack," she said slowly. "You weren't more than a day in Norwich? But you weren't here. Where were you?"

"I had places to go. Business." His gaze dropped. "Whitechapel."

Nina stared at his face, uncomprehending.

"To the factory." He looked up at her with a strange smile. "I ran into a spot of trouble."

"What factory?" She felt an incipient horror, as though she teetered at the edge of an abyss. "What trouble? What are you talking about?"

He leaned forward. "I bark too much, Birdie. I'm easily huffed, God knows. I'm not proud of myself. Proud of you, though. All the good I ever did, right here."

The way he was looking at her . . .

"Are you tight?" She leaned in and sniffed. He smelled of cologne and sweat, only mildly beery. "Jack, what factory?"

"I've been planning too. You think this is what I want for us? Holed up like rats in Laddie's attic. So much varnish in our lungs we crackle when we breathe." He laughed and spoke even more rapidly. "No, we'll have a fine house. A carriage for rolling around town. We'll do what we like, when we like it. Infinite French bonbons. Shrimp for Prince Fritz. If you fancy a bloke, you'll marry him and live happily ever after." His smile was brilliant, then his lips curled. "Unless he's an eejit or a bounder," he added. "Then he'll feel my boot on his arse, and you'll have to pick another one."

Her horror intensified. He was tight. Had to be. "I'm not looking for a *bloke*."

"I know. *Much comfort in cats, little in men.*" He did a fair, musical imitation of their mother's lilt. "Grow up hearing that, and seeing the proof of it, and why would you be, if not for necessity? But that's what I'm trying to say." He sounded gruff suddenly, as though the delicacy of the subject made him too conscious of his own clumsiness. "It won't go like that for you. If you do fancy a bloke, you won't be at his mercy. You'll have money of your own."

She couldn't make sense of his words.

"I already have money of my own." She whirled and returned to the paint box, picked up her other account book. "Nearly four hundred pounds. Shall I work the sums for you? I have it all written down. Every painting, every drawing, what you told me it fetched, my percentage of the profit—"

"Are you such a fool as that?" Jack came to his feet. As soon as he reached her, he wrenched away the book. "This is the first thing you pitch in the fire. Do you mean to tie a bow around yourself for the bobbies? *Christ!*" He raised a fist. She flinched, and he pressed the fist to his mouth, sneering at her, furious and *hurt*. As though her flinch accused him, and falsely.

He'd bumped her, shaken her by the shoulders, dragged her by the wrist, thrown her palette across the room, knocked over her easel, punched through her canvas, countless times. But he'd never aimed a blow at her. Most often, he rampaged around her, his fury a cyclone, and herself the eye, frozen, waiting for it to pass.

"I could be arrested tomorrow." He began in a softer voice that rose in volume as he spoke. "And you could walk free. But not if you leave a blasted *catalogue* crediting yourself with the crimes!"

She stood, frozen, staring. Her sweet-faced bullying brother. Easily huffed. Forever yelling in her face, out of abiding love and concern. The years stacked up, pressing her stomach into her throat. She couldn't endure another minute.

"That's mine." She sprang to life, grabbing for her account book, but Jack thrust his arm behind his back. Fritz started to chirp out alarmed sounds.

"Don't trust me? I keep my own accounts here." He tapped his forehead. "You'll get every penny." His face darkened as he thrust the account book inside his jacket. "But not now."

"Yes, *now*." She followed close on his heels as he stalked to his chair. He didn't sit but lifted Ruby's unused cup and splashed it with tea.

"Can't do it, Birdie." His color was up, bloodshot eyes glassy. "Funds aren't currently available. De'Ath has cost us. Ruined our auction. Diverted our capital to Mrs. Beechey."

She blinked. "He hasn't cost us to the tune of four hundred pounds. You're holding my entire savings."

"Your savings went into the factory." He rotated the teacup in his hand. "Bought it last year, the building at least. Takes longer to put the rest in place. You're a co-owner, entitled to half the profit."

"What factory? You never . . ." Her lips had gone numb. "You never told me."

"Yes, well, I thought I'd surprise you. A new venture, one that requires my oversight but not my hands, and not yours either. It's a very small works, but we'll end up cracking a tidy crust. I've good lads to work for us, potters and painters. They'll make reproductions of Sèvres porcelain, Worcester, the best brands. It's not difficult if you understand the process, know the right marks. American tourists will pay through the nose."

Her voice shrilled. "That's where my money went?"

"Your money, my money. *Our* money." He shrugged. "The factory frees both of us. From this." He took a large step and kicked a heap of canvas. "From everything. Baking is hot, hard work. You might not like it any more than you do painting, once it's day in and day out. Have you thought of that? With income from the factory, you'll never feel the pinch. Open your bakery every other Tuesday if you choose. Sell only thimble-sized cakes to the wee folk holding fairy banquets in the hills."

"*My* bakery? Ha!" Rage gave her strength, swept away the doubt that had shot to the surface at his words. "I can't buy the bakery without money."

"You can't buy it because it's not for sale." He looked at her narrowly. "Not last I heard. Steady, now. No need for dramatics."

Rich, coming from him. She crossed her arms, trapped her hands beneath them, glaring.

"Once we start production, we'll start getting paid, handsomely." He took a sip of tea and grimaced. "But at the moment, we're strapped. Worse than strapped. The factory's on a street run by a gang of roughs. So long as I fork over money for protection, they don't smash it up. That's how it goes. But the scum just upped the price. And let's just say, they're bloody unhappy that I don't have the blunt. Which means I need that paper." He pointed to the pile, to the stack of ruined books. "I can manage a few drawings, followers of Rembrandt. And we have your young man in green to sell, the Titian. I've got us a new dealer, sharper than Sleaford, country squires for clients. And you can turn over that fine wage De'Ath promised you, and keep an eye on him. I'll clear out if he gets too close." His voice flattened. "You're safer with De'Ath, anyway. The Whitechapel gents aren't what I'd call friendly."

"You've always protected me." She only breathed it. "From everyone but yourself."

He brought his hand down, a swift motion that sent the cup flying. It exploded against the table. Nina gasped at the sound. Fritz charged for the door with a long, shrill screech.

"Slipped," Jack muttered, folding his arms, then unfolding them to brush the droplets of tea and specks of porcelain from her skirt. She stepped back.

"Birdie," he said.

She began to walk away, mechanically. Her ears were ringing.

"Where are you going?" he called, and she turned to answer him honestly.

"I don't know," she said.

CHAPTER FOURTEEN

NINA WALKED TO Liverpool Street, Fritz gnawing a scavenged whelk too close to her ear. When the terminus came into view—towers rising to the sky, rows of arched windows reflecting the light—she stopped. She saw herself boarding the train to Norwich, traveling on to Hensthorpe, thumping through the cottage door, and throwing herself into Miss Lolly's arms. She'd have a good cry as Aunt Sylvia tsked and laid out jam tarts. If Jack landed back in Pentonville, or got beaten within an inch of his life by Whitechapel roughs, so be it. He'd purchased his fate with her labor, at the expense of her dreams.

But then, in either case, she'd lose any chance of recouping her coin.

The world looked hard and cold, every person jostling past distinctly outlined.

She didn't take the Great Eastern Railway to Norwich. She took the underground to Sloane Square.

Once she'd reached Casa De'Ath, she wavered again, veering away from the gate piers, crossing the street. As the setting sun rouged the clouds above the river, she stood on the embankment. A persistent foulness twitched her nose.

"Your breath is like brimstone." She scowled at Fritz and scooted him off her shoulder. "Brimstone pickled in bad milk. No more whelks."

She watched the river. Every now and then, a little yapping dog chased Fritz around her legs. He'd scale her skirts, then drop back down to play, his cries good-humored. As dusk descended, detail faded from the scene, which allowed memory to surge into the void. The time Jack had decided that Dutch still life was the next rage and covered every surface in their dingy flat with fish. They'd painted those fish for days, until the stink summoned the landlord. All those summer Saturdays they walked to the Strand and ate penny licks of ice cream in the sun. When she was very small, and Mr. Nelson's horrible daughters pushed pillows on her face in the night, he'd let her sleep with him in the alcove under the stairs, giving her the cot, even though the space was so cramped he had to sit up all night, his back against the door.

Fritz regained her shoulder, and she gave him her fingertip and tilted her head, rubbing her cheek on his fur.

Maybe Jack had been wise to buy that factory. They'd make a fortune on forged bric-a-brac. His plan didn't preclude her plan. The revenue would serve to increase her freedom, like he'd said. In the end, she'd lose nothing, except a little time.

And the remainder of her self-respect.

And her peace of mind.

All the smoldering embers of her anger burst into flame.

She turned away from the river. Casa De'Ath was lit up, windows glowing with warmth.

How would she be received?

The very idea of facing De'Ath turned her knees to water.

Somehow, her legs carried her back across the street and between the gate piers. She was reaching for the door knocker when Fritz ran down her body and pelted around the side of the house.

"Oh blast," she said, and charged after.

She reached Signorina Bonaccorso's chestnut tree several moments too late. Fritz was high in the branches.

"*Fritz.*" She put as much force as she could into a whisper. "Get down from there."

Music was drifting faintly from the house, McAdams on the piano.

She placed her palms on the tree trunk and craned her neck. "You think this is funny?"

Now her knock at the front door would seem even cheekier.

Hallo, she'd say to Mr. Kuznetsov. *I was held up a bit, but here I am, and first things first. Fyodor's up the chestnut tree. Can you fetch some candied fruit? There should be a pound in the kitchen. I put it on the shopping list before I bolted. Fyodor likes the cherries best. My thanks.*

"Fritz!" she tried again, louder. He gave a chirrup and leapt to a higher branch.

"Dammit!" She curled her fingers around a thick ridge of bark, fit her foot into a furrow. "I'm coming up," she warned him.

"This tree is like Piccadilly Circus." The drawl drifted down from above. "Don't tell me you're going to sing."

Nina pedaled backward. The light spilling out from the study window reduced De'Ath to a silhouette. But even if he'd kept silent, she could never mistake him. She'd memorized his proportions, the shape of his shoulders, the tilt of his head.

"It's Fritz," she said with an embarrassing rasp. "I followed him back here." She cleared her throat. "I fully intended to knock on the front door."

"I was beginning to think you never would." His deep voice vibrated with subtle shades of meaning.

Nina vibrated too. Their kiss seemed to flutter in the darkness between them. The speech she'd prepared unwrote itself word by word.

"I told you my house rules," he continued. "And then I broke one."

"Rule three." Nina felt short of breath. That was what this was to him, then. A dalliance. One of many, if Miss Holroyd was to be believed.

"I apologize for my conduct," he said, and strangely, it stung. He didn't dally with employees, as a point of pride. She had her pride too.

"Don't apologize," she said. "It's not the reason I stayed away."

"No?" He spoke in a voice deeper still, and he shifted forward, leaning against the balcony railing.

"No." She shook her head. "My brother caught a fever. I should have written."

A mercy, that this exchange was taking place outdoors, in the night. She hated to think of all her expression must reveal.

"How is he now?"

"Improving. Nothing keeps him down long." She realized she was holding her throat, fingers pressing her jugular.

"I'm glad," he said. "And I'm glad you're here."

Was he smiling? Nina edged away from the house, to ease the angle of her neck.

"You'll find the kitchen awash in orange flower water." He was definitely smiling. She could hear it. "The other day, there was an avalanche of golden sultanas."

"I forgot the cake tins." Nina's stomach kicked. Supposedly, she'd gone home *for* cake tins.

He was quiet, perplexed, perhaps, or putting together incriminating pieces.

"Miss Finch," he said at last, and paused again. "I should warn you. I've devoted a sizable portion of the previous three days to speculations about your hair."

"My hair?" Nina's heart pounded faster. *Dear God.* The odor of deceit . . .

"Is it brown?" he mused. "Or is it blond? I haven't been able to settle my mind on the subject. And then it occurred to me that your hair is the color of moth wings, the exact color of their softness, and that to see it properly, I need to touch it."

Her breath puffed out. "My hair is dull. It's no particular color at all."

"Nothing about you is dull." His voice tugged at her, beckoned her like a finger. She was rocking onto the balls of her feet, as though she could lift her lips to his. Float up to the balcony.

Madness.

She ground her heels into the grass.

"I've looked for Ariadne's crown in the sky every night," he said. "I've imagined setting those eight stars on your brow. I won't say what else I've imagined. It's bacchanalian in nature."

Her head was spinning, like she'd had too much wine. Bacchanalia. Bacchus's festival.

His posture was loose, one elbow propped on the balcony railing, one arm dangling.

"You said that what happened between us didn't keep you away. Tell me—is it part of why you came back?"

Surprise jolted through her, and more: an echo of the giddy heat that surged when he'd lifted her against him in the vestibule.

"If it's not," he said. "I won't speak of this again."

She gripped her elbows. Fritz rustled in the leaves overhead.

Now she wished she could see his eyes. She wished she could float to the balcony, that she could touch down before him, that he'd wrap her in his arms. She wished she was the person he imagined her to be.

She knew what she should say.

Let us never speak of this again.

Her mouth had gone dry.

"It is a part of it," she said.

In the silence that ensued, they both remained still.

What relief, to offer him this shred of truth. She felt a second's joy. And then a new ball of dread formed inside her.

A shred of truth. That implied there was no whole, only hopeless tatters. *She* was shredded, by the teeth of the trap she'd sprung around her.

"I had a row with my brother." It burst from her, as though a vent peg had been loosed from a barrel. "That's another part of it."

"A row," De'Ath repeated.

"Like the one you had with your brother." She was speaking thickly now. "With a little less broken china."

"Any slogging?" He'd changed his tone. Dark emotion strung the question tight.

He thought that Jack . . .

"No," she said quickly. "No, he'd never . . ." Her hand moved reflexively over her skirt, still gritted with dust from the exploded cup.

There *was* a distinction between bluster and a beating. Sometimes that distinction stretched gossamer thin.

"It's complicated." Her shoulders sagged.

"It's very simple," said De'Ath softly. Such gentleness in his voice. And yet each word carried down to her, clear as a bell. "As soon as one essential misconception is corrected."

"What misconception?" she whispered, but her voice carried too.

"Harm isn't care," he answered. "That's it. Simple. But the one is so often confused with the other."

Unblinking, she gazed up at him, a tall figure haloed by light. Every feature blotted out.

"You were confused, once." Understanding dawned. "Someone harmed *you*."

Someone he loved.

He straightened.

"Do you like to swim?" he asked. "I was going just now. Perhaps you'd join me?"

"Swim?" She took a step forward. "*Now?*"

"I swim at all hours. I'm the captain of a swimming club."

This time she saw his smile, a faintly luminous crescent. His mood had lightened, sincerity giving over to sarcasm.

"It's too cold," she said. "And I splash rather than swim. And I'll have to wear my knickers."

"Details." De'Ath waved his hand.

"And then there's Fritz. I need to get him down." She peered up into the tree and saw a flicker of white. Fritz was scampering along a bough. And then he was in the air, flying toward the house. He landed on the balcony railing and leapt again, past De'Ath, through the French doors, and into the study.

"Any other objections?" De'Ath laughed as he turned. "Good. I'll meet you at the coach."

Chapter Fifteen

HYDE PARK BELONGED to the human peacocks by day. They strutted the footpaths, preened on the lawns, perched on horses or in carriages. But before dawn, and after seven in the evening, it belonged to the swimmers, professionals and amateurs who gathered on the banks of the Serpentine, to plunge and race, for love of the sport. And earlier still, or later, at the hour when early and late crossed over, it belonged to Alan.

"The most popular bathing place is farther on." He led Miss Finch through a dark gap in the trees. "Where Claud met me for swimming lessons, until the present impasse." He glanced in the opposite direction, toward Park Lane and Umfreville House.

"But you're not taking me there?" Her hip bumped his thigh. Every band of muscle in his body contracted.

He looked down at her. "I'm taking you elsewhere."

They were almost to the water, a flat, gleaming expanse.

Kessler and McAdams reached it first and set down the steaming kettles and the linens.

Kessler flung out his arms. "And gentle winds and waters near," he cried. "Make music to the lonely ear!"

"There's an awful fine line," approved McAdams, crouching to test to the water.

"Lord Byron." Kessler dropped his arms.

"Cold as a dog's nose." McAdams said it cheerfully, scooping water with his hand and flinging it at Kessler, who smacked him on the back of the head.

They started up the bank toward the coach, McAdams whistling a jaunty tune.

"Lord Byron was a swimmer." Alan moved closer to Miss Finch.

She turned halfway toward him. "I thought he was a poet."

"He was. He also swam the Hellespont."

They didn't know yet how to be near each other, now that pretense had fallen away, replaced with mutually acknowledged desire.

What else does the future hold? Alan seemed to hear Neal's question.

"It's a swim I've always thought to make myself," he said. "Have you ever considered a journey to Constantinople? Or Troy?"

"Never." She laughed. "But I like Turkish delight. I'm sure I'd find other things to like in Constantinople, if I happened to end up there."

Her voice told him she thought it less than likely.

She paced to the water's edge and dipped a finger.

"It *is* cold," she gasped, and hopped back, sitting on the grass. "We'll catch our death!"

"Cold never hurt anyone in measured doses." He approached and sat beside her.

"I prefer my doses of cold by the spoonful," she said. "Pineapple ice cream."

"You like everything sweet," he observed, and she drew up her legs, wrapped them with her arms, and rested her chin on her knees. The moonlight illuminated her face but only dimly. He could tell, though, that her smile was more sure. Darkness pooled in her dimples, and her eyes were clear and bright.

"Nina's Sweets is what I'll call my pastry shop."

"Nina's Sweets," he murmured. The breeze blew again, cool air streaming around them. A cove of warmth had formed between their bodies. He leaned toward her, narrowing the space. "Temptation itself."

Her intake of breath thrilled him.

This wasn't a dalliance. It was something more dangerous. With

Nina Finch, he felt his mask slipping, and he forgot the horrors it concealed.

He skimmed his hand over her hair.

"Did your row with your brother do this?" He slid his finger down a stray lock. He hadn't considered until now what it might mean, that her coiffure was slipping down around her shoulders.

Decent, she'd said of her brother. A decent man, rough-spoken.

Such tricks the mind played. Any fact could be reconciled with a ruling fiction. Warped into compatibility with the myth of a mother's love. A brother's decency.

"Did he lay a hand on you?" he asked.

"I lost a hairpin, that's all," she whispered.

He tipped up her chin.

"He's never laid a hand on me." Her moonlit eyes grew deeper the longer he looked. Her lips parted on a sigh.

"Let it be," she said.

He did. He kissed her. Her mouth was soft, sweeter than fruit, sweet as a goblin orchard. The taste of magic itself. If he could learn the secret of this bewitchment, he wouldn't feel so lost, but it was like a spell written in sugar, disappearing on his tongue. He pulled her into his arms, and then, God, he was overcome, drowning already, going down, gloriously, beneath the heaviness of her breasts and thighs, the heat of her breath, even as his cock strained up, and his heart tried to crash through his chest.

She licked his lip, as she'd done in the vestibule, the small, exploratory movement of her tongue eliciting his groan.

He rolled them over, pressing her into the grass, his hand sliding under her skirt to the top of her stocking, and just above, to the satiny skin. She gasped, and he felt her palm on his chest. His heart pounded against it with bruising force.

He lifted away his mouth, leaned his forehead on hers.

"Nina," he said hoarsely.

"Alan," she returned, and *that* thrilled him, too, as did the hitch in her voice.

"I invited you to swim." He removed his body from hers, turning onto his side.

"I'd rather do this," he said, and caressed her mouth with the pad of his thumb. "But I don't want to make myself a liar."

He felt her breath skip. He could see the shine of her eyes, but not their sentiment.

He rocked into a crouch. "Let's swim, then."

"I only splash." She said it to the sky. "I'll wade to my knees."

"You don't have to dip a toe." He stood. "But I promise you, there's nothing like swimming at night."

With that, he shucked off his coat.

She sat up, staring with those wide, dark eyes.

He unbuttoned his waistcoat, one-handed. Her gaze on his fingers made their movement clumsier.

"You taught your nephew how to swim?" She stood and came to him and took his wrist. Her touch was cool, but it stoked a bloody inferno in his groin.

She lowered his arm to his side.

What had she even asked?

She helped him off with his waistcoat, unfastened his braces, and began to undo the buttons of his shirt.

"Taught my nephew how to swim?" His jaw tensed. He could smell her hair, and her skin, and it was all he could do not to fall upon her all over again. He studied her eyelids, the black curves of her lashes, as her fingers moved down his chest.

"I did," he said. "It promotes health. Trains the muscles, regulates breathing."

She sighed as his shirt opened, revealing more cloth.

"Bathing costume," he told her, trying not to smile. That *was* regret on her face. "I'm not swimming in the buff."

"I didn't expect so. A gentleman like you." She gave her head a toss as she stepped back, but she was smiling with adorable chagrin. He pulled his arms through the sleeves of his shirt.

"Promoting health. Is that it? With your nephew?" She gripped her elbows. "You hope the swimming will strengthen his chest?"

He threw his shirt after his waistcoat.

"It strengthened my chest." He shrugged. "I *know* it will strengthen his too." He frowned as he knelt, untying his boot laces as quickly as possible, in case she tried to offer assistance here as well.

"Geoffrey used to admit the lessons were beneficial." He levered off the boots, peeled away his socks, and rose. "Since I've become a persona non grata, he's forbidden them, on medical grounds." He snorted. "And now I'm not permitted to exchange so much as a word with Claud or my nieces. Unless I call off the sale of the portraits."

"That was his response to your letter?" She swallowed as his hands moved to his trousers, watching out of the corner of her eye.

No one had ever watched him strip with such sly fascination.

He watched *her* as he let his trousers drop down.

Her lips parted, and her gaze shot up, shot to his face, then over to the treetops.

His bathing costume did blasted little to conceal a cockstand.

"The scales," she said tightly. "They haven't fallen from his eyes."

"I don't know who ever had the idea that they would." He kicked the trousers onto the pile of discarded garments. "Some rank optimist."

"And what was wrong with your chest?"

He stretched slowly, rolling his head on his shoulders, the keen edge of his excitement blunting.

"Pneumonia," he said at last. "I contracted it as a baby. Gave my mother quite a fright." He'd heard the story innumerable times. How she wouldn't return him to the wet nurse afterward. How she'd known her life's purpose was to keep him close. "She took me to Switzerland, France, Germany, Italy, the United States, anywhere she could find a sufficiently scenic sanatorium."

"It developed into tuberculosis, then? You don't seem . . ." Nina was looking at him now, compressing her lips. What word had she fought back?

Pale. Thin. Dead.

"I was misdiagnosed." He shook out his limbs. "I wasn't tubercular but asthmatic. And I brought the asthma under control by swimming. An American doctor taught me." He smiled. "Dr. Barth threw me in a river in the Rocky Mountains." He turned toward the placid lake. "The Serpentine is like lava in comparison. We swam every morning. The results were . . . eye-opening."

You'll kill him! his mother had screamed at Dr. Barth when she'd learned of their outings.

Mrs. Umfreville, you *are killing him.* Dr. Barth had replied more quietly, so that Alan, bundled between nurses on the sleeping porch, could barely make out the words.

Mrs.? His mother had gasped. *I am the* Duchess *of Umfreville!*

I don't care if you're the Queen of Sheba. Dr. Barth *had* raised his voice then. *I am a doctor, and your son suffers from bronchial spasms. He doesn't have tuberculosis, do you hear me? You should be pleased.*

They hadn't stayed a day longer in Colorado.

"Swimming is the closest we can come to flying." He willed away the memories and turned back to Nina.

He grinned. "Closer than this."

He lunged, swept her into his arms, and spun. Her hands clasped his neck, and her laughter rang in his ear. She felt impossibly good against him, lushly snug. He pushed past his hip's first rebuke, wresting from the pain one final, dizzy spin.

He set her down, and she swayed into him, face tipped up, mouth seeking his.

He kissed her, smiling against her lips, and tore himself away.

Swimming, not kissing. Swimming.

Three steps, and the grass gave way to liquid, the cold drilling up through his feet. He dove, sluicing down into the lake's crystal heart, then shooting up to the surface.

In the water, he was fast.

He struck out, swimming until his sluggish blood began to pump; then he went under again and changed direction, heading back toward shore.

This time, when he surfaced, he saw Nina standing ankle-deep in the water.

She'd shed her dress and petticoat and wrapped herself in the banyan he'd included with the linens. It reached down to her shins, a single layer of silk. The breeze molded it to her body.

He swam toward her, his breaststroke Byronic. Only Byron was likely to have swum in such a state of rampant arousal.

His feet touched the mud.

She walked to him with hands held out. "Teach me to fly."

NINA ALREADY REGRETTED her boldness. The lake was inky black and cold as January. When she flexed her feet, pain went shooting through the soles. Her veins felt like needles. Had the blood in her toes *frozen*?

She was still dizzy from whirling in Alan's arms, and she was drugged from the scent of his banyan, and from the expression on his face when he rose from the water, hungry and determined.

He wanted her.

Here it was at last. Something she might turn to her advantage. A man in lust was easily led.

Nausea bubbled up at the thought.

As he reached her, she made to pull back, too late.

His large wet hands gripped hers. Her heart twinged, and she brushed her thumb over the swollen knuckles of his left hand.

"Ready?" He leaned in, scattering her with droplets. "We'll start with a leg stroke."

"Is that wise?" She frowned. "My feet might break off. They've turned to ice."

"Details," he said. He released her hands and stepped around her, lifting one of the kettles from the bank.

"Follow me." He brushed past, wading out into the lake. His bathing costume was sleeveless, knee-length, the black fabric suctioned to his broad back, to the curve of his high, round bottom. The water rose up his thighs. He turned to face her. That crooked smile—it hooked her like a fish.

Drat it. If only she were a fish. It would be more apropos. And fish weren't frauds.

She sucked in her breath and she went to him. Her skin was *wincing*. She held her arms out stiffly as the water sloshed to her hips. The silk tugged at her shoulders. Her stockings sagged. Clearly, the lake wanted to slurp her down.

"Swimming." Alan pronounced the word grandly, as though the lake were his lectern. "That special mode of progression that enables a person to derive entire support from the liquid in which he is immersed." He looked at her with a widening smile.

She yanked at the banyan, tucking the halves more tightly under the knotted belt, narrowing the closure, keenly aware of his gaze. His pale irises had caught some of the night's wan light. They seemed, suddenly, like chips of the moon.

"You, however, are going to rely on me for partial support as you practice your kick."

She flexed her feet again. Definitely frozen. Her nod was reluctant.

"You'll take hold of my waist. For the kick, you'll draw your knees toward your hips, then shoot them backward."

"Like a frog." She could picture the motion.

"Like a frog," he agreed, and twisting, he lowered himself gently into the lake, onto his back. One arm stroked the water, the other held the kettle just above the surface. He was moving slowly toward shore.

Take hold of my waist.

She lunged forward and grasped him, his motion pulling her onto her chest. A frigid wave slapped her breasts and belly, broke against her mouth, and she sputtered.

"Bring up your heels, then push back," he said. "Heels up, push back."

His legs were moving somewhere beneath hers, propelling them along.

She kicked like a frog, too jerkily.

"Keep going," he said. Suddenly, heat blossomed, tendrils curling around her. Steam billowed. He was pouring the contents of the kettle into the lake. The rush of hot water seemed to lift her. She wasn't *flying*, but she was very nearly horizontal, and her gasp gave way to a startled laugh. She kicked, not a proper stroke, more an expression of glee. Her heart pounded wildly, and she kept kicking, clinging to his hard abdomen, feeling the muscles bunch and lengthen beneath her thumbs. Hovering above him, she could kick forever.

But there was only so far to go. Only so much lake to suspend their bodies. Suddenly, they were in the shallows, brought together by the water's diminished volume. He sat up, carrying her with him.

"I can just reach . . ." he began, stretching his arm toward the grass. A moment later she understood what he'd meant. He tipped her off him. With a giddy shriek, she splashed down on her bottom, then lay back as more hot water swirled around her, and more. He emptied the remaining three kettles. Her wincing skin was *sighing* and tingling. She floated in the shallow water, delirious with the shock of the cold immersion, the licks of heat.

"It's *wonderful*," she murmured, waving her arms, seeking the warmth.

The last kettle thudded onto the bank.

"Should we try again?" he asked. "An arm stroke this time?"

"Not if that's the last of the hot water." She rose onto her elbows. The night air felt mellow on her skin, the soaked silk clammy. "I'd rather swim the Hellespont."

"Maybe you will." He shifted, and a warm current lapped between her thighs. "Maybe we will."

"Together?" She shut her eyes. Dalliances didn't endure across the length of Europe, did they?

He *was* a liar, with his insinuations of limitless possibility.

Suddenly, he was lifting her, turning her. Her knees splashed down. She opened her eyes and stared into his face. She was straddling his hips.

"You'll have to learn an arm stroke first." He pushed the banyan over her shoulders, then ran his fingers up her bare skin. "Or I could stroke your arms."

His smile was mischievous. He seemed almost boyish, wet locks of hair forming disorderly curls around his head, dark lashes in clumps, eyes radiant.

When he discovered swimming, had his face looked something like this?

She gave an agitated laugh, desire and doubt wringing the odd sound from her throat.

The more intimate they became, the worse her betrayal.

The more she cared, the more harm she would do. To him. To herself.

This had to stop.

He kissed her mouth, and she didn't stop him. He kissed her

throat, his hand sliding to her breast, dragging down her chemise, its lace trim scratching her nipple. She hissed and wound her fingers in his hair.

She *wanted*. She wanted beauty and pleasure, stolen moments to remember years from now, when she was living her quiet life, in Hensthorpe, with her aunts, their cats, Fritz.

No, she wanted more.

She wanted him.

He palmed her breast, then latched it with his mouth. The wet heat seared her. She arched her back, hips rolling, the soft flesh between her thighs split by the thick ridge between his. A moan pressed up from her belly.

Sweet, insistent friction thawed every chilled inch of her skin, reliquefied her marrow. She was melting around his hard contours, thighs spreading wider.

His teeth closed on her nipple, and she moaned again, kneading his shoulders.

He reared up, caught her face in his hands. His kisses came in waves, and she realized she was still rolling her hips, working herself over him, the tension torturous, trembling the flesh of her inner thighs.

And now one of his hands was gripping the crease below her hip. His thumb slid down and over, nudged through the slit in her drawers.

At the first slow circle, she dug her nails into his neck.

He paused, hand wedged between them.

"No?" He grated the word.

"No," she gasped, falling forward, burying her face in his chest. His chest seemed so solid, curves of muscle hot and hard beneath damp wool. She found it difficult to imagine it had ever been a source of complaint.

His chin pressed the top of her head, and his arms wrapped around her.

"There are better places than the Serpentine, I'll admit."

"I don't mean not now, or here." Her breathing was unsteady. Her thighs still felt loose and sensitive, shivered by pulses of aimless pleasure, slowly ungathering from a tense knot of nearly unbearable sensation.

"I mean not ever," she said. "Or anywhere."

"Why?" Gently, he touched her shoulders, maneuvered her back so they could regard each other through the silvered shadows. "Because I'm still your boss? I could sack you, and then we wouldn't have to worry."

He gave her his crooked smile. Rejection made him wry, not wrathful.

"No, thank you," she said miserably.

"That wasn't a threat," he said. "Nina, if you don't want this . . ."

"I don't," she lied, looking down. His chest jerked, and she heard his harsh breath.

A droplet of water was rolling down her cheek. It had come from her hairline, not her eye.

"I'd rather continue on like before," she said. "As a secretary."

"Who also bakes."

She lifted her head.

He didn't look boyish now. His face was etched with lines. But the slant of his eyebrow was teasing. "We have to do something with those golden sultanas."

Her laugh was half sob.

"I won't speak of this again." He repeated his words from the balcony, with a formality that pretended she wasn't, right at this very moment, sitting on his rock-hard cock.

She scrambled up. Her legs felt stiff and shook queerly. They didn't seem to belong to her body. A beat later, he stood as well and walked for the linens.

"I'm sorry." She spoke to his back. He bent and turned, draping her in soft, dry cloth. She huddled into it.

"No reason to be sorry," he said kindly, kindly and incorrectly.

She turned her face toward the shimmering black of the lake.

CHAPTER SIXTEEN

"KEEP HUMORING HIM." Narayan Mukherjee shoved a bundle of documents into a cubbyhole in the towering cabinet that dominated his small, book-lined office.

"I wasn't humoring him. I praised the violinist because the violinist played like the dickens." Alan jammed his shoulder blades into the leather cushion of the high-backed chair and grimaced.

"Start humoring him, then." Mukherjee turned back with a shrug. He wore a natty brown suit and a dark blue turban. His look was acerbic.

"Truly." Alan frowned. "I gave you the full story of the current contretemps, sparing no detail . . ."

"None." Mukherjee murmured his agreement, assuming a long-suffering expression.

Alan's gaze narrowed. "And so you must agree," he continued, "that my brother's attempts to control me have no legal basis. Yet this is your counsel? *Humor him?*"

Mukherjee crossed behind his cluttered desk, dropping into his chair. He pressed his fingers together and peered at Alan over the steeple.

"Forgive me for stating the obvious, but the Duke of Umfreville is a duke. Also, a prominent member of the Lords." He tilted his head to the side, as though considering.

"Yes," he said dryly. "*Humor him* is my counsel, as your friend, not your solicitor. As your solicitor, I should demand from you an enormous sum and thank my stars for the business."

Alan rubbed his temple, where a headache was consolidating itself. He was out of sorts. Last evening, Nina had reappeared, a vision in his garden, better than a vision. He'd filled his arms with her. Her presence had filled the hours with meaning, aligning his body and his mind, hinting at a future that didn't flounder under the burden of the past.

And then he'd tried to shag her in the Serpentine.

Of course she'd declined.

His blood was still smoking with remorse, and thwarted desire, and the white-hot urge to crowd her into some corner of his house and try the whole thing again.

He'd said he wouldn't speak of it. He'd make no reference to her hair, or her mouth, or her deep eyes, which seemed to hold worlds. He'd make no reference to his soul-shaking longing to know her and be known by her.

He wouldn't pressure her either, like some boor in a tavern, deluding himself that his passion was permission.

He respected her, and yes, he wanted to sink inside her, to feel her softness all around him, to hear her heated sighs, but . . .

"De'Ath." Mukherjee was scrutinizing his face.

"Yes?" Alan cleared his throat.

"Don't involve the law," said Mukherjee. "You'll waste time and money." A faint smile tipped his lips. "Forget the courts. Rely on your widely celebrated wits."

Alan grunted and stood.

"Fine, then," he murmured, and took his cane from the umbrella stand, his hat from the peg. He paused at the door. "Humor him. Bloody hell."

He lunched at Cassanova's, where waiters poured out wine and dished pork ribbons day and night for revolving parties of musicians, artists, and poets, in smoky subterranean rooms. He didn't eat alone—the painters Redcliffe Davis and Thomas Ponsonby descended on his corner table—but his mind whirred as they gossiped.

Humor him. Cancel the sale of the portraits. Evince an utter change of heart. Claim he was ready to purchase a house in Mayfair and ask for the funds. Invest them instead. Create a new portfolio to generate income. Then he could go back to doing exactly what he pleased.

Except . . . his ability to see Claud, Arabella, and Mary would still depend on his brother's whim. To solve *that* problem, he needed leverage.

A half-formed idea flashed up and vanished as its contours became too clear and too dark.

Davis and Ponsonby erupted in laughter. Alan sipped his wine and gave them his attention. Their talk had turned to the Royal Academy's Summer Exhibition and its attendant controversies.

"Did you hear about the scandal at the Schools?" Davis caught Alan's eye and grinned in anticipation, blowing smoke at the low ceiling. "The sets of life drawings submitted for this year's prize were stolen."

"We think a workman nicked them to sell round the pubs." Davis laughed. "As dirty pictures."

"Hmm," said Alan, drawing out his watch.

"Students were all in a pother." Ponsonby spoke with his mouth full. "It's one for the annals. Like Jack Reeve filching Sir Sloshua's inkstand."

Alan dropped the watch back into his pocket. "So infamous as that?"

Jack Reeve. He hadn't heard the name in years. The Dutchified Dauber. Now his thoughts trended in a new direction.

The waiter began to clear the plates and his companions said their goodbyes.

Outside the restaurant, he faltered, only for a moment, blinking against the light, his hip mounting a delayed revolt against the uneven stair. The moment passed, unobserved.

The next moment, Alan was seated in his carriage, bowling toward Broughton's Auction House.

THE FOLLOWING DAYS were bright and dry. Alan dictated one letter, informing Geoffrey that he'd decided the family portraits should remain in the gallery, for posterity, and another, lauding the fine weather and noting its suitability for an afternoon swim with his nephew. In the letters he sent back, Geoffrey praised the wisdom of the decision. But he doubted that any interaction between Claud and Alan would suit. Not until Alan gave a few more proofs of probity.

The smugness of the replies made Alan grind his teeth. He'd rather humor a hog.

When the invitation arrived to the Duchess of Umfreville's ball, he snorted and cast it back onto the tray. When an invitation to Count Davanzo's musical soiree arrived, featuring the Sicilian nightingale Signorina Bonaccorso, he groaned aloud.

Nina looked at him, intrigued, so he handed her the card.

"How lovely," she said. "It's finally her turn." The dimples winked in her cheeks, and he strained a muscle in his neck as he kept his mouth at an appropriate distance from hers.

The days were not without their tortures.

Each day after breakfast, Miss Finch would knock on his study door with the letter tray, and he'd read and dictate responses to anything pressing. He'd dictate a notice, or part of an article, or— for the fun of it, as much to make her smile as to progress on the project—a page or two toward his novel of Mars.

After lunch, he'd send her from the house to Hyde Park to keep watch on the entrance nearest Umfreville House. If Arabella and Mary appeared with their nursemaid, she was to sneak Mary toffees and pass Arabella an envelope enclosing printed paper figures for her paper theater and a letter for Claud, along with an Italian astronomer's map of the Martian canals and an advertisement for the Bramleys at the Royal Aquarium.

It was ridiculous, to involve her in a covert mission to communicate with children. But he couldn't call on them at the house or direct letters through his brother or Fanny. To show his nieces and nephew that his affection was constant, he *required* a secret messenger.

Once Nina had departed, he felt a bittersweet alleviation of the ache in his heart. Then he began to count the minutes until her return, when he could linger with her in the warm, fragrant kitchen, receiving her report from Hyde Park, getting in the way of the baking, winding himself up again with lust and frustration.

He liked to lean on the glazed brick wall and watch her arrange copper bowls on the table and measure out flour and sugar. He liked to watch her precise motions as she cracked and separated eggs.

She talked as she whisked or sifted, wiping her hands from time to time on the light blue apron he'd sent Mrs. Dormody to buy, along with the cake tins, the dough docker—everything Nina had forgotten when she'd left home after that row with her brother.

On Wednesday, while making Victoria sponge, she informed him that Casa De'Ath was lacking in cats.

"And there are abundant candidates," she said, as a prelude to revealing that Kuznetsov had been feeding a feral colony of the creatures in the back garden for the past year. "Won't you let us put a hole in the door?"

"A hole," he repeated, glancing at Rouget. The old communard came and went from the kitchen as Nina worked, but that day he was watching, too, as Nina uncapped the orange flower water and added it to the batter.

"Not in the front door," she clarified, looking up. "And just a small hole. I'm a great hand at sawing."

"You?" Alan raised his brows, then recalled her description of life with those spinster aunts. Baking, berry picking. Building hedgehog houses. "Should I assume you can also plane and hammer?"

She only smiled. "Butter the pan?"

"This hole," he pursued, as he buttered the pan, a task he'd never imagined himself performing, but which at least—like the other tasks she gave him—provided a pretext for his spending so much time belowstairs. "It's bound to admit all the wildlife in London. I won't share my home with squirrels."

"Sugar it too," said Nina, peering. "As for the squirrels, the cats will scare them off." She rounded the kitchen table, brushing past him to fling open the kitchen door. Kuznetsov nearly fell into the room. Listening in, the rascal. Nina beamed at him, and he joined the little party. His hands were splotched with black, as though *he* were the one who'd blackleaded the range until it shone.

Alan rather suspected he knew who'd tidied and polished and converted his kitchen into the house's center of gravity.

She was explaining to Kuznetsov that you could spoil a sponge cake by mishandling the flour.

"You sift and sift, and then you fold it in gently," she said, and made slow rotations with the spoon. Sweat broke out on Alan's brow and he sidled away from the oven, which helped not a whit.

On Thursday morning, he found a scrawny orange tabby in his study.

"That's Max," said Nina, and then to Max: "You belong in the butler's pantry."

Max, however, preferred the study.

That evening, when Alan returned home from the theater, his feet led him downstairs rather than upstairs. His entire household was in the kitchen eating cake off his best china.

Nina saw him first. "Mr. De'Ath."

The salutation struck him like a slap of cold water.

"What's all this?" he asked gruffly. Kessler and McAdams parted, and he saw the remains of the cake on the table. He gave a twitch of his head.

Aristocratic weddings often featured cakes like marble sculpture, blinding white and yards high, each tier decorated with elaborate sugar flowers. This cake was simple in comparison, one tier, circular but bumped out at regular intervals with crenellated towers. The icing was textured like a stone wall.

"A castle?" He looked at Nina. Her cheekbones were flushed.

"It's the Bastille," said Kessler. "For Rouget's birthday."

"We stormed it," added McAdams helpfully.

Rouget handed him a plate.

The cake was chocolate. The stone façade was marzipan and royal icing.

He could tell that his appearance had introduced an element of constraint into the revelry, so he took himself back upstairs.

The taste of sugar on his lips disquieted his dreams.

By Saturday, he admitted what he'd realized on Friday.

He sat at his desk in his study wiggling his injured fingers, picking up his pen. *Twirling* his pen.

He could write.

He could write in a flowing hand. When Nina knocked, he

dropped the pen, and then he dropped his head, in self-disgust. Was he going to pretend he'd lost the use of his fingers forever? Resort to subterfuge so that Nina could misspell her way through his essays and he could stare like a besotted clod?

Some men preferred to dictate.

He preferred to write.

"Good as new." He held up his hand as she passed into the room.

"You mean you can hold a pen?" She stopped.

He gave his pen another twirl to demonstrate.

"I have other things for you to do," he said, because her face was clouding, and he wondered if she still thought he might sack her. "Citations to check, for my book. And I still need you to watch for the children."

It didn't sound like much.

"You can bake in the mornings," he said, "if that's to your liking."

He hardly needed constant baking. Perhaps, though, if he started entertaining for tea and hosted a salon . . .

He might dry up his lines of credit before Geoffrey turned over a shilling, but until then he'd keep Nina in almond paste and citron.

She'd baked the *Bastille*.

He wanted to see—and taste—subsequent creations.

"Is it?" he asked. "To your liking?"

She nodded, hands linked at her waist, very much as though she awaited dismissal. Her high-necked dress was plaid, blue and white, and fit her poorly. He knew that because he'd felt her breasts, and her hips, and her thighs, their perfect proportions.

He looked away, through the French doors, at the leaves of the chestnut tree.

"I hope Signorina Bonaccorso is splendid tonight," Nina murmured.

He glanced at her. "Is the soiree tonight? I'd forgotten."

She narrowed her eyes. "You forgot on purpose."

"Maybe." He leaned back in his chair, relieved that her pall had lifted. "Maybe I have good reason. This soiree—it's hosted by Count Davanzo."

She gave a small shrug. "Another Italian bloke?"

"Ambassador. Tied up with my brother's political ambitions. I've insulted his taste before. This is my chance to redeem myself, by rhapsodizing about the signorina's voice. Do you see the problem?"

She responded instantly. "You don't want to anger the duke. But you won't praise the signorina if you don't admire her performance. So you'd rather not go at all."

"Well. It seems you do know me." He cleared his throat. "Elegantly put."

"But what about the signorina?" Nina's eyes were rounded now with earnestness. "It's her chance too."

He sighed and gave her a dark look. "I believe you've collected the signorina like one of your strays."

"My strays?"

He pointed to Max, curled in his chair.

"Oh," she said, and laughed. "He's Mr. Kuznetsov's stray, really. His full name is Maksim." She paused. "You collect strays too. You met everyone who works here at a rally or a music hall."

He laughed too. "Not everyone."

Their gazes caught and held.

"I suppose I'll go to the kitchen, then," she said.

A dozen alternate suggestions rose to his lips.

He gave a nod and lifted his pen.

When the door shut behind her, he wrote a letter to Sir Cunliffe-Owen, the director of the South Kensington Museum.

It was high time he took a close look at the pictures Syme had acquired from Chips Sleaford.

He found that his eyes kept drifting to the French doors, to the chestnut tree.

What if he risked the soiree and gave the signorina her chance? If she did perform splendidly, sang like a nightingale, he'd have the opportunity to mollify Geoffrey while sacrificing none of his integrity.

He rested his chin on his fist.

Would Nina ever get her chance?

She was talented, intelligent, and winning, but as she'd pointed out, she was a woman in service, and what was more, entangled with her brother, who sounded like the type to drink her wages.

Nina's Sweets. How would she ever buy a bakery? *He* could buy one, along with the fruit market, if all went according to plan. Buy it for her. Act as a patron. Patrons funded artists, writers, musicians. Why not a baker?

Her Victoria sponge was light as air. He'd felt as though he was eating a cloud.

He stood, and he knew that unless he exerted effort, his feet would direct him down to the kitchen.

Only Laocoön struggled more, but he managed to gather hat, gloves, and overcoat and head out the door.

On the ride to the Royal Academy of Art, he jotted down questions for anyone who might remember Jack Reeve.

CHAPTER SEVENTEEN

NINA SAT ON her favorite bench, watching children fly a kite over the meadow. The wind was fitful, and the kite kept diving to earth, which caused the children to shriek and fight one another for the string. Nina had seen them yesterday too. Across the week, she'd come to recognize several of the afternoon regulars. There were many children, children galore, children of all shapes and sizes.

But never the Duke of Umfreville's.

According to Alan, their nursemaid often took them to the park after lunch. But which nursemaid? The duchess was jealous of the girls' affections. The kinder the nursemaid, the shorter her tenure.

Today, Nina had brought Fritz on her vigil. He'd seemed a bit jealous lately, of the cats. And he loved Hyde Park, big and green, littered with picnickers' detritus, which he found so irresistible.

He was emitting mellow cheeps on her shoulder, and she reached up to rub his fur.

Eventually, she abandoned her bench and walked between the trees, up the gentle slope of the hill. She had a better vantage from the hill and could surveil the park gate properly.

In the two days since Alan had proclaimed his hand good as new, she'd let herself fall under a cozy domestic spell. She baked, and then she wandered Hyde Park, and then she baked more, and at various intervals Alan presented himself in the kitchen to dock biscuits or to ask her some unexpectedly fanciful question, most recently, how she imagined ambrosia, the food of the Greek gods. She was lulled by the regularity, and pleasantness, of her routine, and by the company, Kuznetsov, Rouget, and the rest. And of course, Alan himself, who overflowed her heart when he tasted the vanilla extract and grimaced, and when he whipped egg whites, laughing in delight at the moment they came up in peaks.

Now that she didn't write out his letters—some of which had continued his queries into Sleaford's whereabouts—she could shove her real life out of her mind. She could pretend her greatest concern was overbrowning the puff paste for her lemon cheesecake. She could pretend that she had no ulterior motives.

But real life kept niggling away at her.

She monitored Alan's movements, so that Jack could evade the net.

It was soothing to bake and soothing to look for the duke's children. In these two arenas, she didn't play Alan false, or Jack either.

Her gaze stayed trained on the sky. The low, scuttling clouds threatened rain. Their silver was ominous, and beautiful, and very like the silver of Alan's eyes.

Night after night, she replayed their kisses and grew sweaty and restless in the narrow bed, and her urge for release felt perilously like an urge to confess.

And if she did? What then?

Her stomach lurched, and she lowered her gaze.

For a time, she watched people passing through the arched gate into the park. Redheaded twins in knee pants with a big, twinkly, white-haired lady who looked like a fairy godmother. A widow walking three Pekingese. Courting couples.

She decided to return to the benches and resume her seat.

She started down the hill and almost tripped on her skirt.

Those two girls on the path. One was gangling, with a black fan of hair on her narrow shoulders. The other, a tinier girl, had a birthmark on her cheek and a halo of dark curls. Lady Arabella and Lady Mary. They were following a nursemaid. Miss Milford trailed behind them, and so did the little marquess himself.

Nina straightened her skirt and walked briskly after them.

The little party was heading for the Serpentine. When they

reached the shore they stopped and surveyed the scene. Heart tripping, Nina sat on an empty bench at a few yards' distance. The
nursemaid opened her basket and handed bread to the girls with a
sweet smile. The little marquess skipped forward to claim his own
piece of bread, but Miss Milford called him back sharply. The
nursemaid's smile faltered, and the girls studied their bread, lower
lips bumped out.

"Come along, moppets," said the nursemaid gently. "The poor
ducks are famishing."

"The ducks prefer Claud." Lady Arabella looked up hopefully.
"Can't he feed them too?"

"Perhaps next time." The nursemaid's smile reappeared, and she
took Lady Mary's hand.

Nina watched Claud wave gamely to his sisters as they were led
to the water.

"Come along." Miss Milford passed right in front of Nina and
flapped out a sheet at the base of the oak that shaded the bench. She
situated herself atop it and propped her back against the tree. With
obvious reluctance, Claud approached. He knelt just within the
outer limit of the tree's shadow, picked up a stick, and stabbed it
determinedly into the dirt. He wore long white drill trousers with
his middy blouse and jacket, and Nina could see the damp seeping
into the cotton. He dug with furious concentration. Miss Milford
said something indistinct, which he ignored. She raised her voice,
and he threw down the stick and joined her on the sheet, sitting
cross-legged on the farthest corner, displaying the stains on his
knees. He slumped, chin on his hand.

Now that Nina was confronted with these closely guarded children in the flesh, sneaking anything to any one of them seemed
patently impossible. The girls seemed to have forgotten the ducks
and were running pell-mell after a grossly fat brindle pug. All at
once, the poor thing gave up, panting, and flopped down to submit
to their embraces.

That was when Miss Milford began to drone. Whatever she was
reading, it sounded like the very soul of dullness. She needed a lesson from Aunt Sylvia, who read aloud from novels with a spirit that
made her audience explode alternately into cheers and sobs. Or she

needed a change of material. Nina heaved a sigh and accidentally sucked Fritz's tail into her mouth.

"Gah." She batted it away.

What to do? The sight of three members of the Metropolitan Police crossing the lawn produced a nasty jolt. Right. She wouldn't try to lure Lady Arabella into private conference. If the nursemaid sent up a cry, Nina might find herself tossed into a wagon by a brawny constable. Too many sensational stories these days of procuresses haunting parks, spiriting away young girls, selling them to brothels. Nothing for it but to address the nursemaid directly. Perhaps she'd agree to take the little package herself and distribute the contents. Miss Milford seemed unlikely to look up from her dreary book, and even if she did, she'd assume they were simply passing the time of day. Her eyes had already swept over Nina without a glimmer of recognition.

The nursemaid was drifting farther away along the shore. Nina rose, and at that moment, she realized that Miss Milford droned no more.

She turned slowly toward the oak, afraid to hope. But . . . *yes*. The woman's head nodded on her shoulder. Her hands rested on the pages of the open volume in her lap. Thank the angels and the saints! Nina walked toward the oak with an exaggeratedly casual step. Should Miss Milford's eyes fly open, she'd ramble on, as though she'd never planned to stop.

The nurse's eyes did not fly open. She looked surprisingly young and defenseless in sleep, eyelids smudged lavender with exhaustion. Did she sit awake all night, making sure her high-spirited charge stayed abed?

Nina circled to the boy and saw him looking at her curiously.

"Is that a squirrel?" he asked.

She smiled and crouched down carefully by the torn earth and discarded stick.

"Fritz is a marmoset," she said, and scooped him from her shoulder. She set him down on the grass. He darted instantly to Claud and scampered over his legs on his way to the tree. Claud laughed—too loudly. Nina's whole body tensed, but Miss Milford didn't stir.

"A marmoset is a kind of monkey," she added in a low voice. "Fritz is a friend of your uncle's."

Claud's eyes fixed on hers, big eyes set in a sharp-featured face. His dark curls peeped from beneath his cap.

"Uncle Alan," he breathed. "Is he here?" He looked around hopefully.

"He had another engagement," she said, and Claud's face fell. "He gave me something, though, for you and your sisters."

Claud came up onto his knees. "What is it?"

Miss Milford made a strange sound, and her head tipped toward the other shoulder. Nina hesitated.

"Let's try to be quiet," she whispered. "Your nurse is in sore need of rest."

Claud's eyes narrowed. "She said I wasn't to see Uncle Alan anymore."

"Ah." Nina sat back on her heels. "Well. That's not for her to decide."

"I know." Claud's lips twisted. In that moment, he was Alan's spit and image. "My father decided. Do *you* think Uncle Alan has too many whims?"

Nina stared, at a loss. Her instinct was to defend Alan from the duke's aspersions and to point out that the duke was a detestable ass. But the detestable ass was the boy's father. She bit her lip.

"I think," she began, feeling her way cautiously. "I *know* that your uncle Alan is very, very fond of you. And the rest is for him and your father to sort out."

Claud nodded, and then his chin puckered.

"Will they?" His eyes were full of worry. Nina's heart swelled painfully.

"Certainly," she said, with firmness. Claud looked relieved, and also expectant. She fished in her chatelaine. "These are for Lady Mary."

Claud whisked the toffees into his pockets with the speed of a stage magician and held out his hand for the envelope. Instead of tucking it into his jacket, he tore it open and shook out the treasures. He put the paper figures delicately to one side and unrolled and rotated a small map of strange islands and waterways, eyes glowing with delight. He rolled and retied it with reverence and slid the string from the other tube. He spread it flat on the sheet and they regarded it together, a vividly colored handbill.

"Who are the Bramleys?" asked Nina. Claud was tracing the bold type at the top of page. ROYAL AQUARIUM.

"The greatest swimming family in the world." He pointed. Sure enough, it said exactly that. The chromolithograph depicted a handsome, jolly couple in bathing costumes posed in front of raging surf, surrounded by seven circular images of adolescent boys and girls diving and somersaulting. "Uncle Alan's going to take me to see their show, and afterward I'm going to ask them if I can be a Bramley too."

Nina could tell he was in earnest. Claud, Marquess of Stancliff, future Duke of Umfreville—an aspiring *Bramley*. That would flummox those who put wealth and social consequence above the humbler consolations of a united, affectionate family.

Claud cocked a brow, and again, the resemblance to Alan was uncanny.

"My father doubts I can eat a chocolate cake underwater." He lifted his chin. "I *can*."

"I didn't know anyone ate cakes underwater." Nina blinked. "Cakes should be *moist*, of course, but . . ." She trailed off. Moist within reason.

"The Bramleys do *everything* underwater." Claud's volume rose as he reported on that remarkable family's aquatic exploits. Nina's eyes kept sliding to Miss Milford, but she couldn't bring herself to interrupt. The boy was embellishing, describing balls and banquets at the bottom of the sea. He spoke breathlessly, caught up in his inventions. No wonder Alan took such pleasure in composing him a novel of Mars. Claud existed most fully in imaginary worlds.

He finished with a dry, hollow-chested cough, bending over and covering his mouth with both ends of his neckerchief. Miss Milford's head bobbed forward and jerked back.

"That's all marvelous," Nina murmured, eyes on the nurse. "They must eat a special sort of cake at the bottom of the sea."

"Tiny green cakes," offered Claud. "And big blue ones."

She looked back at him and smiled. "I bake lovely cakes, but none are green or blue. And they're meant to be eaten on land."

"You bake cakes?" He leaned forward. "I would eat them anywhere!" He said this last with a knightly boldness that made Nina laugh.

"I'll keep that in mind," she promised, and his chest moved with a quick, excited breath that once again exploded into body-rattling coughs.

Drat secrecy. Concern for the boy overrode every other consideration. She touched his shoulder. "What do you need? Should I wake your nurse?"

Claud wheezed and shook his head. He began to roll the handbill, concentrating on the task. His face had blanched. As Nina stared, uneasy, she saw a drop of water hit his pallid cheek. And then the skies opened. Fritz bounded up her dress and jammed himself beneath her chin. Everywhere, people were opening umbrellas, or scattering, or both. Claud barely had time to stuff the contraband down the front of his shirt before Miss Milford came to her feet.

Nina stood and ran with her head down and her skirts bunched in her hands. By the time she'd passed through the gate out of the park, she felt grimy and bedraggled, and she stared at the traffic with stinging eyes. A coach from Casa De'Ath collected her each day, but never so early. She'd have to find shelter, or she'd have to find her own way back to Chelsea. *Bother.* She fumbled in her chatelaine to see if she had the coins for a cab, ducking down to avoid the umbrellas of the passersby. One pair of legs entered her field of vision and stayed put. Muscular legs encased in fine gray trousers. A pair of legs, and the shaft of a rosewood cane.

Alan. She straightened with a gasp.

"I was in the area," he said with a twirl of his umbrella. "And aspired to save you from the elements." He raised his brows as his gaze traveled from her wilted bun to her muddy boots. "My timing was off." He gave his head a rueful shake.

"Your timing is wonderful." She smiled up at him. "I have something to tell you."

"I have something to tell you too." He slipped his fogged, dripping spectacles into his waistcoat pocket. "I just left the South Kensington Museum."

A clap of thunder sounded.

"Precisely." Alan grinned at the heavens and held his umbrella over her as she climbed into the waiting coach.

Chapter Eighteen

———————————————

Fritz kept butting her neck with his hard, cold little face. Nina fidgeted too. Her excitement had transformed to dread.

"What happened at the museum?"

"You first," said Alan, tossing his hat onto the seat.

"I saw the children, all three of them." Her nerves made the story tumble out in a rush. She told him about her conversation with Claud, the green and blue cakes at the bottom of the sea. He kicked up his leg and listened, ankle resting on his knee, eyes bright.

"He's well, then," he murmured and inhaled like a man who'd been holding his breath.

A new pressure built in Nina's chest, unrelated to her own predicament.

"Geoffrey tells me otherwise."

She chewed her lip, picturing the boy doubled over, thin shoulders shaking. He'd looked, and sounded, far from well. She'd omitted those details, instinctively. She'd wanted to present a happy account, one that brought exactly this expression to Alan's face, soft and warm.

She met his eyes.

"What?" His voice sharpened.

The coach took a wide turn, swaying gently. A foul odor wafted through the compartment. The air was humid and close, redolent of Fritz and whatever horrible thing he'd been eating. She dumped him onto the seat and wrapped her arms around herself.

"I don't know that he's well. He's skin and bones."

Something dark flicked in Alan's gaze. "You said yourself his parents' faces curdle milk. Is it surprising he lacks appetite?"

"He coughed." She persisted now that she'd begun. Alan deserved as full a picture as she could give. "He coughed *violently*."

Alan put his fist to his mouth and regarded her over it. She remembered that look from the garden at Umfreville House, when he'd interrogated her about Claud's doctor and nurse. He'd claimed, then, to seek information about his nephew's welfare. He'd claimed, too, that he and the duke inhabited different realities.

In Alan's reality, Claud didn't suffer from a wasting disease.

He sought information, but he resisted it when it contradicted what he wanted to believe.

Sad. Sad and human. Alan De'Ath *was* human, however much lauded for the infallibility of his judgment.

She wanted to touch him, but she was the one who'd told him never again. She slid her boot forward, not quite far enough to bump his. He saw the motion. He didn't slide his own boot forward, only clenched his hand at his side.

After a beat, he raised his eyes. "There wasn't blood?"

"No."

He nodded slightly, a bit of the warmth returning to his face.

Fritz had crept onto his seat and was nosing around his hat.

"In that case, it could have been anything. Smuts and pollens in the air can produce a cough." He stiffened, brows shooting up his forehead. "So can a stench. My Lord." He looked at Fritz. "He's pungent."

"At present." Nina watched as Fritz rolled over and kicked the hat, which tipped. She sighed and leaned forward to collect him, but he sprang onto Alan's chest.

"Hello." Alan scratched between Fritz's ear tufts.

"When I'm home," said Nina, righting the hat, then returning to her seat, "I lather him regularly with almond shaving soap and give him rosewater soaks. And clean his teeth. And sprinkle him with jasmine oil."

"Do you? What a glamorous toilette."

"He hates it. I have to chase him all about. Fritz, come here."

Fritz bumped his head against Alan's hand and curled up into a ball.

"Your turn." Nina drew back her boot. For a week, she'd been telling herself that if they didn't touch, didn't kiss, it would all hurt less in the end.

But this hurt.

"What do you have to tell me?" She crossed her arms over her chest. "About the South Kensington Museum."

"I examined the pictures, the ones Syme acquired from Sleaford." He was grinning now, like a cat that got the cream, pleased with himself, and pleased to share his triumph with her.

She couldn't share it. There was nothing they could share, not truly. Even when he whipped eggs or teased her for suggesting ambrosia was Aunt Lolly's hedgehog cake—the camaraderie was tainted. Amazing it didn't come out in the biscuits.

"The museum director has been relying on Syme to grow the collection, allowing him to authenticate his own selections, and to hell with the art referees, the staff, the board." He brushed back a lock of hair. "Those pictures hadn't been properly inspected."

She braced herself. "And?"

"Fakes. Less persuasive than the Berneys. Same pattern of pin-drawn cracks on the surfaces."

"It's your eye, then, against Syme's."

"My eye is better." He laughed. Oh, he was in a very fine mood now, his sweets and messages delivered, and his verdict, too.

That invisible bulwark was rising between them. She felt lonely, on the outside of his merriment.

"The director agrees," he said. "But there's more."

She shuddered.

His face changed. "You're cold."

His quick concern flooded her eyes. She would feel safe with his arms wrapped around her, and she'd melt against the heat of his chest.

He glanced toward the window and sat up straighter.

"Ah," he said. "Let's continue someplace warmer and more celebratory."

Minutes later, when he'd stopped the coach and they stood again on a wet street, Nina beheld the shop that had caught his eye. A pretty, blue-painted storefront, with big windows divided into leaded glass panes, PATISSERIE FRANÇAIS written out in gold letters above.

"One of the best French bakeries in London," he said. "Has mademoiselle considered adding éclairs to her repertoire?"

He offered her his arm, playful, and she clutched it, her grip too tight.

The shop *was* warm, and just as pretty inside as the outside had promised. Round tables with white cloths were set with vases of spring flowers. A pianist played in a recessed corner. Ornately framed mirrors hung on the walls. The waiter's expression didn't betray what a glance at the elegant clientele confirmed: Nina was far shabbier than the usual customers, even on days when the hem of her skirt hadn't dragged through the mud. He and De'Ath were speaking in French with the ease of old friends, and before she had time to feel too out of place, he settled them at their table and returned with a teapot and tiered tray of pastries.

Nina's mind blanked as she took her first bite of éclair. Thank God. She needed a reprieve from time and space. She existed only, calm as cream.

"They pass muster, then?"

She opened her eyes, licking chocolate from her bottom lip. Alan was lounging in his chair across the table's small span.

"I'll order more," he said.

She felt the familiar, painful tug, his proximity magnetizing every fiber of her being.

And she felt ice trickling down her spine. It wasn't rainwater. She was nearly dry.

It was panic.

"Lord Alan."

Alan turned his head. The man who hailed him had a protrusive stomach, saffron-colored teeth, and very friendly blue eyes. He moved nimbly between the tables. When he reached them, he nodded graciously—and incuriously—at Nina.

"Lord Kilderbee," said Alan. "Allow me to present Miss Finch. Miss Finch, Lord Kilderbee."

The introduction rolled off his tongue. No explanation of their relationship followed. He simply sipped his tea.

"Pleased to meet you. Wretched weather, what?" Lord Kilderbee spoke heartily. "But tell me," he addressed Alan. "What *did* you make of the signorina's performance last night?"

Nina's gaze shot to Alan. He gave her a half smile and set down his tea.

"The signorina was divine. The performance revived my faith in the bel canto."

"I thought the same!" Lord Kilderbee pressed closer to Alan's chair.

"Great minds," said Alan blandly, and then he inclined his head. "Lady Kilderbee."

A lovely woman in a primrose silk walking dress came up behind her husband. Her thick, pale hair was swept back with jeweled combs, and her white smile seemed glazed on her face.

"Lord Alan." Her eyes skimmed Nina on their way back to her husband.

"My dear Patricia missed the final arias," Lord Kilderbee told Alan, tucking Lady Kilderbee's arm beneath his. He gave Lady Kilderbee's arm an indulgent pat and tutted. "Gossiping in the garden."

"Not gossiping." Lady Kilderbee's smile retracted into a rosebud pout. "Lady Ashbee was in need of my support."

"Can't fault a loyal friend." Lord Kilderbee patted her again. "But the signorina was *divine*. A shame you missed a moment of it."

Alan selected a colorful macaron from the tray. "My poor brother missed the latter half of the performance, too. Truly a shame." He looked up with a sarcastic smile, lost on Lord Kilderbee, if not his wife. "There's always next time."

Nina watched the Kilderbees make their way toward the door, still awkwardly linked at the arm, their steps out of rhythm. When she turned back to De'Ath, he was offering the macaron to Fritz, who was curled inside his waistcoat. Her heart skittered.

She picked up her teacup. "You went to the soiree."

"Someone suggested I give the signorina her chance."

She flushed.

"My review will be rhapsodic." There was a shade of mockery in his voice. "And I'll be rewarded. If I signed my surname to it, my brother would rhapsodize to his banker. My account would be opened before the ink was dry. But I can't bring myself to go that far."

"Your surname." Nina added a mille-feuille to her plate. "It's not De'Ath?"

"Not originally. I adopted it at Oxford."

"A pen name." She worked the tines of her fork into the mille-feuille, piercing the layers of puff pastry and custard, a delicate operation. It steadied her. "Why De'Ath? You liked the morbid puns?" *Lord Death.*

"More than I liked the puns suggested by my surname."

"How bad can it be?" She looked up. He was baiting her, grinning. And it wasn't so very hard after all, in this sparkling shop, to lull herself again into a sense of complacency. "What *is* your surname?"

"Lord Alan Daft." He sketched a bow. "At your service."

"Your name is Daft." She blinked. "*Daft.* Daft? But that's . . ." A giggle tickled her throat. She coughed.

"Daft," she repeated.

"Your mistress is cruel." Alan bent his head to Fritz. "I show her where to thrust the knife and she drives it home and twists the blade."

Fritz fixed her with his glossy eyes.

"What was I supposed to say?" She put down her fork. "*Daft.* How venerable. Tell me of its ancient and distinguished origin."

"Check your *Debrett's.* It's a fine old name. Geoffrey has always considered my refusal to use it an affront to the family."

"But really it was necessity." She paused. "A man of letters can't be . . . Daft."

"That too." He gave her an inscrutable look. "I make things worse by calling Geoffrey, Geoffrey, as though we're mates who go round the pubs. I should call him *Umfreville,* of course. I used to call him *Umf,* but he liked that even less."

"Umf." She laughed aloud.

"I'm going to have to burn this waistcoat." He offered his thumb to Fritz, who grabbed it. "He really does smell like a pestilence. So. The rest of my news. Do you want to hear it?"

All the sparking light seemed suddenly to slice at her. The outside world, crashing through the glass.

"What is it?" she asked, a question, not an affirmation, not a lie, as though that mattered.

He stretched the pause deliberately, and she realized she could see him reflected simultaneously in two of the shop's mirrors, and herself as well.

She froze, watching a dark, handsome man lean toward a frozen woman from different angles.

"I know the forger's identity," he said.

She cut into her éclair. She had the crazed urge to gobble it, to devour every pastry on the tray.

"A sensational revelation." He tilted his head. "It will bring down the house."

She swallowed. Yes, the roof seemed to be caving in, the walls tipping forward.

"Who?"

He wasn't wearing his spectacles. His eyes danced.

"It should have occurred to me at once. He was notorious for a time. Flooded the market with fakes. Rembrandt was a favorite. Brueghels. Van Dyck. He served a sentence at Pentonville over a decade ago, and no one in the art world has seen hide nor hair of him since."

"But why should it be him?" She lifted her cup and set it back on the saucer with a clatter. "You've made it sound as though forgers are in every corner."

"There are plenty of middling forgers. To possess such skill, and to misapply it so colossally—that's rarer. It indicates a man who received the best training and yet holds everything it represents in contempt. A man with an ax to grind. A man who spent a decade improving his methods. I saw a few of his Rembrandts back then. He's gotten better." Alan paused, thoughtful.

Nina lifted her cup again and this time she drank. The liquid felt cold all the way down to her stomach.

"His name is Reeve. The forger." Alan glanced at the cup as she returned it to her saucer, took up the teapot, and poured out more tea with casual grace. "He was a student at the Royal Academy. I talked with Academicians who knew him then. They said Reeve was as ill-mannered as J. M. W. Turner, with twice the talent."

Absurdly, the compliment shattered Nina's composure. She felt her lips tremble.

Twice the talent of *Turner*, the greatest British artist of all time. Had anyone ever said it to Jack himself?

"Reeve went to earth after Pentonville. Not to reform. To plot new crimes. The more I consider it, the more certain I am." Alan didn't notice her emotion. He was toying with his spoon. "If Reeve *is* working with Sleaford, the colormen and suppliers on the street might know him, if not by name, by description." He glanced up, smug. "It won't be long now."

For a single blinding instant, Nina hated him with all her heart.

He credited himself with winning the game when people like him had rigged it all up in the first place. It was Jack's voice in her head.

She couldn't bear to see his elation, his self-congratulatory expression, the smirk on his lips.

His lips. When he'd asked her about ambrosia, she'd remembered the taste of his lips. Thank God she hadn't told him.

"He's a thief as well as a forger."

"A thief?" She did look at him now, her gaze like flint.

"He was expelled from the Royal Academy for theft. Of the founder's silver inkstand no less."

No. She shook her head. Jack hadn't stolen anything. The wealthy, powerful men who'd made the accusation—their only proof was his relative poverty, their own assumptions.

After his expulsion, he couldn't join the faculty of an art school or give private lessons as a painting master. Respectable society slammed its doors. No one would hire him to paint a portrait of a bride, a child, a *dog*. His name was ruined. He was all but forced to borrow someone else's name, to paint as anyone but himself.

She had to write to Jack at once. He had to leave London immediately.

"Nina?" Alan sounded far away. She turned her head, but he was everywhere, reflected, black hair, white teeth.

"Excuse me," she managed, pushing back her chair. She walked briskly to the door and pushed out onto the street, where she vomited exquisite French pastry into the gutter.

CHAPTER NINETEEN

THE DAY AFTER Alan's performance review of Signorina Bonaccorso appeared in the *Illustrated London News*, he received a call from his brother, the first Geoffrey had ever paid to his Chelsea address.

"Shall I give you the tour?" he asked. He'd come around his desk in greeting. Geoffrey's ice blue eyes were pinned to a charcoal drawing on the study wall, an elephant, indubitably Rembrandt's.

"I've seen enough." Geoffrey swung around and shrugged. "This isn't a proper residence. It's a boardinghouse for poets, heretics, and foreign riffraff. When you return to Mayfair, you'll dismiss them all."

"When I return to Mayfair, I will." Alan smiled. He might as well have said, *when pigs fly*.

Geoffrey nodded. "Here."

Alan leafed through the papers, then took the leather folio case back around his desk. A yowl alerted him that Geoffrey had tried to sit in the green Chesterfield armchair.

"That's Max's seat. Try the sofa." He didn't look up. "The allowance is generous. But I require more if I'm to relocate."

"I can let a house for you."

"*Buy* a house." Alan wrote the figure across the top page. He closed the folio. "And I have to do it myself. It's a question of taste. I won't live in some high-walled monstrosity on a noisy thoroughfare."

Geoffrey was still standing. His smile showed that Alan's bargaining conformed—pleasantly—to his expectations. He believed that he now set the rules of engagement.

Humor him.

Alan walked over and presented the folio.

Geoffrey took it and tucked it beneath his arm. "Before you judge Mayfair, remember Mayfair will judge you. High walls or a haircut. You need one or the other."

Alan laughed. "Brother, was that a bon mot? How entertaining. Even so." He curled his lips. "Our solicitors had best conclude this conversation."

He saw Geoffrey to the front door, where Kuznetsov handed him his overcoat, hat, and gloves. The gloves—buff colored—looked as though they'd been used as an ink blotter, which perhaps they had. Kuznetsov seemed lost in thought as he held open the door. Geoffrey's lips thinned. But he put his smile back in place.

"We'll invite you to tea," he said to Alan. "Before the end of the month, with the children. You'll like that, won't you? You can say goodbye to Claud."

"Goodbye?" Alan accompanied him down the path.

"The warmer weather hasn't relieved his complaint to the extent we'd hoped." Geoffrey paused at the gateposts. "All this damp we've been having."

"Where are you taking him?"

"I'm not." Geoffrey's eyes slid away. "I'm needed in Lords."

"I see." Alan stared at his brother's face, the sour lines carving down from his nose. "Fanny will take him, then." He gave a mirthless laugh. Her absence would make Geoffrey's liaisons easier by half. "*Where?*"

"Italy, the mountains this time." Geoffrey returned his gaze. "Pistoia."

Alan felt a wash of cold. "That was where . . ." He ran a hand over his face. The air seemed thinner. It wouldn't fill his lungs, even if he heaved, panted, clawed his chest. The old terror expanded inside him, expanded the time between one breath and the next.

He stood as straight as he could.

"Where you had your accident. I know." Geoffrey hadn't donned the soiled gloves. He turned them over in his hands. "I know every detail. You were lucky it happened there."

"Mother thought so." Alan drew a slow breath. "She adulated my surgeon. They seemed to share a singular accord."

"Dr. Barbieri. The best in the world." Geoffrey's eyes were washed of color in the sunlight, more white than blue, with pinprick pupils. They flicked down Alan's leg. "You wouldn't walk if it weren't for him."

Dr. Barbieri had also had blue eyes. He used to sing under his breath when he checked the bandages. He always greeted their mother with a deep bow. Principessa, he'd called her. When Alan had written the hospital, years ago, he'd learned the man was dead.

"You can appreciate my choice." Geoffrey inclined his head. "I'm sure Fanny would prefer Davos. But we have history in Pistoia, as a family."

"Don't send Claud there." Alan's tongue felt thick in his mouth. "Find another pretext for banishing your wife."

Geoffrey's teeth ground audibly. He didn't separate his jaws to speak. "Claud is my son and heir. He is afflicted with tuberculosis, a wet disease that ameliorates in a dry climate. Mother swore by Pistoia. He goes. Fanny goes with him. End of story."

"Entrust him to me." Alan blinked against the sun, which felt too yellow, as though displaced from those Tuscan afternoons, when he lay on the terrace, the steep, parched landscape dropping away, the lonely cypresses beckoning.

"What?" Geoffrey stared. The garden was queerly silent. Alan took a step closer. His throat was too tight for his voice to carry.

"I'll act as his guardian. You'll see his health improve under my roof."

A muscle leapt in Geoffrey's jaw. "You. *My* son's guardian. *My* son, the future Duke of Umfreville."

"You use his frailty when it serves you." Alan felt as though he were pushing the words through a jagged fissure. "The rest of the time, you shun him for it. He's dejected and friendless. I'll provide him with tutors, company, varied entertainment, nutrition, exercise. He will *thrive*."

Geoffrey lunged forward, his boots overlapping Alan's at the toe, their faces so close Alan could count the red threads in his eyes.

"Say goodbye to Claud before he leaves for Pistoia. Or don't." Geoffrey slapped the gloves against Alan's chest. "It's the only decision that's yours to make." He turned, bowling over a slight, blond man who had the misfortune to step into the garden as he stepped out.

"How do you do?" He said it coldly, without stopping. The other man inclined his head with an admirably pacific expression, considering he'd been knocked into an artichoke plant. He'd kept his feet at least.

Moments later Alan heard carriage wheels bumping over the paving stones. He looked at the high, blue sky, at the gloves he'd caught in his hands, at his visitor. His heart beat an alarming tattoo, and his lungs felt flat.

In the drawing room, Herr Steucklen spread out samples of his wares—tube paints, pencils, paper. Alan's heart slowed as he watched the man's methodical, unhurried movements. With a silent apology to his stationer, he placed a large order, then rang for tea.

By the time Steucklen was repacking his box, Alan had queried him comprehensively on his corner of High Holborn and its denizens.

Steucklen sometimes mounted drawings for Sleaford but had no notion of where the dealer had gone. He did know a Jack, Sleaford's friend. Not an artist. Jack worked at a knickknack emporium at Cow Crossing Yard and gave him bargains on poured-wax dolls for his wife's collection.

"This Jack?" asked Alan, and showed him a sketch. Augustus Burgess, whose studies at the Royal Academy had overlapped with Reeve's, had dashed it off with a bemused smile.

Steucklen's smile was also bemused.

"I think perhaps," he said.

Alan didn't waste a moment after Steucklen's departure. He went swiftly to the library. Nina was sitting cross-legged on the high-backed painted settle bench that faced the stained-glass windows, a typed copy of his current manuscript divided into two piles on the cushion beside her, a book in her hands. She looked up, jolted, and frowned. Since she'd taken ill at the patisserie, she'd seemed strained and skittish.

"I'm not a quarter of the way through," she said. Stacks of books surrounded the settle, bristling with slips of paper. She'd been finding and marking lines he'd quoted from memory so he could correct any imperfections of recall.

"There's no rush."

Her hair was scattered with colored light.

His fingers twitched, and he made his hands into fists.

He wanted her with him when he entered that emporium. She'd been a part of his investigations from the beginning. She'd been there when he'd discovered that first forgery. It was fitting that they saw this through, together, to the end.

Any excuse, dammit.

He wanted her with him all the bloody time. And never more than today.

His vision swam. The colored light. The *Tuscan* light. Those cypresses like spikes.

Splintering pain.

He was going to fall.

"Mr. De'Ath?" She hovered just outside his reach. And then she stepped closer. "Alan?"

"It's nothing." He shook his head. "A goose walked over my grave." The pain was gone. His leg felt dead.

She looked apprehensive.

He smiled. "I prefer the thought of more poetic creatures on my grave. Ravens. Snow-white palfreys. Perhaps a stag."

Now her brows pinched.

"Not important," he said. "Let's go catch a thief."

Cow Crossing Yard opened off Clerkenwell Road, a collection of tall, dilapidated houses squeezed around a narrow court, all blistered bricks and treacherous verandahs.

"Do you mind?" He threaded his arm through hers as they approached the emporium. "We're a happy couple, with space on the walls for charming old pictures. Ask after every painting you see. Your indulgent husband will buy whatever you desire. If Reeve himself sells us a slapdash faux-eighteenth-century oil, well." He shrugged. "Our work is done."

Straight to Scotland Yard.

Nina had been quiet during the carriage ride. Now she seemed mute.

Before he could ask what was wrong, the door of the emporium burst open, framing a pair of pimply mashers in too-tight suits, one green, the other blue. They lingered in the doorway below an ancient barber's pole, the faded paint of its red spiral flaked off in patches.

"Mind the bloody bird," boomed a voice from within. Too late. A gray-and-red parrot flew between them. Instead of veering up into the blue sky, the bird arrowed toward Nina, tipped up its wings, and perched on her shoulder. He felt her body tense.

"Give me a kiss," said the parrot.

"What cheek." Alan laughed as a blond giant bounded down to the cobbles, shoving the unfortunate young men to either side. "Your bird, sir, is overly familiar with my wife."

"Your wife." The man's suit matched the bird's plumage, gray jacket and red trousers. He looked too long at Nina, fondling the rose in his buttonhole. "Polly's just being sociable. Here, Polly." He raised his arm, and the parrot flapped to it. He gave Alan a toothy smile.

"Lawrence Ladbrooke," he introduced himself. "Curiosity dealer, furniture broker, antiquarian, barber. Tell him, Polly."

"Penny for a shave," said the parrot.

"Sixpence and you know it," said Ladbrooke. He had to duck under the lintel of the door. Alan followed him inside, the pressure of Nina's arm on his increasing slightly, a sign that her steps lagged.

The emporium's antechamber was chockablock with the tackle of the barbering profession. There were chairs along the walls alternating with sinks and tall tables from which various pots, bottles, and tongs threatened to topple. Gilded fish and stuffed songbirds hung from the ceiling, and a taut web of wires anchored in the moldings, clipped with tufts of hair for false whiskers and toupees. Alan passed beneath this singular curtain, cologne burning in his nostrils. The scent was strong enough to mask even vapors of varnish and turpentine. If Reeve's workshop was in the building, he wouldn't know by smell.

He released Nina's arm so he could maneuver into the back rooms. As in any curiosity shop, they presented a mishmash of rubbishy, mediocre, and marvelous objects, both decorative and natural. Piles of rugs made transit difficult, as did massive pieces of Gothic furniture and customers. Three of them blocked his access to the depths of the back parlor.

Alan changed course, weaving around cabinets that displayed collections of fossils, painted teacups, gems, fans, snuffboxes. He slowed.

Dip pens. Enameled, silver, tortoiseshell. Reed. That one. Identical to Nina's. It meant nothing, taken by itself. Such pens weren't rarities.

He lifted his gaze and searched for her. She stood beside a suit of armor, her proximity to its rigid plates emphasizing the vulnerability of her soft, rounded figure. Her hands were clasped behind her back, and she seemed absorbed in her study of a pink Chinese vase on a walnut stand.

He heard a thud. A young woman balanced on a Glastonbury chair had just knocked an ormolu clock from a shelf. She was frozen, feather duster in hand.

She was staring at Nina.

Something tingled down Alan's spine. He made his way to the parlor's perimeter and leaned close to a murky, worm-eaten portrait. Innocent junk.

He slid his eyes to the next painting. Less innocent. An unsigned landscape, pointedly familiar to anyone acquainted with the subjects of John Constable. The average collector would pounce, thinking himself lucky. He'd pay far less for his "Constable" in Cow Crossing Yard than he would at Broughton's.

Any amount was too much. The topographical inaccuracies alone proved that Constable's hand had never touched the canvas. Reeve had known better than to send it to auction.

"Give it an ogle." Ladbrooke appeared beside him. "I can't tell what's o'clock with pictures myself. Not my specialty."

"No?" Alan raised a brow and lowered his voice. "I do believe it's a Constable."

Ladbrooke whistled. "You shouldn't ever have said so. Constable? His daubs aren't cheap." He shook his head and heaved a mighty sigh. "But I'm on the square. I can't swear it's a Constable, and it's not my way to palm off a picture as this or that. Pity an honest fool and pick your price."

Alan laughed as he met Ladbrooke's shrewd, twinkling eyes. The man was no fool, honest or otherwise. He didn't take Alan for a husband on a lark with his wife, long in the purse, easily rooked. What had given him away?

Maybe his eccentricities of style were a hindrance, not only in Mayfair. He was too recognizable. Swindlers identified him on sight.

Or he was asking himself the wrong question?

Who had given him away?

He looked again for Nina. She'd drifted away from her corner, and he had an unobstructed view down a tunnel of giltwood chairs and sofas. A marmalade cat stirred from a nest of old lace on a sofa, sprang to the floor, and stalked to her, pushing at her skirts, insistent and familiar. She made an involuntary movement, a dip down to stroke the cat's arched back, then froze. Her eyes brushed his as she straightened, but she couldn't hold his gaze.

Alan removed his spectacles. He felt, suddenly, that he'd never seen her so clearly.

"Or don't you want it?" asked Ladbrooke in a level tone.

"I want a word with Jack Reeve." Alan swung around and gave him a frank stare. "I understand he works here."

"Not anymore." Ladbrooke picked a feather off his sleeve. "Rum cove. I'll miss him. Went to New York. Or did he? Ruby!" He raised his voice. "*Was* it New York?"

"New York." The young woman hopped down from the chair. Her thick coil of coppery hair looked heavier than the bronze upon which she rested her palm. "Definitely New York. If it wasn't Dublin."

"He'll have taken his leave recently." Alan's eyes returned to Nina. Immediately after their conversation in the patisserie would be his guess.

She gave no sign she heard what they were saying. Perhaps she didn't, standing there, halfway across the room. She picked up a shell and traced its spines with her finger. Was *this* her milieu? He'd thought her an unlikely maid when he'd met her. A clerk's daughter was his supposition at the time.

A forger's sister.

His spine tingled again. Pain began to saw around the ball of his hip. He needed to sit and think.

"He left me shorthanded," said Ladbrooke with a shrug. "Feels like he's been gone a century."

Alan plucked at his side-whiskers, which he'd begun to cultivate the day he'd purchased his first pair of antique spectacles in a shop much like this one, in Oxford.

"Do you have a hand free for the razor?" he asked. "As it turns out, I'm a decade overdue for a shave. A penny, is it?"

Ladbrooke's smile gleamed. "Sixpence."

"Sixpence," Alan repeated, and showed his own teeth.

"And a haircut," he added. "While you're at it."

THE INSTANT ALAN and Laddie disappeared behind the folding screen, Nina sidestepped a sofa, slipped behind the tapestry that concealed the door, and let herself into the narrow hallway. She shut the door behind her and stood, gripping her sides. She felt as though she were going to shake apart.

The door creaked open. Ruby flew to her, tugging her into a tight embrace. Mop circled around their skirts.

"Tell me he really left," Nina managed. She'd written Jack with a warning, but, of course, he couldn't send a reply. If he'd been too stiff-necked to listen . . . If he were still *here*, instead of in Hensthorpe . . .

"He went the other day." Ruby stepped back. She grabbed Nina's elbow and pulled her into the kitchen.

"I only have a moment." Nina sagged against the sink. For years, this squalid little kitchen had been her refuge, the place she'd tried—and failed—to keep in order, while daydreaming about a kitchen all her own. It looked the same. But it offered nothing now, by way of peace or protection. She took a deep breath. Mop hopped up to the counter, drawing her eye to a pan of coffee. Jack's, for tinting paper. Stupid. What else had he left behind? She seized the pan and dumped the liquid, jamming it lengthwise into the sink behind the crusted dishes.

"He emptied the studio?" She paced the kitchen, threw a lidded tin of charcoal in the dustbin, wiped out the mortar in which Jack had crushed rotted acorns for oak-gall ink.

Ruby nodded. "But I don't think the coppers were his chief concern. Some rowdies came by, wanted their blunt. Laddie had to reason with them."

Nina stopped pacing and pressed her middle, which was sick and quivery. She'd seen Laddie *reason* with plug-uglies before. "They won't find him, not before he figures out where to go next." She tried to smile at Ruby.

Ruby's expression was fierce. "I'm worried for *you*."

"Don't be." Nina shook herself. She needed to return to the Knack's parlors and devote herself to her wifely shopping. "Alan doesn't know I've anything to do with Jack."

"Alan." A line formed slowly between Ruby's thin brows.

"De'Ath," said Nina.

Ruby stepped closer. "You're blushing."

"I'm going to be sick is what I am."

"Now I'm more worried." Ruby looked her up and down. "Has he taken you to bed?"

"No!" Nina choked. "He'd have me in jail sooner than his bed if he knew the truth."

"I saw the way he looked at you." Ruby took her hands. "Do you know what you're doing?"

"Oh bloody hell, of course not." She sounded hysterical. "My life's on fire. Jack made a hash of everything. My savings are gone. And the only man I've ever . . ."

Ruby's fingers tightened on hers. "You ever what?"

Nina shook her head. "I used to think, if I felt some way about someone, *he'd* end up deceiving *me*. Not the reverse."

"It's usually both." Ruby sighed. "But the blokes are worse, more often, because they can be."

"I don't want this." Tears burned Nina's nose. "I always saw myself like Aunt Sylvia and Miss Lolly. I want their life. None of *this*, this feeling like my heart is going explode out of my chest."

"You've got it bad." Ruby released her hands with a sympathetic squeeze.

"I should go." Nina rubbed her face. "He'll wonder where I've gone."

"French letters," said Ruby. "Sneak 'em from Laddie. Is there anything you want to ask me?"

Nina drew a long breath, her head a blaringly explicit jumble of lovers' limbs and images of love's aftermath, which the stereographs never pictured: abandoned women with extinguished eyes. Could French letters protect your heart?

The most urgently practical question trumped all. "Will you take out the dustbin?"

She slipped back into the parlor, stationed herself in front of a random picture, and focused on it with all her might. The artist's talent, while small, matched his ambition exactly, with happy result. A small, welcoming landscape. She'd suggest Alan buy this one. Three of Jack's fakes did hang on the walls, but they were badly lit and sandwiched between framed prints and carved masks. Easily passed over. Alan might neglect them. And *she* could certainly be excused for failing to notice.

"Dearest."

She pivoted. Alan sauntered toward her. His black hair was clipped short. His cheeks had been scraped clean. His jaw was sharply chiseled. All that hard definition—his lips looked softer for it.

"Dearest," he drawled again, when it became clear that she could only gawp. "I've already selected three pictures for our nuptial bower. Mr. Ladbrooke's about to wrap them up."

"That's right, guv." Laddie sidled past him, toward Nina, and took one of Jack's pictures from the wall. "I shall cocoon the goods. Best daubs in the house." He glanced at the picture in his hands. "Don't I wish I could remember where they came from." His eyes slid over Nina as he turned, the left fluttering, the most furtive of winks.

She felt a little throb of gratitude.

Laddie might have squealed, tried to barter his information for money. But he hadn't given up his friend, or her, for that matter. Maybe he wouldn't sell his own mother. She'd apologize for that particular quip.

Alan handed her into the coach and waited outside to see the pictures packed. She expected him to speak as they rolled down Clerkenwell, but he looked steadily out the window. His profile seemed *finished* somehow, framed by the clean edge of his jaw. His starched cravat folded snow-white against his tanned neck. He looked more, and less, like himself.

"Nina," he said at last. "You know about my surname. Now I find I'm curious about yours." He turned his face to her, his expression oddly blank. "*Finch.* How did you come by it?"

"By my father." She hesitated, the quiver in her stomach sharpening to a pain. "Same as most." She couldn't see his eyes behind his spectacles. Light flared on the lenses.

"Your father," he repeated softly, shuttering the window. He stretched his body in the opposite direction and shuttered the other window too. The compartment dimmed. Now his pale eyes dazzled.

"But your father was *Reeve*, was he not?" He removed his spectacles and slid them into his coat pocket. His gaze never left her. "Or so your brother's surname leads me to believe."

For an instant, the world seemed to stop. She had the sensation of hanging in space, everything dark, Alan's eyes distant stars. Then the pavement juddered the coach's wheels and a word puffed out of her.

"No." She blinked, and her vision cleared.

"No?" He lifted his brow. "Jack Reeve is not your brother?"

She caught her breath. Beneath the panicked roaring in her ears, some other emotion sang. The truth—uttered at this late stage—would not redeem her. And yet, as she opened her mouth, the pain in her stomach began to relent.

"No, my father *was* Finch," she said. "Jack's father was Reeve, the man who died in the carriage factory." She exhaled shakily. "Jack is my half brother."

Alan's expression grew cold and masklike. Did rage churn beneath?

"Christ," he swore.

She went rigid. His body seemed larger, the compartment too small for sudden movements. A punch directed at the shutter was liable to bring an elbow near her face.

She wouldn't flinch. She was already retracting into herself.

He saw it. A new light flared in his eyes, pure horror.

So slowly he seemed scarcely to move at all, he leaned forward. She watched his hand extend toward her, her mouth as dry as sand.

When his fingertips touched her wrist, the rigidity streamed from her. She went watery and weak. There was no defense against this tenderness.

"Jack didn't steal that inkstand." She sagged, looking down, watching his thumb slide into the tiny hollow above her wristbone.

She wished she hadn't said it, spoken as though the inkstand were the linchpin, and without it the whole case against him fell apart. Both of them exonerated of their falsity, their falsifying, by that one false accusation.

I'm sorry, she might have said instead, the apology as meaningless as the excuse.

She forced her head up. He'd slid to the edge of his seat, his knees a whisper from hers. Everything about his face was hard. Yet his thumb still stroked her skin, the pressure light.

She understood. It wasn't forgiveness, but a promise.

He wouldn't handle her roughly.

Paradoxically, she felt *more* breakable, or newly aware that she was already broken.

"How do you know he didn't steal it?" he asked, and his faint smile mocked her faith. That was what it was, after all, not knowledge, but faith. Jack had said he didn't do it, and she'd believed him.

She had no direct answer to give.

"My father left when I was four." She closed her eyes. "Went out for milk and never came back. I remember staring at the door, willing him to walk back through it. I can picture that door more clearly than I can picture his face. The door, and the drawing tacked up beside it, Jack's. Of Kipper, our cat."

She opened her eyes. Alan's face was still hard. But he turned her hand, and his hot thumb pressed into the dip of her palm.

"Our mother couldn't sit and wait." She cleared her throat. "We lived for a time with Mr. Farrar, then Mr. Nelson. Then there was . . ." She pressed her lips together. She wouldn't list the serial evictions, each brought on by the whim or waning interest of the next Mr. Such-and-Such.

Alan considered her, silent. The heat of his thumb in her palm was spreading through her body.

The contrast unbalanced her—his hard, cold, withdrawn watchfulness, and simultaneously, this point of contact, equally devastating.

It loosened her tongue.

"Jack is older," she continued. "By the time he was sixteen, he'd gone out on his own, and he was doing well for himself. He'd started studying at the Academy Schools. But he always called, wherever we were. He'd bring me pomegranates. His friends bought them by the crate, to put in their pictures. But no one ever ate them. Too much of a nuisance." Her chest was rising and falling, fast. She really was going to be sick.

"They weren't a nuisance to me." Her voice grated. "I loved to uncover the seeds. I shared them with Mr. Mucklow's parakeets."

"Of course you did," murmured Alan, and she saw what she'd thought she might never see again: a warm, amused light in his eyes.

"When our mother got sick . . ." Her throat had clogged but she pushed on. "When she died, Jack swore he'd keep me with him, and he did, even though it meant letting little rooms with bad light, missing his lessons and lectures. Falling out with all of those lily-sniffing friends." The lump in her throat had a sharp edge. "Not one of them stood up for him at the Royal Academy."

"*You* stand up for him." Alan's gaze became piercing. "And stand by him. A loyal sister." The muscles in his jaw leapt. "But at what cost?" His thumb skated over her palm, trapped the racing pulse at its base. "Why were you in Umfreville House?"

"To recover a letter Sleaford wrote to Jack." The truth emerged, unvarnished and instantaneous. "He mixed up the envelopes. If his grace had read the letter carefully, remembered who Jack was . . ."

"He might have guessed that Rembrandt van Rijn had nothing to do with the portrait of the woebegone old man that now glooms beside Fanny's shelf of Dresden medallions." Alan released her hand and sat back.

She curled her fingers and jammed her fist into her skirt.

"My brother has secrets of his own." Alan tilted his head. "He doesn't leave his correspondence lying about."

"It was in a drawer."

His lifted brow dared her to confirm his suspicion.

She wavered, only for a moment. "A locked drawer."

His glance traveled over her. "Reeve has you thieve for him."

"I learned to pick locks from a friend. Not for any purpose. More of a . . ." She bit the inside of her cheek. She couldn't explain the particulars of the education Ruby offered.

His slitted eyes prepared her for the question she'd been dreading. "Where is he?"

She barely breathed it. "You know I can't tell you."

"Can't? Or won't?" His mouth compressed, creating caves beneath his cheekbones. "What I *know* is that your brother has spent over a decade coercing your obedience. You *didn't* lie about wanting a life apart from him. The bakery. Your dream of gooseberry tarts."

"I didn't lie," she confirmed, his certainty giving her a flicker of directionless hope. "Not about that. Or the village, and my aunts' cottage, and the hill with the gooseberries."

"Reeve's jaunt to Pentonville." How gray his eyes looked, gray as iron bars. "It coincided with that prolonged visit to your aunts?"

She made no reply. He didn't need one. The set of his mouth became grimmer by the second.

"In fact, your brother *failed* to keep you with him. His choices led to your separation. He proved himself unfit as a guardian. When it became clear that you were safe and happy elsewhere, he should have kept away. Instead, he took you back and put you to work, in that emporium. He sent you on risky errands. Sent you to me, to snoop." His smile looked dangerous. "He should have sent you back to the countryside."

His gaze bored into her, bored through the dark and light rings she'd grown around her love for Jack, year by year, layers of solace and hurt, hope and fear.

"He should never have put you in this position. He should have used the money he plundered to establish you far from the orbit of his misdeeds. Instead, he makes you party to his crimes. That's harm, Nina. He has harmed you. And it's in your power to stop it, *now*."

Wildness rose in her.

"You don't know as much as you think you do." She was shaking, cold sweat breaking out on every inch of her skin. "His crimes *are* my crimes."

Here was the edge. She could scramble back. Nerves jumped in her skin and she flung forward. "Jack didn't paint the pictures you saw at Broughton's, or the ones Syme bought for the museum."

His face darkened, but his eyes, they looked strangely vulnerable, a profound bewilderment in their depths. And then his pupils flared.

She nodded. "I did."

CHAPTER TWENTY

When the coach rolled to a stop, he wondered if she would run, and if he'd try to chase her down, or simply let her go.

She didn't run. She walked with him into the house. He paused in the vestibule, where he'd *inspired* her with his lips, and his heart twisted. That sketch. Had he really thought that her emotion had spontaneously overflowed, swept along her untrained hand?

He'd ignored every sign that she wasn't what she seemed.

She looked at him with bottomless eyes, and turned. He followed her down the hall into the library, shut and locked the door behind him. She was already disappearing behind the settle.

Slowly, he crossed the room.

"I'll tidy up." She stared down at the stacks of books for far too long, avoiding his gaze. "I don't suppose I'm still your secretary."

"You were never my secretary." He studied her: navy dress, severe chignon. She appeared, at first glance, such an average specimen of English womanhood.

She was anything but.

He could tell she felt his eyes upon her. Her cheeks washed with pink.

"You were your brother's spy." He propped his cane, sat on the settle, and gestured to the empty cushion. "Sit."

She joined him, folding her hands on her lap. Capable-looking hands, the knuckles little divots at the bases of the sturdy fingers.

Capable. Christ. They were more than capable. *She* had twice the talent of Turner, yet she'd been confined to imitation and aspired to a career in cakes.

A dark laugh loosed from his throat, and she tensed, as she had in the coach. She anticipated a violent outburst. He sobered at once.

To hear her talk, rough-spoken Jack Reeve was a hero. That implied she'd endured even worse treatment from Mr. Mucklow, or Mr. Nelson, or one or several of the additional father surrogates who'd lurked in her ellipsis.

She was looking at him now without blinking, a wary line between her brows.

"This situation has its ironies," he said. "Kate Holroyd might initiate you into her Sisterhood. If you pledged to paint original work."

"I pledge never to paint again." She stared fixedly at the window. The sun had moved, and its beams had ceased to carry the colors of the panes into the room. "I hate painting, in fact."

"Because your brother ruined it for you. That's a crime in itself." What compositions might she have created if the right mentors had nurtured her artistic vision?

He sighed. "I doubt you'd hate painting if you'd studied with the Sisterhood."

"I could never have studied with them." She didn't shift her eyes. "I *am* a sister. I've been Jack's sister since the day I was born. That alone would have barred me from the Academy Schools."

"Your surnames obscure the relation. No one need ever have known."

"I should have hidden who I am, then? From everyone, forever? I'd have substituted one kind of fakery for another." Now *she* laughed, a harsh sound.

She pushed into the far corner of the settle and faced him. "I'm sorry for my lies. I do wish I hadn't lied to you. Or really, I wish I hadn't any cause to lie in the first place." She sighed—or scoffed— the expulsion of air seemed both fretful and sardonic. "I could wish so many things. It's a pointless exercise."

"It doesn't change the past, but that doesn't make it pointless." He shifted, knees slanting toward her. "Acts of imagination can help us change the future."

"The future." She echoed him in a hollow voice. He could guess what she imagined. The gray walls of Pentonville.

The pause stretched. She seemed to nerve herself for speech.

"I haven't the right to ask you for anything," she began.

"You haven't the right," he agreed, and gritted his teeth. She was a liar and a fraud. For Christ's sake, she'd stood at his side and let him explain Berney's techniques to her, let him describe her own bloody brushstrokes. She'd let him introduce her to that old Italian bloke, Botticelli. He'd never felt such a thoroughgoing fool.

Part of him wanted to rail. Part of him wanted to pull her into his arms. Their mouths had fit together like they'd been fashioned for each other.

Perhaps he was double the fool, but he couldn't believe it was false, the emotion in her eyes after they kissed, his sense of their bond.

"Ask," he said hoarsely. "Ask for what you want."

She released her breath. "I'd be grateful if you permitted Fritz to stay here."

"God above," he muttered. The favor she begged wasn't for herself but for her pestilential little monkey.

A bit of the bleakness left her face. "Mr. Kuznetsov will take care of him."

"He won't," Alan responded before he could think. "Fritz stays with you. Nina." He raked a hand through his hair. "I'm not turning you in to the police."

Her gaze flicked to his, and her throat moved but no words came out.

"I'm going to see your brother arrested, him and him alone."

Their gazes clung. Her eyes were widening, irises smokey dark.

"You're still afraid." He pressed her. "Will he implicate you?"

At that, she lifted her chin. "Never."

There was a fervent, prideful note in her voice. It raised his hackles.

"No, he wouldn't, would he?" He proceeded with a touch of cruelty. "He bullies you all day long, but God forbid anyone else does. That's *family* to men like him. A means of holding a monopoly on mistreatment. Honorable. Or maybe that's his version of loyalty?"

Her lower lip trembled. "I'm the one who forged the pictures you saw. I *imperiled* art itself. Isn't that what you said forgers do?" She smoothed her hands over her skirt. "But now you say you won't turn me in to the police." The look she gave him was sharp. "Why would *you* show such loyalty to *me*?"

He pressed his back into his corner of the settle. Because forgers in the abstract weren't *her*, the woman who invaded his dreams. Because he wasn't falling in love with *forgers*.

He cleared his throat. "Your crimes and your brother's are qualitatively different."

"I painted more of the pictures."

"The Berneys." He nodded. "Everything but the Jan Steen at South Kensington. Not the Rembrandt."

Obvious, in retrospect, that the forgeries hadn't all been painted by the same hand. He'd been too focused on the techniques used to age them, on evidence they came from the same workshop.

He rested an elbow on the settle's hook armrest. "I'm not concerned with the quantities. Who taught you how to paint? Or rather, how to *hate* to paint?"

She firmed her lips.

"Jack Reeve did," he answered for her. "And while you painted, he colluded with Chips Sleaford to find patrons for your pictures and fabricate provenances. Or was that your idea?"

"I agreed to it." Her eyes began to shine.

"When did it begin, your artistic training?"

"Right after he got out of Pentonville." She hugged herself miserably.

"Which made you what? All of thirteen? Is that when you agreed? As a child?"

She smiled a thin smile, its irony cutting inward. "Everyone has a story of woe. You think the jails aren't filled with men and women who were once children? Who grew up hungry and exploited, or worse? By your logic, no one should be imprisoned."

He stared. "You *want* me to turn you in."

"Or neither of us." She slumped. "It's your choice."

His breath sawed. She was looking down, and her lashes were moist. He had the strange notion that if he stroked them, his thumbs would smear their darkness across her cheeks.

"I knew what we were doing," she whispered. "I knew we could make more money on forgeries than anything else. I knew I'd never get a bakery selling combs, or dipping matches, or marrying a *bloke* who'd take what was mine, then take himself off."

"All right," he said, staring at her face, her downcast eyes. "You win. I'm not being logical. I don't bloody care. I'm not letting you go to Pentonville, not when I know where you belong."

With me.

God, the unconsidered phrase had almost slipped out.

"Nina's Sweets," he said.

She looked up at him then, with a bright, wondering expression, already darkening as she shook her head. "Impossible, regardless. My money's all gone, every farthing."

He held himself still. "Where did it go?"

"Jack put it into a different venture." She uncrossed her arms and pressed her knuckles to her satiny cheek.

He flexed, then curled his fingers. "This new venture of his. Is it as wholesome as baking?"

She slid her eyes away.

"I didn't think so. He'll continue on, in the same vein as before. Unless I put a stop to it."

Her spine stiffened. "I won't help you find him."

"Nina," he said softly. "I don't need your help. Scotland Yard will happily track him down."

"You'll be happy too." She closed her eyes. "What a fine feather for your cap."

He swore under his breath as a bolt of anger shot through him.

"I'm not happy," he growled. "I feel as though I've been turned inside out." His heart accelerated. "You have caught *me*, dammit, and it should be the other way round."

Her eyes opened. Her lips parted. A tiny noise emerged from her throat. And she leaned forward. She leaned forward just the barest fraction.

He slid to meet her, bracing his arms on the side of the settle, pinning her between them. He lowered his face inch by inch.

He didn't want to reason. He wanted to drown in her eyes.

Her breath eased out. "Your spectacles."

He'd forgotten to put them back on.

She licked her lips. "You don't need them, do you?"

"No." He could feel the heat of her skin, smell its scent, honey-suckle and rose. Her pupils had expanded.

"The frames are fitted with plain glass," he said. "I started wear-ing them at Oxford."

"A disguise." She tilted up her chin, which brought her mouth achingly near to his own. "Lord Death, with spectacles to symbol-ize wisdom, and a cane instead of a scythe."

The hush that descended felt enormous. It pushed him back from her. He lowered his arms, sliding away on the bench.

"What are you hiding from?" Her voice was very low, and she paled as she searched his face, hesitant but determined. "You know who I am."

He could hear her unspoken question hang in the deafening si-lence.

Who are you?

Holy God. He could barely breathe, lungs flattening. What she searched for in him—the self he hid from the world—offered noth-ing but annihilating darkness. The honey that seemed to well within him whenever they drew close—that was *her* sweetness. He drained it from her. If he got *too* close, he would leave her dry and bitter and lost. He was triple the fool, because he was still imagin-ing it, imagining that he might lay himself bare. The two of them unmasked. Naked souls.

His hip was a ball of fire. His heart was a ball of fire.

"Alan." His name hitched in her chest. He watched, as though in a dream, as she came forward and laid her hand to his jaw, still stinging slightly from the blade. "I don't deserve your trust, but—"

He fell on her, burying his hands in the silk of her hair, captur-ing her lips, groaning at the swipe of her tongue inside his mouth. He bent her back over his arm, nuzzling her throat, returning—desperate—to her mouth. The rhythmic give-and-take of their tongues worked him to a frenzy. He dragged her onto his lap, wad-ding her skirt. Her knees clamped around his thighs. A few but-tons, a cloth flap, a scrap of lace—the flimsiest obstacles prevented him from burying himself inside her.

He was burning up, the pain and the pleasure merged in his groin, a monstrous desire.

He broke their kiss with a gasp. "This." Frustration flared his nostrils. "*No.*"

Her eyes found his. "What, then?"

He pulled her into his chest, his chin on her shoulder, fingers playing in the fine hair at her nape. He stared at the window, at the colored enamel design—the cypress trees, their dark green going darker as the last of the daylight faded.

Naked souls. It was far too late for that. They could hurt each other straining toward some beautiful potential that could never be realized, or they could help each other within the wicked limits of life as it was.

The idea had been writhing, half-formed, in the darkest corner of his mind.

She provided the missing piece.

"We will strike an agreement," he said, relaxing his arms, letting her lean back.

Her lips were swollen in her pallid face, her eyes wide.

"I won't give up my brother," she whispered. "I told you I—"

"Hear me out," he interrupted. "I don't expect you to give him up. The action required has to do with *my* brother, not yours."

NINA HEARD ALAN out. When he'd finished, she stood and paced to the window, staring blankly at one tiny piece of painted glass. When she turned to face him, all she could do was repeat his words.

"You'd give me what I need to buy the bakery." She pressed a finger to her lips. They felt shockingly tender, bruised from the pressure of his mouth.

He was slouched in his corner of the settle, watching her.

"I'll give you whatever you're asked to pay in cash. I'll provide equipment, too, and inventory." He gave her a strangely poignant smile.

"And I'll give you . . . letters. Letters I steal from the duke's study." Her legs didn't feel entirely solid beneath her.

He knew the truth. He hadn't lashed out. He'd unleashed his

desire, not his rage, and she'd met his wild kisses with her own. Until he'd ripped himself away. She hadn't *caught* him. He'd broken the kiss, broken free of the magnetism that pulled them together. As should she.

He didn't condemn her. But he did condemn Jack. Her stomach kicked.

"May it be the last time you pick a lock." Alan's voice was light, but his smile twisted his mouth. He was fully aware that he'd introduced another irony into the situation. He sent her on an errand to Umfreville House that mirrored her first.

"Why are these letters so valuable?" Her voice sounded frayed.

"They were penned, and perfumed, by Lady Kilderbee." He stretched out his long legs, careful to avoid the stacked books. "You met her, in passing."

She nodded. The uncommonly pretty woman from the patisserie.

"And Lord Kilderbee," she said, recalling her fulsome husband.

"Indeed." He raised a brow. "My brother's staunchest ally in Parliament. Terrible shame if long-standing cuckoldry came between them."

She approached the settle. "How do you know about these letters? And where they are?"

"I've rifled through every drawer in that house." His gaze wandered away from her. "I was in residence the year before last. Geoffrey left his keys in plain view. He must have been distracted, packing in a white heat. He was rushing Claud to the Adriatic—an advantageous choice, for Geoffrey, given his political hobbyhorses. He spent those months abroad courting Italian foreign ministers." He sneered. "I wasn't looking for his personal papers. I was looking for . . ." His face slammed shut. "I was looking for something else."

"What?" She wished she hadn't asked.

He wasn't going to let her in.

As she expected, he ignored her question. "It's just as well I found Lady Kilderbee's billets-doux instead." He folded his arms. "Once those letters are in my possession, Geoffrey is in my power."

"Blackmail." She mouthed it gingerly, an ugly word.

"A last resort." His eyes narrowed. "I'd have continued to play

Geoffrey's ridiculous game on his terms, if the stakes were purely financial." Muscles tightened in his jaw. "But he risks my nephew's life."

"The coughing fits." Ice formed in Nina's chest. "They've taken a turn for the worse?"

Now Alan's eyes were slits. "The coughing fits provide my brother with a pretext. They justify his shipping Claud to Italy, along with his wife."

"He's sending them to Italy," repeated Nina, and Alan's expression became vacant.

"Pistoia," he said, his voice hollow. "Because his *marriage* has taken a turn for the worse."

Nina's throat felt dry. Perhaps the duke acted for the wrong reasons. But even so . . .

"Won't Italy do your nephew good? All the blue sky and pure air."

Stark lines carved down around Alan's lips. "In my experience, the ills of exile outweigh the benefits of the particular environment."

The hairs stood up on her arms. He'd gone too rigid, as though braced beneath an unendurable weight.

"*Your* experience." She took a breath. He'd mentioned its outline—the journey from country to country, chasing a cure he didn't need—but he hadn't filled in the details. Looking at him, the ice kept spreading from her chest, crackling through her veins. How bad had it been?

"I don't understand, of course, what it was like," she began.

"No point in trying," he interrupted, so coldly the icy feeling spiked all the way to her fingertips. "It defies understanding."

She began again, the memory of Claud's hectic eyes spurring her on. "You weren't consumptive, though. And Claud . . ." This time she stopped herself, as color leached from his face.

"Claud *is* consumptive?" His gaze was as cold as his voice. "I've heard no affirmation from Dr. Thayer, and if I did, I doubt I'd find it convincing. West End physicians are biddable creatures. They diagnose in response to social cues as much as science. *I* will decide the best course for Claud. He's not going to Italy, to *Pistoia* of all places."

She stepped forward, the impulse to soothe materializing with no sure path to travel. She returned to her cushion on the settle. He followed her with his eyes. She opened her mouth, but he shook his head, dismissing the subject.

"It's love," he said, and her heart flipped, even though his tone was scathing.

"According to Geoffrey," he continued. "A great love that he shares with Patricia, Lady Kilderbee. Our fathers were friends, with neighboring country houses. Both spendthrifts. Geoff and Patricia would meet in the beechwood and bemoan their fates. Geoff poured out the whole story to me after our father's funeral. The straitened young duke required an heiress. But the equally impoverished Patricia was his very soul."

"That's the reason you gave over those investments." She could hardly believe it. "Because he told you he was in love?"

"I enjoy theater." His lips curled. "Romantic drama in particular, and the stormier the better. I felt compelled to introduce another plot point. And frankly, I preferred the normality of the new arrangement—my elder brother, the duke, disbursing funds as a duty. Rather than a fortune I'd earned selling properties that *pity* conferred upon me."

Sitting there, chest broad, folded arms swelled with muscle, teeth bared, he looked not like a man to be pitied, but a man to be feared. She felt a frisson of excitement, chased by disquiet.

"They decided not to marry, though," she said. "Each other, I mean."

He gave a one-shouldered shrug. "Love matches aren't the aristocratic way. Neither are business enterprises. I couldn't guarantee my investments would yield as much as they did. And regardless, the dukedom's debts were considerable. Geoff would have needed to reduce expenditures. He made his choice as a duke, not a man." His lips tipped into a contemptuous smirk.

"You mean he chose to make himself miserable."

"And he makes others miserable, which concerns me more." His eyes had turned stone gray. He focused those eyes on her. The force of his gaze pressed the air from her lungs.

"Do we have an agreement, then?" He extended his hand. "I won't ask any more questions about your brother." He paused, considering. "Or about your friends at the knickknack emporium. You'll stay here until we've completed our exchange. And you won't attempt to contact Reeve."

Her heart pounded in her ears. Was she selling out her brother to buy her own freedom? She'd thought, perhaps, a letter to Hensthorpe, dropped in the pillar box, to apprise Jack of the situation, to *explain*. He might be expecting her . . . waiting for her.

She could refuse Alan's bargain, but refusing would do Jack no good. And she'd lose all. She was shaking as she nodded, as she took Alan's hand. His fingers tightened around hers.

They looked at each other. It was a twisted agreement, odd, awkward, and morally gray. They were allies *and* enemies. And hell's bells, she wanted nothing more than to crawl back into his lap. "I don't know how I'll get anywhere near those letters." She withdrew her hand. "I doubt the duke will rehire me. If that was your plan."

"Oh no," said Alan, and the quirk of his lips became a very crooked smile. "You are going to enter Umfreville House on my arm, when we attend the duchess's ball."

CHAPTER TWENTY-ONE

THE NEXT SEVERAL days flurried with activity. The first notable outing was to a lovely Georgian home, redbrick with crimson window arches. After Casa De'Ath, the interior struck Nina as pointedly conventional in its elegance: rich wood paneling and white plasterwork, vase after vase of gardenias. Alan nodded to the butler and led the way to the back garden himself, where he intercepted the owner of the house, shoveling in the shrubberies.

He and Neal Traymayne were on the most familiar terms, and that familiarity extended instantly to her.

"You're Nina." Neal addressed her with such obvious delight, she wondered what Alan had communicated by letter—or hadn't. "Did you work this transformation?" He squinted at Alan, barbered and crisply tailored, then grinned and swung his shovel over his shoulder. "This way."

He whistled as they passed between the purple lilac and the yellow laburnum into the wild heart of the garden, the most spectacular garden Nina had ever seen. It was small but so varied and seemingly haphazard that it gave the impression of immense, untrammeled space. Dandelions grew in sunny profusion. Only the rose-swathed trellis showed signs of the impeccable manicuring the whole must have required. The woman writing beneath the trellis at a wrought-iron table was impeccably manicured herself, from her blond coiffure to the pointed toes of her ribboned boots. That was

Neal's wife, Lavinia, who'd agreed to ready Nina for the Duchess of Umfreville's ball.

After Neal made their introduction, Lavinia rose, took Nina's arm, and marched her out from under the trellis into the early-afternoon sun. She stepped back, and to the right, and to the left, sizing Nina up.

She sighed. "It won't be easy."

With that sigh, Nina felt her own lungs deflate.

Lavinia crossed her arms. "I'd hoped *something* of mine might do. Unfortunately, you and I differ point for point."

Nina's smile curdled on her lips. All of Lavinia's points corresponded to ideals of delicate, feminine beauty.

"If we let out my Worth with the gold brocade, added *panels*," Lavinia spoke as though to herself, in a musing tone. "No. No, you'd look like a Bergère chair."

Nina wondered how to put an end to this particular humiliation. Tell Lavinia "Bergère chair" was just the thing?

"We need a gown designed especially for your figure. A *very* low neck. Rich color." Lavinia began to circle around her. "We're going for full-blown rose. You'll *devastate*."

Nina blinked. Now she had a touch of vertigo.

"The challenge is *time*." Lavinia stopped short. "Three days isn't enough for Miss Stirling. She's the only dressmaker I'd trust, and she's in the highest demand. I'll have to ask her as a personal favor. The sooner the better. *Although*—" Her voice dropped and she leaned forward, putting her lips to Nina's ear. "The way he's staring at you now, the gown I envision might stop his heart. I'd hate to bring about the early demise of my husband's dearest friend."

Nina twitched her glance toward the trellis. Neal and Alan stood near the little table, locked in conversation. And yet . . .

Alan's eyes were fixed upon her.

"It's a risk we'll have to take." Lavinia lifted her hand, wiggling her fingers in farewell.

"Goodbye, darlings," she called, and lowered her voice again. "I'm desperate for the story. You'll tell me *everything* in the carriage."

In the carriage, Lavinia accepted disappointment reluctantly. "You're sure you're not engaged?"

"Quite sure."

"Not engaged *yet*," suggested Lavinia. "You met at Umfreville House, you said. Where you worked as a *maid*." Her lashes fluttered as she sighed. "That's absolutely marvelous. I adore a mésalliance. Was it love at first sight?"

He didn't see me at all. He saw a fake Rembrandt.

Nina smiled weakly.

"You'll tell me someday," Lavinia assured her. The fashion house was a whirring, parti-colored blur. In the cheerful blue-and-gold-papered fitting room, two focused young women helped Nina strip and then set about encircling her body parts with their tapes. At some point in the process, Miss Stirling herself appeared, stern and lynx-eyed and disinclined to accommodate last-minute whims. But it wasn't long before Lavinia's high-spirited, appreciative chatter had her shaking her head in fond exasperation, agreeing that, yes, Nina did resemble—in coloring and figure—the opera singer Eliza Gerard, whom she'd always costumed so beautifully. By the time they departed, a half dozen seamstresses were gathered around Miss Stirling, preparing to rush Nina's evening gown into production. And Nina had discovered—via one of those seamstresses— that Lavinia was *the* Lavinia, Lavinia Laliberté, author of *The Bluebell*. Ruby had read chapters of *The Bluebell* aloud to her, with uncharacteristic sighs and giggles. It followed the fantastically thrilling piratical exploits of a runaway duchess.

"Are you working on a new novel?" she asked, as they settled back into the carriage.

"A romance of the civil wars." Lavinia gave her a secretive smile. "Can I put you in it?"

"I think I'd rather stay out of it," said Nina. "If you don't mind."

For a moment, Lavinia looked crestfallen, then she brightened. "It's all right. Your real-life romance will be nearly as exciting. Now, what are we going to do about your hair?"

Talk of tiaras and curled fringes carried them back to Bennet Street, where they joined Neal and Alan for lunch in the garden, a leisurely, comfortable meal that reminded Nina of lunches with her aunts in the garden in Hensthorpe.

No chickens underfoot, though. And in Hensthorpe, she didn't feel a constant tug, her whole body attuned to someone else's, his every movement, every glance.

After lunch, she accompanied Alan to painters' studios, to the theater, and to dinner. No matter the venue, Alan's eyes sought hers, even as he laughed, made notes, bantered with friends and acquaintances. He found moments to whisper in her ear, rapid précis of the people around them, observations, questions. What did *she* think about this picture, that poem, her bouillabaisse, the play, her wine? Maybe he kept her with him because he didn't trust her. He thought she'd break her word, post a letter to Jack, flee herself. But it didn't feel punitive. It felt as though a flame flickered between their bodies, attracting them both like moths.

When they finally returned to Casa De'Ath, she was half-asleep, half-drunk, dizzied by the night. In the vestibule, she bumped into him, and he steadied her with a firm hand. And then he stepped back. He walked on. He wouldn't kiss her again.

The next day, Nina spent the morning in the kitchen, baking ratafias for trifle. When she went upstairs to bring Mr. Kuznetsov a hot biscuit, crisp and almond scented, she glimpsed two visitors trooping out the door, respectably dressed men of middle age, neither with the flair that typified Alan's Chelsea set. Alan appeared a moment later, took Fritz from Mr. Kuznetsov, and whisked her into his waiting coach. They made a brief call to the office of a publishing firm, then a longer stop in a gallery, followed by lunch with literary personalities who traded brilliancies and only picked at the curry and rice.

"And?" Alan asked as the coach began again to roll. He sat across from her, Fritz in his waistcoat.

Nina wrinkled her nose. "I liked the curry more than the conversation."

"An unfair comparison. Curry and conversation should be evaluated independently."

"The curry was perfect. The conversation was overseasoned."

He gave her an owlish look, which wanted spectacles for maximal effect. But since she'd asked about them, he hadn't returned his customary pair to his nose.

"Finley is an excellent playwright," he said. "I think you'd like his latest. It's a farce. I'd invite you, but it doesn't open until mid-summer."

"Oh." She sounded disappointed to her own ears.

"You'll be in your village by then." Alan rolled a shoulder. He'd swapped his frock coat for a morning coat that hugged his broad shoulders. "Baking tarts."

"Not to the exclusion of all else," she responded automatically, and blushed. He'd think she was angling for that invitation.

His eyes had begun to glitter. "Bakers work long hours."

She frowned. Was he going to explain baking to her? Like Jack had tried to do? *Baking is hot, hard work. Have you thought of that?* Why, yes, she had. She'd thought of everything.

"I'm going to buy Mr. Craddock's bakery," she said. "It's old and small. The parish has a newer, bigger bakery, and everyone in the village buys bread and biscuits there. Mr. Craddock sells buns and rolls and cakes, nicer things in small quantities. I'm going to specialize even more. Uncommon sweets for important occasions."

"A cake shaped like a dragon for St. George's Day?" He laughed. "Dear God, you baked Rouget the *Bastille*." He shook his head admiringly. "I imagine, with your combination of skills, you could sculpt Michelangelo's *David* out of marzipan."

"Probably." She was blushing more fiercely now. She didn't have to lie anymore, and a tremulous joy trickled out from her heart. "I'll bake uncommon sweets for everyday occasions too. Those I'll have ready, for anyone who comes in. And I'll make pastries to order, for all the squires. And the Cricket Club. And the Beowulf Society."

She worried her bottom lip with her teeth. She'd guessed at frequency and size of orders, totted up prices, subtracted costs.

"I'll work long hours," she said. "But I'll decide when and how many." She hesitated, trying to smooth the doubting lilt from her voice. "And if people like what I bake, they'll be willing to pay a little more for it."

"They will." The brightness in his eyes seemed to fill her with light.

He crossed his legs. His trousers were different too, not his usual style. They were gray and fit him snugly. "Where *is* your village? How far from London?"

"Middling far." Her core went cold, sucking the blush from her cheeks. She dug her shoulder blades into the soft leather of the seat.

"You've never told me the name."

Her heart stood still. And started again at a chirp.

Alan looked down, adjusted the lapels of his coat, and stroked between Fritz's ears.

"Jack found him," she said softly, and Alan looked up, his expression neutral. Did he wonder at the change of topic?

"In a menagerie," she continued. "Half-frozen, pecked at by peacocks. We nursed him back to health together."

"You're a brave little chap." Alan scratched Fritz's head.

"So," he said, after the pause had drawn out. "Jack is a *parfait gentil* knight." His voice was wry.

"He can be." Nina's heart had stopped sending out those little ripples of joy. "He saved Fritz from the jaws of death. Not only Fritz. Kittens. Once, near the village, he even rescued a baby hedgehog. We took her with us to London. She slept in my chest of drawers and lived to a ripe old age."

"This hedgehog . . ."

"Nettie," she supplied.

"Nettie." Alan sounded increasingly skeptical. "Was she wounded as well? Pecked by feral peafowl?"

"Not wounded. Abandoned."

"Ah." His eyes probed hers. "How did he know? Her mother might have been out hunting. Or it might have been time for her to leave the nest."

"What are you after?" She stared at him.

"I'm only trying to ascertain the facts."

"I told you the facts."

His ironic look wasn't without sympathy, which made it worse. "You told me your brother rescued a baby hedgehog. And yet you can't be sure that she needed rescuing."

"You think he just *snatched* her, for no reason." She wasn't cold any longer. The heat gathering inside her was the sort that collected around a bee's stinger, a smarting, poisonous fire.

"Probably not for no reason."

"Why then?"

Alan held her gaze until hers wavered and dropped. A dreadful realization choked her.

She knew why.

"We'd been fighting." The words grated in her throat. "He'd said we had to go back to London a day early, and I was miserable. We went to sketch in open air, and I dropped my sketchbook in a puddle and ruined it—on purpose, he said. I told him it was an accident, and when I knelt down to pick it up, he bumped me, and I fell into the puddle."

The memory came back with the surprising force of that blow. She glanced up. Alan was considering her, brows level, face grave.

"He said that was an accident too. I threw mud in his face. He stormed off, and I hid in Mr. Middleton's barn, to teach him a lesson. But I was too cold and hungry to last long. When I heard him calling, I came out. He had Nettie bundled in his coat. And the fight was over." She shut her eyes briefly in case Alan's face registered his triumph. When she opened them, she saw that his expression hadn't changed. "We wore gardening gloves to touch her and wrapped her in old shawls with a hot-water bottle. The children on the train tried to feed her their hard-boiled eggs. We laughed the whole way home."

Her mouth tilted up at the corners. Alan's didn't.

"It turned out all right," she said. He looked as though he meant to object.

"For Nettie," she added.

Alan rubbed his forehead and sighed. "He's there now, in the village."

Her whole body jerked.

"That's why you won't tell me the name."

"I can't . . ." She sucked in a breath.

"Don't." He shook his head. "It wasn't a question. I promised I wouldn't ask you."

A lump rose in her throat. Alan cracked the happy memories she'd enshrined in amber, threatening the foundation of her world. But he held himself back when he could push his advantage and gain ground. He respected the boundaries they'd established. She was safe with him.

"Jack—he's probably gone already." *Dammit.* The lump kept rising. She sounded hoarse. "If he's still with our aunts, it's because he's waiting for some word from me, waiting to hear whether or not I mean to join him. He should go, of course. He shouldn't wait." She balled her fingers, drilling her knuckles into her thighs. "You're not the only one searching for him, and the others aren't so mannerly. He owes some Whitechapel roughs some money." She felt sick, saying it. Men who ran protection rackets and smashed up businesses would think nothing of smashing up Jack.

Where would he go? North, maybe. To fleece those industrialists. She might never see him again. He'd have left her at last. She realized her eyes were closed when Alan spoke.

"Nina."

It took effort to force her lids apart. He was staring at her, no, *reading* her, the volumes of turmoil in her face.

"I'll be the one who finds him." His square jaw hardened. His smile looked like it could cut. "And he'll receive fair treatment, under the law." Slowly, he slid across the compartment, folding his large body into the space beside her on the seat.

"I'd like to throttle him myself." He said it philosophically. "But it wouldn't undo what he's done."

"The forgeries," she began, not knowing where she was going.

"I don't mean his forgeries. I mean his manipulation, or carelessness, or both. His filling your life with people to fear. The police. Whitechapel *roughs.*"

She glanced up at his profile. The set of his mouth was murderous.

"Himself," he said, more darkly.

"And if it *could* be undone?" She fixed her eyes straight ahead. "If I really could wish everything different, I don't think I'd do it. Not because I'm deceived. I do see the bad. Piles of bad. Heaps." She gave a raspy laugh. "The good is still there. Jack also filled my life with people to love. And non-people." She reached out to touch Fritz's head, but laid her hand instead on Alan's side and felt his muscles clench beneath his coat. She pulled back.

"Without Jack, I wouldn't be who I am." She licked her lips. How exposed she felt, and foolish. So, this was honesty. "I can't cut him out."

He angled her a look, shaded by his soot-black lashes.

"You're Nina Finch," he murmured. "You can do anything." He wrapped his arm around her.

She froze, then she melted into his solid warmth. His scent flooded her, Brown Windsor soap and that dark, delicious, nameless spice.

Chirp.

She let her gaze travel down. Fritz stared up at her, half-levered out of Alan's waistcoat, eyes wide and mischievous. He stuck out his tongue, ear tufts vibrating.

She blinked back sudden tears and stuck out her tongue in return.

Alan stretched out his legs and leaned back, so Nina could settle her head more comfortably on his shoulder.

Much later, after a visit to a watercolor exhibition, a hot, surprisingly enthralling hour in a lecture hall, another dinner in a subterranean restaurant, and a quartet concert, Nina found herself back at Casa De'Ath, standing with Alan at the foot of the front staircase.

She was as breathless as if she'd run up those stairs three times over. She'd fallen into step with him and hadn't thought of splitting off toward her own room.

Now, she was lingering. *They* were lingering, turning toward each other.

"Nina," he said, and in the pause that followed she had time to imagine too many things. She couldn't think at all, could only stare up into his face.

"Here." He reached into his waistcoat. Fritz stirred and sprang into her arms.

She lowered her burning cheek to stroke his fur and heard a murmur so deep and low she could only assume it was *good night*. And a moment after, she heard the sound of Alan's slow steps as he ascended the stairs.

CHAPTER TWENTY-TWO

NINA AWOKE WITH a gasp. A wave of pleasure was rolling through her. The covers bunched between her legs; her arms cinched the pillow. She sat up, pushed away the hair plastered to her sweaty cheeks. Her rapid breathing had dried her throat. The room was pitch-black and too warm.

Water. She scrambled out of bed and banged into a chair. She clutched at the handle of the wickerwork basket before it sailed off the chair into the washstand. Nested inside, Fritz gave an admonishing cry.

"Go back to sleep," she whispered. "It's the middle of the night." Was it? Or was it the earliest hour of the morning? She'd lost all sense of time. She lit a candle and shadows swarmed. The walls seemed unbearably close, furniture squeezing together.

Air. Air first. She went to the tall window, pulled the silk curtain cord, and yanked up the sash. Welcome coolness seeped around her. She rested her forehead on a pane of glass.

She registered Fritz's presence, his quiet leap onto the sill, but her sluggish body reacted too slowly, even as he pressed into her waist, gathering himself. Even as her brain anticipated his next move.

"Don't—"

But he'd already hurtled into the darkness.

"Blast!" She canted forward, jamming her whole upper body

through the window, thrusting her arms down into the prickly landscaping. Where had he gone? She craned her neck to squint up at the house's brick façade, mantled heavily with ivy. That ivy was rustling.

"*Fritz.* Don't move another inch." He was climbing for the balcony above.

She retracted herself, wiggling her shoulders and knocking her head on the sash. She spun, seized the candleholder, and raced from the room.

Once she'd climbed the tightly spiraled servants' stair, she stopped to catch her breath, candleholder shaking so violently in her hand the long hallway seemed to flicker. That door there, by its location, opened onto the room possessed of the relevant balcony.

She tiptoed to the door. She should have put on stockings, shoes. The room—it might be a guest bedchamber. It might be . . .

The door swung open.

Alan stood framed in the doorway, in a spill of golden light. She'd swum in that banyan he was wearing, pale blue silk patterned with vines. His broad shoulders spread the simple robe to capacity. She could see a wedge of bronzed chest between its front folds, the dusky channel that divided his pectoral muscles. The hem hit well above his knee. He wore trousers, darker blue, loose. They looked soft, curving with the hard muscle of his thighs.

She swallowed. Just now, in dreams, his lips had played over hers, until her blood had thickened and flowed through her veins with the sweet lassitude of syrup.

The left corner of those lips tipped up in a crooked smile.

"Your monkey, madam." He held Fritz in the curl of an arm. "Again."

She swayed. Heaven help her. Her bones were also syrup.

Gently, he lifted her hair over her shoulder, smoothing it down her back. He set Fritz on his preferred perch, the slope of her neck.

"I'm sorry we woke you."

"I wasn't asleep. I was reading." His pale, black-rimmed eyes narrowed. "It's the middle of the night."

"Is it?" She cleared her throat, so dry it tickled. "I wasn't sure."

"You should be in bed."

Of their own volition, her eyes swerved around him. From where she stood, the foot of his bed was visible, two posts of a dark four-poster.

Fritz chose that moment to launch from her shoulder to Alan's, a light, brief landing. His next bound carried him into the bed-chamber.

"Bugger. Drat it. Pardon."

Alan stepped aside to let her hurry after.

"It was a dull book anyway." His voice followed her.

Low-burning lamps and the coals in the fireplace gave the room its golden glow, along with the gold-framed pictures hanging on the burgundy walls. She averted her eyes from the bed, looked instead at the mahogany wardrobe, the large, worn armchair. Behind the armchair, glass-fronted bookcases rose as high as the wainscoting. Fritz posed among the statuettes and vases arranged on top.

She put the candleholder on a low table and changed course, darting to the French doors. As she shut them, she heard another click. When she turned, her heart hammered her ribs.

Alan was walking toward her with a slow, deliberate tread. No cane. His steps were ever-so-slightly uneven.

"What are we going to do?" he asked.

Her heart skipped a beat, and her courage failed. "About Fritz?"

He shook his head, eyes bright. "About *this*."

This. No.

She took a breath. "Nothing. You don't dally with employees."

He kept walking toward her. "We've established that you're not my employee."

"You don't dally with forgers, either. You seemed to remember that the other day. When I . . ." She flushed. "And then you . . ."

She had leaned toward him on the settle, and, in the end, it was he who had pulled away.

"I didn't stop kissing you because you're a forger." He stilled, a yard away.

"That's why *I* should have stopped." Her gaze slid to the notch at the base of his throat. "It's too confusing. You've forgiven me— or it seems you've forgiven me—by making the blame Jack's. But the blame is also mine."

"I do forgive you." His pulse flickered, hypnotic. "And you *are* your own person, accountable for your actions."

"But you don't hold me accountable."

"You hold yourself accountable. That's enough for me."

"I know what you'll say." She dropped her gaze to the carpet. "Jack doesn't do the same. He deserves what he gets. But I feel like a bloody traitor, enjoying your company, when you're trying to hurt him."

His bare feet entered her field of vision.

"I didn't think I was lonely before," she whispered. "But when I'm with you . . ." She gulped for air. "I feel as though there's more of me."

She slid her foot between his feet. His feet were much larger than hers, more finely shaped.

"You have nice toes," she said.

"Nina."

She didn't look up. "Why *did* you stop kissing me? Miss Holroyd said you've kissed a lot of people."

"I have."

"So, it doesn't affect you that much, one way or the other?"

"You affect me," he growled. "And I want to do more than kiss you."

She raised her head and almost quailed. His expression was fierce, wolfish with hunger.

She felt a flutter, deep and low, that made her clench her thighs. She swallowed. "You want a tumble?"

A strangled sound emerged from his throat. Her crass language amused him. And aroused him. She could sense it. The atmosphere in the room thickened by the second.

"You stopped," she continued, faltering, "because you could tell I . . ."

He looked perplexed. But wasn't that it? He'd understood what her inexperienced kisses implied. He'd decided to protect her virtue.

"You could tell that I haven't . . ." She was hot with embarrassment.

"You haven't? No. Lord." He stepped back. "I assumed the opposite."

She must look like a beet. She felt her cheeks turn screaming red.

What she'd lacked in experience, she'd made up for in wantonness. Of course it wouldn't have struck him as virginal, her straddling his hips in a park.

"I shouldn't have assumed anything." He was wincing. "Do you want a drink? I want a drink." He strode from her and returned with two glasses.

She wet her mouth with the brandy gratefully.

"Nina," he said, on a breath. "I can't give you what you need."

She lowered her glass and stared.

"Do you think I expect you to marry me?" She gulped the rest of the brandy and handed back the glass. "I've never had the slightest interest in marriage. I saw my mother. And I see my aunts. I'm not marrying anyone."

Her eyes latched again to his throat, the pulse beating there like wings.

"But you should marry someone," he said. "For love. A wholesome village lad, with a soul as pure as a dewdrop. Someone as truehearted as you are."

"Truehearted?" Her chest cramped. "I've built my life on lies."

"Nina."

Slowly, she raised her face. He stared down at her, bright gaze transfixing.

"When I look into your eyes," he said, "I see all the way inside you. And the beauty there is enough to bring me to my knees."

She wasn't breathing. A spiraling sensation threatened her balance. She'd felt this before, with him, as though they were both about to topple.

"When you look into my eyes," he said, gaze darkening, "you try to see all the way inside me. But there is nothing inside me. No beauty."

He swallowed his brandy and set both glasses on the table. "You should keep your distance." He was warning her, or begging her, or both. He stepped toward her. "Because I can't seem to do it myself."

They were chest to chest. With each quickening breath, her breasts brushed the slippery silk of the banyan.

Her voice trembled. "Do you want me to go?"

"No." The dim light gilded the high planes of his face and left the rest in shadow. "But you should."

"I should," she agreed uncertainly. She didn't feel certain of anything, not even the floor beneath her feet. "I'm tired." Tired, yes. Dizzy. Spiraling, up or down, she couldn't tell.

Her gaze slid to the side, to his bed. "We could sleep." She licked the traces of brandy from her lips and met his eyes, their frightening intensity. "I could stay here, with you, just to sleep."

He released her. The angles of his jaw sharpened to knife points.

"I've never slept beside anyone." He said it roughly. "Not by choice, not in my life."

Her brows pulled together. "But your . . . the other women you kiss?"

He shook his head. Her eyes moved over his tense face, scored suddenly with anguished lines.

"I want to stay with you," she breathed and reached up, touched the sharp edge of his jaw. The skin was hot, cat's-tongue rough with stubble. He sucked in an audible breath. And then she watched him turn to marble, gaze dull and remote, face drained of life and color. She withdrew her hand. She waited for three excruciating heartbeats, and then she made herself turn. She was halfway to the door when he caught her wrist and spun her back around.

He wasn't marble now. His eyes were blazing. One hard arm came under her, and she was off her feet, cradled high against his chest.

He took three strides to the bed.

A TRILL PIERCED the hush and brought Alan halfway back to consciousness. Everything around him felt soft and warm, tender as cake. Everything within him too. He didn't want to move or think. He wanted to exist in this state forever.

Where was he?

In bed. With Nina. His arm draped her waist.

The trilling continued, rising in pitch, then ceased.

"Tell me that was the nightingale," he murmured, eyes closed, "and not the lark, the herald of the morn."

"It was Fritz." She made a sleepy movement, which pressed her bottom into his groin. He almost groaned. Now he was fully awake. And slightly less content.

He wanted more.

He opened his eyes. Her hair streamed across the pillow. He could turn his face and tickle his nose with it. Instead, he inhaled, rose and honeysuckle, mixed with something citrusy, lemon verbena.

"I didn't have any dreams," she said, a scratch in her voice. "Did you?"

"No." He raised his knees, dragging her into the defined space he created between his chest and his thighs, clamping her there, his chin coming down to rest on the silky crown of her head.

God, she was so soft, nestled against him. The morning light seeped softly through the window. The world was softness, with a glow like a pearl.

Fritz stopped trilling. The hush resumed.

"Sometimes dreams are just a feeling, though." She shifted against him. "You're scared, or you're happy. I might have had one of those."

"How did you feel?" He closed his eyes again.

"Happy." It was a sigh.

He felt her inhale.

"Alan," she whispered, "is this really the first time you've slept beside someone?"

"Yes," he said, throat constricting as he waited for her to ask him why.

"Was it as bad as you feared?"

He opened his eyes. "I never said I was afraid. I prefer to sleep alone." He was squeezing her more tightly as he spoke.

"When I was young," he finally began, and hesitated. "Nurses tied me to the bed."

He measured time by Nina's breaths. When she didn't speak, he understood that she was making time, all the time he needed to say what he would say.

"Those are my earliest memories." He lowered his face, so his lips touched her hair, its faint, sweet scent stronger than the ghostly odor that clung to the memories themselves. Boiled linen. Rancid linseed. His mother's heavy powder.

"The poultices they'd put on my chest were too hot, like wet fire. I'd flail but it tightened the knots. My mother would remove them, untie me. She was my savior. I'd cry if she left the room for an instant. That's how it all started, with my unnatural attachment."

Nina twitched, and he forced himself to continue.

"By the time I was five, she was spending every day at my side, and some nights too. My father didn't try to stop it. He was always affable, with her, with me. He had his own obsessions . . . horses, parties, other women. He liked chess. He liked playing with me because he could win. Until he couldn't." Chess made sense. Sixty-four squares, thirty-two pieces, the movements of which were clearly defined.

"My mother—" He hesitated again. No squares here to guide him. To speak was to descend into disorder. "My mother would lie in my bed for hours. She'd sob and sob and bend my neck until I thought it would snap. Her tears would run into my ear or my mouth. Torrents of them. I'd picture my lungs filling." A laugh dragged from deep in his chest.

"And you picture it still?" asked Nina in a low voice. "If there's someone in the bed?"

"I can't breathe if someone is lying next to me." He pressed his face into her hair, inhaling more of her scent. "But I could last night. I can now."

They lay for a moment in silence.

"Your poor mother," whispered Nina. "She was afraid you would die."

"She would sob and call me her angel. She would beg me not to go." He relaxed his arm, allowed Nina to turn over.

"But it wasn't because she was afraid I would die. She was afraid I'd get better." He touched Nina's cheek, traced the pink line left by the pillow. Suddenly, it seemed miraculous: beholding the uncomposed face of a woman in the morning, beholding *this* woman's face. Showing his own face to her.

"In my suffering, I was hers, entirely. If I was an angel, she was God. I existed to prove her beneficence and power. And I wanted to please her."

He could feel the slight contraction of Nina's facial muscles beneath the pad of his thumb. The clear honey of her irises layered a darker shade of brown. She did have the deepest eyes he'd ever seen.

"She was pleased . . . that you were ill?" Her eyes searched his. His thumb traveled the satiny crest of her cheekbone, and then, slowly, he drew back his hand.

"She gave me pills to swallow. *Nightmare pills*, I called them. I'd take them and monsters walked around in my head. When I started spitting them out, the nightmares stopped, just like that. I had more strength in the morning. My mind was clearer. I think I knew then, at ten years old." His mouth twisted. "I didn't trust myself. Or maybe I didn't want to be right. I was afraid of what being right made her. A monster." His smile felt monstrous, all wrong on his face. "The monster wasn't inside my head. She was hovering over me. She was real. It was real, the nightmare."

She comprehended. He could see the change come over her, her nostrils flared, and she reached for his hand. He felt her squeeze hard as he continued.

"In Colorado, I heard a doctor tell her I didn't have consumption. That should have been the instant I rebelled. I was fourteen. Old enough to run away, to find work at a miner's camp or a lumberyard." He laughed. "If they'd have had me. I was barely strong enough to lift my Latin grammar book. I would have made an unlikely frontiersman. I did nothing. I hid in my books. I kept trying not to know what I knew. We went to Italy next. Pistoia."

"Pistoia." She was hugging his arm close, his skin in contact with the stiff frills and cool buttons of her nightgown. The soft heat of her breast rose through the cotton. "Where Claud and the duchess are going?"

"Won't be going," he said automatically, then nodded. "Yes. A health resort in the mountains." He paused. "She lied to the doctors, in front of me. She didn't realize my Italian had improved, or perhaps she believed what she was saying. That I coughed blood. That *I* had stained handkerchiefs she showed them. She pleaded for a surgical intervention. She pleaded for them to resection my lungs."

"Did they?" There was horror in Nina's voice.

"No." He sounded mesmerized to his own ears. "No, but I ended up in the operating theater anyway. I took a fall, a bad one. After the surgery, I spent months on my back. With her beside me."

He rolled onto his back, freeing his arm in the process. He folded both his arms beneath his head.

"Does anyone know?" She propped herself on her elbow beside him. "What she did to you?"

"I told Geoffrey, after she was dead." His jaw clenched. "He already thought I was an ingrate. Once I left for Oxford, I never went home again, not while our parents were alive. But after I told him, he thought me a delusional ingrate." He formed his lips into a smile. "It's hard to believe, after all. That a mother would do such things."

He realized that he was tense with anticipation.

Nina's gaze met his. "I believe you."

His smile slipped away. This, too, was miraculous. Air rushed into his lungs.

"The person you most want to listen to you"—she spoke cautiously—"it's yourself, isn't it? As a boy. *He* couldn't believe it, and so it took him longer to free himself."

His teeth tapped together, and he tasted blood. He'd nicked his tongue. He kept staring into her beautiful eyes, all the way down to her beautiful heart.

He'd said so much, and yet, not nearly enough.

He wasn't free.

His nightmare had become his reality.

It was the worst part of the pain. That no doctor he saw could pinpoint a physiological cause for its shattering force. He should tell her that, reveal not only his scars, but his wounds, so she didn't take this for a story of redemption.

"I believe you," she said again. "Alan, it wasn't your fault. It didn't happen because you were too attached to her. It happened because *she* was sick."

He opened his mouth, changed his mind, gave a slight nod instead. He'd made a mistake, letting her stay, absorbing her light. And he was selfish enough, even now, to rise up onto an elbow, to grasp her hand, spreading her fingers with his. He brought their clasped hands to his mouth and kissed her knuckles.

When he lowered their hands, he was going to kiss her mouth. No better angel could stop him. She was watching him with half-lidded eyes, parted lips.

He lowered their hands. She started, breaking his grasp.

"Blast." She turned her head. "Is that Boyd?"

"Blast," he echoed. His valet was an aspiring actor and paced the hallways of a morning, running lines, before he burst into the bedchamber.

Today he was reciting *The Vicar of Wakefield*.

Alan sat up, leaning his back on the headboard as Nina scrambled from the bed. She spied Fritz on the bookcase and gathered him into her arms. She was blushing—at the idea of Boyd catching them in bed—and looked back at him shyly.

He grinned. Mistake or no, he was happy she'd stayed, happy she was here. Tonight, they'd attend the ball. She'd steal Geoff's letters. And that would conclude her part of the bargain. Someday he'd visit Nina's Sweets. He'd taste her gooseberry tarts, and meet her truehearted village husband, and content himself with knowing that all her dreams had come true.

She was smiling at him now, smiling a dimpled smile, in her cotton nightgown, long hair streaming over her shoulders, a monkey clasped to her breast. He hoped his expression wasn't wistful.

As soon as she'd left the room, he pushed back the covers and stood. He slid an ebony cane from the stand, walked to the French doors, and flung them open. The morning was blue and rose and gold.

I believe you, she'd said, instantly, easily, and it was the truth. She did. She believed him. The ache in his hip felt oddly soft, no hot coal, but rather cool gray cinders. He stood for longer than was his wont, looking at the clouds.

CHAPTER TWENTY-THREE

THE GLOBE LIGHTS in the ballroom had been replaced with chandeliers of tiered crystals, sparkling prisms that scattered stars in every direction. Mirrors in heavy gilt on the upper walls expanded the firmament. Alan wandered in and out of a dozen conversations, gaze straying again and again to the arched entranceway. It was too soon for Nina to reappear. The house teemed with errant guests who spilled out of the downstairs rooms into the garden and up the front staircase. These wanderers would make Nina's little act of larceny more challenging to commit.

A waltz ended, the sea of silk and tulle parting. He crossed the dance floor, heading toward the orchestra. Fanny had installed whole hedges between the columns. The air was humid with warm flesh and vegetation.

He felt hot breath on his ear.

"Could it be?"

He didn't turn his head. Geoffrey fell into step with him.

"Lord Alan Daft. You look well."

Alan shot him a glance. They looked like each other, a matched pair in their formal suits, expertly tailored to flatter similar frames. All black, but for the gold glitter of their cuff links.

"Your grace," he said pleasantly. "I'm passing a most enjoyable evening."

"You can't be serious." Geoffrey eyed him with suspicion. "It's like bloody Vauxhall in here."

Alan raised his brows. "An excellent characterization." The glittering canopy of lights, the screens of flowering vines, the overflow of invitees—it all combined to evoke a populous pleasure garden, uncomfortably compressed. He suspected the evening's immoderation owed more to Fanny's ire than to her tastelessness. She meant to punish Geoffrey for her imminent banishment.

He laughed. "Ingenious."

"Gauche," Geoffrey muttered. "I'm surprised she didn't sell tickets."

"I paid sixpence." Alan plucked a flute of champagne from a passing tray. "For a shave. And more for the haircut. I gathered from *you* that was the price of admission."

Geoffrey's slow smile looked satisfied. A few pro forma complaints couldn't disguise his good humor. Whatever gaucheries Fanny perpetrated tonight, he thought to be rid of her by the month's end. And here was Alan, no longer styled like an eccentric bohemian, but like an eligible bachelor. All but bending the knee. Small wonder his spirits ran high.

As they reached the room's perimeter, Geoffrey's voice boomed with rare jocularity. "What ho?"

He addressed the Earl of Bettany and Pelham Osborne. They were conferring by a column, their faces beaded with sweat. Osborne leaned toward Geoffrey with the vibrating intensity of a man trying not to hop.

"Lord Salisbury made a compact with Parnell." As he named the leader of the Irish Parliamentary Party, his nose twitched as though he smelled something foul. He lowered his voice. "Gladstone's budget is doomed. It's a fait accompli."

"It's also a party secret." Bettany glanced at Alan. "And now it's going straight to print."

"No, indeed." Geoffrey's voice sounded sleek. He looked at Alan too, with gloating approval. "My man Friday here won't put down a word."

Alan tamped down a flare of temper and shrugged.

"Publishing hearsay isn't in my line." He couldn't resist throwing a wink at Osborne. "Your on-dit is safe with me."

Another waltz struck up. He glanced again at the entranceway. Lord Kilderbee filled his line of vision, pink as a prawn and beaming as he shouldered into the circle.

"Beastly hot." He mopped his forehead with his handkerchief. "Lady Kilderbee and I were steamed on the dance floor."

Alan felt Geoffrey snap to attention at his side. There, a few yards behind her husband, stood Patricia, breathtaking in gold-maize silk. She was conversing with a petite woman who'd bought extra inches dear in the form of a high-gabled diamond tiara.

Patricia wasn't looking at her companion. She was looking at Geoffrey.

Alan had always found her manner supercilious, her beauty cold. The expression on her face now had a feverish intensity. Geoffrey's expression, too, burned with naked desire.

Hell. He had to look away. This reminder of his brother's humanity was bloody inconvenient. Geoffrey was vain and shallow. And yet, he loved Patricia, deeply. It felt fraught, suddenly, his plan to exploit that fact. But the devil take the hindmost.

"If you'll excuse me." He spoke abruptly and didn't wait for a response. He exited the ballroom, pausing in the hall, which was quieter and cooler, banked with white-muslin-clad debutantes. Matchmakers and gossipmongers chatted among them in clusters.

What if Nina had run into trouble? What if one of Geoffrey's drunk, presumptuous friends had stumbled upon her in the act and decided to have his fun with a pretty interloper whose only hope was his silence?

Alan wove his way down the hall and climbed the stairs, passing two defiant-looking wallflowers as they descended. Their loitering must have delayed her. And yes, she was just stepping toward the door to Geoffrey's study when he turned the corner.

She sensed a presence before she knew it was him. She swerved from the study door, not like a startled thief, but like a woman who'd had too much champagne. Her hips swayed, and then she saw him and froze.

Silk roses had been sewn to the train of her vibrant blue gown, rust red, as large as hearts. Her breasts brimmed above the ribbons of the daring décolletage. Her smile was relieved, intimate, excited. The kind of smile that said *Thank God it's you*.

He wanted her to smile at him like that, always. He wanted to push her against the door and take her now, damn the letters, damn everything. The light was dim, and her eyes glowed with radiant darkness. She gave him a curt, soldierly nod.

"Keep a lookout," she said, and then she was at the study door, sliding two pins from the wreath of rosebuds Lavinia's lady's maid had fastened to her hair.

Bloody useless lookout. He couldn't tear his eyes from her. She had one of the pins in her mouth, bending it with her small white teeth. Then she was at the lock, hands moving quickly. He could watch this woman sift flours until the end of time. Pick locks until Judgment Day.

His eyes strayed from her hands to the curve of her waist, the generous slope of her hips.

Click.

She pushed through the door, blue silk trailing behind her. Once she'd passed out of view, he could blink, and glance about, to make sure they weren't observed. He pressed his fist to the cool wall. Time slowed. Then the door opened. A beautiful criminal slipped out and lifted up her wrist, set her reticule to swinging. She had the letters.

She came to him, swiftly, and he took her elbow, escorting her back to the stairs. His blood was pounding through his veins. She smelled like a rose, and she bloomed all over with roses of silk that rustled as she walked, and his every sense was flooded with *her*. Which was why he failed to consider his steps.

They were on the stairs when a bolt of pain made him stumble. He corrected quickly. But she felt it, and he felt her eyes on his face the rest of the way down. He guided her away from the ballroom. His cane tapped the marble floor. Away from the band, the laughter, the clinking glasses. He braced himself.

"Your cane," she said at last. "It's not like your spectacles. It's not for show."

He didn't answer, only slanted a look at her.

"You have a limp." She was worrying her bottom lip.

"A slight limp," he agreed. "Sometimes." He flicked his eyes down at himself. "And yet I wasn't lamed in battle or by disease. My legs are of equal length and development. You can examine them, if you like. I've asked plenty of doctors to do so over the years."

"You told me you fell." She lowered her voice. "And ended up in the operating theater. I assumed . . ."

"I fell," he confirmed, turning them through an archway.

Why not speak of it here, now? He'd just crossed the Rubicon and robbed his own brother. He was falling now, had been falling every moment, for weeks, in hopeless love with this more-than-remarkable woman, whose brother he was also poised to destroy.

His life was teetering out of control.

They entered the picture gallery. It was nearly empty, only a few other partygoers drifting down its length.

"I did fall," he continued. "I initiated it, though. By jumping through the window."

CHAPTER TWENTY-FOUR

A STUNNED SILENCE opened between them. Nina looked from the pictures lining the long room back to Alan. She felt as though her eyes were straining. He'd been right, last night. She did try to see all the way inside him. He'd been wrong as well. There *was* beauty there, a great, troubling beauty.

His silver irises went steely as he looked back at her.

"I wasn't trying to end my life," he said, his mouth edging into a sardonic smile.

Perhaps he'd misinterpreted her pained thoughtfulness for revulsion.

They'd stopped walking, still linked at the elbow, and she pressed mutely into his side. He started moving again, leading her across the room.

"I didn't care if I lived or died, so long as I got away. My room was on the second story, not very high. But the courtyard was stone flagged." He cleared his throat. "The *daftest* thing I've ever done."

She tried to reward this attempt at humor with a laugh and failed. She twined her arm more tightly with his. "The most desperate, perhaps."

"I should have made a desperate dash through the orderlies. But they'd come to move me to the hospital, and instinct sent me in the opposite direction." He slowed their pace as they neared the far wall. "I wasn't about to let a surgeon experiment on my lungs. Take out the upper lobes, and some ribs along with them."

She felt his movement, something between a shrug and a shudder.

"After that day," he said, "I never heard anyone mention pulmonary surgery again. I was already bedridden. It must have seemed superfluous."

"Because confining you to bed was the goal." She had a metallic taste in her mouth. His cane kept ticking, like a metronome.

"When I woke up in the hospital, an operation had been performed, on my hip, or on the neck of my femur. The doctors I've seen since draw different conclusions from the scars. They agree, though, that I have a normal range of motion. Normal strength. If the injuries were crippling, as my mother claimed, then Dr. Barbieri saved my leg."

He stopped in front of a landscape. "I almost wish I'd lost it. An amputee can verify his experience with a glance. He can adapt to new mechanics. I didn't lose my leg." He shifted, and she shifted too, uneasily.

"But I might be losing my mind," he said quietly. "Or my soul. There you go. My dark secret."

His arm felt hard as iron through his coat. Had he told her this part in public so she couldn't embrace him?

"Alan," she whispered, but he was looking straight ahead at the landscape, not at her.

"Ah," he exclaimed, in a changed tone. "This is what I wanted to see."

She turned her eyes from his profile to the picture. They lit first on the scrawl in the corner, the lie she'd signed to it. *James Berney*.

"That tree there." His forward movement pulled her with him, the picture inches away. "You plucked it from his most famous painting. *The Priory Oak*. And mellowed it with midsummer sun. The lichen on the trunk maps where the light falls." He shook his head. "Astonishing."

Her skin shattered into gooseflesh. He didn't want tender words or caresses. In front of this picture, they weren't a man and a woman who'd shared secrets and desires, breathed the same breath. They were art critic and art forger. Entities separate and opposed.

He turned his gaze on her, face shuttered. "You shouldn't have added those cows drinking from the pond."

She slipped her arm from his.

"No," she agreed. "Jack said the same."

She didn't realize she'd been widening the space between them until he closed it with a stride. His mouth lowered to her ear.

"The last thing I want is to cause you pain."

She felt the warm stroke of his breath, and a shiver ran over her. Did he refer to Jack's downfall? Or to this yearning she felt, for him, for *more*?

I can't give you what you need, he'd told her.

But what did she need? Stability. Companionship. What her aunts had. They'd never risked their hearts, gambled on love, the intoxicating sort. The sort that wore off, left you sick and alone.

She pulled away from Alan, began to walk, breathless. But she didn't get far. A picture caught her eye, not one of her own, or of Jack's. It showed a woman, dark-haired, elegant, her brow arched, the bow of her lips tilted at one corner.

Nina stopped and stared at that familiar half smile. Her blood ran cold, as though Alan's mother sat before her and not her painted semblance. Had the duchess been the knowing architect of her son's harm? Or had she persuaded herself she had his best interests at heart? Had she been too lost—too hurt herself—to tell the difference? Alan came up behind her and stood for a moment in silence. "An airy portrait," he said at last. "Idealized and superficial. But it does capture my mother's expression, in a certain mood."

She kept studying it. The amusement on the duchess's face seemed thin and brittle, a touch cruel.

"Uncle Alan!"

The shouted greeting locked her knees. Lucky thing, or she might have toppled as the boy barreled into them.

"Claud." Alan laughed in surprise, hugging him to his side. "Shouldn't you be asleep?"

"It's morning on Mars." Claud wiggled out from beneath his

arm, wheezing as he smiled. His hair went in all directions, and his nightshirt swallowed his thin frame.

"We're exploring," he said, and held up a toy soldier. He looked at Nina and blinked. "Miss Fritz! Is Fritz here too?"

"Miss Fritz." Alan gave a soft snort and raised a brow at her. "No," he said to Claud. "The lady had to settle for my company this evening."

Nina smiled and curtseyed. "Your lordship. You came all the way from Mars?"

Claud nodded. "We're famished by the journey."

"Hoping to sneak into the refreshment room?" Alan ruffled Claud's hair, then crouched to look into his eyes. "You'll be caught red-handed. There are herds upon herds of humans. But Miss Fritz and I might be able to secure you and Felton a few bonbons."

Claud exploded upward in his eagerness, lost a slipper, hopped in a circle, and coughed. A short cough that grabbed something in his chest. He coughed again, louder. Alan passed him his handkerchief wordlessly, and the boy covered his face.

"There you are."

Nina looked over Claud's bowed head. Miss Milford was approaching, weaving around statues and couples gone stock-still with curiosity.

"Give me your hand." The nurse closed in on them, wafting the strong odor of vinegar and Cherry Pectoral. She seized Claud's wrist.

Alan rose to his full height. "He's on a mission of exploration. I'm going to guide him to the local comestibles."

"Lord Alan." Miss Milford froze. "The marquess needs to return to his room."

"Eventually." Alan nodded and winked at Claud. "Explorers aren't exempt from the laws of nature. He does need sleep. When he's tired, he'll return."

"Now," said Miss Milford. "Or I will have to tell his grace."

"His grace is entertaining." Alan smiled. "The ball," he added, as though clarification might be needed. "How did the marquess come to leave his room in the first place? I'm sure his grace will want to know."

Miss Milford's smooth cheeks went waxen. "Please. For the boy's sake. And mine."

Alan's eyes locked with hers. Nina glanced at Claud. He was wadding the handkerchief in his hand.

White silk, blotched with red.

Nina's vision tunneled. She reached out and gripped Alan's arm. He was speaking to Miss Milford.

"Very well. He'll return to his room. But not without a bonbon."

Nina took this as her cue. She spun around and hurried from the gallery, plunging again into heat and noise, making for the refreshment room, grateful that the dazzlement overpowered thought. When she reentered the picture gallery, she heard Claud's exhilarated voice before she saw him. He was going on and on about the Royal Aquarium of Mars, Alan's questions punctuating the breakneck tumble of words.

She drew up to them, and they glanced at her with identical grins that made her heart balloon. It felt too big for her chest. Claud's hands were empty. No sign of the wadded silk. No sign on Alan's face that he'd seen the message written there in blood. She passed Claud the tiny plate of wafers, biscuits, and bonbons. At once, Miss Milford clamped his shoulder and propelled him down the hall.

Alan looked after the boy and the nurse. Nina blinked, and red dotted the darkness. As soon as she spoke of what she'd seen, she would break his heart.

"We did what we came here to do."

Alan had turned to her, his gaze so heated she felt it like a touch on her skin. He waved his hand, waved away the pictures, the house, the world itself.

"Let's forget all of it." Irony tinged his voice, but his face was all urgency. "Tonight, let's dream one of those dreams that's a feeling. Happiness. No—*bliss*. Ecstasy."

She stared into his eyes, quicksilver and brilliant. To dream the same dream—even for one night.

This man was in her blood. She grew more intoxicated with each beat of her heart.

She couldn't fight it.

She was already in a dream as they walked from the blazing house into the night.

WHEN ALAN OPENED the door to his bedchamber, he stepped to the side and let her walk through ahead of him. The fire was low. Only one lamp burned. She kept her back to him, nerves so tightly laced that the *click* of the door made her flinch. She felt his presence all around her. The room itself smelled of him. She closed her eyes and saw red, the shade subtler than blood. As though poppies had dissolved behind her lids.

Let's forget all of it.

"You understand I want you in my bed." His deep voice was a murmur. "Not just to sleep."

She heard a soft slap. He'd peeled off his gloves downstairs. That slap—he'd discarded some other article of clothing.

She turned instinctively, and he was there, his bare fingers hot on the base of her throat.

"You can say no." His expression was dark.

She tilted up her face, offering her lips.

The force of his kiss pushed her gasp into his mouth. She followed it with her tongue, ravenous. Fear coursed through her. What if she couldn't sate this hunger in a single night? God help her, she would try.

She reached for his lapels, touched his shirtfront instead. It was his coat that he'd shed. A promising start. She wanted to strip him to the skin. She wanted to lick down to his bones. She scrabbled at buttons. He caught her wrists in his hand and lifted them over her head. With his other hand, he jerked down on her gown. Her breasts popped free. With a hiss, he pulled away by inches to stare. The raw need in his eyes shook something inside her.

"I've been fighting the urge to do that all night." He ran his hand down from her clavicles, over the swell of her breasts. Her nipple peaked against his palm.

"I feared they'd spring free of their own accord." She confessed it with a laughing moan, her spine lengthening as he raised her wrists higher. "The neckline goes to my navel."

"Not yet." His smile was wicked. He tugged the gown harder.

"Don't tear!" She narrowed her eyes into a glare. "This gown is a work of art."

"Quite right." He didn't sound chastened. But he sighed, dropped her wrists, and set himself to disassembly, unlacing, unhooking, uncasing her. Voluminous layers of silk piled higher and higher. Padding, wires. *Springs*.

"A work of art, and a feat of engineering," he murmured, toeing aside her bustle. "Dressmakers should build our bridges."

She giggled until he knelt to untie her garters, fingertips flicking her thighs. The giggle died in her throat. Her mind slowed, moved at the pace of his fingers as he rolled down her stocking. The world was simpler. It was simply sensation.

He slipped off her stocking and boot, stroked his thumb along the arch of her bare foot before he set it down on a cool gush of ribbons. When he did the same to the other foot, she wobbled and gripped his head to steady herself. His soft, thick hair tickled between her fingers. Tentatively, she shaped his skull, his temples, his jaw, then buried her hands in the cloth at his neck. With a thrill of triumph, she found the loose end of his cravat and laid his throat bare. She retreated a step with her prize, ruffles lapping her ankles.

Her retreat. It gave him a better view. She realized as the corner of his mouth tipped up. She was naked but for her drawers, and he was looking his fill.

"This artful gown," he murmured, slithering its train in a lazy arc over the carpet, a silk rose in his fist. "It was a distraction." He dropped the rose and reached out. He skimmed the backs of both hands down the curve of her belly.

"A disguise." His knuckle dipped into her navel. "Your body." His voice caught. She didn't move. She didn't breathe.

"Your body is the marvel," he said. He moved one knee forward, then the other, and his breath blew hot on her sternum. He put his lips to her breast. He sucked, hard, her nipple swelling against his tongue. The cravat slipped from her fingers. She moaned. The pressure of his mouth made her thighs tighten around the sweet ache at their apex. His hands closed on her hips, and he lifted her smoothly, lifted her up and back. She emitted a cry of wonderment, feet treading empty space. First her toes, then her heels came to rest on a pliant surface. She looked down at the small, round platform. A tufted leather ottoman.

Alan was smiling up at her.

"What are you doing?" Her voice was shaky. The *ottoman* was shaky. His face was shockingly close to the slit in her drawers.

"Nothing, unless you want it." He seemed to be waiting for a sign, waiting for her assent to begin. But begin what? He remained on his knees. Weren't their relevant bits a little too dispersed? Confusion bloomed.

"I've spent time in a village." Her face prickled as she spoke. "Among cows. And sheep. Do you know rams are called tups? That's how we get the verb." She gulped air. "I've seen things in the farmyard. And in stereographs, the ones from France. People *tup* in all sorts of positions."

He made an amused noise in his throat, too husky for a laugh. He didn't look mocking but intrigued.

"They do indeed." His drawl was ragged at the edges. "Human creativity is a wondrous thing."

She adjusted her stance, inner thighs sliding together. "This position is more creative than I can fathom."

"I'd say I invented it." He grinned, skating his hand up the back of her leg. "But there's nothing original about any aspect of the act of love. It's all been done. For millennia. Every iteration. Every variation. And yet." He palmed her buttocks. "Lovers continue to make it their own. I stood you on the ottoman because I want your quim *here*." He leaned forward, hovered his mouth where her drawers split. She shivered at the puff of air. It seeped through the curls that hid her inner flesh.

He drew back, the focus in his eyes disconcerting. "If it pleases you." Now his knuckles brushed those curls. At her gasp, he flattened his hand, pressed with his palm. The beating she felt there—it competed with her heart.

"Does it?" he asked.

"It pleases me." The words emerged, nearly soundless. She heard his swift intake of breath, and he nodded, mouth compressing. He moved his palm in a slow circle. Her vision blurred. His face was a ferocious smear. Black slashes of brows, quicksilver gleam of predatory eyes. Sharp glitter of teeth.

"And this?" The question rasped. She heard a noise she didn't recognize. *She* had made it. His arm braced her, pinned her in place. She bore down, felt herself slicken, swell. His fingers slid over that tensely budded part of her, a rhythmic motion, maddening. When *she* touched it, she sighed, throbbed, a tension building, then releasing, a mild wave. The feeling didn't frenzy. Now she feared she'd burst. The sound gathering inside her was no gentle sigh. If he didn't stop, she'd scream. If he did stop, she'd die.

"This?" he asked. He opened her, thumb rubbing. The pleasure pulsed. Her nod was a kind of collapse. Thank God her quivering legs had been absolved of responsibility, that she could trust him to hold her fast. His finger pushed inside, and another. He began to churn her. She shuddered, moaning. She was beyond herself, pressing back against the heat of his palm, rocking forward. He slid his hand free, and his hot mouth locked on what had become her center. Her whole being concentrated between her legs. She wanted more. She *needed* more. His fingers dug into her hips, his grip ruthless. She felt the bite of his nails. The pain—it snapped her. She cried aloud as the pleasure spilled over, whipped into peak after peak. Her body was falling or floating. And then he had her in his arms. The next thing she knew she was on her back in his bed, and his mouth was sipping hers, slow, delirious kisses. His hand was busy in her hair, loosening pins, disentangling the rosebud wreath, smoothing her snarled tresses over her shoulders. He was lulling her. He was signaling that they'd finished. It was over. He'd hold her now. She could drowse against him until morning.

Her body throbbed in protest. She was sated, God. But her nerves refused to sleep. Dawn would come, but it was night—their night. She moved to pull his shirt up from the waistband of his trousers. He came away from her mouth, rising onto an elbow, and stilled her hand.

"Better we stop here."

"What about bliss?" She was still panting, and his eyes glinted.

"That wasn't bliss?" he drawled. "Do let me try again." His fingers caressed the skin between her breasts, trailed over her belly.

"What about *you?*" She sat up. "All those bacchanalian things you imagined."

"The sound you made coming undone in my arms was enough to satisfy a hundred satyrs."

"I want that too." She scrambled to her knees, grabbed again at the fabric bunched at his waist. "I want to hear you."

He wasn't going to hide from her. Not tonight.

He let her tug his shirt free and slip her hand beneath. His breath hissed as she palmed his stomach, the hot smooth skin, the hard ripple of tensed muscle.

"There's only us," she whispered, palm charting his ribs, the smooth rise of his pectorals. "In this dream, there's only what *we* feel."

There was nothing and no one to come between them.

She leaned forward and kissed his mouth, kissed his bared throat. He didn't resist as she pushed him down and straddled him, the fabric of his trousers rough against the sensitive skin of her inner thighs. He growled as she settled her weight, and she felt his hard, hot arousal pulse beneath her. She could hear his muscles humming with tension.

"You haven't done this before," he grated. "If we stop here, then . . ."

"I won't have to lie to that truehearted village lad who wants to marry me for my virginity and spotless soul?" She gave a gusty laugh. "I'd refuse him anyway. He would never see me, see all of me. I wouldn't risk my independence and my heart for *that.*"

Was she doing it for *this?* For him?

She shoved away all thought of risk. Rapture. Rapture only.

Slowly, deliberately, she put her fingers on his shirtfront and undid the top button. She stared down at his slitted eyes.

"Do you want this?"

"God, yes." He tipped her off him, rising from the bed. She was almost frightened by the speed with which he stripped his garments, and by the body emerging, everywhere thick and muscled, hard and brutal. When he shucked his trousers and drawers, his cock reared, dauntingly large.

"But that doesn't mean it's too late to change your mind." He saw the expression on her face and gave her that crooked smile. "We could play chess."

The lamplight bronzed the width of his chest and limned the heavy muscles. His chiseled abdomen narrowed to lean hips. Only the scars that wrapped his hip looked pale and bloodless. The sparse hair on his chest and stomach thickened below his navel.

She swallowed. "Do you have a French letter?"

"I do." He arched a brow. "In the match holder." He gestured at the nightstand. "I also have a chess set."

"I'm bollocks at chess." She met his eyes and took a deep breath. "Come here," she said, the command thrumming her throat.

He did, eyes flaring. He put a knee on the bed, and then he launched himself upon her. They gasped together as skin contacted skin. He dwarfed her, pressing her down, his weight just shy of crushing. She wiggled, and his thighs wedged between hers, spreading them wide. The stretch alone made her moan. He plunged his hands into her hair, his tongue into her mouth. She flexed her hips, the shaft of his cock pressing against her. He groaned, breaking their kiss, reaching for the match holder. He was quick to roll on the French letter, quick to ease back between her thighs. He dragged his tongue over her breasts, then kissed her hard. The heat and pressure were overwhelming. His chest, hips, legs, covered her completely. As he devoured her mouth, his cock nudged her opening.

She raked her hands down his back, clasped his hips, arresting his motion. He lifted away from her, just a fraction, enough to show he understood. He'd wait. He'd stop at her slightest signal. She exhaled, sliding her hands, and beneath her palms, she felt them, his scars. Thin flesh dense and immobile, stripes of alien tissue in his supple, living skin. She stroked their length, the one that curved with his hip, the one that ran down his thigh.

He went still. She looked up into his face, and she kept stroking. Nothing of him would be strange to her. Every particle of their bodies belonged to them both. He closed his eyes, a sweep of black lashes. Her fear was gone.

"Alan," she whispered, and his lids parted, his gaze fierce. He trapped her face in his hands, stared down at her.

"Yes?" he asked.

She canted her hips, ground them against his, eliciting his gasp. "Don't stop," she said, and he entered her, the movement controlled, slow. She tensed anyway, clamping her thighs to his flanks, struggling to breathe. Above her, his eyes were bright, unwavering. He kissed her, reaching between them to tease her center, stroking until her thighs butterflied. He pushed then, deeper, and the burning was quenched by a rush of liquid, her body opening a floodgate. Her body, wet and ready. He thrust, pulled back, thrust again. She gripped the hard curve of his buttocks, following his motion. She could have laughed—something was effervescing inside her, giving off tiny, tickling bursts of pleasure—but instead she was crying out, goading, begging. *More. Don't stop. More.*

He hooked her legs higher around his waist. She could feel his muscles tightening, feel every animal jerk as he drove into her, faster now. She was catching the rhythm, each hard, deep thrust making the gasps burst from her throat. He surged within her, no control now, their bodies wild, heartbeats one thunder. She latched her mouth to his neck. Dear God, the *taste* of him. It was everything. It was impossible. His thumb pressed her quim, and she flung her head against the pillow and convulsed.

He kept moving, his cock striking the very core of her sensation. She bit his neck as he jolted and gasped, arms rigid, a howl tearing from his throat. He subsided over her, still lodged deep inside. She licked the little indentations she'd left in his skin. She couldn't decipher the taste, its components. He tasted *right*. That was the closest she could come to describing it.

Exactly, infinitely, eternally *right*.

Chapter Twenty-Five

SOMETHING'S WRONG. THE moment her sleepy gaze traveled up to Alan's face, Nina felt her skin prickle, anxious hairs stirring on her nape.

He was leaning against the headboard, arms folded across his naked chest. Had she ever seen him look so grim? Or so beautiful? Her next shiver of anxiety was edged with a desire so keen it seemed to cut.

He turned his eyes on her. She squeezed hers shut. Ridiculous. Cowardly. Also, there was no fooling him.

"You're awake," he commented, and she forced her lids to part, propped herself on her elbow, and met his eyes.

"You've *been* awake." She sounded strange, as though her throat were clogged with velvet. As though her voice itself had been pleasured.

She flushed. He didn't blink.

"Doing what?" she asked, in the same embarrassingly rich tone.

"Thinking."

She cleared her throat. "That's the problem, then." She managed a wry smile. "Maybe you should think less."

He kept staring for a beat, then gave her a lopsided smile in return. "I'll *think* about the possibility."

She sat up, the sheet slipping momentarily below her breasts. His gaze flicked down. Suddenly, it was all there, between them.

The air thickened with the excruciating, soul-bearing intimacy of the night. Everything he'd done to her body, everything she'd done to his.

She warmed at the recollected sensations, at the inner echo of her own voice sobbing brokenly for more, *more*.

He reached out, not for her, but for the bellpull. His hand hovered by the tassel.

"Hungry?" It was a question. It had a rasp she could *feel*, that made her catch her breath, too aware, suddenly, of the linen's skimming contact with her nipples. She fixated on his hand, then her eyes followed the vein that snaked under the skin of his forearm.

Her mouth watered. She dampened everywhere.

She *was* hungry, insatiably hungry, for *him*. The fact should worry her. For now, though . . . he hadn't tugged the bellpull.

She'd worry later.

With a twist, she flung her knee across his thighs, dropping into his lap. Their gazes locked. He laughed the laugh she loved and lowered his hand.

"Good morning," he drawled, his expression amused and surprised. The proof of his arousal pressed against her, hot as a brand. She stroked it, his cock, nearly overwhelmed by her sense of achievement as he gasped.

"Good morning," she said, and fit herself over him. Boldly, slowly, she sank until he was buried inside, until his lips parted around a groan. She ground in a small, hesitant circle. These slow revolutions—she could feel them inside her. She could feel how they affected *him*, winching his muscles until he was rigid beneath her.

He gripped her face. His eyes were slits. She stilled, flushed and horribly excited. *She* had done this, made them both shake, nerves lacing tight. She'd done it in the light of day, no shadows to lend concealment. Every facet of her need exposed.

This wasn't a dream.

He regarded her, that silver gaze screened by his lowered lashes. She acted instinctively, moved to obliterate that whisper of distance, his maddening self-control. She gave his mouth a voluptuous lick. She consumed his smile. With a growl, he seized her hips, and she felt a thrill, the balance of power shifting. He had unleashed his own appetite. Now *he* was devouring, his teeth on her throat. He lifted her up, then drove her back down, hard, straining to meet her. The bed creaked as the urgency of their coupling increased. Her breasts slapped his chest. She fought his grip, writhing, found her own rhythm, which became their rhythm. *More. More.* Thank God, thank God, they were both gluttons.

The pleasure built from below, from where they rubbed together, and from within, where his thick cock stroked, her moans timed with each deep, lubricious glide. She was arching back, taut as a bow, and then, as he jerked, her name hoarse on his lips, the tension broke. She was dissolving into liquid, the spasm rippling from her head to her toes. Her cry surrendered even her bones.

After, she lolled in his lap, her soft thighs spread over his hard ones, her forehead on his shoulder. His arms were linked loosely around her.

"I meant," he said finally, a low rumble, "hungry for breakfast." He traced her clavicle as she straightened, his tone playful.

"It's early for breakfast," she protested, although she hadn't a notion of the time. The curtains glowed with clear sunshine. But the end could still be deferred. And her awful knowledge: she could hold it, alone, a trifle longer.

"I have a train to catch."

"Oh?" She looked at him more closely. He was flushed, cheekbones glossed with sweat, mouth relaxed and humorous. But his eyes were darkening, lines bracketing his smile, which flattened as she stared.

Her stomach hollowed with foreboding. "Where to?"

She knew, though. She knew as he bent over her, as he rested his lips on her crown. He said it almost below the threshold of hearing, warm breath sifting her hair.

"Hensthorpe."

She didn't shrink, although in her chest, something crumpled. She put her palms on his pectorals and pushed. He leaned back against the headboard.

"That's your village," he said. He should have sounded smug. She wished he did sound smug, so she could muster dislike, maybe even despise him.

"I've been there." He looked at her steadily. He sounded serious, bleak, something just short of apology registering in his tone as a slight hesitation. "It was years ago, when I was writing my essays on English landscape. I wanted to see the oak from *The Priory Oak*, and other sites that appear in Berney's pictures. There's quite a cluster in Hensthorpe."

She was starting to cool. Her damp skin felt clammy. He'd spent himself against her belly. How strange, these traces of their fusion, their intermingling, when suddenly they were so clearly distinct.

Art critic. Art forger.

"It only occurred to me this morning." His large warm hands settled on her shoulders, smoothed the gooseflesh from her upper arms. "The picture I saw last night, and the pictures at Broughton's—I was too focused on compiling the faults, noting everything false. I didn't let the truth of your painting speak." A brief smile lifted the corner of his mouth. "They brim with love." His hands tightened on her arms.

She couldn't utter a word. For the second time that morning, she squeezed her eyes shut.

"*Your* love." His voice continued in the darkness. "It was there on the wall for anyone to see. The light you painted so truly as it brightens the lichen on the Priory Oak—that same light ripens the gooseberries you put in your tarts."

She opened her eyes. She'd given herself away. And given Jack away too. Alan would find the cottage easily, in two steps. First, detrain at the Hensthorpe station. Second, ask for Sylvia and Lolly. Ask anywhere.

"It's Sunday, isn't it," she said. The days had begun to blur. "Aunt Sylvia will make a roast. If it's fine outside, they'll eat in the garden. Miss Lolly will have invited her cousin, Mrs. Swales, and Mr. Middleton will stop by whether invited or not. That's what you'll encounter. Elderly villagers eating under a plum tree." She crossed her arms over her breasts. "Jack won't have waited this long."

Alan nodded. "It might well be a fool's errand." That nod, his tone—he meant to comfort her. Her nose burned. She blinked rapidly and dropped her gaze, which landed on that notch at the base of his throat. She stared at his fluttering pulse.

"Ask me not to go," he said, and brushed back the damp hair that had curtained her face, tipped up her chin.

"No." She shook her head. He'd always made his own intentions clear. She'd accepted the terms. His fingertips slid to her cheekbones. He framed her face and looked at her with lowered lashes.

She took a breath. "But I'm going with you."

She reached out and tugged the bellpull herself.

THE SUN WAS high when they detrained in Hensthorpe. Alan turned to Nina, who sidled away from him on the platform. Now, as at every moment along the journey when she'd shifted to avoid contact, he felt a strong pang of unpleasant emotion.

Her big-eyed pallor made clear the intention behind the distance. She wasn't punishing him. She was struggling to preserve her composure.

He carried her portmanteau and they walked into the village center, like strangers who happened to find themselves on the same path. Fritz skipped ahead and veered toward the churchyard. Cursing under her breath, Nina raced to retrieve him. She looked—briefly—like herself again, and the strength of his relief bordered on ridiculous.

They passed the church itself. He wasn't sure if he remembered its round Saxon tower from his previous visit or from Berney's painting *Afternoon, St. George's Church*. They turned down a cobbled street lined with shops. Brick and flint façades, pantile roofs. The tavern had a Dutch gable that seemed about to topple.

As they passed the last shop, its large bow window caught Alan's eye. He stopped and considered the display. Cakes and buns. Jars of jams, glinting jewel bright where the sun struck.

Here it was.

Nina retraced her steps and stood beside him. The bakery was closed for the sabbath, but even so, Alan thought the air seemed warmer, faintly sugared.

"That's Aunt Sylvia's hedgerow jelly." Nina's skirts brushed his leg. "As a girl, I went with her to deliver the jars and collect the empty ones the customers returned. And sometimes I'd stay and pit cherries or crack eggs for Mr. Craddock, in exchange for hot biscuits."

The corner of her mouth had tipped up at the memory.

"And now he wants to sell his bakery, to you." Alan smiled at her as she looked up at him, with more color in her cheeks, and life in her eyes. Then she dimmed.

She looked again at the window. "He'd rather not sell at all. He'd prefer to convince his sons to take over the business."

"Will they?"

"When marmosets go to Mars." Fritz peeped on her shoulder, and she scratched his belly with an absent-minded fingertip. "They're too busy drinking and gaming." Her brow creased. Before Alan could touch her hand, she drew away from him. "This way." She put her back to the bakery, and to him, with deliberate forcefulness. "We'll cut across the green."

The green buzzed with conversation and pollinating insects. Villagers filled the acre, loosely bunched into laughing cliques that followed no logic discernable to the London eye.

Several hailed Nina as she passed, including a square-jawed young man whose salutation conveyed so much bashful enthusiasm his friends hooted and clapped his shoulder.

Wholesome fellow. Truehearted, maybe.

Not a match for Nina Finch.

She wanted someone who'd see all of her. Someone from whom she wouldn't have to hide her past, or her glorious carnal greed, or her talent, or her irreverence, or her adorable, impudent smile. Someone for whom she wouldn't have to sacrifice her dreams.

And that was *him*, dammit.

Alan speared the ground with his cane.

She was leery of marriage, understandably. Her mother had been abandoned. She idolized her spinster aunts.

Ask her anyway. The edict struck like a bolt from the blue. He kept covering ground, eyes fixed on Nina, who looked as beautiful in the afternoon light as he'd ever seen her.

Ask her. He could attribute it to exterior forces. He'd despoiled the woman, and the voice of convention commanded him. Act honorably. Do your duty. But no, it was his heart commanding.

They'd reached a rutted, unpaved lane. Nina stopped in front of a lovely two-story cottage climbed all over by wisteria. She turned to face him, and the world reduced. Shining brown eyes, purple blossoms. Warm sun.

He stepped forward, a molten wire corkscrewing from his hip to his knee. The resultant gasp dispersed in his diaphragm, a warning. It almost silenced his heart's command. Almost.

Ask her.

But if the pain meant the worst? If he *was* losing his mind?

He'd handle it, somehow. He'd never let his own burdens weigh her down.

"Birdie." The masculine voice rupturing the silence wasn't his. Nina spun. To the left of the cottage, a man was leaning on the fence, a cigarette between his lips. He had Nina's mouth.

"I knew you'd turn up," he said. "I didn't figure you'd bring a friend."

Chapter Twenty-six

Jack Reeve lifted the latch and opened the gate, scooting a chicken to the side with his boot. Alan couldn't read the look he exchanged with Nina. She stalked into the garden. Alan strolled after and Reeve pulled the gate shut behind him.

Fritz went leaping up into the boughs of a fruit tree, which showered white blossoms onto the table beneath. Nina circled around the table and turned, arms crossed tightly, expression bleak. She'd positioned herself defensively, an iron barrier between herself and the volatile males. That she felt a need to guard herself made Alan's nostrils flare, for what it proved about her life to date.

"Your sister didn't bring me here." He rounded on Reeve. "She supports you to the point of reckless self-endangerment. I can't convince her that you aren't worth it."

"Blood is thicker than water." Reeve smiled and blew a stream of smoke into the air. He was a short man, bulked with muscle. Armed, if Alan gauged the bulge in his jacket pocket correctly.

"Our blood anyway," he continued. "Maybe water *does* run through the veins of nobs such as yourself. That's why they call it blue." He shrugged, then gave a mock start, flourishing his cigarette at a chair. "Where are my manners? Have a seat. You're in time for dinner. We eat early on Sundays." He glanced at Nina. "My dear sister and Aunt Sylvia's roast are the only two reasons I'm still in England."

"I'll be the first to wish you bon voyage." Alan ignored the chair, over the protest of his hip. "After you stand trial and serve whatever sentence is meted out to you."

"And why would I do that?" Reeve flicked away his cigarette, shifting his stance, squaring off with him.

"Jack." Nina interjected, her voice low and furious. "You'll make things worse. We need to talk."

"Sure we do." Reeve didn't take his eyes from Alan. "But first my fists will have their say."

"Sporting of you." Alan lifted his brows. "You could just shoot me."

Reeve didn't deny it. His hand brushed his jacket pocket. "I try not to shoot company. But if you're making a recommendation . . ."

"*Jack*." Nina tried again.

"There's more company coming," Alan said softly. His hip screamed. Before setting out, he'd written a note to the inspectors in the Criminal Investigation Department who'd taken his statement on the forgeries in the South Kensington Museum. He doubted they'd caught the same train he and Nina had. The next one more likely.

"How's that for sporting?" Reeve had gone still, his smile fixed.

"The police." Nina's voice throbbed. She cut Alan an agonized look. The dead feeling in his knee—where the burning nerve endings grounded out—spread through his body. What had she expected?

"Are they already here?" Reeve glanced toward the gate.

"Seems not." Alan shrugged. "Soon enough."

"Birdie, see if they need a hand in the kitchen." Reeve said it flatly. Alan waited for Nina to refuse just as flatly. Her eyes darted between them. Then she whirled and strode for the cottage.

Alan couldn't help it. He watched her go. Her chignon had collapsed its pins, the soft locks of hair trailing down to her midback. She'd picked up her skirts, exposing her ankles, the curve of her calves.

"Remember yourself." Reeve spoke near his ear. "That's my sister you're dogging."

Alan wheeled, braced for the exchange of blows. "I'm not forgetful of anything about her."

Reeve didn't flinch, but he didn't lunge either. He studied Alan for a moment, then drew away and dropped into a chair.

"You understand, then, that she's never been involved in any wrongdoing. She's a good lass, a bit naive. Lawful as a parson."

Alan expelled a breath. He'd gambled on this outcome, with near total certainty. But his muscles eased at the confirmation.

"I understand perfectly."

"Your seat." Reeve pointed with his chin. Alan sat. Reeve flashed him a thin smile and removed a small cigarette case from his trouser pocket, flipping it open. He fumbled to extract a cigarette. Alan stared at his fingers, the crooked phalanges and inflated joints. They registered the damage of chronic affliction.

"Handsome, ain't they?" Reeve caught the direction of his gaze and winked.

Alan frowned. He'd gawked at the deformity like a fairgoer. It was behavior he despised in others. He stretched out his legs, diverting a chicken from her course.

"Alan De'Ath." Reeve shook his head, a facsimile of admiration. "The top-loftiest toff ever paid to prate." He used the pad of his index finger to stand a cigarette, which he rotated into his mouth. "I'll break *your* fingers if I hear you laid them where they don't belong."

"You hear what you want to hear." Alan sneered. "Have you ever *listened* to Nina? No, why would you have? Easier to play the protector when you can pretend it's what she wants. When you can justify using her for your benefit."

"Well, well." Reeve's eyes had narrowed. "Seems I will be breaking your bloody fingers."

"Try," Alan suggested. His pulse pounded in his temples. The moment Reeve so much as twitched he'd slam him to the ground. He forced mildness.

"She can make her own decisions," he said.

Reeve struck a match with surprising grace and puffed his cigarette.

"They still get the job done." He regarded his hands. "Pentonville mitts, I call them." He stuck the cigarette on his lip, then fisted and flexed his right hand. "Some days I need the brush tied on."

"That happened at Pentonville." Alan said it levelly, but his stomach turned over. Prison meant hard bed, hard board, hard labor. It was supposed to be punishment, not torture.

"Oh aye." Reeve tilted back his head and produced a perfect ring of smoke. It warped as it rose. "That and more."

Their silence filled with country noise. Chickens, cockchafers, rustling leaves.

Alan asked without thinking, "Did you steal Reynolds's inkstand?"

Reeve lowered his chin and barked a laugh. He sneered. "The Royal Academy was stealing. It's a bad thing to hoard riches as wee girls go hungry. Did you learn nothing in church?"

Alan raised his brows. "Wee girls going hungry. That excuses the theft of bread."

"Only a rich man sitting behind his mahogany desk thinks a silver inkstand is a silver inkstand." Reeve snorted. "For everyone else, a silver inkstand *is* bread. A year of it. Should we ask the baker herself?"

Alan twisted and saw Nina marching back to them, flushed, more of her hair loose around her shoulders. She held a bottle in each hand, long green necks in a white-knuckled grip.

"Birdie." Reeve waved with his cigarette. "Mr. De'Ath thinks it's all right to steal so long as it's from bakeries. What do you think?"

"*Stop* it," demanded Nina, eyes flashing. "*Please.*"

Reeve's smile held more than a hint of hostility. "I can, if he can."

"When the police come . . ." Nina walked forward, put the bottles on the table, and took a breath before she faced them. "I'm turning myself in too."

"Like hell you are." Reeve's face blotched with red.

"We worked together." Nina wrapped her arms around herself. "A team."

Alan rose, and Nina looked at him. Now that she was here, in this garden, he could tell that her eyes were the color of spring earth, of life itself. Her hair a canvas for shifting shade and light.

"It's the right thing to do," she said. She sounded firm, her calm rehearsed. She hadn't been crying on an aunt's bosom inside the cottage. She'd been fortifying her resolve. "I forged dozens upon dozens of pictures. Write the full story. Leave nothing out."

"No." Something clawed was rummaging in his guts.

"I'm with De'Ath on this one." Reeve leapt to his feet, pistol in his hand. He trained it on her. "Not another word out of you."

Nina stared. "Oh, please." Alan was stepping around her before he realized this particular *please* wasn't an entreaty but an expression of disgust.

"Put the gun down." He moved toward Reeve. Nina tried to sidle between them, to shield him with her body.

"Out of the way." She shoved again. "He won't shoot *me*."

Alan didn't budge. He felt the pistol's barrel dig into his ribs. Reeve directed a fierce glare at Nina.

"Concerned for him, are you?" He cocked the pistol, frowning. "If he's concerned for you, he'll help me lock you in the henhouse." He met Alan's gaze and gave an infinitesimal nod. The two of them could settle this for her, without her, in her best interest. Alan took a breath, overwhelmed by the desire to do exactly that. He was slow to shake his head.

"She can decide what she says to the police."

Reeve cursed a steady stream of filth.

"And so can I," Alan said. Anticipation—and suspicion—flared in Reeve's eyes.

The gate banged. Reeve jerked backward, shoving the pistol into his pocket.

"*You* get in the henhouse." Alan shouldered past him. "And tomorrow get on a bloody boat."

A man shambled into view. Not one of the detectives. Not a detective at all. Father Time, perhaps. His flowing white beard reached midway down his chest.

The gate banged again. Up in the tree, Fritz shrilled, a warning cry. A rotund dog bounded into the garden.

"Opal!" A rotund woman dressed all in pink appeared at the top of the path. "Catch her, Mr. Middleton!"

Father Time made an ineffectual swipe at the dog. Poultry scattered. The dog waddled straight to Nina.

"I missed you too," she said, dropping into a crouch. The dog wiggled and licked her face, tail thumping the grass.

"These hens are a menace!" The woman in pink swatted one

with her hat. "Lolly! Why are the hens out? You knew I was bringing Opal."

A broad, aproned woman with a serving dish had emerged from
the cottage. Her red hair circled her head in a braided crown.

"Bring her to the kitchen," she sang out, inclining her head toward the door she'd left open. "Sylvia saved her a bone."

The woman in pink jammed her hat on her head and bent to tie
a length of pink ribbon to the ring on the dog's collar.

"Hello, Nina dear," she said, as Nina stood, smoothing her skirt.
She raised her voice accusingly. "No one told me Nina was here. Or
that she was bringing a guest." She fixed Alan with her small sky
blue eyes. "I'm Millicent Swales. Oh, botheration. Lolly, the hens!"

She gave the nearest a vigorous swat. She and the dog were off,
beelining for the kitchen door. Alan reached Nina at the same moment Father Time clapped her in a grandfatherly embrace. He
stepped back with smiling eyes—his mouth was invisible within
the extraordinary expanse of beard—and nodded at Alan before
continuing on through the chickens.

After the sudden commotion, the garden seemed eerily quiet.

Nina resumed smoothing her skirt. It took her a moment to lift
her gaze.

"You told Jack to hide," she said, with a hitch in her voice.

So he had. He scratched his brow. "That's the long and short of it."

"What about the detectives?"

He shrugged. "They should have come quicker. Reeve *was* here,
like I said." He glanced about, as did Nina. No trace of Jack remained. He might have climbed into the henhouse or escaped
through the back gate. "Now he's gone."

"Because you let him go." The clouds shifted and the light
painted her hair gold.

"You can stop reminding me." He leaned more heavily on his
cane. "I'll make my case about the forgeries regardless."

His success—sensational success—would be guaranteed if the
forger confessed, hell, if *both* forgers confessed. Syme's career would
be over.

He sighed. "It will be more of a challenge this way, that's all."
He paused.

"Do you want to go with him?" he asked, and realized he was holding his breath.

She shook her head.

"Will he make you?"

She shook her head again, more defensively.

"He pointed a gun at you."

"He'd fire it at himself first." She lifted her chin, daring him to contradict her. He said nothing, and she took a deep breath. "Jack will go. I'll stay. Here." She shifted her gaze. Alan followed it.

Millicent Swales, Miss Lolly, and Mr. Middleton had gathered under the fruit tree, at the table, which was now stacked with crockery. Another woman stood with them, tall and slender, with a high silver bun. She was staring back at him with pursed lips.

Aunt Sylvia.

He tipped his head to her, trying to communicate all his most noble intentions with that slight bow, then angled his body, screening Nina from prying eyes.

"Make your offer to Mr. Craddock," he said to her. "Make your offer, and then, while he deliberates, come back to London." His voice dropped. "Come back to me."

Her eyes rounded.

"The talk in town will be awkward for you." He cleared his throat. "Word about Reeve will spread in artistic circles, about the investigation. But barring an arrest, a trial—interest will wane quickly. In the meantime, we can dine in."

"You hardly ever dine in." Her mouth flattened. "You won't like missing the excitement."

At that, he let a smile drift across his mouth. "I won't be lacking for excitement."

For a moment, she twinkled, a little burst of gratified surprise, then she frowned. "You find art and politics exciting." Her brows came together. "You find *poetry* exciting."

"I find you exciting." He watched the crests of her cheeks flush. "I'd rather hear your recipes than sonnets. In fact, your recipes are more poetic than most poetry. All the dissolving sugar and butter washed in rosewater. Wonderful imagery." He shook his head.

"Recipes don't have imagery." She gave him a grudging smile, dimples like two dark currants in her cheeks. "They have ingredients."

"I wonder if you could bake using a poem instead of a recipe."

"I wonder if you've taken leave of your senses." She firmed her mouth, deepening the crease in her lush lower lip. He could detect a hint of the perfume she'd worn to the ball on the breeze, and the creamy honey scent of her skin.

"You've taken over my senses," he murmured. "I wanted to say this somewhere more private . . ."

He glanced toward the table. The elderly villagers were seated, except for Aunt Sylvia, who'd begun serving the roast. They seemed occupied and were out of earshot.

He looked back at Nina. "Nina Finch. Will—"

"You're going to propose." She was clearly aghast. "Because of last night."

"And this morning," he teased. Pink tinted her throat. Her breasts were rising and falling with her quickened breath. Their plump swell made him feel positively carnivorous.

"If you need to ask as a sop to your conscience, go ahead." She stood taller. "The answer is no."

"Conscience can go hang." He met her eyes squarely. "It's not because of last night, or this morning. It's because of all the nights and mornings to come."

He reached out and touched her hand.

"It's because your whole being is like a melody repeating not in my head, but in my heart. My very blood hums with you."

"Poetry," she whispered, her tone dismissive. But her eyes were shining. She hadn't pulled back.

"A recipe, then," he said slowly. His thumb slid down the slope of her palm. She made a small sound in her throat.

"A recipe for a life. We combine ourselves. Bodies, minds, hands, hearts. Joys, fears. Dreams. Then we divide the mixture. Not *you* in Hensthorpe, and *me* in Chelsea. Us, in both. With Fritz, preferably washed in rosewater, and whatever and whoever else we want to add. Poultry, perhaps."

The chickens were circling.

Nina's fingers closed over his thumb. Then their palms slid together.

"I'd planned to open my art gallery in a fruit warehouse." His heart was rising on a tide of hope. "Why not a farmstead? The literati adore an out-of-the-way locale."

"You'd put on exhibitions in a barn?"

"I'd remove the cows." He arched a brow. "But yes, in essence. And Londoners will come by the dozen, by the baker's dozen. They'll buy you out of cakes."

The sun on Nina's tipped-up face illuminated the faint smattering of freckles on the bridge of her nose.

"I meant what I said to you," she whispered. "I never wanted to marry anyone. *Much comfort in cats, little in men.* My mother used to repeat that like a lullaby."

"There's risk in love." He acknowledged it, a muscle ticking in his jaw. He leaned forward, and his shadow fell across her.

Her eyes held turbulent emotions. She put her other hand on his chest. "Alan. There's something I have to tell you."

Dread snaked through him. He shifted, and the sun flashed in her eyes.

"Lady Kilderbee's letters," she said. "You have to give them back."

Chapter Twenty-Seven

ALAN LOOKED UP at the spun-sugar clouds. The sun was warm on his face. He wasn't sure if Nina had broken his heart or his brain.

Her voice sounded far away. "You can't blackmail the duke."

He stirred himself. "I don't understand. You've developed an eleventh-hour respect for the rule of law?"

He did understand that he'd proposed, or nearly, and she hadn't said yes.

"It's not about the law. It's about Claud."

He stared, a strange, sick shiver moving over him.

"It's about what he needs," she said.

"Well, then." He jerked a nod. "That's exactly why I had you take the letters in the first place."

"What *he needs*." Her eyes began to shimmer. "Not what you want."

Heat radiated from their conjoined palms. Her other hand was still pressing his chest. He felt as though it were pressing down on his heart. He'd never seen her so pale.

"Claud needs what any little boy needs." He groped for patience. "And I refuse to let Geoffrey make—"

"There was blood."

Something like fog billowed in his head. The greenery of the garden grayed before his eyes.

"Last night, after he coughed. On the handkerchief. There was blood."

He released the hand he held, then stepped back, away from the pressure of the other.

"The monogram is surrounded by pimpernels." His own voice seemed to come from elsewhere. "You mistook the scarlet thread."

"*Alan*." Her eyes were galaxies, big and dark. He felt small, awaiting cosmic judgment.

"The blood was blood." She breathed it. "It was *his* blood. You don't believe me?"

There was new horror in her voice, and a note of shock.

He heard a serrated laugh. It had sawn its way through his windpipe.

"You suffered in Pistoia." She clutched his wrist. He couldn't look at her, so he gazed over her shoulder. "Going there might save Claud's life."

He flicked his eyes to her face. "Do you suppose I would deprive Claud of medical attention? I'm friends with several doctors I respect highly. Once I have guardianship, they'll advise me. If he were to have consumption, then . . ."

"He does have consumption." Her certainty was terrible. "I know he does. Everyone knows. Alan, you're . . ."

"Deluded," he finished for her. "Yes, I may be. I admitted as much." She used the admission against him now. His heart gave a violent lunge.

He ground his teeth. "But not about Claud."

"I wasn't going to say deluded." Her pale face was fierce. "I was going to say afraid. You're afraid to face it. But *we* can face it. Together."

"No." He spoke abruptly, broke her grip on his wrist.

He could picture the London skyline, Umfreville House, Claud in bed, the red counterpane. He could picture the handkerchief in his hand.

White. The handkerchief was white as snow.

He became aware that Nina's eyes were melting under his gaze. Tears spilling over.

"Not to worry," he murmured. "The detectives and I will repair to London on the next train."

She brushed at her cheeks. "And then?"

"Make your offer to Mr. Craddock," he said, and paused. He

could feel that the smile forming on his lips was cruel. "Or does your objection to blackmail mean you renounce your payment?"

Nina drew a sharp breath.

"Come to London for your money, if nothing else." He turned from her, a rapid motion, like ripping off a scab.

"My apologies." He approached the table, summoning everyone's attention. The two aunts wore identical expressions of concern. How had Nina explained his presence? And how much of their little show had they witnessed? Miss Lolly and Aunt Sylvia exchanged a look.

"I'm sorry I didn't have the pleasure of a longer acquaintance," he said.

"Or a proper introduction." Aunt Sylvia raised a thin brow.

"Or that," he acknowledged, and departed.

SLEEP WAS IMPOSSIBLE. Finally, Nina crept downstairs, careful not to wake her aunts as she passed by their bedroom doors. She sat in the parlor, cuddled under a blanket warmed and weighted with the fattest and fluffiest of the cats. Charlemagne vibrated against her. The clock ticked on the mantel. Last night, at this hour, she'd been wrapped in Alan's arms.

He was back in Chelsea by now.

Her throat felt full. She hadn't managed a bite of roast at dinner.

The seconds ticked by. She heard a thump and drumming paws and Billie joined Charlemagne on her lap. At some point, she dozed. When she opened her eyes, the candles had burned low, and Jack stood before her in the flickering shadows.

"You should get yourself to bed."

She sat up straighter. "Where were you?"

"Here and there. The King's Arms." He dropped onto the sofa. Bits of straw stuck to his dirt-rimmed boots.

"Did you track that all through the house?" She realized she was speaking too loudly and scowled, lowering her voice to an emphatic whisper. "You smell like a cow."

"Spent some time in a hayloft." He shrugged, then squinted, trying to read her expression. "You're sore with me." He leaned forward.

"Shabby play, taking your money without asking. But I swear on our mother, I'll make it up to you."

She glanced down, fingertips sifting through Charlemagne's soft fur. "I'd rather you didn't."

Parting would be easier—simpler—if he were shabby to the last.

"What's that supposed to mean?"

"Keep your voice down." She cast a meaningful look at the ceiling.

"I didn't burn your ledger." He matched her whisper. "Makes me stupid as a turnip, but I have to show you somehow I'm not diddling." His voice rose. "You *will* get every penny, and tenfold."

She returned her attention to Charlemagne, began to pick at his fur, like Fritz would do.

"And the trouble's over with Whitechapel. No one's going to crack my head. Laddie's paying the protection."

She stilled her fingers as the pause lengthened.

"For a share in the factory."

She looked up with a snort. "Right." She should have known. Laddie hadn't squealed, because he stood to gain by his silence.

"And he can run it. Not my first choice, but as it turns out, I'm getting on a bleeding boat."

"Trouble's over," she repeated, and frowned. "Why the gun, then?"

"Matches my cuff links," he said evenly. "Did you notice the engravings on the brass?"

"I noticed the steel barrel." She glared. "When you poked it into my face."

"That was . . ." He grimaced and draped his arm over the back of the sofa. "Sorry for that." He tilted his head and studied the ceiling for a moment before he leveled his gaze. "Birdie."

"Jack." Charlemagne rolled, and she stroked his belly.

"What would you say to Paris?"

"I wouldn't say anything." She felt something hard-cornered with her fingertip, a sticky fragment of leaf, and removed it gently from Charlemagne's fur with her nails. "I don't speak French."

"*Merde.*" Jack flashed his teeth. "In that case, you'll learn."

Slowly, she shook her head. "*I'm* not getting on a boat."

Billie's back paws kicked against her thighs, and he was off, slinking toward the fireplace.

She swallowed hard. Alan's voice was in her ear. *Make your offer to Mr. Craddock.*

She exhaled. "I can buy it now. The bakery."

"And how's that?"

She pressed her cheek to Charlemagne's head. "An agreement I made. With Alan."

"*He* is buying the bakery." Jack said it carefully, too carefully.

She shut her eyes. A mess. From the very moment she and Alan had met. Broken china and betrayals. And yet, when she was with him, she felt whole, solid, every part of her put to rights.

"In return for what?"

She opened her eyes and the look in Jack's made her wish she hadn't.

"What did the bastard make you do?"

"It's my affair," she said, an unfortunate phrase. Jack's eyes caught more of the room's light and blazed.

She knew that expression. He'd detonate at a heartbeat.

"I'm not a child." She locked eyes with him. "You're not either, so stop your huff."

He raised his clenched fist. She flinched, barely. His fist reached his lips. She registered for the first time that he'd stripped his rings. Maybe Laddie had demanded collateral.

"Tell me one thing." He lowered his fist, drilling his knuckles into the arm of the sofa.

"Should I be sorry I didn't shoot him?" His eyes darkened. "If so, I won't be sorry long."

"Sorry?" *She* detonated, rising from the chair. "I'm so sick of *sorry* I could scream. I don't want you to *be* sorry, or not sorry."

"Don't you, now?"

"No!" she snapped. "I want you to *be* someone who keeps his head!"

"Doing a bang-up job of that yourself," he observed. "Where's *your* head, Birdie? De'Ath turned it, that's clear as day. Bit of advice. Don't pin your hopes on a ponce. You're lower than dirt to the likes of him."

"And to you I'm special?" She was staring at that naked fist. "Your beloved sister, who you can browbeat and knock around and use when and how it suits you."

His fist jumped, and she hunched her shoulders, sheltering Charlemagne with her body. Jack didn't sweep the lamp from the table or punch the arm of the sofa. He froze, looking up at her. She froze too, tense, miserable, not bothering to hide it. Hoping he *saw* it, saw her every strained nerve. Layers of fray, telling the worst story of their lives together. An undeniable record, like the rings in a tree.

He blanched.

"I'm sorry," he muttered.

The word hung in the air.

He tried again. "You know I love you."

"Love isn't an excuse." She didn't blink.

He sagged. "Jesus God." It was a supplication rather than a curse. He released a long breath. "I'm not a saint. But I'm not a bloody ogre. I try my best. What more can I do?"

"Don't ask me." She gave a small shrug. "Ask yourself."

His fist collapsed into loose fingers, each bent tip distinct against the dark upholstery.

"Fair enough," he grated. "I will."

Silence yawned between them, sudden and profound. On the periphery, she heard, again, the tick of the clock.

Her arms felt slack. Charlemagne twisted and went limp, slipping under her elbows, hopelessly floppy. She bobbled, trying to keep her hold. No good. She bent her knees so he could roll down the ramp of her skirt, and she heard Jack laugh.

"As though he were cooked in a soup."

She met his gaze. His eyes were damp, his smile uncertain. His face—it was more familiar to her than her own.

"A noodle with fur," she agreed, sighing, and wedged herself beside him on the sofa.

At last, Jack spoke, so softly she had to strain to hear him. "I'll go tomorrow."

She nodded, eyes on the fireplace. Charlemagne had joined Billie, the two of them flanking Fritz's bed.

"Without you," he said, and the hint of a question in his voice meant she had to nod again.

She could tell he was studying her. Tears pricked her eyes. She bit her quivering lip.

"Chin up," he murmured. "You'll be all right." No question in his voice now. "More than all right."

She curled her legs under her, leaned into the arm of the sofa, rested her head. She wasn't so sure. His hand was a warm weight on her shoulder. Neither of them moved. As soon as they did, it would start, their new apartment. She concentrated on her breath, let her lids drift down. When she opened her eyes again, she had to blink against the morning light. She was still there on the sofa, and Jack was gone.

LATER THAT DAY, after she'd shaken out the rugs and swept up the straw and the cat fur, she walked to the bakery and lingered outside by the window. The bell was tinkling as customers came and went. She watched Mr. Craddock moving about behind the counter, wrapping orders in paper. After some time, she walked on, no longer taking in her surroundings. She felt disoriented, *here*, in Hensthorpe.

Nothing seemed right.

Back at the cottage, she found her aunts in the kitchen. Aunt Sylvia was hovering over a huge pot of milk on the stove. Miss Lolly stood at the table, squeezing the liquid from boiled nettles into a vat.

Nauseated, Nina sat on a stool. The sour-sweet odors of cheesemaking didn't usually repulse her. Her throat worked as she swallowed, and swallowed again. The door to the garden stood open. She could see the very spot where she and Alan had exchanged their final words. The desire to see *him* struck with such force it dislodged every buried emotion.

"Squeeze," directed Miss Lolly, pointing to the vat of nettles on the table.

Nina burst into tears.

"My heart alive!" Aunt Sylvia dropped the spoon and went to her. "Is it Jack? He won't be gone forever."

"Tears aren't for Jack, I reckon." Miss Lolly murmured it as Aunt Sylvia pressed Nina's head to her sternum.

That made Nina cry harder, until she managed to choke off her sobs and straighten.

"It's the bakery." She scrubbed at her wet cheeks, gulping for air. "I'm going to buy it."

Now Miss Lolly hugged her. "But this calls for celebration!" She pulled a pair of stained gloves from her apron pocket and brandished them. "Just as soon as we squeeze these nettles."

"I thought you and Jack were in some . . . financial difficulties." Aunt Sylvia uttered this cautiously as she turned back to the stove. She and Miss Lolly never pried. They were private themselves. And sharp-witted. Nina had long suspected they knew what she and Jack did in London. Or knew enough to know they'd do better not to ask.

"We've had setbacks." Nina took the wadded gloves from Miss Lolly and smoothed them flat on the table. She ached to unburden herself, to let every detail pour forth.

"I earned the money when I worked for Alan, the man you met, or didn't meet, rather." Her cheeks burned.

"Enough to buy the bakery." Aunt Sylvia was studying the milk in the pot.

"If I collect it." Nina shifted on her stool.

"If." Miss Lolly's brows crept up to her hairline.

"When." Nina gripped her elbows. "I'll go tomorrow, I suppose."

"To London. To collect your money." Miss Lolly used the strainer to scoop nettles from the vat.

"Yes. No. Perhaps." Nina felt sweat sliding down her back. She turned her eyes again to the garden. A mess. A royal blasted buggering mess.

"That's what you said the other day, isn't it?" Miss Lolly sounded suspiciously bland. "When he proposed."

Nina started, gaze snapping back. Miss Lolly was doing a poor job hiding her smile.

"Lolly, please." Aunt Sylvia put her hands on her hips.

"Fancy *you* couldn't tell." Miss Lolly shot Aunt Sylvia a triumphant look. She transferred the nettles to her gloved fist and gave a gleeful squeeze.

"Your aunt," she said to Nina, "received more marriage proposals than a decade of debutantes."

"It was extremely tiresome." Aunt Sylvia sighed. "*Did* he propose?"

"He did, almost." Nina's voice was a croak. "But then *he* rejected me."

"My," said Miss Lolly. "That's unusual."

"I added a condition." She gripped her elbows harder. "He's clever and kind and funny and *fizzing*, absolutely gorgeous, you saw him, and I love him—I love him—even though I've always been certain it's not worth it, loving someone, because it can end so poorly, and I might lose myself in the process, like Mother did. But he makes me feel like I've found myself, like I can do anything, because *we* can do anything." She gulped, dizzy. "But I'm afraid too. I'm afraid to love him, because *he's* afraid, of some part of himself he won't show me. And if he's already hiding, eventually I won't be able to find him, whether or not he's run off. And by then, losing him will feel like losing myself. Maybe it already does." Her chest was heaving.

Miss Lolly and Aunt Sylvia were looking at each other.

"The condition you mentioned, what was it?" Aunt Sylvia asked.

"To face a very painful truth, about his nephew. I'd face it *with* him, of course. I said that. And he said no. And that means he's going to harm the boy, inadvertently."

Her breathing stayed shallow, as she glanced from aunt to aunt.

"Are you sure *you* didn't reject *him*?" asked Miss Lolly.

"I don't know. He might have thought so." Nina bent double. "Does it sound like I rejected him?"

Aunt Sylvia cleared her throat delicately.

"Bugger." Nina stood up so abruptly her calves bumped the stool's lowest rung. "What's the time?"

Aunt Lolly fumbled a watch up from a pocket, damp gloves smearing the face with green.

Seventeen minutes to the next train. Perhaps Alan hadn't yet gone to the duke. Perhaps, if she went to London now, she'd get another chance to stop him from making a terrible mistake.

"Did you ever regret it?" She fixed her eyes on Aunt Sylvia. "Refusing all those suitors?"

"Never." Aunt Sylvia gave her a radiant smile.

She nodded, heartbeat slowing. "You're happier alone."

"Alone?" Aunt Sylvia's expression shifted between concern and amusement. "My dear, I'm not alone." She glanced at Miss Lolly, who lifted her chin.

"*We're* not alone." Miss Lolly dropped her handful of spent nettles on a dish, a plop of punctuation.

Again, Nina glanced between them. She had the distinct impression they were communicating something of vast importance.

She wet her lips. "I meant something different. I meant, you're happier because you didn't choose *that* kind of love. You know, romantic love."

She blushed. She wasn't about to describe the love she'd experienced with Alan, composed of hope and agony, longing and giddy, unbearable pleasures.

Aunt Sylvia looked pensive. "Nina dear, there's a great deal we should have said to you."

"We thought it went without saying," interjected Miss Lolly.

"Oh." Nina stood for a moment, flummoxed, eyes flitting from woman to woman. "Will you say it, then? Or not?"

Aunt Sylvia's gaze met Miss Lolly's.

"We will," she said. "But not now. You look as though you have somewhere else to be."

Nina realized she was on her toes, half-twisted toward the door. "Do I?"

She was wringing her hands together, as though that action would keep her from tearing apart.

"Most certainly," said Miss Lolly. "You go, now." She smiled at Aunt Sylvia. "We'll be here."

Nina went. She sped upstairs to grab her portmanteau and the ledger Jack had left for her, and she clattered down again, gasping her goodbyes to her aunts, and to Fritz—snoozing with Billie in the parlor—then bursting out the front door. She reached the train station with mere seconds to spare. It wasn't long before she'd caught her breath. But her heart raced on.

CHAPTER TWENTY-EIGHT

"THREE NEW PAINTINGS, and six works in progress. And you're looking at the door."

Alan turned to face Augustus Burgess. The man feted as England's greatest living painter was shaking his head.

"I'm crushed," Burgess added, a hand pressed to the frogs of his colorful smoking jacket, light green velvet and rose madder silk. "Surely *Love in Avalon* is worth a second glance."

Alan's gaze swept the vast painting studio, crowded with aspirants and notables and with Burgess's easels. He hadn't given the pictures a first glance. Nor could he bear to do so now. The pigments seemed dangerous, as though they might stain his corneas. Make him see red where it didn't belong.

"You're looking at the door again," observed Burgess. "Come, now. The picture's not as bad as that."

Alan allowed himself a beat, to compose his face, to mirror his friend's teasing smile.

"It's worse," he drawled. Burgess laughed, easy and unoffended.

He should have stayed home. He'd hoped the salon would provide a recess from his roiling thoughts. Instead, he felt overstimulated, every sight and sound an irritant.

"I worried something was wrong. Not with *Love in Avalon*." Burgess flicked a lock of black hair over his shoulder. "With you."

Alan reached up to adjust his spectacles and remembered he wasn't wearing them.

"Standing in the corner," continued Burgess. "Perhaps you're saving your strength?" At Alan's blank expression, he grinned wickedly. "For a more important battle."

"You invited Syme." Alan waited for his own reaction. This news should organize his mind, give him purpose.

"Of course I did. My guests don't come for the canapés. They come to see history being made. Syme's fired up. Did you hear? He got that prominent American critic, Ingalls, to inspect the paintings you disputed. And Ingalls agrees with him. Says they're originals." Burgess clapped his hands. "I'll clear the dais. You and Syme can have it out. Tit for tat."

"An exciting opportunity." Alan shrugged. "Sadly, I must decline." He started to walk, trying not to catch anyone's eye.

"You aren't leaving?" Burgess fell into step with him.

Alan veered around a sofa, focused on the door.

"You can't leave." Burgess jogged to catch up.

"I have a pressing engagement." Alan frowned at the half-truth. But *pressing engagement* was a more socially expedient explanation than *unannounced visit to a duke with intent to blackmail*.

"No one's on time for those." Burgess was undeterred. "Syme will be here any minute. Stay long enough to reel off a few of the clues that convinced you. For God and country. And for Henley, who'll put it in the papers."

Alan grunted. And the door opened. Disclosing not Syme, but . . .

"Dear God, a doublet!" Burgess called out with sufficient volume to draw all eyes to the new arrival. Kate Holroyd paused on the threshold, grinning. She was, as ever, equal to the attention. And most definitely dressed in a doublet. It was deep purple, and she'd paired it with black knee breeches and hose. She winked and gave an exaggerated bow. Alan saw in a flash who stood behind her. Compared to Holroyd, this woman faded into the background. She wore a plain brown dress. She had hair of an indeterminate shade, a round, sweet face. An unassuming presence. If you didn't overlook her entirely, you might think her ordinary.

His extraordinary, impossible love.

He stopped dead and stared.

Her face was *too* expressive. Staring wouldn't help him solve its mystery. He needed to hear her voice, feel her touch.

He didn't glance back at Burgess. The painting studio winked out. Everything winked out but Nina.

He went to her.

"May I have a word?" he asked, his voice low.

At her nod, he led the way to a small library. She entered ahead of him, and after he pulled the door shut, he leaned against it. She turned and looked at him, fingers playing nervously over the chain of her chatelaine purse. He realized she was travel worn—skirt rumpled, wisps of hair escaping her chignon—and weary. The shadows beneath her eyes attested to a wakeful night, much like the one he'd spent himself.

He pushed off the door. "I didn't expect to see you here."

"You weren't at your house."

He tipped his head. "I take it Holroyd was at my house. Doing what?"

"She'd called to collect you for this party. She thought you were driving together."

"Driving together." He walked forward, forcing himself to stop before he closed the distance between them completely. "Perhaps she sent a note I didn't open." The corner of his mouth kicked up, a minor effort. "It happens. As you know, I don't have a secretary."

The light was dim, but Nina flushed. "You should go to an agency."

She looked fatigued, but she sounded spirited as ever.

"You spoke with Mr. Craddock?" He assumed a businesslike demeanor. "I haven't yet spoken with my brother. I tried him at home, twice. I even visited that bastion of feudal thinking he calls a *club*." He gave a slight grimace. "I was about to return to Park Lane when you arrived." He paused. "You won't leave London empty-handed."

"That's not . . ." Her hand closed convulsively on her chatelaine. "I brought something for you." She dug inside the purse. The notebook she extracted was unfamiliar. She held it as though it were fragile.

"I used it as a ledger." She stared down at it, then thrust it toward him. He tucked his cane beneath his arm and took it, thumbing it open. He recognized her neat handwriting. Rows of phrases, names, numbers. Calculations. He turned a page, then another.

"*Bust of a Man in a Plumed Beret*," he read. "Rembrandt. Sleaford. Twenty-five." He looked at her.

"Twenty-five pounds," she said. "That's what we got from Sleaford. The debits are on the left, for materials and the like. The final tallies are at the bottom of each page."

"*Portrait of a Knight of Malta with a Rosary*." He frowned. "This went to Edward Whitcombe."

"Do you know him? You can tell him, then, that Titian didn't paint it." She laced her fingers together.

Alan kept turning pages. There. The titles of the paintings Syme had acquired for the South Kensington Museum.

This notebook proved they were forgeries.

It proved so much more than that.

He drew a breath, raised his eyes. "Why are you giving this to me?"

"I knew you'd find it useful." She averted her gaze. "I thought Jack had burned it."

"He should have."

That made her gaze swing back to him. "He returned it instead. He wanted to show me that he respected what was mine."

"Charming." He bit his tongue. The library's oak fireplace was massive. He could burn the notebook himself. Or he could hand it back to her. He flipped it closed and hesitated. "This isn't part of our bargain."

"You decided not to catch a forger." Her eyes grew brighter. "I decided to give you that ledger." She hesitated, shifting her weight. "I decided something else too." She blinked rapidly, as though she couldn't quite believe what she was saying. "I renounce the payment. If you blackmail the duke . . . I renounce it."

He must have made a small shocked movement. A muscle in his hip wound tight. Time stood still.

He shook his head. "Nina's Sweets. You must know I'll do anything to make it yours. Because . . ." He heard the gravel in his voice and stopped.

Because I love you.

He cleared his throat. "Because shortbread needs its Da Vinci."

"Mozart." Her face had changed. She was looking at him with higher color, shinier eyes. And he was looking at her . . . with neutrality, he hoped. Not with desperate, thirsting desire. Her lips parted. Something tugged behind his ribs.

"I prefer Mozart," she said. "Da Vinci makes me think of amber varnish and Lavender Spike Oil."

His brow creased with horrified awe. "You forged Da Vincis."

"Check the ledger," she murmured, dimples flickering as she gave him a sheepish smile.

"I want the bakery." She swallowed, smile fading. "But I can find another way."

"What way?" He stared.

"I don't know," she admitted. "But this is more important."

"This?"

"You. Us." He could sense her frustration unraveling into something frantic. "Claud." She took a ragged breath. "I understand how hard it is to let him go, but—"

"You understand?" Goaded, he leaned over her. "Then how can you insist that I abandon him?"

Her chin was tipped up. She didn't flicker an eyelid.

"You *don't* understand." He leaned closer. "The feeling of isolation that makes the days run together. The sheer *terror* of being powerless and alone."

Suddenly, the air went thin, and his lungs bucked in his chest. The world slipped from him. Everything was gone. He hung in darkness.

And felt soft pressure, the touch of her hand.

"Alan," she said gently. "It's not the same as what you experienced. With Claud—it's not the same."

He planted his heels, focused on her face. He gave her his fiercest stare. "I *won't* abandon him."

"Don't. Don't abandon him." She held his gaze. Clear brown eyes. No pity in their depths, but rather a compassion so profound it dizzied. "Accompany him, however you can. When he goes to

Italy, write him every day. Write him adventure stories. Help make his life full. Help him heal."

He straightened abruptly. His pulse was leaping.

"You *are* abandoning him," she said, "if you can't see him as he truly is."

"I see him." His throat was so tight.

"You don't see him. You see yourself," she whispered.

The white handkerchief unfurled in his mind. He couldn't see anything through it. Or else it was the sudden flare of pain blinding him. His leg was a spike driving toward his spine.

"I'm going to fall. I'm going to fall down."

In an instant, she was pressed to him, small and soft, unbelievably strong. Bearing his weight. The sofa was only steps away. They tumbled onto it. He collapsed backward, stretching out his leg.

"Are you all right?" she asked, breathless.

"No." He wanted to disown the truth as soon as it passed his lips. To shape his lips into a sardonic smile. Fix his mask in place. Instead, he let his head tip back.

"No, I'm not all right."

She didn't say anything. She resettled herself carefully beside him. In two tentative movements, she laid her cheek on his shoulder, her arm on his chest. His breath shuddered out. And then the ice in his chest melted. His taut muscles began to ease. He inhaled deeply, a bigger breath than the pain wanted to allow.

He wrapped his arm around her and held her close.

CHAPTER TWENTY-NINE

SOMETIME LATER, NINA stirred. Alan's heart thumped beneath her, the beats steady but far too quick. His hand slid up her arm, then smoothed her hair back from her temples. She stilled and let him stroke. He repeated the slow, soothing motion. *She* found it soothing. But she understood why he did it. Alan was soothing himself. A lump formed in her throat.

"I feel like Charlemagne," she said at last, pressing her nose into his coat. Alan paused his stroking, hand cupping her head.

"The cat," she clarified. And then, to clarify further: "It's a favorable feeling."

His hand grew heavier.

Her own heartbeat quickened. "How do *you* . . . feel?"

"As though I finally understand why you prize cats." His hand began to move again.

She pushed her whole face into his coat. He smelled better than good. She couldn't get enough, not through the fabric at any rate. She sat up, and he lifted away his arm so she could readjust next to him. He sucked in his breath. She saw his cheeks hollow, his cheekbones leap forward.

"Alan?" His name was the question. She wasn't sure what else to ask.

He didn't look at her but instead looked straight ahead.

"Greek romances." He angled his gaze and met her eyes. His

were narrowed, a silver gleam. "The Song of Songs. Old French epics. Elizabethan sonnets." His face regained a hint of drollery. "Love is a wellspring of language." He paused. Stark lines appeared on his brow. "Pain, on the other hand. Pain makes language run dry."

She felt dry, as though she might crumble and blow away. "You don't have to say anything."

She'd needed him to show himself, the hurt part he hid away. But now she worried she'd rushed him, that she should have trusted, and waited.

"I'm here," she whispered, flushing at the inadequacy. His expression softened. When he reached out, she thought he'd resume his stroking. Instead, he framed her face with his hand, studying it as only he ever had, with an enraptured intensity that sent a shiver through her entire body.

"With me, the pain comes and goes. Now it's going." His thumb grazed her jaw as he withdrew his hand. He let his head fall back on the sofa. "Sometimes it keeps me up all night. Sometimes it strikes by day, and I can barely keep my feet. I do, though. Usually."

"Usually you smile." She pictured him in the Olgilvie Gallery, his waxen face, the curve of his lips.

"Part of the act." He was smiling now, a dark smile. He stretched out his leg again, a long, muscular leg, encased in black cloth. It looked solid.

"Your injury still pains you." She spoke slowly as she tried to work it out.

Pain, not as a constant, but as a constant possibility, introduced that hesitancy into his gait. He was never certain his next step wouldn't hurt.

"You don't know why." She watched his face. "And that makes it difficult to accept."

More than difficult. He'd told her he thought he was losing his mind. *Or his soul.*

Right now, he had the look of the damned.

"The *doctors* don't know," he corrected. "I have a theory." His mouth twisted. "A story. A nightmare, perhaps."

"Tell me." She could hear her own heart. He looked at her, and something seemed to snap behind his eyes. Smothering a groan, he folded over her. The ridge of his brow ground against her forehead. She felt herself sinking into the cushion, his weight bearing down, his breath featherlight. At that moment, she wanted to sink with him forever.

He ripped away, pushing his back into the corner of the sofa.

"What if I *didn't* break my leg?" His gaze seemed to pour into her. "A concussion, bruising, yes. But no shattered pelvis, no un-united fracture of the femur. What if . . . my mother had the surgeon cut me anyway? What if she had him operate for no other purpose than to create this, this pain? I can *feel* something, like a thorn. So sharp, so . . ."

He gritted his teeth. She was afraid a single word would silence him. She took his hand and placed it on her chest. Her heart was pounding a refrain.

I'm here. I'm here. I'm here.

"What if my mother gave her ruby earrings to the surgeon? What if he cut into my hip and put one inside? One red teardrop." Every little muscle in his jaw stood out. "It makes perfect sense. Monstrously perfect sense. Which is no sense at all." He approximated a laugh. "I've searched for hospital records, correspondence between my mother and the surgeon. I've searched for those infernal earrings. I've considered"—his voice grew hoarse—"I've considered asking a doctor to cut me open. To look."

Her gasp slipped out. His gaze slid over her hungrily, as though he craved reaction. As though he wanted her to revile him.

"What if there's nothing? What if I have myself hacked apart for no reason?" His voice dwindled.

His face was perfect agony. Denials surged, nearly tripped off her tongue. She wanted to reject his anguish, his theory, everything that hurt him.

She swallowed hard. "You do have a reason."

"The earring." His head jerked. "You think it's there?"

"I don't know. The pain is there. Pain is a reason. Confusion, fear—those are reasons. Taken together, they motivate most of human behavior." She paused. "Along with greed, I suppose. And pride."

"Now you're naming sins." His eyes began to glitter strangely. "Are those mine?"

She felt her color rise. "I'd begun to speak more generally."

"Rather dark view," he murmured. His smile was less awful to behold.

"I wasn't finished." Her breath whooshed out. "There's enough pain in this one world to spread across a hundred others. But you *can* act out of something else instead. You can find other reasons, for different actions. Hope." Her pulse crashed in her ears. "Love." She swallowed the lump that had re-formed in her throat. "You can open your heart."

"Metaphorically." His smile was . . . his smile. Crooked. Humorous. His gaze slitted, speculatively. "My heart . . . instead of my hip."

She swallowed harder. "No saw."

"I didn't want to bring you into this nightmare," he whispered.

"We're not going to live in a nightmare, or in a pretty dream either." She stared into his eyes. "We're going to live in the world together, the beautiful, terrifying world."

He nodded. She felt as though her heart was beating into his hand.

He shut his eyes, and when they opened, his lashes were spiky with damp.

"The poet John Keats had consumption." His conversational tone jarred with his expression. "One night, he saw blood on his pillowcase. He said that was his death warrant."

"And?"

"He died." There was a slight hitch in his voice. "At twenty-five, in Italy."

She looked away. It wasn't in her power—or anyone's—to tell him what course Claud's disease would take.

His hand crept higher, fingertips brushing her collarbone.

"Claud isn't you," she said. "And he's not John Keats either." She drew her legs up onto the sofa and knelt beside him, their faces level.

"We all die," she said softly. "But love gives life fullness. No matter how brief. We don't any of us know how much time we have. We should—"

He kissed her like she was his next breath. She fell back, circling him with her arms, dragging him with her. His heaviness pressed everywhere. She had no air in her lungs. They were extracting what they needed to survive from each other, with their tongues and their teeth.

They were still kissing when a cry rang out.

"There you are!"

Nina was slow to understand. Alan's tongue was gliding over hers, most distractingly. She held a fistful of his hair, and her other hand had somehow traveled beneath his coat to better knead the frankly nonmalleable muscles of his hard, wide chest. As for the placement of Alan's hands, one entire arm was up her skirt, fingers fanned between her legs. His visible hand was groping her breast.

He turned his face to the side and growled. "Holroyd. Do you ever knock?"

Kate—she'd insisted Nina call her Kate—bounded across the threshold.

"I beat down doors from time to time," she said. "Does that count? I hate to interrupt, but a certain old windbag is maligning your intelligence in the studio."

Alan sighed, tugging down Nina's skirt and doing up her buttons with unnerving facility. He rose to sitting, and Nina scrambled up too, less composedly. Her hair was a mess. Her limbs were trembling.

"I thought you should know." Kate folded her arms.

"Now I know." Alan gave her a pointed look.

"You're missing an opportunity."

Alan raised his brows in answer. Nina almost choked. Neither he nor Kate seemed remotely abashed.

"I respect your priorities." Kate grinned and tipped her head to Nina with the barest suggestion of a wink. "I'll be going. I'll let you drive her home, then." Kate slanted a smile at Alan, who ignored her.

"Right," she said. "I was going, wasn't I?"

She went.

"I want to take you home," said Alan softly as the door clicked shut. "Unless"—he spoke more softly still—"you want me to take you here."

"We can split the difference." Nina's voice was too hoarse to carry the joke. "The carriage?"

His eyes glowed like falling stars. A flare, and then darkness as he claimed her mouth.

At last, they were moving down the blue hallway. When they reached the door to the studio, Alan paused.

"This won't be but a moment," he promised.

The crowded room went silent when he rapped his cane on the floor, except for Kate, who gave a victorious yawp from the sofa. Nina edged away from him, out of the sight lines of the eager guests.

"I have something to say, regarding the pictures you acquired for South Kensington." Alan addressed Lloyd Syme, who stood in the middle of the floor, snifter in hand, mouth screwed up as though filled with lemon juice.

"More tripe." Syme had a deep, carrying voice. "From a man who confuses art criticism with criminology."

A few titters here and there. Holroyd's hiss. Then, again, a silent expectancy.

Now was the moment for Alan to whip out her ledger—Jack's ledger, he'd have to say. Syme would crumble. Kate would yawp. Alan would bask in glory.

But a moment, he'd said.

She'd fade into the background. He'd want more than a moment, certainly. To revel.

He turned his head. He looked at her, not Syme.

"I was mistaken." His voice was deep and carrying.

"What?" Syme exclaimed.

"I shouldn't have attributed the pictures to Jack Reeve." Alan looked back at Syme. "Terribly shortsighted of me. I'll let Sir Cunliffe-Owen know I've seen the light." His gaze flicked again to Nina. His smile was richly satisfied. He gave one more rap with his cane. "I think that's all, then."

You could have heard a hog bristle drop from a brush.

No one moved.

"Adieu," said Alan brightly. Voices erupted. Nina might have stayed rooted in place, but Alan took her hand in front of all assembled and led her from the room. Tugged her, in truth. She was too dazed to keep pace with him, her laggard mind trying to catch up to the implications, her feet faltering.

He'd called it off, the hunt for Jack, the excruciating public conversation about pictures that *she* had painted. He'd put her feelings before his reputation.

At the top of the stairs, he turned and crowded her into the wall, kissing her until she was dazed *and* senseless.

"Make haste." He interspersed the words with licks to her neck. "Our carriage awaits."

That helped. She hastened.

He must have given the coachman the opposite instructions.

The drive back to Chelsea took an exquisitely long time.

NINA SLEPT STUNNINGLY late and woke all at once.

"It isn't noon?" She opened her eyes and gasped, sitting bolt upright.

"It's one." Alan was lounging beside her, wide awake but seemingly disinclined to bestir himself. He gave her a lazy smile.

"You must have somewhere to be." She pushed her hair back from her flustered face. "Or do you feel too humbled to show your face?" She bit her lip. Saying he was wrong in front of dozens of artists and critics, not to mention his nemesis—did he regret it already?

"Humbled?" Alan lifted a brow. "No man would feel *humble* after such a night."

Nina's blush started behind her navel.

"Perhaps you've forgotten the things you said?" He rolled over and trapped her between his arms. "Does this sound familiar?" His lips were at her ear, the murmurs breathy and hot.

"I never said *that*," she gasped.

"No?" He maneuvered his lower body, braced himself above her. "Maybe I got ahead of myself."

She melted beneath him, opening to bring him deep inside. His tongue, his cock. They moved together, and she kept silent at first, smiling her challenge against his mouth, her eyes wide so she could see the wicked glint in his. He gripped her knee, angling it up. His next thrust made her groan. She clung to him as he took her and took her. She didn't know what she said, what she did, only that the pleasure made something clench right in the very pit of her being, and that when it exploded, she'd scream. His hand wedged between them, his thumb rubbing *there*, as he pumped his hips. She screamed, and his smile pressed into her neck. The words *he* muttered as he jerked in her arms made the most obscenely gratifying music she'd ever heard.

AN HOUR AFTER breakfast, they lazed into the drawing room for tea. As Alan flipped through the newspapers, Nina nibbled a biscuit and gazed out the window at the garden.

"No articles yet." Alan discarded his paper. "That look—you're thinking of your brother."

"He's in France." She put the half-eaten biscuit on the rim of her saucer. Jack didn't know of his imminent exoneration. He'd find out at some point. She supposed he'd return. What kind of contact would they have then, if any?

She gave her head a shake. "I hadn't been thinking of Jack, actually. I was thinking of Kate Holroyd's picture. The one we saw in the smoking room at the Olgilvie Gallery."

He smiled. "*The Dreamers.*"

"They're both women." She smiled back at him. "I hadn't realized."

"It's ambiguous." Alan raised a brow. "Viewers will interpret the painting differently."

She drew a breath. "I should have realized . . . something else."

She could spend the rest of the afternoon reviewing touches, glances, a thousand little signs that comfort was but a small portion of what Aunt Sylvia and Miss Lolly gave each other.

"Which is?" Alan reached for her hand.

She hesitated. Her aunts kept their relationship secret. It wasn't for her to tell.

"Maybe I always did want to live a love story." Her smile felt watery.

"Ah." He played with her fingers, grinning. "What would you say, then, to a marmoset, a dozen cats, and a husband?"

She made a sound between a giggle and a gasp. "A *dozen* cats?"

He slid off the love seat, onto his knees.

"A dozen between this house and our farmstead, not in each. I have my limits." He laced their fingers together. His eyes shone. "You'll bake the bride cake, of course."

Her pulse was galloping. "You still want to marry me?"

"I do." He frowned with laughing eyes. "Wait, I'm getting ahead of myself. No *I do*s. Not until you say *yes*." He paused. "Do you? Don't answer. That was too abrupt. I'm going to start again, more ceremonially." He cleared his throat, and she could tell he was trying not to smile. "Nina Finch—"

The door flung open.

It was the Duke of Umfreville.

CHAPTER THIRTY

"WHERE IS MY SON?"

The duke strode into the room, hat under his arm.

"I'd assume in his bedchamber, as per usual." Alan rose slowly to his feet. "But for your very unexpected presence."

"He's not in his bedchamber." The duke didn't seem to notice that Alan had been on his knees, didn't seem to notice Nina at all. He paced a circle, peering behind furniture.

"He's not hiding in a vase in my drawing room either." Alan reached for his cane. Nina stood, moving close beside him in case he needed to steady himself.

The duke cast his hat onto a chair. He reached the windows and began to shake the curtains with the industry of one of his tormented housemaids.

"Nor is he in the curtains." Alan touched Nina's arm, then walked toward the duke. "Before you pull up the rug, why don't you tell me what's going on?"

"You tell me." The duke pivoted, his expression rancorous.

"What does Miss Milford have to say?" Alan's expression was unreadable. "She never leaves his side."

"I dismissed her. Yesterday. I think you knew. *You* were skulking around Park Lane. You called twice." The duke poked his finger into Alan's chest. "You orchestrated this, didn't you? You've been plotting something."

"I have been plotting something, yes." Alan laughed a laugh with too many edges. "Not a kidnapping. And not anymore."

"How do you explain the fact that my son is missing?" The duke all but yelled it.

"He seized an opportunity to run off."

"He wouldn't dare disobey me."

"No, in your household, the consequences of disobedience are most unpleasant." Alan's smile was breathtakingly sardonic. "But then, unpleasantness is the status quo. Which might dilute the deterrent effect."

"He is Marquess of Stancliff." The duke's nostrils flared. "I instilled in him a sense of duty."

"And the sense that he has already failed," said Alan in a low voice. "That he has already dashed your hopes. That *he* is the source of your abject misery."

"I'm not miserable."

"Brother, you are *rancid* with it." Alan leaned forward. "Misery permeates your house. Your foul mood is as bad for Claud as a wet climate."

"Here it comes. *I'm* making Claud ill." The duke sneered. "Like our mother made you ill."

Alan's face turned white.

Nina started forward. The duke turned his head and gave her a look of vague surprise.

"I don't think you invented Claud's illness, or that you're the cause." Alan was still as stone. "Claud has tuberculosis."

The duke's head snapped back around.

Alan rolled his shoulders, straightening. "He should go to Pistoia, if that's what the doctors recommend."

The duke froze, jawbone straining against the skin. He stood for three heartbeats in silence, then twitched into motion. "I need to find him."

He was halfway across the room when Alan called out.

"Let me help."

The duke kept walking. Nina gave herself a shake, picked up her skirts, and ran. She beat him to the door, with enough time to whirl around and—

"Dear God." He recoiled, just avoiding the collision. "Remove yourself from my path." He flicked the air, grimacing his distaste, then whipped around as Alan came up behind him and laid a hand on his shoulder.

"Where is he? You *are* hiding him, dammit."

Alan glanced at Nina, a question in his eyes. She nodded. *Tell him.*

She'd guessed too.

"I'm not hiding him." Alan sighed. "But I know where to look."

The duke shrugged off his hand. "After you, then."

THE ROYAL AQUARIUM was an enormous building, with a soaring barrel-vaulted roof of glass ribbed with iron. Nina's heart sank as she entered the great hall. It was chaotic and noisy, crowded with hothouse plants, fountains, statues, and above all, spectators, hundreds of them, cheering and heckling the different acts. She craned her neck and watched a pretty girl dance on a wire in a costume that resembled satin smallclothes with stockings. It was only a moment's distraction, but it was enough. The people around her had reconfigured completely. She'd been separated from Alan, and the duke as well. Now that she was on her own, the search felt more overwhelming.

She asked after the aquatic entertainments, but they didn't begin for half an hour. She ducked into annex after annex, peered into the faces of the little boys clustered by the strong man and the conjurers. Back in the great hall, she started marching, determined to search it end to end.

"Why the hurry, pet?"

The question followed her. She rolled her eyes at each grinning masher in turn. The Royal Aquarium reminded her a bit of the Knack.

At last, she veered around a perfume stall and felt her insides unknot.

A tall man faced one of the fish tanks. His black coat hugged an unmistakably magnificent set of shoulders.

"Miss Fritz!" Claud leaned around Alan and waved to her.

In her haste to reach them, Nina stomped the toe of the next man who tried to bob along beside her.

She didn't apologize. Or slow down.

Alan had turned, and she felt his gaze arrowing straight to her heart.

"Thank God," he murmured when she'd drawn up beside them, panting. "I was about to enlist the assistance of the orchestra conductor."

"Oh?" Her heart was pushing quicksilver through her veins, and his warmth was expanding it.

"I thought if he lent me his tenors, and they called to you in chorus from the central stage, our reunion would be secured."

"It is. I am." She took a flustered breath. "I'm here."

Claud nudged her. "Do you want to learn the names of the fish?"

At this cue, she dutifully peered into the tank. The creatures swimming *were* fish. But a far sight prettier and more colorful than their dead brethren in the market.

"I don't know any of them," she admitted.

"I didn't at first either." Claud turned back to the tank with satisfaction. His complexion looked better than it had on the night of the ball, and his chest sounded clear.

"What's the little blue-and-gold one?" she asked.

"Emilia," said Claud promptly, and pointed. "That's her brother Bertram."

Nina laughed at her own surprise. Had she expected Claud to recite a taxonomy? He was far more interested in make-believe than natural science. Like everyone else at the Royal Aquarium.

She glanced at Alan. He was looking at her, his face alight with relief and amusement. He took her hand as Claud continued naming fish. His strong grip anchored her. She gazed into the marine world behind the glass, the dreamy undulations of the seaweed so beautiful she wanted to weep. Or else it was the emotion of these past days, these past weeks, catching up to her.

"And that's—" Claud stopped. Nina swung her gaze to him. He'd gone ramrod straight.

"Papa."

"We will discuss your misconduct later." The duke loomed by a spindly, drooping palm tree. His posture seemed ever-more rigid by contrast. "But you should know that you have caused your mother a great deal of worry."

"I'm very sorry for it." Claud had assumed the morose dignity of someone much older. "I understand I'm to be punished."

"Then we understand each other." The duke's eyes swept the hall. "This isn't the place for you."

Nina could feel Alan tense. He was about to speak.

But Claud hadn't finished. He stepped toward his father, wide-eyed and earnest.

"Mr. Bramley drinks a bottle of milk underwater." He pulled a crumpled handbill from his pocket. "And Mrs. Bramley eats cake. And the children do imitations of porpoises. And they all somersault and dive. I wanted to see. You wouldn't allow Uncle Alan to take me. The two of you are still quarreling." He bunched his forehead.

Nina felt a guilty prickle. She had promised him his father and his uncle would work out their differences.

"I wanted to see," he repeated. "So I could remember it, when I'm in Italy."

The duke shifted awkwardly. "There's no excuse."

"No, Papa," agreed Claud, somber. Then he gulped and rose onto his toes. "But if you punish me more, might I stay a little longer?"

"It would be a shame to miss the Bramleys now." Alan pulled out his watch. "Only ten minutes to go." He smiled his crooked, beautiful smile. "Best swimming program in the world. Geoff, you might even enjoy yourself."

The duke frowned and plucked the handbill from Claud with two fingers.

"We've already paid the shilling," offered Nina.

The duke ignored her. Just as well. A silly point to make to an aristocrat. They relished wasting shillings.

His brows rose as he scanned the handbill.

"*Swimming* program? I see smoking, waltzing, undressing, everything but *swimming*." He folded the paper sharply then folded it again, and again.

"There's a demonstration of the sidestroke." Alan bent and extended his arm, repeating the motion.

"We did that one," said Claud, and tipped his head, moving both his arms.

The duke looked between them. His expression stirred a feeling akin to sympathy in Nina's breast.

"Go," he rasped, and cleared his throat.

Claud dropped his arms, his grin too big for his face. "Truly?"

"Go watch the Bramleys with your uncle." The duke glanced at Alan. "If he doesn't object to taking you home."

"Of course not. But . . ." Alan had a line between his brows. "Come with us."

"No," said the duke shortly. "No, I spotted half of the House of Commons in the North Gallery. I, too, must seize opportunity when I see it."

He spun on his heel, holding the folded handbill like a riding crop against his thigh. Claud looked after him until Alan ruffled his hair.

"On to the show," he said.

FANNY WAS YELLING in the entrance hall when Alan and Nina delivered Claud to Umfreville House. She was yelling at Geoffrey, who, from the sound of things, had only just arrived himself, bearing news that their son was safe.

"And I find out *hours* later? You show no consideration for me as your wife. But as the mother of your children, I should—"

She broke off at the sight of Claud. He gave her a nervous smile and began talking excitedly the moment she wrapped him in her arms. She let go and put her hand on his forehead.

"You're not feverish."

"I'm not." Claud bent backward.

"You're filthy." Fanny stepped away. "You'll have a bath before dinner. Upstairs with you."

Claud put down his head and ran with his arms stretched behind him. Imagining himself a porpoise. Alan's mouth quirked. Claud reached the stairs and waved. Fanny eyed Alan, then Nina, then turned without a word.

Geoffrey swung around to face the butler, a pale man, reactive as a waxwork.

"I'll receive my guests in the drawing room," he snapped, and then he, too, spun on his heel.

In the drawing room, Alan stared at the fake Rembrandt on the wall with an increasingly powerful sense of unreality. As though he had stepped back in time.

Geoffrey sat motionless in his chair, blinking at the tea tray on the table.

Alan could almost hear the corresponding click inside his brain.

"You!" Geoffrey jolted. He looked at Nina, eyes blazing. "You are that incompetent, insupportable maid!"

Nina winced and clasped her hands. "I wondered if this would happen."

"Mind your tongue." Alan gave Geoffrey a threatening grin. "Or I'll yank it out."

"Me? Mind *my* tongue?" Geoffrey frowned. "I believe this baggage called me a rich, stingy crosspatch."

"Your grace," Nina cut in. "We got off on the wrong foot."

"Wrong hand, if I recall." Geoffrey glared at her. "You dropped a full tea tray."

"I did." Nina nodded gravely. She paused, then nodded again. "Twice." Her lips trembled. She was going to laugh.

Geoffrey turned his glare on Alan. "You hired this woman?"

Alan raised a brow. "Most recently I asked her to marry me."

Geoffrey blinked. "That's a jest."

"I've never been more serious in my life."

"Married to a maid." Geoffrey's smirk was disbelieving.

"She hasn't said yes," Alan confided. "And in point of fact, she's not a maid."

"But I'll happily bring that tray to the kitchen." Nina bounced to her feet. "And leave you to talk among yourselves. You need something stronger than tea, I think."

She bent over the table.

Geoffrey leapt up. "Don't you dare."

"It's no bother. I was going to the kitchen anyway." She lifted the tray. "It's the most wonderful kitchen I've ever seen. If it were mine, I'd appreciate it. And I'd appreciate the people cooking my meals and cleaning my messes." Her brow furrowed as she studied him. "You have so very much to appreciate."

"Ha." Geoffrey's laugh sounded thin and unconvincing. "I'll *appreciate* it if you refrain from dropping that tray."

Nina kept staring, with mixed dislike and goodwill.

"That's a start." She sighed. "Appreciation takes practice. Keep trying, and you'll improve. Even in the absence of natural talent." She curtseyed and the tray rattled.

Geoffrey opened his mouth and closed it.

"Your grace," she said, and rattled from the room.

CHAPTER THIRTY-ONE

THEY WENT UP to the study. As Geoffrey poured the whiskey, Alan removed the bundled letters from his coat and dropped them on the desk. All things considered, Geoffrey took it well. After a few fits and starts of questions and curses, he drained his glass and poured another. Alan put down his own glass and reached for the bottle.

"Do you remember?" he asked, and lifted the bottle high.

That long-ago night, when they'd passed a bottle between them, and then another.

Of course Geoffrey remembered. They'd said things they'd never forget and probably both regretted. Truths that they'd each flung back in the other's face.

"I remember the headache the next day." Geoffrey rubbed his temple.

Alan laughed and tipped the bottle back again. Their father's funeral had passed in a pounding blur, the alcohol only partially to blame.

"I wish I'd never told you about Patricia." Geoffrey flung himself into an armchair. "You judged me then for the choice I made, the only choice I could have made. And now I discover you planned to blackmail me because I didn't surrender the woman I loved."

"Your affair with Patricia gave me an opportunity." Alan held Geoffrey's eyes. "I planned to blackmail you because you closed my account. Because you tried to control what I write, how I live. Who I am."

Geoffrey looked away. "Why return the letters, then?"

Alan pictured Nina, and his chest went warmer than the whiskey warranted. "Maybe I got my soul back."

"*Blackmail.*" Geoffrey emptied his glass and peered into it. "Did you think to keep Claud in London?"

Alan didn't answer.

Geoffrey set the glass on the floor and looked at him. "I wouldn't have capitulated to any demand detrimental to his health, even under pain of death."

His stare was fierce. It was written all over his face—how badly he wanted Alan to credit the statement.

"I see that." The words felt sharp in his throat. "And I see that Claud is sick." He hesitated. "But, Geoff, he's not *only* sick."

Geoffrey was still looking at him, mouth twisted. Alan held out the bottle, and after a moment, his brother took it and drank.

"I found something." Geoffrey set the bottle beside the glass and rose. He went to the chair by the fireplace. A dark, ornate box sat beside the reading lamp on the side table.

"The Staunton chess set." Alan shook his head, confused. "You've had it for years."

"I never opened it." Geoffrey approached. "Sunday, I took out the pieces. I was considering a game, with Claud." He stopped, looking down at the box with vague accusation. "We didn't end up playing. I went to the club instead." Bitter lines bracketed his mouth. "I don't show fondness easily. None was shown to me."

The old story. Weary, Alan tilted back his head and waited.

"I found pills," said Geoffrey, face white as bone. "Under the velvet lining. It was torn, and . . . You hid them there. Pills you were meant to take."

Alan's eyes felt hot. A shudder was locked inside his spine. "I hid them wherever I could. When I was alone, I'd destroy them. Not all of them, apparently. I wasn't often alone." His mouth had gone dry. He took the bottle and drank. "I kept the chess set by the bed. It was a convenient receptacle."

"I asked myself why." Geoffrey turned the box, ran his thumb over the carved mahogany. "Why hide pills? Some caprice, I decided. An early sign of your unreliability. I tried to put it out of my head. But . . ."

He looked far from decided. He looked broken open by the question he couldn't ask.

"She gave them to me." Alan held the bottle against his cheek.

"They sickened you." Geoffrey's jaw worked. Finally, he thrust the box into Alan's chest, wrenched the bottle from his hand, and gulped.

"Get them analyzed," Geoffrey grated. "Find out what's in them."

Alan opened the lid of the box and touched an ivory chess piece.

"For years," Alan said, "I was obsessed with proving . . ." What? That he had been hurt in a knowable way. That he had a right to hate her, his mother. That he *was* right, to hate himself.

He sank over the box. But he felt no urge to dig to the bottom, dig down to the decades-old pills that he'd pretended to swallow, that he'd palmed or spit out.

When he lifted his head, he had the sensation that he was throwing off a weight. He met Geoffrey's eyes.

"I wanted to dissect what happened, to pin it all down." He waved his hand. "A postmortem pursuit." His smile felt defenseless, its irony fled. "Now . . . I want to live."

Geoffrey's eyes slid away. "They're there. If you change your mind."

Alan nodded. "Geoffrey—thank you."

Geoffrey gave a stiff nod in return.

Alan figured he'd say what he had to say now, lest the next chance come at fifty. "You could get a divorce, you know."

Geoffrey choked.

"Disastrous choice, obviously. You'd be a walking scandal for a time. But perhaps . . . less of a miserable bastard."

"Miserable bastard." Geoffrey echoed him. He didn't look affronted. He was staring into space. "Miserable husband. Miserable father." He shook himself, with a slight intake of breath. "Miserable brother."

His expression had a strange, half-fledged quality. Several emotions too new and too unfinished to identify played across his face. Helped by habit, he formed a frown. "Do you think that maid has vandalized my kitchen?"

"Nina Finch." Alan felt his smile burst out, like the sun from behind the clouds. "No. She's only dangerous when provoked, or when she's chasing after her marmoset."

Geoffrey's frown deepened.

"Small monkey," explained Alan. "Smells like a tannery." He pulled a knight from the box, a stallion's head, with an arched neck and rippling mane. Beautiful. He sighed. He returned the piece, shut the box, and rose to his feet.

"These games between us," Alan said. "They end now."

Geoffrey folded his arms. "What do you propose?"

"I take back my investments. You take everything else. All the cherishable goods. We'll have our solicitors make it official." Alan paused. "Except I'm keeping the ancestral portraits. Unless you'll trade, for certain of your new pictures."

"Such as?"

"The Rembrandt in the drawing room."

"The one you think is fake." Geoffrey's brows lowered in perplexity.

"That's the one, yes. And a few others in the gallery, also valueless."

"You will always baffle me." Geoffrey's tone wasn't hateful. In fact, his voice held a note that wasn't entirely unlike affection. He must have heard it too, because he stiffened.

"We're agreed, then." Alan held out the box. "Care to play?"

Geoffrey narrowed his eyes.

"Not with me. With Claud. I doubt he's interested in his dinner."

"And why is that?" said Geoffrey.

Alan cleared his throat. "Because earlier he was rather interested in the food vendors. And I provided him samples of their wares. No cake. I wasn't trying to undermine your authority."

Baked potatoes, crumpets, pineapple slices, cherries, ginger beer . . .

Geoffrey snorted and went behind his desk to put back the bottle.

"He'd welcome your attention." Alan slid the chess set across the desk and took up his cane.

As he shut the door behind him, he saw Geoffrey lean forward, open the box, lift out a knight, and close it tight in his hand.

NINA CURLED INTO Alan as the coach swayed. She felt languorous, with his arm draped over her, the hard muscles of his chest comfortable as goose down, despite possessing opposite properties. A paradox. One of many. He stroked down her shoulder, and she shut her eyes and listened to him describe the tentative new peace he'd made with his brother.

"I trust it," he murmured, after a long pause. "Although I did hold back a letter just in case. If he notices, I'll apologize for the oversight and return it, *after* we meet with our solicitors."

He buried his face in her hair, and instead of scolding him, she sighed. He was hers. Nina's Sweets would be hers too.

"I'm going to hire Ruby," she said, eyes closed. "She'll prefer the bakery to the Knack, even if she thinks Hensthorpe a hole-in-the-corner backwater."

"It has a Beowulf Society." Alan nuzzled her ear. "And uncommonly lovely cows. And soon, the world's best gooseberry tarts, and a gallery that shows the most daring modern art . . ."

She must have drifted off. When she opened her eyes, the coach was stopped and her heart was singing.

She said as much to Alan, drowsily. He pressed his smile to her cheek, a crooked kiss, and he didn't mention that the singing might be coming from the house. She realized it when he opened the front door. Music poured from the front parlor. When she reached the threshold, Nina saw McAdams at the piano. Kuznetsov was shuffling cards, head turned toward Boyd, who sat to his left at the table. There were two other players. Kessler.

Jack.

The last person Nina expected to see in Alan's house, bar none.

He was slouched, chin propped on his fist. He glanced at Nina as she lunged forward.

"What are you doing here?" she gasped.

"Bankrupting your pals." He winked.

"You are also pal of Nina?" asked Kuznetsov, beaming, the cards arcing between his fingers.

"I hope so." Jack rose.

"Intermission, gentlemen." Kessler rose, too, and retrieved a bottle of scotch from an open packing crate. McAdams didn't pause his number. Jack sidestepped the crate. He and Alan reached Nina at the same moment. She stood between them, the air snapping with tension. They both looked ready to snarl. Jack acted first. He gave himself a shake, palmed back his hair, and smiled at Alan.

"De'Ath," he said. "You let me slope off once, and if you let me slope off again, I swear this will be the last time you ever see my pretty face. I didn't come to make trouble." He held up both his hands, then reached slowly into his coat. "I asked myself what more I could do, for Nina, and I did it."

His hand emerged, fingers pinching an envelope.

"Here." He handed it to Nina. "It's thin but the notes are fat. Your money. I sold the factory. Buy the bakery from Old Craddock. You don't need *him*." He moved his gaze back to Alan.

"Jack." She turned the envelope in trembling hands. "How did you know where to find me?"

"Don't want to embarrass you." Her brother was the one who looked embarrassed. He rocked on his heels. "But you're gone on the man. Wasn't hard to guess you'd go back." He glanced at Alan and frowned. "I'll shoot you clear across the Channel if you give her one second's sorrow."

"You don't have to get on a boat." Nina's stomach cramped. "Alan told Lloyd Syme, told everyone, that he was wrong, that the paintings were authentic. There won't be an investigation."

For a moment, Jack stared. Then he hooted.

"Thank you kindly," he said to Alan, and then to Nina: "I see why you like him. I'm starting to like him too." He shot Alan a grin. "We could collaborate on your next book. Call it *Secrets of a Forger's Workshop*. My pen name is Anonymous, of course. I'll help you make forgery detection into a science. Think about it. Together we're unstoppable."

"*Jack.*" Nina made a sound like a laugh that turned into a strangled sob. "You never change. You're always on to the next scheme. This time it won't involve me. It won't involve Alan, either." She was definitely laughing *and* crying. "*I've* changed. Do you hear me?"

Jack looked at her, lips pressed together.

"I don't want you so far as France," she said. "But I need you farther than you are right now. For I don't know how long."

She shut her eyes. When she opened them, he was still looking at her, white and still.

"All right," he said in a hoarse voice. "I'll just win this last game of cards. And then—au revoir." He knuckled his eye, hard, then fixed her with a familiar squint, shaking his head. "That's enough, now, Birdie."

She realized she was crying harder, and Alan was pressing his handkerchief into her palm.

"Let's say it's not forever." Jack reached out to touch her arm, and Nina felt Alan go rigid beside her. But he didn't move, and neither did Nina, and Jack's touch was gentle.

"And next time you see me," he said, "you'll have cause to be glad of it. How's that?"

She nodded and covered his hand with hers before he drew it away.

"Deal me in, lads," he called. Kuznetsov waved him over. For his part, Kessler had lost interest in cards.

"I have a new poem," he declared. "Who wants to hear it?"

Nina turned to Alan, and they moved as one, out of the room, down the hall, out the door into the garden, into the cool night. They wandered around the house.

"I'm proud of you," said Alan, drawing her into the deep shade of the chestnut tree. "Proud of us."

He leaned against the trunk, and she leaned into him, her back against his chest, his arm tight around her. His lips nuzzled her nape.

"How do you feel?" he asked.

"With my fingers," she said, walking them up his arm.

His laugh made her smile.

"And with my heart and my soul," she added in a softer voice. "Because you're here."

"Does that mean you *will* marry me?"

"Oh." She shivered, then laughed as Alan kissed her temple. "Right. I didn't say yes."

"And?"

"Hmm."

"Christ." His lips moved on her neck.

"Yes," she said, and he turned her.

"I still imagine setting the stars on your brow."

She could just barely see his eyes in the darkness, their faint shine.

"I like the stars where they are." She found the edge of his face with her thumb. "What else do you imagine?"

"This," he said, his mouth so close she felt his smile curve the air.

"This," she whispered. "It's so much better than anything I ever dreamed of." Her smile touched his.

"And it's real," she breathed.

He kissed her, the taste sweet beyond all measure.

EPILOGUE

Two Months Later

THE SUN SLANTED through the clouds as Nina cut across the meadow. Fritz bounded ahead, leapt through the rails of a fence, and spiraled up the trunk of the old crabapple tree. Before she'd left the cottage, she'd tried to tuck him into the satin-lined basket with Lucinda, to no avail.

A princess for Prince Fritz. That was what was written on the card that came with the lovely young marmoset. No signature, but Nina knew who sent her. Jack's wedding gift was a true beauty, with silky fur and bright black eyes. Fritz seemed dazzled, at first. But he'd quickly resumed his roving. Of late, Lucinda had been doing her best to make him jealous, or else—Alan's theory—she'd developed a preference for Charlemagne. For her sake, Nina hoped she *had* formed an attachment to the gentle, constant old cat. Fritz was handsome, but rather a fiend. She reached the hedgerow beyond which the ground sloped to Priory Pond. The tiny, twisted branches were massed with green leaves. Too early in the season to glean for Aunt Sylvia's hedgerow jelly. But the gooseberries on the hill were ripening. Her soon-to-be nieces, Mary and Arabella, would arrive tomorrow to help pick them.

Nina's Sweets hadn't yet opened for business. There'd been too much to do, finalizing the sale, replacing equipment, stocking ingredients for the wedding and beyond. But Nina had been baking in the new ovens, testing recipes. And Kate had painted a resplendent sign, which hung now above the door. NINA'S SWEETS. Gold and pink and pale green, berries and birds in the corners.

It was nearly time to begin on the bride cake. Nina had decided on classic fruitcake, with an emphasis on plum. Massive, round, and multilayered, tiers separated by column stands. A labor of love *and* an advertisement, with sculptural elements, figures worked in marzipan.

She already knew the piece of cake she and Alan boxed to post to Italy for Claud would include a marzipan Fritz. The duke had made the trip to Pistoia with his son after all. When he'd returned last month, he'd had happy news to share with Alan regarding Claud's improvement. Since then, the doctors' reports had only gotten more encouraging.

Next summer Claud would join his sisters, picking berries on the hill. Join Alan for a swimming lesson in Priory Pond. And perhaps, join his father for a game of chess at the table beneath the plum tree in the cottage garden.

She could see the pond now, shining at the bottom of the hill, shaded on one side by the ancient oak, the tumbled-down stone walls of the ruined abbey protruding here and there from the thick green grass.

Birds twittered behind her in the hedges. The pond was placid.

For the past two months, she'd been mostly in Hensthorpe, but Alan had been coming and going, taking rooms at the inn and calling on her at the cottage.

Last night, he'd arrived to Hensthorpe late. Their visit in the parlor had been brief. But she couldn't have mistaken his words— he'd told her to meet him here in the morning.

She stopped. And he surfaced. The ripple shimmered as it spread. He was cutting through the water, fast, and she raced the rest of the way so he'd see her before he turned.

He put down his legs and stood. He stood more easily these days. The pain still came and went, but without the same force. Fear and doubt no longer gave it fuel.

He grinned, flinging back his wet hair, long enough now to get in his eyes. He wore his black bathing costume. The thin fabric clung to his muscled torso, his lean hips. She couldn't help it. She stopped again and stared. Windswept clouds flirted with the sun. One moment he was in shadow, the next, the light sparkled on the droplets rolling down his bare arms.

Gorgeous day. Gorgeous man.

A breeze at her back urged her to the water's edge.

"What did you want to tell me?" She felt herself smiling, a huge, silly smile, and clapped her hands to her cheeks. As though it might otherwise overflow her face.

Alan raised a brow. "Come closer."

"You're waist-deep in frigid pond water."

"It's temperate." Alan beckoned. "And if you come close enough, I can keep you warm." He smiled his crooked smile. "I'm *intemperate* when I'm around you. Burning with immoderate desire."

She tried to frown. No good. The corners of her mouth kept rising up.

"I'll dip my feet," she conceded, and set about unlacing her boots, tugging off her stockings. The day would be hot. A bee lazed by.

She curled her toes as she splashed into the pond. The water *was* temperate, at such shallow depth. The mud felt soft.

"So?" she asked.

He approached slowly. "We have our farmstead. It's a half mile toward Potesham. The river on one side, rolling fields on the other."

"Not the old Haylett place?" She gaped. "The house is enormous. We could live comfortably in the dovecote."

"The dovecote is attached to the barn." He was right in front of her now. A droplet of water rolled over his cheekbone, heading for the corner of his mouth. "Barn and dovecote are for public exhibitions. The house is for us, and we need the room. For one thing, my picture collection has recently grown by dozens upon dozens of canvases."

The sun burst out. His eyes sparkled between wet, black lashes.

"Just the other day I acquired several more. Sir Cunliffe-Owen and I reached an arrangement."

She furrowed her brow. "You acquired the pictures *Syme* acquired?"

"The ones you and your brother painted, yes. The museum couldn't hang them, after Sleaford's disgrace."

Chips Sleaford hadn't been apprehended, but several forgeries had been definitively linked to his showroom. Luckily, none of them were her doing, or Jack's.

Sleaford's disgrace had attached to Lloyd Syme as well. Kate was still crowing.

"Golly." Nina gave Alan an uncertain smile.

He was grinning. "Broughton was delighted to sell me that lot of your Berneys. And I've tracked down most of the other pictures, thanks to your ledger. A few elude me, but not for long. I won't stop until I possess the complete oeuvre of Nina Finch."

She laughed, then did manage to frown. "You're spending a fortune, on fakes."

"Not a fortune. I give the pictures a stern look and shake my head, and the owners are generally willing to part with them for next to nothing, plus advice on what to buy instead. A few cost more, but I consider every penny well spent. For one thing, I'm restoring credibility to our nation's museums and private galleries." He sounded wry. "For another, I could look at those old masters all day, finding all the little ways in which *you* appear. You have a slightly elfin take on ears, did you know that? All the ears you paint look faintly like your own."

This laugh melted her frown away.

"Alan," she began, and licked her lips. She'd been parched when she came here to meet him, and now her mouth felt horribly dry. And there he was, glistening with moisture. Her next step sent her skirt dragging through the water, but she reached him and put her mouth on the notch at the base of his throat. His skin felt deliciously damp and cool.

Water scattered down as he wrapped her in his arms.

"You didn't catch a forger, but you rid England's walls of many a fake." Her smile did overflow that notch. She slid her face over and kissed below his collarbone. "That's half of what you set out to accomplish."

"What do you mean?" His arms tightened. He stepped backward, and her skirt billowed, water rushing around her legs.

She gasped, and he took one more step and tilted. They fell together, and a wave rolled over them, cold and shocking. She clung to his chest, sputtering and laughing, and he began to swim, pulling her with him, stroking back with one arm.

"I did catch a forger," he murmured, and when she kissed him, they both went underwater. It wasn't so deep they couldn't stand, so they stood, locked together, the clouds reflected all around them, so they felt as though they were kissing in the sky.

Author's Note

Two of the more whimsical elements in *Artfully Yours*—Nina's pet marmoset and the Bramley family—have a firm basis in reality.

Fritz's character was inspired by Mitz, the marmoset who lived with Virginia and Leonard Woolf in the mid-1930s. Mitz appears in Virginia Woolf's diaries, and more recently in Sigrid Nunez's novel, *Mitz: The Marmoset of Bloomsbury*, which paints a wonderfully intimate portrait of the tiny monkey and the Woolfs themselves.

The Bramleys are based on the Beckwiths, a famous family of professional swimmers headed by Frederick Beckwith, a swimming professor and promoter. His daughter, Agnes Beckwith, swam five miles from London Bridge to Greenwich in 1875, when she was just fourteen years old. She went on to become one of the Victorian era's most famous "natationists," performing in tanks at the Royal Aquarium and at baths and music halls. Natationists thrilled crowds with feats of athleticism and endurance and with their underwater stunts, such as dancing, smoking, and eating cake. Caitlin Davies tells Agnes Beckwith's story (among many others) in *Downstream*, a fun, informative social history of Thames swimming. When Alan swims with Nina in the Serpentine, he defines swimming using the words of Charles Steedman, the author of the first manual on the sport. I encountered that quotation in *Downstream*. I also encountered the anecdote that became the seed for the scene, a reference to a lifeguard warming the cold river with hot water from a kettle.

While writing, I spent some time delving into forgery scandals and testing out cake recipes. Neither activity was strictly necessary to the book, but both proved highly enjoyable. One forgery anecdote interested me because of its outcome. While still an unknown, Renaissance sculptor Michelangelo artificially aged a sculpture by burying it in a vineyard and passed it off as an antiquity—or his art dealer did. Either way, the fraud was discovered and it only helped Michelangelo's career. Impressed by the young artist's skill, the collector who'd bought the fake antiquity became his patron and commissioned him for more (modern) sculptures!

As for my forays into British baking, I loved Jane Brockett's *Cherry Cake and Ginger Beer*, which gives recipes from (mostly English) children's books I grew up reading, like *The Lion, the Witch, and the Wardrobe* and *The Wind in the Willows*. I recommend Paddington Bear's Favorite Marmalade Buns! Definitely my sweetest research yet.

ACKNOWLEDGMENTS

THIS BOOK WENT through several iterations, and I would never have been able to see it through without my brilliant agent, Tara Gelsomino, and my marvelous editor, Kate Seaver. Heartfelt thanks to you both for the insightful feedback. Thanks to Bridget and the whole dream team at Berkley. Thanks to Wake Forest University for the research support, and thanks as well to my inspiring students and colleagues. Thanks to my comrades in narrative: the Berkletes, Joanna, John, Radhika, Brian, Sarah E., Art, Brad, Dona, Marream, Caren, and Julia. I'm eternally grateful for your commiseration, celebration, perspective, and advice. The cakes in this book are for Kallista, except for the Bastille, which is for the Wolves. Special thanks to Mir, for everything, but also particularly for reading and commenting on a draft of this book in appropriately heroic fashion. And loving thanks as ever to Ruoccos.

ARTFULLY YOURS

Joanna Lowell

QUESTIONS FOR DISCUSSION

1. Nina and Alan come from radically different places and have radically different goals. Their marriage will depend, in part, on their willingness and ability to compromise. What kinds of compromises do you imagine them making? How important is compromise in a relationship? How important is staying true to individual values and needs? How can couples strike the right balance?

2. Art forgery increased dramatically in the nineteenth century. This boom in fakes responded to the demand created by new national museums and the rise of a Victorian middle class with a penchant for collecting. Throughout history, many art forgers have been caught, and some have become famous—or infamous—in their own right. There has never been a famous female art forger. Do you have a theory as to why?

3. Across the first half of the book, Nina deceives Alan in multiple ways. Despite their shaky beginning, they build trust with each other by the end. Is this trust justified? Are some forms of deception more forgivable than others? Do you think Nina will deceive Alan again? Why or why not?

4. At Augustus Burgess's salon, Alan gets the opportunity to prove that he was correct about the forgeries in the South Kensington Museum. He doesn't take it, choosing instead to put Nina before his personal ambition and his principles. Would you have done the same in his position?

5. Nina struggles to establish boundaries with her brother. How would you describe their relationship? Is there any advice you would give her?

6. Pets played an important and complex role in Victorian domestic life, from Buckingham Palace—where Queen Victoria kept pedigree dogs and Angora cats—to the working-class household, which might include mousers, birds, squirrels, and mutts. How are pets depicted in the story? Do you have a strong bond with a nonhuman animal? How has it affected your life?

7. As a famous critic, Alan is a tastemaker, with the power to shape public opinion. What if you had this level of cultural influence? What underappreciated artist, writer, actor / actress, or musician would you champion? Is there a fashion item or hairstyle you would make popular?

8. What constitutes art, and who counts as an artist, changes depending on historical, social, and cultural contexts. How do you define art? Do you consider baking an art? Do you consider yourself an artist? What are your creative outlets?